Matter
OF
T.

Scriptures are taken from the King James Version of the Bible. Songs cited are from *Our Hymns,* or *Songs of the Civil War*, complied and edited by Irwin Silber (Bonanza Books, New York, © 1960). Article about Stuart's Second Ride Around McClellan taken from the front page of San Francisco's *Daily Alta California* Newspaper, dated November 12, 1862. *Poem of the Cavalier* is an original work by the author, dated July 11, 1991.

A Matter of Trust

Copyright © 1995 T. Elizabeth Renich
Published by Emerald Books
P.O. Box 635
Lynnwood, Washington 98046

Printed in the United States of America.

Library of Congress Cataloging-in-Publication Data

Renich, T. Elizabeth (Tammy Elizabeth) , 1964–
    Matter of trust / T. Elizabeth Renich.
      p.   cm. — (The shadowcreek chronicles ; bk. 2)
    ISBN 1-883002-14-1 (pbk.)
     1. United states—History—Civil War , 1861–1865—Fiction.
  I. Title.   II. Series: Renich, T.Eelizabeth (Tammy Elizabeth) , 1964–
Shadowcreek chronicles ; bk. 2.
PS3568.E593M38   1995
813' .54—dc20   95-21653
                                                                CIP

4/96 Pas-Time 8.09

Dedication...

*T*his book is dedicated to all the people who finished reading *Word of Honor* and wanted to know *"Well, what happens next?"*

Acknowledgments...

There is something about seeing your own name in print on the cover of a book. When I opened the box containing my first published novel right there in the Chargers reception area, I had to smile, scream softly, and then admit that dreams do come true. I am now a published author, even though I sometimes have to stop and blink and remind myself that I have indeed written *that* many words to fill all *those* pages—twice now! There are tangible indicators that serve to jog my recollection: television interviews, book signings, mail orders, reviews, royalty checks, newspaper articles, letters and cards, knowing someone's done a book report on your book for a class, seeing your own book on a library or bookstore shelf, and reporting sales tax to the state of California. I'll never forget the first time I was introduced as, "This is Ms. Renich, the *author* I was telling you about...." It certainly has a tendency to make one's day! The challenge of writing that first novel has progressed into the challenge of a series of historical novels. I do love a good challenge. *Matter of Trust* is the second installment of Salina's story.

I've had many encouraging people, once they've finished reading *Word of Honor*, tell me, "Come on, there's got to be more to it than that!" I reply with delight, "Yes, there is!" Within the pages of this book, I've answered some of the questions posed in the *Word of Honor*, but I've also presented some new questions for the readers to ponder. The research, reading, and travel are paying off, and for that I am glad—especially since I haven't studied this much since college! All I ask is for the readers to keep in mind that this is historical *fiction*—a made up storyline mingled with real historical fact. I enjoy weaving the facts and details in a manner which allows my created characters to interact with genuine figures and personalities in America's past. While I write, I make a concentrated effort to be as accurate as possible so that no one might take offense to my literary manipulations.

It is my desire that this writing will bring glory to my Lord, for He is my constant inspiration and my ever-present Guide. In reading these pages, perhaps one life might be touched through the words He has blessed me with. Throughout the work done on this second novel, He has been dealing with me in my own "matters of trust" (Proverbs 3:5-6). There is scarcely a day that goes by that I don't praise Him for the amazing things He's accomplishing through me—and for sending those angels to the rescue out in the New Mexico desert...

My circle of "historical" friends and business associates continues to grow, and it is through their influence, connections, assistance, and supplying of valuable resources that I am truly thankful. Included among the many are: Ambler Travel—for their assistance in travel arrangements for my research trips; Debbie Perry Balch at Barnes & Noble—for showing me that I really exist in Books-In-Print; Margaret Brown—for the interesting Virginia Tech newspaper clippings and mentioning me to Dr. Robertson; the clerks and reference librarians at the Carlsbad Library who don't scold me for all my overdue fines, manage to locate inter-library loan requests, and customarily call me back with the little-known details of interest I'm looking for; Bruce Carney—who took me on a whirlwind driving tour of places in the last three days of General Stuart's life; Sal & Joan Chandon, formerly of the Doubleday Inn—who jokingly (?) insist that I should "think mini-series" as I write; Tina Fair, Civil War Institute—who has allowed me to sit in as a guest during lectures and for keeping me on the mailing list; Cal & Betty Fairbourn, Inn of Antietam—for their warm hospitality; Carol Drake Friedman, Author/Historian—for sharing information, advice, and impressions; John Hague, Museum of Culpeper History—who helped me acquire reference books and showed me the old town map for the sake of perspective; Jim Heuting, Battlefield Tour Guide/Gettysburg—for "customizing" my battlefield tour; Dr. Susan V. Heumann—for her assistance concerning the Stuart-Mosby Historical Society and for her postcards before the Super Bowl; Doug Knapp, Museum of the Confederacy—for taking the time to offer encouragement and let me wander among the displays; Ben and Debbie McVeety—for their willingness to help with long distance research, compilation of my "book of articles," and faxing information in quick order; Patty Melton—for bequeathing tickets to the director's cut showing of *Gettysburg*; James I. "Bud" Robertson—who initially wrote and offered his assistance to me and doesn't seem to mind my many queries; J.E.B. Stuart, IV (Colonel, U.S. Army-Retired)—for responding to my letter and following up by sending a most useful book containing his great-grandfather's letters; Robert J. Trout—who has provided ideas and sent me useful material in several fact-filled letters. I also wish to thank the various tour guides and park rangers—at Antietam, Alcatraz Island, Ashland, Chancellorsville, Chatham Mansion, Fort Craig-New Mexico, Fredericks-burg, Manassas, the Stonewall Jackson Shrine, Richmond/Chimborazo, the Sully Plantation, and at the San Diego Mission and Presidio—who willingly stayed after the tours came to an end to answer countless inquiries and/or provide me with reliable facts and figures.

In addition, deep gratitude goes to my coaches and their wives, my players and their wives, and my co-workers within the San Diego Chargers organization. Their encouragement and support means a great deal to me. I also want to thank Danny Brisco; Patty Harter; Janet Hoffman; Joe & Irene Jacoby; Jan Palmer; Nancy Proclivo; Fred, Sue, and Elizabeth Renich; Linda Shimamoto; Betsy Stuart; Auntie Jan (Tornell); the Wisner-Jahnsen-Johnsons; and Warren Walsh at Emerald Books—for being there for me. There are others, some who I know and some I don't, who continue to keep me in their thoughts and prayers, and for that I am most grateful. Thank you to those who have let me use their names in vain—obviously you know who you are—and there may be more of you in the future. And I will certainly never be able to thank my darling Momma enough for again allowing herself to be dragged across the country in search of my tidbits of information. She has been companion and trooper, and I'm proud to say she has come to the point where she recognizes the *"teams," and which "players"* wore blue and which wore gray.

To all of the above, and then some, thanks much!

T. Elizabeth Renich
June 5, 1995

Prologue

October 11, 1862
Near Cashtown, Pennsylvania

Confederate Private Jeremy Barnes pulled a faded, patched quilt close around his broad shoulders. Leaning against a tree trunk, he sighed, watching the white steam of his breath disappear in the cold, pre-dawn darkness. His teeth weren't chattering as much now as they had a few hours before, and he repeatedly curled his toes inside his sturdy boots, just to make certain he could still feel them. He was thankful for the two pair of thick socks he wore. Some of his companions weren't as fortunate. Until the raid on Chambersburg—where the Rebels had seized food, supplies, and clothing—many had used rags to bind their shoeless feet. Three of the fingers of Jeremy's leather gloves were worn clean through, but his hands seemed warm enough.

Sifting amid the meager contents of his haversack, he located a piece of hardtack. Nibbling away as best he could at the corner of the flat, square, hardened biscuit, careful not to break off a tooth in the process, he wished for some hot coffee. But General Jeb Stuart had ordered that there were to be no fires. Extracting a piece of jerky from his haversack, Jeremy chose not to dwell on what warmth a fire would have provided, knowing that the light would expose their position to any Yankees in the vicinity. Instead Jeremy contented himself with the fact that maggots hadn't gotten into his food supply—yet, anyway.

A scant yard from where Jeremy sat, Weston Bentley stretched out on his ground cloth. In the next instant Bentley was snoring, and Jeremy shook his head in wonder. He was convinced that his comrade-in-arms could sleep *anywhere*, *anytime*—even through a skirmish—if just given a chance to lie down. Jeremy hadn't been able to sleep at all in the last forty-eight hours. He'd been too keyed up to think about sleeping, and too cold to get comfortable.

He continued to nibble gingerly at the hardtack, surrendering to reminiscence. It had been nearly a month since *she* had risked coming to see him at Harewood Hospital in Washington City. The memory made him smile. It had taken a combination of courage and audacity to pull off such a feat, and Jeremy was well aware that she possessed a full measure of both, right along with her stubborn independence.

A Yankee captain by the name of Duncan Grant had been the one responsible for Jeremy's transfer to and confinement at Harewood. Once Jeremy was moved from prison to the military hospital, he received sufficient medical attention to aid in the healing of his wounds. Jeremy's injuries—some nasty cuts and bruises and a pair of broken ribs—had been sustained in the grisly confrontation between the Union's Army of the Potomac and the Confederacy's Army of Northern Virginia on the seventeenth of September, during the Battle of Sharpsburg, near Antietam Creek in Maryland. That engagement on Northern soil had since come to be known as the single bloodiest day in the War Between the States.

Jeremy shook his head, turning his dark thoughts away from the battle and the horrifying images of the front lines. Instead he recalled the depth of emotion he'd felt when his dark-haired sweetheart left him at Harewood. He fondly remembered their kiss good-bye. "*Dear God*," Jeremy whispered into the stillness, "please let my darlin' Salina be safe. Let her finish the work she set out to do in San Francisco, and let her come back to me. I love her!"

He *did* love her, and he'd told her so. Salina Hastings knew him well enough to know that he'd not voice words he didn't mean. Jeremy supposed that the love he felt for her was borne out of lifetime friendship and confidence fostered from working closely together along with her late father—a Confederate spy prior to his untimely death. Through Salina's influence, Jeremy was learning that love and trust were entwined. These ideas, however, were new to Jeremy. In his nineteen years, he'd had rare encounters with either love or trust. Often he didn't understand *what* he felt, or *why*, so he merely put up an independent, bold front. What he did know, though, was that Salina was different, special to him. His shadowy past made him slow to trust people, and there were few at best whom he did. Yet Jeremy had given his trust to Salina, and she had his love as well.

Jeremy removed his left glove and stared down at the gold filigree ring he wore faithfully on his little finger. At their parting that day at Harewood Hospital, she had given him the prized token as a keepsake. The dark green emerald gemstone served as a constant reminder, as it was the exact color of her twinkling eyes.

Jeremy sighed again, tipping his sandy-blond head back against the tree trunk and closing his eyes. The very next day after Salina's departure, Jeremy had been part of a prisoner exchange: negotiations between the warring governments required four privates for one lieutenant. Besides himself, three other Rebel privates were set free in exchange for a captured Yankee lieutenant, a young man who was reportedly the grandson of a Federal Congressman. General Stuart himself had seen to the necessary arrangements. Volunteering as a scout and courier had been motivated by gratitude, but now Jeremy served his obligation out of loyalty to the commander. Had it not been for the General's providential intervention, Jeremy might have ended up rotting away in a Northern prison camp somewhere.

"Get up, Barnes. We gotta get a move on." Weston Bentley, one of the other Confederate privates who'd been exchanged with Jeremy, was suddenly wide awake and rolling his ground cloth into a wad, impatiently stuffing it into his saddlebag. "We ain't got all night, ya know. General Stuart's orders are to be up and at 'em. I heard tell we ain't goin' to Gettysburg after all. Seems we're headin' for Emmitsburg instead."

Jeremy cocked a black eyebrow, baffled at his companion's insinuation that he was the one dozing. "Look, *I'm* not the one who's been snoring for the last thirty minutes. I've been awake ever since we left The Bower."

Bentley yawned, stretching both arms above his head. "We done covered quite a bit of territory since we left camp at The Bower, but we got a ways to go still. Reckon the Federal cavalry is lookin' for us yet?"

"Let them look," Jeremy muttered, an anxious, expectant glitter appeared in his sapphire eyes. "The boys are spoiling for a fight, and it seems General Stuart is just itching for a clash with those people."

"Might be so." Bentley grinned. "But them Yankees are just plain too slow for the rate we're movin'."

Jeremy nodded in agreement, tucking the remainder of his hard-tack and jerky into his breast pocket. Effortlessly, he pulled himself up into the saddle atop his chestnut horse. "Giddy up, Comet," he coaxed his reliable mount into position within the column of Rebel cavalry.

Bentley reined up next to Jeremy, alert to his friend's pensive mood. "What's eatin' at ya, Barnes?"

"It's nothing," Jeremy hedged, riding straightforward in line.

"*She's* more than *nothing* if she affects you like this." Bentley rubbed his bearded chin. "Been away from her long?"

Jeremy cast a cool glance at his fellow scout, one that was meant to discourage further inquiry.

Bentley chuckled knowingly and continued, "I'll wager she's pinin' away for you just as bad as you are for her. I bet she's real purty, an' I s'pose she's thoroughly in love with your sorry excuse for a hide..."

"Don't push it, Bentley. She's none of your business," Jeremy said curtly.

Bentley chuckled again. "So it *is* a lady who's got ya all knotted up. I figured it had to be somethin' like that. Well, just put her right outta your mind, Barnes. We got work to do."

"Yes, sir." Jeremy snapped a sarcastic salute, but silently he knew the command was easier said than done. Even while his thoughts focused on their mission, he still couldn't put her completely out of his mind—especially not when she took up so much of his heart.

☆☆☆☆☆☆☆

Dawn had yet to break on the thirteenth of October when General Jeb Stuart's Rebel cavalry returned to headquarters at The Bower, situated at the Dandridge House near Darkesville. The raid on Chambersburg, along with a handful of other small towns in Pennsylvania and Maryland, was a smashing success for the gray cavalry. This was the second time Stuart had boldly encircled enemy forces—the first being back at the end of June, outside of Richmond. In this second ride, accomplished in just three days, Stuart's eighteen-hundred troopers traveled in a 130-mile circle all the way around McClellan's Union Army of the Potomac—eighty of those miles coming in the last twenty-four hours. The gray-clad horsemen cut telegraph wires, damaged bridges, burned machine shops, destroyed warehouses of ammunition and arms, and obstructed the Baltimore &

Ohio railroad. They collected horses, Federal prisoners, and much-needed supplies, all the while managing to evade the blue cavalry's attempt at ineffective pursuit.

Jeremy crawled into the white canvas tent he shared with Bentley beneath the spreading branches of a barren tree. He thumbed through his journal and tore a blank page out to begin another letter. *My Darling Salina,* he wrote, as he had so many times since she'd gone away. He didn't know when his letters would reach her, but he believed that Reverend Yates would find a way to deliver them into her hand. Before he sealed the envelope, he enclosed the poem he'd penned. With a smile in his heart and her name on his lips, Jeremy finally slept.

Chapter One

San Francisco, California
November 13, 1862

Salina Rose Hastings leaned over a glass display case, studying the gold pocket watch which had captured her attention. It was a lovely timepiece with a chained fob, and she smiled instantly, thinking how it might make a nice gift for Jeremy's birthday in January—or maybe even for Christmas, providing she was back home by then. She shouldn't hope too much, Salina knew, but she did anyway. After all, it wasn't quite the middle of November yet.

November. When Salina left Northern Virginia, heading west by rail and then by stagecoach, it had been the last of September. How long ago that seemed! So much had happened in that space of time.

Salina had left her home at Shadowcreek, near Chantilly, in order to complete a task set for her by her daddy, the late Captain Garrett Hastings, Confederate States Army. When he was alive, the Rebel Captain had been heavily involved in an intelligence-gathering Network comprised of mostly civilian spies sympathetic to the Confederacy.

Though her association with Daddy's Network had been voluntary at the outset, Salina found herself irrevocably enmeshed. Because of the Captain's untimely passing, Salina had been left to fill his place. Her remarkable translating skills, her penchant for following instructions to the letter, and her devotion to Virginia had led Salina westward to finish the work Daddy had begun. She knew his plans and his purpose, for he had shared with her in secret what was to be done. Out of duty and honor, she followed in his footsteps.

Fleeing Virginia had also been the only way to avoid the contingent of Yankee soldiers armed with arrest warrants bearing her own name and that of her best friend, Taylor Sue Carey. Suspicion against the two girls had been running high when they boarded the train on a late-September morning. Their journey across the country had been closely monitored by Yankee soldiers—led by a Lieutenant Lance Colby.

Salina and Taylor Sue had arrived in San Francisco late yesterday afternoon on Drake's stagecoach run, where they had been taken into the home of Salina's Aunt Genevieve. Last night had not been spent resting, though. Instead of sleeping, Salina and Taylor Sue transcribed crucial documents contained in a package forwarded by Daddy to Aunt Genevieve prior to his death. Just a few short hours ago, the girls managed to pass the Yankee-sought papers on to the designated Confederate contact. That was all they were instructed to do—get the documents, make the translations, and send them on to the proper authorities. With the assignment successfully carried out, Taylor Sue and Salina could return home at the first opportunity which presented itself.

The shopkeeper came over and stood across from Salina on the opposite side of the glass display. "May I show you something, Miss?"

Salina pointed to the gold pocket watch with curling ivy vines etched on the cover. "I'd like to see that one, if you'll allow me."

"Here you are." The aproned shopkeeper set the watch in the palm of Salina's left hand.

Self-consciously, Salina cupped her right hand under the other, hoping the shopkeeper would fail to notice the severe dryness of her left hand. Beneath the long sleeve of her new dress, purchased during the morning's shopping excursion, the skin of Salina's left arm was even more rough and dried than that of her hand, her muscles stiff and sore from lack of use. Six weeks ago, one day prior to her departure for California, Salina had taken a nasty fall from her horse, suffering a broken left arm in the process. Ethan, Salina's eighteen-year-old brother and an apprenticed doctor's assistant at that time, skillfully set the broken bone. Then he encased her injured arm in a thick, sturdy, plaster cast.

Earlier today, Dr. Ben Nichols had removed the cast from Salina's arm, examined her, and pronounced the break fully mended. He had warned her about the soreness, indicating that the stiffness would work itself out with use, and he had given her some lotion to ease the itchy dryness of her skin.

The shopkeeper cleared his throat and said, "I can have engraving done this afternoon, if you'd like."

"Might it be ready to be picked up by tomorrow morning?" Salina inquired.

The shopkeeper nodded. "Certainly." He told her the amount and Salina paid what was owed. He placed a pencil and pad of paper in front of her. "Write down whatever message you're wanting on the inside of the lid, and I'll see to it."

Salina snapped the watch closed and fingered the ivy-leaf design engraved on the cover. She pondered for a moment, then wrote: *To J.B. from S.H., All my love to my own Horse Soldier.* She smiled to herself again, adding the date which in a few weeks would be his twentieth birthday: *January 15, 1863.*

For a long moment Salina held the gold watch, staring sightlessly at the diminutive black numbers on the small pearl-white clock face. The numbers blurred together, and she saw beyond the timepiece itself to the face of the watch's future owner.

Jeremy Barnes had a handsome face which contained a pair of thickly-lashed, heavily-browed, sapphire-blue eyes. His squarish jaw was shadowed with a hint of black whisker stubble, and his firm mouth boasted a most disarming smile. All this was topped by sandy-blond locks of wavy hair. Salina had memorized each detail about him, down to the rich sound of his voice, the good-natured rumble of his laughter, his towering height combined with the wide expanse of his shoulders, and the feel of his kiss...

"Very good, Miss," the shopkeeper interrupted Salina's reverie. He glanced at Salina's written words and nodded his approval. "Come back tomorrow and I'll have it for you then, all boxed and wrapped up real nice-like. What's your name, Miss? In case my Missus is here tomorrow while I'm gone to run errands," he explained, "she'll need to know that you're the one who's purchased it."

A small shudder chased along Salina's spine, and she wondered about the wisdom of giving her name. *Don't be ridiculous,* she admonished herself silently, *what's done is done.* After a moment's hesitation, she replied in a low tone of voice, "My name is Salina Hastings."

"All right, Miss Hastings." The shopkeeper nodded. "The watch'll be ready for you tomorrow."

"Thank you." Apprehension again washed over her. What if someone were to come looking for her?

Salina mentally shrugged and silently repeated, *What's done is done.* She turned toward the middle of the well-stocked general store where she spotted her aunt, Genevieve Dumont, and her cousin, Sophie. Esther Nichols, Ben's sister, was with them, poring over a mail-order catalog. Salina's green eyes scanned the store once more, still searching.

"Looking for me?" Taylor Sue Carey stood just behind her. "What did you find?"

"A pocket watch. I bought it for Jeremy. I intend to save it for his birthday, if we don't make it home by Christmas," Salina answered. "Did you find anything that caught your eye?"

Taylor Sue wrinkled her freckled nose and shook her head. "No, not really. Where's the watch?"

"The shopkeeper is going to engrave it for me. He said it will be ready by tomorrow. We have to come back downtown anyway—I have to pick up that other dress from Madame Lucy's Boutique," Salina reminded her friend. "Madame Lucy assured me the alterations would be completed by then."

"I'd almost forgotten about that." Taylor Sue looked down at Salina's feet. "How are your new shoes?"

"They feel tight." Salina wiggled her toes inside the newly purchased, fashionable footgear. "It shouldn't take too long to break them in." She shook her dark curls and rolled her expressive emerald green eyes. "At least Aunt Genevieve has no call to be ashamed of my appearance today."

Taylor Sue giggled. Yesterday, when Salina had climbed down from the driver's seat of the stagecoach, her mamma's sister had been absolutely beside herself to find her niece decked out in a pair of denim britches, a threadbare flannel shirt, an oversized buckskin jacket, a dusty old hat, and dirty boots. Aunt Genevieve had hurried Salina and Taylor Sue, who thankfully was properly dressed in acceptable feminine trappings, into the carriage that whisked them to the Dumonts' Spanish-style *hacienda*.

"You look like a proper young miss today, Salina, so you should have nothing to fear in the event we might encounter any of your aunt's high-society friends," Taylor Sue said teasingly.

Salina mischievously yanked one of Taylor Sue's russet-brown curls in mock retaliation. "Aunt Genevieve gave me quite the scolding." Salina clearly recalled the stinging tears caused by her aunt's scathing words. But it wasn't so much the comments about her bedraggled appearance or her boyish clothing that had hurt Salina, it was the way Aunt Genevieve constantly belittled Daddy. Under her breath Salina whispered adamantly, "I'll be thankful when Drake comes to fetch us this afternoon. He'll hide us away tonight, and then I'll somehow persuade him to bring us back here and to Madame Lucy's tomorrow morning before he takes us with him to the Express office."

"I thought that the stagecoach ride from St. Joseph took forever to arrive here, but after all that's happened in the past twenty-four hours, I'll gladly climb back in for the return trip," Taylor Sue whispered emphatically. "Like you, I want to get away from San Francisco and back to Virginia just as soon as possible."

"We'll wire Reverend Yates from St. Joe. He can get a message to Ethan telling him to apply for leave. Then the two of you can be married just as quickly as we can arrange for it—just as he promised before we left."

Taylor Sue flushed a becoming shade of pink. She glanced down at the solitary diamond of her engagement ring, glittering on the third finger of her left hand. "I love your brother very much, and I can hardly wait to become his wife."

"I know." Salina squeezed Taylor Sue's shoulders in a one-armed hug. "It's written all over your face."

"Is that so? Well, then it must be the same telltale look you get on your own face whenever you speak of Jeremy Barnes," Taylor Sue returned with a laugh. "Do you think the two of you will ever marry?"

Salina shrugged, her fingers instinctively closing around the heart-shaped locket that dangled from a golden chain around her slender neck. "I know that Jeremy loves me, and he knows I love him, but there's been no talk of a marriage between us."

"How can there be when the two of you are on opposite sides of the country, for Pete's sake!" exclaimed Taylor Sue. "Drake will see that we get safely back to Missouri. God will watch over us the rest of the way—just as He did on the way here. You'll see."

Words from Daddy's last letter came to Salina's mind: *Be strong and courageous.* Yet Salina had come to realize that she had little strength on her own behalf. The true, unfailing, inner strength came from her faith in Jesus Christ alone. Salina smiled to herself. Mamma had attempted to teach her that principle, but Salina was admittedly a bit headstrong. She found she had to weather the storms for herself in order to fully understand.

A sudden chill raised gooseflesh on Salina's arms, and in that moment Virginia, her family, and her friends seemed farther away than ever: Ethan, Mamma, Jubilee, Reverend Yates, Tabitha Wheeler, the Armstrongs—all except Cousin Lottie—the Tanners, and especially Jeremy. Even the war seemed far removed, though Salina perceived a degree of discontent here in San Francisco, a sense of tension lying coiled just beneath the surface.

Last night their trusted friend, Drake, the half-breed stagecoach driver who once rode with Jeremy and the Pony Express, had given Salina a newspaper article taken from the *Daily Alta California*. A brief paragraph made reference to General Jeb Stuart's daring ride around the Union army back in mid-October. If not for that newspaper clipping, or the subtle attitudes of some of the people she'd met since her arrival, Salina might have wondered if San Francisco *cared* about what was happening between the North and South. She knew, though, that there were people in this far-removed city that cared very much what was going on in the East—so much so that they, too, were willing to fight for what they believed was right.

Dr. Ben Nichols was such a person. He was Daddy's contact here in San Francisco. Salina had seen with her own eyes his name on the lists, as well as many additional names belonging to other organized Southern sympathizers. Salina could not deny that she had contributed to the Southern conspiracy efforts here. She knew that the date for launching Daddy's western campaign was the fifteenth day of November—just two days from now. The plans called for simultaneous attacks in key western cities, led by armed Confederates plotting to capture the territories between Texas and California, and California itself, all in the name of The Cause. Salina shuddered, relieved to know she and Taylor Sue would be well away from San Francisco by then. In two days, Salina would be that much more safe, and that much closer to returning to Virginia, her loved ones, and whatever was left of Shadowcreek.

☆☆☆☆☆☆☆

Genevieve ordered the driver of the closed carriage to make two stops on the way back to the *hacienda*: the first to drop Esther Nichols off at her brother's medical office; the second at the office of the Dumonts' lumber mill.

"I'm just going in to see if Gerard is in need of a ride home," Genevieve said of her eldest son. "You girls wait here," she told Sophie, Taylor Sue, and Salina. "I'll be back shortly."

Noticing that her friend was impatiently wringing her hands, Taylor Sue leaned over and whispered, "Be still, Salina. Relax. You're as skittish as an unbroken colt. Drake won't leave without us, you know. He promised he'd come for us, and I doubt he would let anything stand in his way of fulfilling that vow."

Salina stopped fidgeting with her hands and absently scratched at her left arm. "I know. Drake will come through. I have no doubt of that, it's just that I feel..."

Taylor Sue took a small bottle of creamy lotion from her handbag. "Here, Salina. Roll up your sleeve and put some of this on your arm. It'll soften your skin." She poured a dab into Salina's palm. "You feel what?"

"I feel like we're being watched...again," Salina whispered in small voice. She glanced at her cousin Sophie who was too absorbed in her new edition of *Godey's Lady's Book* to pay much attention to the two of them. Salina peeked out of the carriage, her attention drawn to an upper-story window in the brick building across the street from the lumber mill. She was *certain* that she had seen the shade drop swiftly into place at the very instant she'd glanced up.

"What is it, Salina?" Taylor Sue persisted, following Salina's gaze.

"I thought I saw something up there, but perhaps I'm mistaken." Salina rubbed both arms to dispel the gooseflesh that prickled there. "The feeling that someone might have been watching is passed now."

Taylor Sue did not see what Salina evidently had, but she believed Salina. Taylor Sue had grown up with Ethan's sister, had known her all her life, and she had come to trust Salina's uncanny instincts without reservation. Taylor Sue could recount many occasions when Salina's intuition had been unerringly correct. If Salina felt they were being spied upon, most likely they were.

"The Yankees have been on our trail ever since the circus in St. Joseph," Taylor Sue whispered. "You don't think Duncan Grant is here in San Francisco, do you?"

"I don't know." Salina squinted her eyes, pausing to consider the possibility. "We know Lieutenant Colby's here, and their female operative, the Widow Hollis. But I'm not sure that Duncan would be sent unless..."

"Unless what?" Taylor Sue prompted.

"Unless those people in Washington ordered him to follow us. They have warrants for our arrests. Daddy often used to say that the Yankees would stop at nothing to retrieve the information he gathered."

"I'm glad we're rid of those documents!" Taylor Sue squeezed Salina's hand. "We did what we came to do. We're out of it now."

Salina sighed heavily. "How I pray you're right about that!"

☆☆☆☆☆☆☆

"Do you think she recognized you?" Lieutenant Lance Colby asked the woman clad in black widow's weeds. Mrs. Irene Hollis was a Union secret agent, and a very good one. Duncan Grant wouldn't have assigned her to this case otherwise.

"Of course she didn't see me!" the Widow snapped. "How could she possibly recognize me? From that distance, if she saw *anything*, it would be merely shadows, nothing more." The Widow cast an impatient glance at the young lieutenant at her side. He was Duncan's right-hand man, and Duncan was resolutely teaching him the art of being a successful operative. But admittedly Lieutenant Colby had much to learn. "Did you find anything?" the Widow wanted to know.

"No, ma'am." Lieutenant Colby lowered his pale blue eyes and studied the toes of his boots. "If she is in possession of the documents we're looking for, then I am of the opinion that Miss Hastings carries them with her at all times. I might be able to make more headway if I enforce the order for her arrest."

"Then what's stopping you?" the Widow challenged. "Duncan..." She cleared her throat and amended, "Captain Grant suspects that the Rebels will make a move soon after her arrival here in San Francisco. She's been here for twenty-four hours, for goodness sake! If she succeeds in contacting any of the members of the inner circle of the Southern conspiracy leaders, I want to be there. I have already established an acquaintance with several of the participating members, but what I want to know is who is in charge, and exactly what they plan to do. That Hastings girl has the answers I want, and I mean to get them. If that calls for taking her into custody, then so be it, Lieutenant."

"I'll make the necessary arrangements with the commanding officer at the Presidio," Lieutenant Colby coolly replied. "Will you want to question her there?"

"Perhaps," the Widow did not commit herself. "Don't let her slip away again, Colby. I'd hate to think that the Rebels would pin all their hopes on her. But then, that would be to our advantage, wouldn't it?"

"Yes, I suppose you're right," Lieutenant Colby answered. "She is the one who filled the gap created by the death of her father, but Captain Grant insists that Garrett Hastings would have a contingency plan for whatever it was he was working on."

"I believe we've established that Salina Hastings *is* Garrett's contingency plan. This time, we'll prove what a monumental mistake he made in thinking an inexperienced sixteen-year-old girl could handle the job he left for her. She is way over her head in this thing." The Widow's laugh was sinister. "Talk to Gerard Dumont about her first. He tipped you off about the shopping plans for this morning. It might be that he has learned even more since her arrival. Bring her in, Lieutenant. That's an order."

☆☆☆☆☆☆☆

"Odd, but Henri said that Gerard had gone home for the day," Genevieve Dumont spoke more to herself than the other occupants of the carriage. "I hope he hasn't taken ill. It's not like him to leave work all of sudden like that. He's been acting so strangely these past few days..."

Salina's eyes locked silently with Taylor Sue's, a rush of apprehension racing along her taught nerves. Late last night, Drake had come to the Dumonts' house to assure himself that the girls were relatively safe. He'd informed Salina that he'd seen her cousin Gerard in a saloon with Lieutenant Lance Colby and Lieutenant Malcolm Everett, who was the husband of Salina's cousin, Marie. Drake warned Salina to be on her guard more than ever, especially since he'd witnessed Colby showing Gerard and Everett a tintype photograph of her.

Genevieve, too, had warned Salina, cautioning that everyone in the Dumont household firmly believed in the Union. They disagreed with secession and had little tolerance for the Rebel Cause, actively working to suppress it. Though Genevieve had been born in Virginia, she had adapted to California and embraced her husband's political views. Yet Salina knew that while her aunt detested Daddy and his Secret Service ways, Genevieve would not hand her over to Federal authorities for Mamma's sake.

Salina ought not have been so surprised as she crossed the threshold into the guest room, but the scene took her breath away just the same. "Oh no!" she moaned, hands clenched in tight fists at her sides. "No!"

Taylor Sue stepped around Salina into the room. She stood mute with disbelief.

The guest room was utterly ravaged. Pages had been torn from books, clothes and draperies shredded, furniture broken, and glass strewn across the tile floor. Down-filled comforters and pillows had been knifed open, their feathery contents flung in all directions.

"This is worse than what happened to our hotel room in St. Joseph," Taylor Sue whispered when she found her voice. "Oh, Salina, the Yankees think we are still in possession of the documents and information that belonged to your father. They don't have any idea that we've passed them on to..."

Salina quickly put a finger to her trembling lips, causing Taylor Sue to pause before she spoke the name *Dr. Ben Nichols* aloud. "No one must know about him," Salina whispered. Even Esther Nichols herself, whom the girls had met on the stagecoach from Carson City in Nevada Territory, was unaware of her brother's involvement with Captain Hastings's Network.

At his office, while removing the plaster cast from her arm, Ben Nichols had instructed Salina to leave the secret information in a vanity drawer in the dressing room at Madame Lucy's Boutique. Dr. Nichols was to fetch the documents from the hiding place when he deemed it safe to do so. During lunch at Chin Li's restaurant in Chinatown, she had wordlessly conveyed to Ben that the papers had been secretly deposited in the drawer. Ben's nod of acknowledgment told Salina that her part in the scheme was successfully completed.

Salina now knew that she and Taylor Sue were in grave danger. Inspecting the devastation, she discovered that she was left with little more than her new purchases and the money she had concealed in a small drawstring pouch she wore beneath her petticoats—money enough for their stagecoach fare home. A dull rage boiled as she sank to her knees, picking up the splintered cherry wood lapdesk that had belonged to Daddy. Hot tears stung her eyes, but they did not fall.

In the far corner of the room was the traveling trunk that had also belonged to Captain Garrett Hastings. Ax marks ruined the wooden finish, and the false bottom, where additional information concerning the Western Campaign had been secreted, was torn asunder. "Oh, Taylor Sue...It's all gone."

Hot, salty tears trickled down Salina's blanched cheeks. There was no sign of any of the items which had been packed inside the trunk: the military uniforms of both blue and gray, a small leather-bound book, Northern newspapers, some photographs, and the remainder of Daddy's personal belongings.

Taylor Sue picked through a pile of items beside the damaged trunk and recovered a well-worn book. "Here, Salina." She put Garrett Hastings's Bible into her friend's empty hands. "At least the vandals had some respect for the Word of God, if nothing else."

Clutching the Bible tightly to her chest, Salina began to search frantically. "The doll. Where's Celeste?" Celeste had been a special gift from Daddy on Salina's sixteenth birthday. The doll was especially unique because it possessed a hollow body and had once been used to smuggle contraband items through the Northern blockade of the Southern ports on the Atlantic Ocean.

"They took everything I had that would remind me of Daddy!" Salina cried furiously as her search for Celeste proved futile. "Everything but this," she indicated the Bible she held in her trembling hands.

Taylor Sue put her arms around Salina in an effort to console her. She didn't know what to say; she was too frightened to speak. A cold chill stole around her heart, and she silently prayed that Drake would come for them—quickly. "At least they didn't get the information we translated. For all we know, it's already on its way to the proper contacts."

Salina nodded. The information included the names of volunteers and leaders who were willing to form civilian regiments necessary to fight against any Yankee resistance; the locations of each cache containing guns and ammunition; maps of southwestern territories and California detailing Union troops concentrations and movements; the shipping schedules for gold and silver from the nearby mines; and the mail routes with delivery schedules.

On Saturday, November 15, the plans called for simultaneous action in Virginia City, Santa Fe, Tucson, San Diego, and San Francisco to strike against the unsuspecting Federal government offices and strongholds. The goal of the Rebels was to capture California with its vast resources, and to secure all the land between Texas and California in hopes of extending the Confederacy from the Atlantic to the Pacific.

There was one item Salina had not forwarded on to the Southern sympathizers by way of Dr. Nichols: a sinister plot to assassinate President Abraham Lincoln. This particular item, she was much relieved to discover, was not in her daddy's bold handwriting, but someone else's. Instinctively, Salina had destroyed the details of the assassination plot by tearing up the pages and discarding them in the cold grate. Being involved with the Western Campaign was one thing, but cold-blooded, calculated murder was another matter entirely.

Salina collected herself, heaving a shuddering sigh. She had to think. Drake would be here soon, and there was work to be done. Her tears continued to spill unchecked, even though she angrily wiped them away with the backs of her hands. "Drake will know where we can hide until tomorrow when the stage leaves."

"We're in a serious mess," Taylor Sue stated the obvious.

Salina nodded and said with some difficulty, "Yes, I think we are at that."

Chapter Two

*L*andsakes!" Genevieve exclaimed loudly when she saw the disarray of the guest room. The girls had already been working for nearly an hour to straighten things up, but their efforts had made only a slight difference, and the room still stood in shambles. "What on earth is going on here?"

Quietly, Salina answered her aunt's question. "Someone broke in while we were shopping in town today. It appears that anything not stolen was reduced to tatters."

"What about that package your father sent here to me. Is that a part of all this? Is *that* what they were after?" Genevieve queried, making a strained effort not to shriek.

Salina nodded. "Yes. They found the lapdesk that belonged to Daddy, but it was empty by the time they got to it. The information it contained is already gone, delivered into the hands of those who will put it to use. Drake will be here at any time." Salina saw her aunt cringe visibly at the mention of the half-breed Indian who worked as an

Express company stagecoach driver. Salina continued, biting back the anger caused by her aunt's disdain concerning Drake, "He has offered to take Taylor Sue and me back east tomorrow morning. We'll be out of your way and will cause you no further embarrassment. Thank you for allowing us to stay here as long as we have. I do apologize for being such a bother."

"Tomorrow?" Genevieve questioned. "Salina, really. Let's do think about this. Understandably, you're a little distraught at the moment. If these people—whoever they are—know that you don't have your father's documents anymore, I'm sure you'll be safe enough here. You haven't even had the opportunity to wire your mother and tell her you've arrived. I should have thought of it sooner myself. We'll take care of it right away. Come, I'll drive you to the Express office and we'll send off that telegram."

Salina shook her head. "We're still under suspicion, Aunt Genevieve. There's a very real chance they might come after us."

No sooner were the words off Salina's lips than a loud thud sounded downstairs. "Someone's in the courtyard." Genevieve looked out the window. "You two girls stay right here," she ordered. "We'll discuss all this nonsense in a minute."

Genevieve advanced only two steps before Gerard led several armed, blue-coated soldiers into the guest room. "She is Salina Hastings." Gerard pointed to his cousin. "The other one is just her friend."

Two soldiers took her by the arms and stood her in the center of the room. "What's in this for you, Gerard?" Salina's heart ached at her cousin's betrayal. "What do you stand to gain?"

"The knowledge that another Rebel traitor will be punished for treason," Gerard shot back.

Lieutenant Lance Colby entered the guest room, and Salina was stunned at his appearance. At a first glance, he looked like Jeremy Barnes, but Colby's hair was a lighter blond, his eyes a paler blue, and his stature didn't quite measure up to the six-feet-two-inches that Jeremy stood in his stocking feet. Colby was a vague, watered-down reflection of Jeremy, Salina thought, and the resemblance was a bit unnerving.

"Good afternoon." Lieutenant Colby nodded politely to Taylor Sue, then stood directly in front of Salina. "Miss Hastings." He touched the brim of his hat with one hand and in the other he held the warrant issued for Salina's arrest. Colby was startled to discover how much more beautiful the girl was in real life than in her tintype photograph which he habitually carried with him. Clearing his throat,

Lieutenant Colby stated, "Salina Hastings, you are under arrest for conspiracy against the United States of America. My orders are to take you into custody for questioning and eventually you'll stand trial for your offenses. Do you understand the charges?"

"What proof have you in any of this?" Taylor Sue stepped forward between the Yankee lieutenant and her friend.

"Yes, Lieutenant," Genevieve added, "what proof do you have?"

"With all due respect, ma'am, I don't need any proof so long as there is sufficient suspicion. As I'm sure you are well aware, President Lincoln has suspended the *writ of habeus corpus* for the duration of the war. Besides, Miss Hastings herself can probably tell you that I have quite enough proof." He looked beyond Taylor Sue, into Salina's dark green eyes. "Don't I, Miss Hastings?"

Tilting her head to a defiant angle, Salina retorted, "Do you, Lieutenant Colby?"

"I do," Colby snapped affirmatively between clenched teeth. He bristled at the green fire in her eyes. "Will you come along peaceably, or shall I have to make an example of you?"

Salina thrust out her arms, extending her clenched fists. "If I am the criminal you seem to believe I am, Lieutenant, why not use the cuffs?"

She was mocking him, and he didn't like it. "By all means," Colby barked orders to a subordinate, "put the cuffs on her—and on the other one as well."

"Taylor Sue is not involved in this," Salina interjected.

"I beg to differ with you on that point, Miss Hastings. Miss Carey is *with* you, and that alone is enough to make her an accomplice to conspiracy." Colby glared down into Salina's vivid, snapping green eyes. "Both of you are prisoners of war, Miss Hastings. It would serve you well to remember that spies are usually captured, and if not shot—as your father was—then hanged. You are at my mercy, and I have little tolerance for Rebels such as yourself or your father before you. My advice to you is not to do or say anything that you will come to regret. Understood?"

Salina swallowed hard, feeling the awkward heaviness of the confining iron handcuffs. "Yes, Lieutenant, I understand," she said, squaring her shoulders, wondering if he detected the catch in her voice. Salina called to mind words she had read in a telegram sent to her by Duncan Grant: *On the night I visited your father in prison...I made a solemn promise to him...I would do whatever I could to see to the well-being of you and your family. I gave him, as I give you now, my word of honor that I will do all in my power to fulfill that vow...*

Captain Grant was Lieutenant Colby's superior officer, and Salina was certain that Duncan would have given Colby very specific orders on the way she was treated. After all, he'd given his word of honor, and even Mamma had believed that should mean something.

"Let's go," the Lieutenant ordered the men under his command. "Come along, ladies."

☆☆☆☆☆☆☆

How much time had passed until they were incarcerated at the Presidio, Salina did not know. It could have been a matter of minutes— or hours. Taylor Sue was weeping openly, but Salina refused to give Colby the satisfaction of knowing how terribly frightened she was. "Taylor Sue?" she whispered into the quiet stillness of the cell they shared.

"Yes?" Taylor Sue answered, wiping tears from her freckled cheeks.

"I'm sorry for dragging you into all of this," Salina apologized. "I never meant for it to go this far."

"We're in this together. I've told you that from the start. I was involved from the time Celeste fell off your bed and broke open and together we discovered the contraband items inside. It was together that we nursed the wounded at Chantilly after the battle at Ox Hill. Together we crossed enemy lines to visit the Tanners in Alexandria so you could see your father when he was held at the Old Capitol Prison..." Taylor Sue's voice trailed off. Then she added firmly, "Put it out of your mind, Salina. There's nothing to be sorry for. I am here with you by my own choice. We're friends, you and I. What are friends for if they can't help each other and be strong for each other? I know you would have done the same for me had I been in your shoes."

"You know Ethan's going to kill us, if the Yankees don't beat him to it." Salina shrugged and tried to smile. "He'll never forgive me if something happens to you. He didn't want to let us come west anymore than our mammas did."

"Ethan knew we had to leave," Taylor Sue said simply. "We had to do what we could to keep your father's Network going."

When Salina made no reply, Taylor Sue asked gently, "What are you thinking, Salina?"

"Of a psalm I read: *Save me, O God; for the waters are come in unto my soul. I sink deep in the mire, where there is no standing: I am come into deep waters, where the floods overflow me. I am weary of my crying: my throat is dried: mine eyes fail while I wait for my God.*"

Taylor Sue shook her head. "God will not fail us, Salina. He's with us, even now, and He'll take care of us. We must have faith and trust in Him. Whatever happened to being strong and courageous?"

"That was few thousand miles ago," Salina whispered sadly.

Taylor Sue nodded. It had not been an easy journey for them, but they had survived. "Be encouraged, Salina, and let us make this psalm our prayer: *Make haste, O God, to deliver me; make haste to help me, O Lord. Let them be ashamed and confounded that seek after my soul: let them be turned backward, and put to confusion, that desire my hurt. Let them be turned back for a reward of their shame that say, Aha, aha. Let all those that seek thee rejoice and be glad in thee: and let such as love thy salvation say continually, Let God be magnified. But I am poor and needy: make haste unto me, O God: thou art my help and my deliverer; O Lord, make no tarrying."*

The girls joined hands and prayed together, committing themselves and their predicament into God's hand.

"Well, well, well." A rough, masculine voice filled the prison cell, causing both girls to jump. "I see the tendency for spying *does* run in your family after all, Miss Hastings."

Salina bit her tongue to keep from answering, and the man came closer. It was Lieutenant Malcolm Everett, Cousin Marie's husband. He gripped the bars of the cell, his leering face close to the opening. "Marie said there was something about you that was different. Gerard, too. I see now that they were quite right."

"I am no different that anyone else, Lieutenant Everett," Salina insisted. She only met this man last evening during supper at Aunt Genevieve's, but she had not liked him then, even when he was putting on his good behavior. Now his true colors were showing, and she liked him even less. "What would lead you to believe that I am different?"

"There's something odd about a girl who's father was supposed to be hanged for treason, but was shot trying to escape instead. Being a spy is no better than being a common thief, as far as I'm concerned. It's dishonorable, especially in a lady, if in truth that's what you are," Everett taunted. "You came unchaperoned on the stagecoach with that half-breed Indian and his mulatto shotgun rider. Your disregard for social convention combined with your misguided Southern sympathies are enough to draw a conclusion that you are Rebel scum. And I, for one, believe that you deserve whatever punishment you're sentenced to pay for what you've done!"

Salina's eyes narrowed. "And what is it that you think I've done?" She took a step closer to where Everett stood, with only the bars between them.

"Spying, of course. Treason against the United States of America. You're just like your father. A traitor," Everett spat. "You're a disgrace to the family. If word ever got out that I had married into a family of Confederate spies..." His voice trailed off, his eyes glaring at Salina. "I shouldn't even be seen talking with you!" Everett turned and left as abruptly as he'd come. Silence hung heavy between Salina and Taylor Sue.

Just like Daddy, Everett's implication echoed in Salina's mind. And Daddy was dead. He gave his life for his devotion to Virginia and the Confederacy, Salina knew, but her resolve wavered for a moment. She didn't want to die; she wanted very much to live and go home. "Dear God," she whispered inaudibly, "I have a great need to feel that You are with me. Be close, and provide us with a way out of this dilemma, if it's Your will. I know You are in control and have the power to do whatever You see fit. Yet I am afraid, and I desperately need Your peace at this time."

Taylor Sue's grip on Salina's hands nearly cut off the circulation in Salina's fingers. "Oh, Salina!" Taylor Sue cried. "I'm frightened!" Great convulsive sobs wracked Taylor Sue's petite frame, and Salina's heart went out to her.

Newly-found courage, certainly God-given, filled Salina, and she said softly, "We're going to get through this, one way or another. God has promised that He will never leave us or forsake us."

☆☆☆☆☆☆☆

With morning came a kindly sergeant who brought two mugs of steaming black coffee and two bowls of thick porridge flavored with cinnamon and brown sugar. "I'm Sergeant Thayer. I'll be looking after the two of you for a spell. Is there anything else I can do for either of you?" he asked solicitously.

"Might I have a bit of cream to put into the coffee?" Salina dared to ask.

"I don't see why not." Sergeant Thayer shrugged. "And you, Miss?" he directed his inquiry to Taylor Sue.

"Some sugar, if it isn't too much trouble." Taylor Sue nodded.

"I'll be right back." Sergeant Thayer saluted.

The confining iron cuffs caused the girls to make rather clumsy attempts at eating, but they managed in spite of their shackled hands. When Sergeant Thayer returned, he brought the cream and sugar with him, lingering at their cell. He didn't seem in a hurry to leave and began telling the girls about San Francisco. He mentioned that he had been stationed at the Presidio for fifteen years.

"I remember your father well, Miss Hastings," Sergeant Thayer admitted. "I recall that you, Miss, were just a wee little thing when he was assigned duty at this post. Garrett Hastings was only here a short time, but he was the sort who made a lasting impression. Brilliant officer, he was, cunning like a fox. I suppose when it came down to hard choices, he did what he thought was right. And knowing Hastings, he never was one to do things in half-measures," the sergeant said with a wistful smile. "You appear to be quite a bit like him, Miss."

"Thank you." Salina took his remarks as a great compliment. "Is there any more coffee?" she asked after taking the last sip. She noticed her throat hurt when she swallowed.

"Yes, please." Taylor Sue added.

"Coming right up." Sergeant Thayer left, but it was Lieutenant Everett who returned with their mugs half-filled with straight black coffee. The girls knew better than to request cream and sugar this time.

Salina met Everett's angry glare straight on and stated boldly, "I should like to see Lieutenant Colby."

"He's not here," Everett said bluntly. "No doubt he'll be back later this evening, and I hope, for your sake, that you have the right answers to his questions."

Salina knew a few hours passed because the patch of sunlight on the floor moved at a snail's pace from one side of the cell to the other, then faded away altogether. Sergeant Thayer returned as twilight set in.

"You've a visitor, Miss. I told him he'd have five minutes, no more." Sergeant Thayer leaned nearer to the bars and confided, "Lieutenant Everett is off duty now, but if he finds out I let the half-breed in, I swear I'll deny it."

Salina nodded quickly. "I understand. Where is he?"

Sergeant Thayer stepped aside.

A tall, copper-skinned man with arresting turquoise eyes stepped from behind the wide sergeant.

"Drake!" Salina instantly recognized the man with waist-length black hair, a gold hoop earring, and a jagged white scar that marred his forehead. She was genuinely glad to see him.

Taylor Sue, too, rushed over to the bars that separated them from the stagecoach driver. "How did you know we were here?" she asked.

"Genevieve Dumont told me. It seems I just missed you at her house. I've been outside for most of the afternoon, demanding to be let in," Drake told them in his gravely voice. "They haven't hurt you, have they?"

"No." Salina shook her head in a quick answer. "We're as well as we can be, under the circumstances." She allowed him to take her cuffed hands into his.

"What happens now?" Drake demanded.

"I don't know yet." Salina shrugged. "Lieutenant Colby isn't here, but he will be later to question us, I would suppose."

"Little One," Drake sighed, using the nickname he'd given her on the trip from St. Joseph.

Salina gazed for a moment at Drake's tanned, attractive face before dropping her eyes self-consciously to his leather boots. Her fingers absently brushed the fringe that edged the sleeve of his buckskin jacket. Last night in the courtyard of Genevieve's house, for whatever reason, Drake had kissed her when he shouldn't have.

Drake lifted her chin, but Salina didn't meet his eyes. Her glance stopped at his mouth, and she found it took a great deal of effort for her to tear her eyes away. Drake was Jeremy's friend, someone he trusted, and it was by Jeremy's request that Drake be Salina's protector.

Drake sensed Salina's confusion. He was again drawn to her as he had been the evening before. He rested his forehead against the bars, his voice heavy with determination. "I'll find a way to get you out of here, Little One."

"No, Drake, don't." Salina shook her head. "We've put you through enough just getting us here. I don't want you entangled in this thing any more than you already are. I need you on the outside, not locked away in here with us. You've got to get a message home for me. The Network must be informed that we've been captured. I want you to wire Reverend Yates. He'll pass the word along to Mamma and Jeremy, and he can notify Taylor Sue's family and my brother. Will you do that for me? Please, Drake," Salina pleaded.

"I'll do it, Little One." Drake squeezed her hands. "But I don't like this."

"Nor do I," Salina said honestly, "but there's little we can do about it. At least not now."

Drake nodded slowly. "I'll send the telegram," he promised. "And after this run, I'll be back to get you out. Do you hear me?" A dark thought flashed through his mind. "Little One," he added seriously, ominously, "don't let them take you to the Island of Alcatraz. Prisoners taken there don't get released. There's something not right about that place. It's shrouded with foreboding. You can feel it even across the bay. If you're taken there, there's not much I can do to help you." Drake caressed her cheek lightly. "I'll be back in six weeks. Just hold on."

Salina doubted whether she and Taylor Sue had six weeks to wait, but she smiled bravely. "Do be careful on your run, won't you?"

"I'll be fine, but I'll be worrying about you," he admitted gruffly.

Sergeant Thayer returned to take Drake away. "Time's up."

"Good-bye, Drake," Taylor Sue said. "We'll keep you and Josiah in our prayers."

"Yeah." Drake touched Salina's shoulder gently. "Maybe I'll find a way to bring Jeremy to rescue you."

"Then he'd be in as much trouble as we are," Salina pointed out. "He's better off with Jeb Stuart."

"I suppose you're right. I'll be back," Drake vowed. "You take care, as best you can, Little One."

"I will." Salina nodded. "Good-bye, Drake."

"Good-bye, Little One." Drake tapped the tip of her nose. He tried to fight the feeling that she might not be there when he returned from his run. He wondered if he would ever see her again.

Sergeant Thayer led Drake away. When he'd gone, Salina lay on her musty bunk, crying until her tears were spent.

☆☆☆☆☆☆☆

Colby returned to the Presidio cell at a late hour. The key grinding in the lock woke both Taylor Sue and Salina with a start.

"Come on," he beckoned to them.

With a yawn, Taylor Sue asked, "Where are you taking us?"

"For a boat ride," the lieutenant answered curtly.

"Boat ride? What?" asked Salina, still rubbing her tear-swollen eyes.

"No time to explain. Just come with me," Lieutenant Colby ordered.

Salina shivered with apprehension. "You're taking us to Alcatraz, aren't you?"

"That's right, Miss Hastings," Colby answered coolly. "We're going out to the fortress, since that's where the Federal government holds people who possess the convictions you do. You'll be kept there at least until the authorities can decide what's to be done with you."

It was intensely cold at the dock. The chilling wind cut through the woolen cape Sergeant Thayer had given to Salina just before they left the Presidio. Taylor Sue had one as well, and Salina could see that hers wasn't keeping her any warmer than Salina's did.

Thick, white, swirling fog was everywhere, severely limiting visibility. Water that had appeared gray-green by daylight was now inky black, lapping greedily at the sides of the bobbing little boat.

Lieutenant Colby assisted the girls into the craft. Each was seated between two large soldiers to guard them. Once Colby was aboard, the men rowed their oars in simultaneous, repetitive strokes. In a matter of moments, the distance between the small boat and the shoreline increased, and the dock was completely swallowed by the murky fog.

Silent questions filled Salina's brain. How could the oarsmen see through the clinging white mists to where they were going? How could she be sure they were going to the island? Surely they wouldn't row her and Taylor Sue out to sea to let them suffer their fate at the hands of the elements. Panic flooded her soul. *Get a hold of yourself, Sally,* she scolded inwardly. *They need us alive to question us.*

The little boat was shrouded by the mists until a beam of bright light sliced through the thick fog. Suddenly, a huge mass of sandstone protruded from the black waters. *Alcatraz.* Salina remembered Drake's mysterious words about the island.

Lieutenant Colby was the first ashore. He talked to the men standing on the wharf, and one of them nodded in response to the lieutenant's question. Taylor Sue was helped up to the landing first, and then Colby went back for Salina.

She stood up without his assistance. Her next step caught her heel on the hem of her skirt, and she lost both her footing and her balance. Salina fell overboard before Colby could grab her.

"*Salina!*" Taylor Sue's scream pierced the dark, damp air. At the top of her lungs she screamed again, "*Salina!*" One of the blue-uniformed guards held her fast as she helplessly witnessed her friend's head plunge beneath the surface of the inky water.

"C-Col-beee!" Salina wailed when she came up for air, but she sank under the water again all too quickly. Her petticoats, hoops, and the yards of material that made up her skirt tangled between her legs, weighing her down. Terrified, she furiously kicked, but she was unable to get her head above the surface again. *I am come into deep waters, where the floods overflow me.* Her arms were of little use with the iron handcuffs locked tightly around her wrists. *I am in God's hands. I am committed to His will for me. Jesus, take me to heaven to be with You...and my daddy...*

Lieutenant Colby dove into the icy-cold water, grabbing Salina and pulling her to the surface. The weight of her wet clothing nearly threatened to drown both of them. Through sheer determination he managed to bring her up to the surface so she could breathe the air once more.

Salt water stung her nose and throat as Salina took in a deep breath. She gasped repeatedly to fill her lungs with cold night air, coughing and choking and crying all at the same time.

Colby handed her up to the soldiers on the landing. "Take her to the Citadel, quickly. See that she's given dry clothes immediately and hot soup or tea."

"Yes, sir, Lieutenant Colby." One of the soldiers saluted.

Colby watched the guard carry Salina away, Taylor Sue hurrying along by their side.

"And what of you, sir?" the soldier who remained with him asked.

"I'll be along directly," Lieutenant Colby replied. "See that Miss Hastings is settled in a warm room and let Miss Carey tend to her. I want a guard posted outside the door. Bring the staff physician—and get her out of those confounded handcuffs!" he ordered.

He coughed a few times himself, bending to rest his hands on his knees. He dropped his head, resting his chin on his chest, arguing with himself. *She had merely slipped, lost her footing,* his mind screamed in a feeble attempt to convince himself that her fall had been nothing more than an accident. Surely Salina Hastings realized how futile an attempt to escape would be. The island of Alcatraz was surrounded by a mile of water on all sides. Yet, she was her father's daughter, he mused, and she should not be underestimated by any means.

Chapter Three

*T*he dream invaded Salina's restless slumber. She could feel herself growing cold, the harsh wind whipping all around her...alone, on an island, surrounded on all sides by deep, impassable waters. Hundreds of sheets of paper blew in the force of the wind, some landing in the water, floating on the surface, others consumed by lapping waves. Clearly she saw faces belonging to Daddy, Jeremy, and Drake, eerily replaced by those of Duncan Grant, Lieutenant Colby, and the Widow Hollis. Each of them was trying to get to Salina, but the water was far too deep for anyone to reach her. She was abandoned, only the sound of harsh, mocking laughter ringing in her ears...

"Salina, wake up." Taylor Sue shook her shoulder gently. "Salina, you're dreaming again."

Salina's green eyes opened wide and her fingers clutched the gold heart-shaped locket hanging from her neck. To lose Jeremy's locket would have been a devastating blow, and she was grateful that the clasp had held strong.

Salina had had the dream once before, during the first night of their arrival in San Francisco, and it had been virtually the same. She'd been on an island where no one, not even the Yankees, could reach her. She rubbed her arms to ward away the chill caused by the memory of the odd premonition. She was still very cold, and her teeth chattered involuntarily.

"Here." Taylor Sue wrapped Salina in another quilt. "You need to get warm."

The staff physician, Dr. Frank Laurence, arrived to check on Salina, as Lieutenant Colby ordered, and he shared Taylor Sue's opinion. "We'll get a fire going in here, and some more blankets." He gave Salina a hot cup of tea thickly laced with honey and lemon. "Drink all of that. It'll warm your insides," Dr. Laurence encouraged, watching her carefully. Her lips were a purplish shade of blue, and her small hands were icy numb with cold. If they weren't careful, pneumonia would set in, and that would never do. The Major would be heartily displeased if something like that were to happen.

"If she starts coughing, give her a spoonful or two of this," the blue-uniformed doctor gave instructions to Taylor Sue. He set a brown bottle of cough syrup on the table against the far wall. "If that doesn't help, be sure to call me."

Taylor Sue nodded, trying to hide her growing concern. "Thank you."

The Yankee doctor touched the brim of his cap. "Good night, both of you."

Salina nodded and wrapped herself more snugly in the quilted blankets. Her eyes brimmed with tears which spilled only after the door was locked again.

"Sssshhh." Taylor Sue rocked Salina in her arms. "Don't cry. Tears aren't going to help anything. We need to pray. God will supply us with the strength to get us through and off this bizarre island."

Salina's tears slipped silently down her pale cheeks while Taylor Sue offered her prayer to the Lord. Salina's body ached; she was desperately cold. The next time she slept, however, it was only Jeremy's face which appeared in her dreams.

☆☆☆☆☆☆☆

For most of the next day, the girls were left to themselves except for a few interruptions: visits from Dr. Laurence, the delivery of a satchel containing the remainder of the girls' few belongings, and punctual meal trays brought in by the guard outside the door.

Salina hardly touched her lunch, in spite of Taylor Sue's admonition to eat something. She'd been dozing restlessly on and off through the long hours, but at least the island dream had ceased to haunt her. Salina licked her dry lips and asked, "What day is it?"

"I believe today is the fifteenth," Taylor Sue guessed, staring out the window across the desolate water. They had been captured on Thursday, two days ago. She turned her back to the window; a view of San Francisco must be visible from rooms on the opposite side of the hall, but certainly not from here. "Perhaps they've forgotten about us because the Western Campaign has started and is taking up their full attention."

"I wonder if we would have heard anything," Salina whispered. In her heart, she felt that the campaign had failed, that she had failed.

The door burst open and Lieutenant Colby appeared at the threshold. The dark circles beneath his pale blue eyes and the blond stubble along his jaw made him look tired and worn out. "The Major has arrived, Miss Hastings, and he is waiting to see you."

One of the guards brought in Salina's dried clothing and laid it over the back of a chair. Her new shoes were carelessly dropped on the floor near the pile of fabric.

"Get dressed. I'll be back in twenty minutes to fetch you," Lieutenant Colby said in a tone which brooked no argument. "I expect you to be ready."

Salina nodded. "Yes, sir."

When Colby returned precisely twenty minutes later, Taylor Sue was brushing Salina's dark curls with a silver-handled brush. Salina was clothed once more in the dark green dress with its solid-colored bodice atop a paisley-print skirt. She had purchased it at Madame Lucy's Boutique just a few hours prior to her arrest. Without hoops, the yards of material that made up the skirt hung limply around Salina's feet. She met Colby's pale blue eyes evenly, refusing to show the Lieutenant even a slight hint of her apprehension.

"The Major will see you now," Lieutenant Colby stated. "Would you follow me, please?" It wasn't a choice, and Salina decided to obey his polite command without resistance.

"And what about me? Am I coming, too?" Taylor Sue suddenly asked. She didn't want Salina going to meet this Yankee Major alone and defenseless. She wanted to support Salina, even if it was only by being nearby.

"You will remain here, Miss Carey," Colby commanded, "until the Major is ready to put forth whatever questions he might have for you. He'll deal with both of you, I'm sure, but one at a time."

Squaring her shoulders, Salina lifted her chin to a somewhat defiant angle. Her head pounded, but she said, "Lead on, Lieutenant."

Colby turned his back on the Hastings girl, struggling to conceal the glint of grudging admiration shining in his eyes. Salina Hastings had nerve, and he respected her for that. Yet at the same time he was truly amazed. Did she not have an understanding of the gravity of her predicament? The Major was a powerfully connected man in Washington, and Salina's future might very well rest in his hands.

Salina wordlessly followed Lieutenant Colby. They walked through long corridors and up stairwells with only the sound of her skirt dragging on the floor behind her. She tried to shake the feeling that the walls were watching her every move. Unexpectedly, the Yankee Lieutenant stopped and Salina ran into the back of him. "Excuse me," she apologized.

Colby opened the door to his left. "No harm done," he replied, searching her eyes for a hint of emotion. Her pretty features were expressionless, however, and he could not tell what she was thinking.

Unconsciously, Salina drew a deep breath and swallowed hard. Her throat was sore and the swallow hurt, but she ignored the pain. Instead, Salina focused on the long, polished oak table dominating the room.

The Major sat at one end of the table, his back toward the door where Salina stood. She could see nothing of him except his elbows resting on the arms of the wing-backed chair he occupied. The sleeves of his dark blue woolen dress coat were trimmed with three curling gold braids which bespoke his rank. On his left hand was a plain wedding band of shiny gold.

"Do come in, Miss Hastings. Join us, if you will."

The rich voice immediately struck a certain cord of recognition, and Salina felt her apprehension give way to an inexplicable sense of relief. Perhaps it was because she only knew one Yankee Major—a Major John Barnes, who was Jeremy's uncle—and that certainly was not *his* voice. Major Barnes was a cruel man and, thankfully, he was far away.

She sent up a quick prayer and was rewarded with a sense of calm. *I can do all things through Christ who strengtheneth me.* Bravely she stepped forward into the meeting room, continuing until she reached the empty chair at the foot of the long table. She sat gracefully and purposefully. When at last she cast a glance at the Major, her green eyes widened in disbelief, and she was on her feet in an instant. "*You?!*" she cried out, slamming her palms against the tabletop.

"Hello, Miss Hastings." Duncan Grant nodded and a lopsided grin escaped his restraint. "I trust my being here hasn't caused you too much of a shock."

Salina merely blinked, speechless. The rich voice had sounded familiar because she knew its owner well. *"Major* Grant?" she asked incredulously.

"Yes, Major Grant," Duncan, who had been known to her previously as Captain Grant, confirmed. "I take it you have not heard of my recent promotion. Well, truth be told, I have you to thank for it."

"Me?" questioned Salina.

"I have been promoted on account of your capture," Duncan explained briefly, "which ultimately led to the dissolution of your father's plans for the Western Campaign. But, I am putting the cart before the horse. Forgive me." He motioned toward her chair. "Please, be seated. We aren't here to discuss my military accomplishments. We're here to discuss you, and more specifically, your reasons for being here in San Francisco—along with what part you held in the conspiracy itself."

Salina sat down, looking at the faces all around her. Duncan alone was the one she could trust, if she allowed herself to. But for now, she was on her guard and said nothing.

Duncan proceeded, "I see no cause for delay, so let's get started. For the record, would you please state your full name, your age, your date and place of birth."

"I am Salina Rose Hastings, aged sixteen years, born on the twentieth of August, 1846, at Shadowcreek, near Chantilly, Virginia," Salina responded in monotone.

Duncan formally introduced the committee seated with them at the table. "You know my Lieutenant, Lance Colby, and I believe you are acquainted with Lieutenant Everett, are you not?"

"He is married to my cousin, Marie." Salina nodded, smiling mildly into Everett's disgust-filled glare.

"Yes." Duncan had already learned they were related by marriage. "And you also know Mrs. Irene Hollis. I believe you first encountered one another as passengers aboard the same stagecoach which left Carson City in Nevada Territory, bound for San Francisco. Captain Weller, our committee secretary, is stationed here at Fortress Alcatraz. Thank you for your assistance, Captain."

Captain Weller nodded to Duncan Grant and then to Salina.

Duncan placed his hands on the papers in the open folder in front of him. For a scant instant, he caught the gleam of his wedding band. He mentally shrugged the thought of his recent marriage aside. That was a matter to be dealt with at another time. He couldn't break the news to Salina in front of all these people. He'd wait until he had the opportunity to speak to her alone. He knew Salina would not take kindly to the fact that he had gone and married her mother.

Duncan cleared his throat. "Miss Hastings, I am going to ask you some questions. It would be in your best interest to answer them truthfully." His gray eyes implored her to cooperate with him, to trust him. Admittedly, he was in a rather precarious position. While he was depending on her answers to gain information about the activities of Southern sympathizers, he was determined to find a way to protect her as best as he could without jeopardizing his duty to the Union army.

"What was your reason for coming to San Francisco, Miss Hastings?" Duncan asked.

"I came to visit some relatives," Salina replied. "My aunt lives here—my mamma's eldest sister."

"Did you come to get away from the war raging in Virginia?" Duncan queried.

"In a manner of speaking." Salina shrugged.

"Did you plan to stay for long?" One of his dark eyebrows raised in question.

"No." Salina shook her head. "I don't care much for the West, and I'd rather be back home, war or no. I miss my mamma, and my brother, and my friends."

"You were planning to return east on the fourteenth, scarcely forty-eight hours following your arrival. You traveled a great distance just for two days' worth of visitation with your aunt and her family. Do you know anyone else here in San Francisco?" Duncan asked.

"I do now," Salina replied casually. "I met Esther Nichols on the same stagecoach as I met Mrs. Hollis. Esther introduced me to her brother, who is a doctor. I had broken my arm prior to leaving Virginia, and Esther's brother was kind enough to remove the cast for me since my arm is healed now." She touched her left forearm, kneading it gently.

"And you know no one else?" Duncan wanted to make sure.

"No." Salina shook her dark head. "I do not know anyone one else who lives here."

Duncan went to the corner of the room and retrieved two wrapped items. "You've been on a shopping spree since you arrived in San Francisco. I believe this is a gown, complete with alterations, which you purchased from a dress shop called Madame Lucy's Boutique. And this." He handed her the smaller box. "Would you open it please." His order was in the tone of a request.

Inside was the gold pocket watch, engraved with her words to Jeremy. "It is a birthday gift for a dear friend of mine," Salina said softly.

Duncan made a show of inspecting the timepiece. "Very nice," he complimented, placing the watch with its fob in the palm of Salina's cold hand. "What else did you do while you were in town?"

"We went to Chinatown. Neither Taylor Sue nor I had ever tasted Chinese food before. Esther said we should," Salina told him.

"And did you like it?" asked Duncan.

Salina wrinkled her nose. "It was interesting, and it tasted rather good, but it's not like anything I'd ever had before. I struggled with the chopsticks most of the time."

Duncan allowed himself to smile. "I've had a similar experience." He returned to his seat and glanced over the papers. Then he said, "Miss Hastings, I have a report here that confirms everything you have just told me. It was voluntarily filed by your cousin, Gerard Dumont. Were you aware of the fact that you have been under surveillance since the moment you stepped off the stagecoach?"

"Why?" Salina answered with a question. "I didn't realize that shopping excursions and Chinese lunches were worthy of such attention by the United States Army."

"It was not the first instance you've been followed," Duncan continued. "And you are aware of that fact. You were followed every stop along the way from St. Joseph to San Francisco. Are you claiming you don't know the reason why?"

Salina sat with her hands folded, waiting to hear Duncan's explanation.

Duncan broke the long, forced stare between them. He produced written orders and said, "These, Miss Hastings, are warrants for the arrests of you and Miss Taylor Sue Carey. The grounds for these warrants are based on the premise that you are suspected of conspiracy against the United States. We believe that you have successfully made contact with Southern sympathizers here in the West, and your responsibility was to supply them with information which would set forth a Rebel-led revolt. Do you deny this?"

"What proof have you that I might be involved with such things, such people?" Salina's eyes burned like fire.

"Lieutenant Colby?" Duncan quirked an eyebrow at his young assistant.

Colby retrieved a wooden crate and proceeded to dump the contents onto the table in front of Salina.

"Surely you recognize these items?" Duncan prodded.

On one hand, Salina was relieved to see once more the items which had been taken from her room: blue and gray military uniforms of different rank, caps, boots, coats, several books, field glasses, train and stagecoach schedules, a map of the western territories, a small leather-bound notebook, falsified passports, a china-headed doll, outdated Northern newspapers, and some photographs—including a tintype of Mamma as she appeared as a young bride the day she'd married Garrett Hastings. On the other hand, Salina was saddened to view these things in the possession of Duncan Grant.

Salina met the Major's granite-gray eyes and shivered. This man across from her had once been her daddy's dearest friend. They had known each other for years. Together they had been cadets at West Point and then fought in the war with Mexico. But the War Between the States had driven an insurmountable wedge between them. Yet in spite of their differences of opinion concerning Union and States' Rights, slavery and freedom, they had remained friends—or at least tried to until Daddy's death had invariably severed the close bond between them.

"We're stalling, Major," Mrs. Hollis complained to Duncan. "Shall we get on with the line of questioning?"

"By all means," Duncan conceded. He turned to Salina. "Do you or do you not, Miss Hastings, recognize any of the items that are there before you?"

Salina lowered her eyes and swallowed. She put a hand to her mouth, emitting a soft cough. Finally, she looked up and nodded, admitting that she did indeed recognize the things Colby dumped from the crate.

"Speak up, please, Miss Hastings," the Widow Hollis said sharply. "Captain Weller is accountable for recording all of your replies. You merely nodded. Is that to say that you *do* recognize these items?"

"Yes," Salina answered plainly. "I recognize them." By her simple statement, she was agonizingly aware she was admitting much more than just familiarity with the items. She was caught, and she was in too deep to claim ignorance at this point.

"Did they belong to your father?" asked the Widow.

"Most of them. Some of the others were mine which he had given to me," Salina acknowledged.

The Widow Hollis reached for Celeste. "Such as this doll?"

"Yes." Salina nodded. "The doll was a gift for my birthday."

"You're a little old to be playing with dolls, aren't you?" the Widow goaded.

"I collect them," Salina clarified, taking the doll from the Widow's grasp. "I had a handful of others, but that was before our estate was fired by order of a Yankee officer. I reckon I'll have to start my collection all over when I get back home." Salina gently smoothed the doll's calico print dress.

"What was your father smuggling in the doll, Miss Hastings?" Duncan's direct question jolted Salina.

She looked at him squarely and again sensed his silent command: *Tell me the truth!* She knew she shouldn't trust this Yankee officer, but he had been her father's friend. Daddy had trusted him. Salina could do no less. She answered honestly, "There was money, a map, some medicine, a key, and a small leather-bound book."

"What happened to those things?" Duncan wanted to know.

"The money was spent, the map and book are here." She indicated the pile of items in front of her. "The medicine was used up, and the key was a spare that fit the lock of my traveling trunk."

Duncan searched through the items for the leather-bound book. It was something he'd never expected to see again. "Did you happen to look through here at all, Miss Hastings?" he queried, flipping through the pages. He missed the anxious look that flitted briefly across the Widow's features.

Salina nodded. "Yes, but I couldn't make any sense of it. It's coded by a cipher of some sort."

"And how would you know that?" the Widow inquired caustically.

"I have some knowledge of ciphers." Immediately Salina regretted the disclosure of that secret, but she returned pointedly, "Don't you, Mrs. Hollis?"

The Widow Hollis's eyes narrowed into angry slits. "Don't be impertinent with me, you little Rebel..."

Duncan interrupted, "You never tried to break the code in the book?"

"No," Salina said simply.

"Well, why not?" He was curious, and he did not doubt that she might have been able to do it had she given it a try. Salina learned to decipher codes from Garrett, and he would have taught her well.

"Daddy told me to keep it for him, nothing more. I merely followed my instructions," Salina replied.

"You're here in San Francisco because you followed his instructions, too, aren't you?" Duncan pressed.

"Yes." Salina nodded.

"You are an obedient daughter, Miss Hastings, admirably so. Obedience is a fine trait. So is honesty. Why did you join in his fight?"

"I only wanted to help him if I could," Salina answered. "I got bored just darning socks, mending uniforms, and rolling bandages like the others involved with the Women's Assistance Guild. I wanted to do something to make a difference."

"Such as launching a Confederate takeover of California and the bordering western territories?" Duncan prodded, straining to keep the sarcasm from his voice. He was not surprised when she wouldn't answer. He hadn't really expected her to. He rephrased his question. "Why do *you* fight, Miss Hastings? Do you believe so strongly in the Rebel Cause?"

Salina's mind raced. What *did* she believe? The definition of the Southern "Cause" escaped her. It was a widely used phrase applied to scores of opinions and beliefs all rolled into one. "I...," she faltered. "I'm a Virginian by birth, and I believe the States should have certain rights..."

"That's your father talking," Duncan brushed her reply aside. "Do you approve of slavery as a right of each individual state? Would you rejoice to see Jubilee or Peter Tom or anyone with a different colored skin reduced to a life of forced bondage and hard labor? They are human beings, Miss Hastings. Don't you think they deserve to be treated as such?"

"Well, yes, I do think so, but..." Salina shook her head in confusion. Slavery was *not* something Salina condoned. But like it or not, the "peculiar institution" was part of Salina's heritage and the Southern way of life. But times were changing. "I'm not fighting to keep slavery," she insisted. "We freed our slaves at Shadowcreek. You know that."

"Then what is it that you, personally, feel the need to fight for?" Duncan pressed for an answer. "Do you even know, or have you simply become swept along in the patriotic rebellious fury?"

"I don't think that slavery is right," she repeated. "And while I really don't understand enough about the government to take up issues over states' rights, or the implications of dissolving or salvaging the Union, I do know this: The Yankees invaded the South. They've marched and fought all over Northern Virginia. They've trespassed in our homes and on our property, taking what they will in horses and livestock, food and crops. They've battled in our fields, across our streams, and on our hills. And I have tended to the wounded they have left in their wake. I am not a man, so I must use other means to defend my homeland, my friends, and my family, as I'm sure you would fight to defend yours!"

Her spirited answer moved Duncan. Up to now, he had given little pause to think of how life must be on the Southern homefront. And until a few weeks ago he'd not had a wife or family of his own to worry about. He nodded, accepting Salina's answer, wondering if he might have opened her eyes for the first time to the very reasons which had led her here.

He sorted through the confiscated documents which Salina and Taylor Sue diligently translated on the night of their arrival. Many of these translated pages replaced coded pages which had been taken from his office at the War Department. "Your father appropriated this information and the maps in order to further his plans," Duncan said quietly. "When he knew I was on his trail, he forwarded them here to San Francisco, and sent you after them. Isn't that right?"

"Yes," Salina replied.

"I have here the documents you forwarded to your Southern contact." Duncan laid the recovered pages in front of her. He pointed. "This is a detailed plan of attack approved by the high command of the Confederacy." He rubbed his chin. "Today might have been a Confederate victory if we hadn't caught up with these plans, Miss Hastings, a victory we Yankees could not afford. Fortunately, the plans were recovered before they reached the hands of the Rebel leaders. As you'd expect, I've sent men to scour the area for those people named on the lists, but naturally, they've all managed to go into hiding. Who was your contact, Miss Hastings? I want to know. Who was it was that instructed you to leave the documents at Madame Lucy's?"

Salina would not answer. She mentally resigned herself to answering Duncan's questions when they pertained directly to her, but she could not bring herself to implicate anyone else.

Salina's evident Southern loyalties only served to anger the Widow Hollis further. "We've arrested Dr. Ben Nichols," the Widow shrieked, "and we'll find the others whether or not you tell us their identities. You're a little fool. The Union will prevail. We'll hunt down the miserable Rebel traitors to be punished for their actions. And you..."

"That's enough, Mrs. Hollis." Duncan's icy glare instantly silenced the raving of the female Federal agent. He hadn't intended to let Salina know yet that the Rebel doctor had been taken into custody.

Salina tried to hide her dissapointment that Dr. Nichols had been captured. She tipped her head to one side. "You hate me so much, Mrs. Hollis, though I don't understand why. We've never known each other before Carson City, yet you seem to think that you do know me somehow."

"I know who your father was, and that's all I need to know. He murdered my husband in San Diego—shot him down in cold blood! I won't rest until I see that *you* pay for his transgressions!" the Widow hissed.

Salina's eyes grew round. "What are you talking about?"

"It is not relevant to this case, Mrs. Hollis." Duncan's patience was wearing thin. "Calm yourself and be seated, or I will dismiss you from the proceedings."

The Widow complied, but she leveled a cold stare at Salina.

"Back to the matter at hand," Duncan continued, somewhat agitated. He ran his fingers through his chestnut hair. The inquisition had dragged on long enough. Salina had confirmed what they had already discovered, and she would not voluntarily shed light on anything new. He neatly stacked the papers and replaced them in the folder. "For all intents and purposes, you have answered our questions to the best of your ability, Miss Hastings. We have the proof we need to prove your involvement in the conspiracy. You will remain here until I receive orders from Washington concerning what is to be done with you."

He looked towards Salina, who was coughing again. Throughout the afternoon she'd done more and more coughing, and Duncan noticed that she looked flushed, perhaps a little feverish. "We have you, Miss Taylor Sue Carey, and Dr. Ben Nichols in custody, thanks to Gerard Dumont's devotion to the Union. You see, Miss Hastings, people will do anything if their beliefs are rooted firmly enough. Gerard believes in the Union, and he was willing to supply Mrs. Hollis with information to lead her to you. Lieutenant Colby and his men were at your heels, tracking you all the way. It is rather obvious to me that your father hoped by sending you here, the plans might have a chance, but they failed. Have you anything else to add, Miss Hastings?"

"No, Major," Salina replied, shaking her head from side to side.

"Then this discussion is, at least for the present time, closed." Duncan's words seemed cold and final. He stood, and the other committee members did likewise.

Salina was dismissed, but she knew this was not over. Lieutenant Colby motioned her to follow him, but she halted in front of Duncan.

He looked down at her flushed face and laid a hand on her shoulder, giving her an imperceptible squeeze. "Whether you choose to believe it or not, we are grateful for what help you've given us."

"I've betrayed those who put their trust in me," she lamented in a small whisper.

The depth of pain and sorrow in her turbulent eyes startled Duncan, but his lips formed an uncompromising line. He had no words of comfort for her. She was the enemy, and it would be wise for him to remember that. He watched her go. Shoulders which had been squared earlier were now slumped, and another harsh cough ripped through her.

The committee quickly disbanded. Captain Weller handed Duncan the pages recorded during the session, and silently Lieutenant Everett followed him out. The Widow Hollis delayed her departure. "Will the sentencing be handled by the courts here?" she wanted to know.

"I don't know yet." Duncan shrugged. "But I don't think so. There's more to it than what's on the surface, Irene. There are other things involved with this which I am not at liberty to discuss." Duncan did not meet her angry eyes as he continued to sift through the translated pages. Something he was looking for was missing. It was the one thing which Salina's case hinged upon. He looked up, and the Widow still stood in the meeting room. "Was there something else, Irene?"

"Something's changed you," she said intuitively. "You've lost your edge, Duncan. You let a sixteen-year-old girl get to you. I thought you were a better agent than that."

The Widow's accusation stung. "Thank you for your appraisal," he said brusquely. He reached into the breast pocket of his dress coat and pulled out a flat leather wallet. He withdrew an envelope and handed it to her. "Here is a copy of the report I will be filing with reference to your contributions and work on this project. You, Irene, are a very good agent, and the Union extends her gratitude yet again. I've been granted the authority to offer you a position in Washington, but I don't think that would suit you. You're very much accustomed to the West, and I, for one, want you to keep working here. We've come to rely on your services."

"I will never go back to Washington," the Widow Hollis confirmed. She accepted the envelope. "I will wait here only until I have my next orders, then I will go to work wherever I am assigned."

"Very well." Duncan nodded. He watched the black-clad woman go. It was difficult to distinguish what drove her—the love of her country or the opportunity to seek revenge. Uncannily, she reminded him of Major John Barnes. Oddly enough, they seemed to share a common goal. Both of them were driven to destroy Captain Hastings.

Now that Garrett was dead, they were determined to lash out at those who were close to him.

Duncan sat alone in the empty conference room, thinking of his dead friend's daughter. Salina looked so forlorn, so fragile, so defeated...

Defeated? Duncan wondered at that. Capturing Salina and the Rebels' plans to invade the West might have prevented the Union from having to fight another battle such as those that had been waged at Valverde and Glorieta Pass in New Mexico Territory in the early weeks of 1862, but they were still a long way from winning the war.

The Rebels might not have as many men, or the seemingly unlimited resources, or a way to lift the blockade—but Duncan knew well that the South had pride, spirit, determination, and dependable generalship which kept their Cause afloat. Salina had been correct in saying that some of the Southerners fought against invasion, to keep their land, homes, and property, while others fought for the rights of individual state governments. There were still others, though, who fought to maintain their aristocratic lifestyles, which included the evil of slavery. Conversely, the Yankees fought for ideals such as Union, freedom, equality—noble causes, to be sure, and Duncan believed they were just causes in themselves.

He thought back on the bloody Battle of Antietam, when General Robert E. Lee had led his ragged Rebel army on a northward invasion. A healthy dose of fear had been instilled in the states above the Mason-Dixon Line, because Lee had brought the war to their own Northern doorsteps. *What if Lee and the Army of Northern Virginia had succeeded on that September day? What if he were to try such tactics again? And for that matter, what if Garrett Hastings's plans had been successfully carried out? What might have happened if the Confederacy had actually managed to extend its region all the way to the Pacific Ocean?* Duncan shook his head and sighed. For the moment he chose to let the matter rest.

Duncan pounded the table with his fist. He had to find those missing pages, but he didn't even know where to begin the search. And he had yet to explain to Salina the gold wedding band he now wore.

☆☆☆☆☆☆☆

November 15, 1862
Tabitha Wheeler's Boarding House
Fairfax Court House, Virginia

Reverend Yates entered stealthily through the back door of the boarding house run by Tabitha Wheeler on the edge of Fairfax. "Good evening, Tabitha."

"Reverend." The short, sprightly old woman secured the door behind him.

"Is he here yet?" inquired Reverend Yates.

"No, but I expect him shortly." Tabitha Wheeler revealed a smile that was missing a few teeth. Wisdom and experience glittered in her knowing eyes. At the hearth she stirred a kettle of thick, fragrant stew. "Have you had your dinner already, Reverend?"

"No, I haven't. You wouldn't happen to have a bowl to spare, would you?" Reverend Yates seated himself at the kitchen table. "It smells delicious."

Tabitha set a steaming bowl and spoon in front of the Reverend. She listened for the faint sounds of a rider's approach. "There he is now. I'll fetch another bowl. Knowing him, he's sure to be hungry."

Jeremy Barnes's boots struck the wooden staircase which led to the back door, then clomped onto the kitchen floor. "'Lo, Reverend, Tabitha," he greeted them with a grin, respectfully touching the brim of his plumed slouch hat.

"Well, well, if those aren't *Lieutenant's* stripes! Did you steal that jacket, son?" Tabitha teased.

"No, ma'am." Jeremy gratefully dipped his spoon into the bowl she put in front of him. "Mmmm...this is mighty tasty, Tabitha. General Stuart has promoted me. I find he is quite an interesting man. He believes the highest compliment he can pay to one of his soldiers is to send them to face the enemy, which is exactly what he ordered me to do. He was pleased, though, with my actions under fire and puts my knowledge of the surrounding area to use as a guide and courier. Thus, the promotion."

"There's fine bit of news and a well-deserved honor." Tabitha winked. "I reckon the General's probably had his eye on you since he finagled that prisoner exchange. They say Stuart handpicks the best to serve with his command."

"Well, I thank you for saying so." Jeremy nodded, warmed by the old woman's confidence in him.

"I've some news for you, Jeremy," the Reverend leaned over the table and whispered. "That new commander of the Army of the

Potomac—General Ambrose Burnside—he's heading out of Warrenton. He's headed south."

"'*On to Richmond*,' no doubt," Jeremy said between bites. It was the constant cry of the Federal government in Washington. "Lincoln wants action, so Burnside will have to show him what he can do. Otherwise Lincoln will keep changing generals until he can find one who'll fight!"

"I reckon so." Reverend Yates nodded his bald head and rubbed his gray, bearded chin. He adjusted his spectacles on the bridge of his nose and secured them behind his ears, just below the remaining fringe of his short gray hair. "Scouting for Stuart seems to agree with you."

"It's always an adventure." Jeremy flashed a dazzling white smile, which was tinged with a hint of sadness. "It keeps the hours full of activity, which helps them pass by more quickly." He toyed with chunks of potatoes and carrots in his bowl and asked, "Have you heard anything? Is there any word of when she's coming back?"

Tabitha set a plate of newly baked cornbread between the two men. "I've sweet butter if you like."

"No, thank you." Jeremy shook his head. The Reverend also declined. "Well?" Jeremy prodded.

Tabitha sat down. She took Jeremy's large hand between her two gnarled ones. There was no use in beating around the bush, so she said, rather bluntly, "Jeremy, she's been taken. The Yankees caught up with them in San Francisco, and she and Taylor Sue Carey have been imprisoned at the Fortress Alcatraz."

Jeremy's entire body stiffened, and he pulled his hand away from Tabitha's. His knuckles whitened as he gripped the edge of the table tightly. "No..."

Reverend Yates took the telegram from his jacket pocket. "Somebody named Drake sent this."

"Drake?" Jeremy's blue eyes traveled rapidly over the brief lines which verified what Tabitha had said. "Dear God..." he breathed an unfinished prayer. He looked to the Reverend. "What do you suppose will happen to her?"

"I'm afraid I don't have an answer for you," Revered Yates said. "You know this Drake?"

"Rode with him. He's a trusted friend. We worked for Russell, Majors, and Waddell as Pony Express riders," Jeremy said off-handedly, still trying to come to grips with the news of Salina's capture. "I've got to go after her!" he blurted out impetuously.

"Now, simmer down a second, son," Tabitha said firmly.

"If you leave, Jeremy, it's considered desertion from the army," Reverend Yates cautioned. "You're a soldier now—an officer, even— and your work is here. In that telegram, Drake indicates that he will go after the girls when he returns to San Francisco."

"But that'll take weeks! There's no telling what will happen to them in all that time," Jeremy said, a sick feeling of helplessness settling deep in the pit of his stomach. "I'll ask for leave...I'll...I'll..."

"You'll do no such thing." Tabitha shook her white head. "You'll stay and fight, just as she's fighting. Salina will manage. She's her father's daughter."

"Her father's dead," Jeremy unnecessarily reminded the old woman. "What if..."

"Sssshhh." Tabitha put a quick finger to her lips. "No cause to speak such dark thoughts aloud. I only meant that Salina's young and she's strong, and that if it's truly Duncan Grant who's holding her a prisoner, she might have a chance for a safe return. It is a small hope, Lieutenant Barnes, but one to cling to nonetheless."

"I wish I could believe that." Jeremy sighed heavily. "Captured. I told her I didn't want her to go..."

"She had little choice. We all know that and the risks she took. If she hadn't gone when she did, the Yankees would have caught her here, sooner. Or they might've taken her at Ivywood—you know that as well as I do. There's simply no use in mulling it over again," the Reverend said. "The girls are in the Lord's hand. We'll pray earnestly that His will might be done concerning the two of them—concerning us all."

Jeremy finally nodded. He pushed away the unfinished bowl of stew and the piece of cornbread. His usually healthy appetite had abandoned him. He wiped his mouth with a checkered napkin and was suddenly on his feet. "I've got to go. I can't stay here. I'm carrying dispatches and am expected to report back to headquarters by morning. Please, if either of you hear anything else about her, let me know. Ever since her mother disappeared, I've had a bad feeling something might happen. I'll get word to Ethan. He'll have to be told about Taylor Sue."

Reverend Yates nodded. "You take care of yourself, Jeremy. We'll be praying for you, and Salina and Taylor Sue as well. Give Ethan our best when you see him."

"Right." Jeremy buttoned his overcoat and put his hat on. He mounted Comet and rode away into the darkness.

"He'll not have a moment's rest until she comes home," Tabitha murmured.

"As if he didn't have enough to deal with already," the Reverend mused. "Find out what you can through the Remnant and keep me posted." Though the Network Captain Hastings had established might have dissolved on a large scale, those who remained locally, those calling themselves the Remnant, could still be of use.

"Rest assured, I will." Tabitha nodded. "I get some Yankee boarders from time to time. I'll listen close and see if there's anything worth anything in their conversations."

"You be careful," Reverend Yates instructed. "Don't do anything to jeopardize your position. You're still a valuable link to us, Tabitha."

"I know. Tell Mrs. Yates I have some nice jellies and jams, and I'll expect a visit from her at the beginning of next week." Tabitha escorted the Reverend to the door. "Do you think the girls will be released?" Tabitha ventured to ask.

"I pray to God they will." The Reverend sighed. "As you told Jeremy, we must cling to our hope that they will come back."

"Aye." Tabitha nodded somberly. "Good night, Reverend." She returned to the kitchen, clearing away the evidence of her guests.

☆☆☆☆☆☆☆

The Citadel on Alcatraz Island
San Francisco Bay, California

Duncan Grant still sat at the far end of the long table, sorting through the items that had been confiscated from Salina's room at Genevieve Dumont's house and the packets of information seized from the dressing room at Madame Lucy's Boutique. Lieutenant Colby, having returned Salina to her room, came back and sat down in one of the chairs.

Without looking up, Duncan remarked, "Why is it, Lieutenant, that I get the feeling you're holding your tongue?"

Lance Colby grinned. "Because, sir, I am. I've worked with you for the better part of a year now, and if there's one thing I've learned in that amount of time, it's that you rarely do anything without valid reason."

The Major nodded. "You're right. Everything has got to be planned to the letter, then masterfully executed." A pondering expression furrowed his brow. "How did you arrive at this conclusion, that every move I make has a purpose?"

"Well," Colby replied, "look at the incident this September past, when Captain Hastings was arrested and taken to the Old Capitol

Prison. You explained to me then that you had arranged for his release because as long as he was locked up, he couldn't lead you to the information you suspected he had in his possession. I watched you bide your time, make your plans, and lo and behold, it was Salina, rather than her father, who revealed exactly what it was you were after."

"It wasn't so much Salina as it was Ben Nichols. The Rebel doctor was too careless." Duncan crossed his arms over his broad chest. "It was he who led us to the information, not Salina. She proved to be very elusive, like her father. You know, Colby—and I am loathe to admit this—Salina was very, *very* close to pulling the whole thing off."

"She's a remarkable young lady," Lieutenant Colby spoke frankly. "Not only is she beautiful, but intelligent as well. Dangerous combination, wouldn't you agree?"

Duncan Grant's mouth formed a weak grin. "She is clever..." His thoughts trailed into silence. Colby's earlier comments had hit the mark squarely. Duncan *did* possess a certain degree of skill in manipulating situations so their outcome might best serve his purpose. He absently twisted his wedding band, another such testimony to his ability to maneuver certain circumstances.

Colby watched the Major quietly for a minute as he kept going through the same papers over and over. The restlessness led him to believe that Duncan Grant might not be satisfied with the way Salina's interview had concluded. "Sir, if you'll permit me to speculate, am I correct in guessing that you are still in search of *something*, and that Salina Hastings has the capability to lead you to it? Otherwise, why would you let her off as easy as you have?"

"Oh, she's not free and clear, Lieutenant, no, no." Duncan shook his head. "I simply didn't want Mrs. Hollis to make any more of a scene than she already had. For the most part, Salina answered the way I suspected she would, given her circumstances. You were there. You heard for yourself. There was no new information elicited from Salina's testimony. We knew everything she told us prior to questioning her. She merely supplied the confirmation. However, you are correct, Colby, there *is* something else—one missing piece to the puzzle. Yet judging by her replies, I don't think Salina herself knows what it is. And if she isn't aware of it, then perhaps Taylor Sue Carey might be. Guilty by association or not, I'm bound to question Miss Carey in order to find out whatever I can."

"What will happen to them, sir?" Colby asked in an attempt to sound lightly inquisitive and not overly curious. "Surely they won't have to stay locked up here at Alcatraz, will they?" The guardhouse was already overflowing with soldier prisoners incarcerated for punishable offenses. And civilian prisoners suspected of Southern sympathies had been brought to the remote island after their arrests were made without due process of the law. Those boldly outspoken for secession were mixed in with those who refused to take an Oath of Allegiance to the Union.

Duncan shrugged. "What happens to the young ladies will ultimately depend on the reply I receive from Washington. Since Fortress Alcatraz is where they bring anyone whose loyalties are in question, they might well have to stay here on the island. From what I've been told, the authorities in San Francisco aren't taking any chances on anyone even remotely connected to the Confederacy. They don't want trouble here."

Colby was inexplicably bothered in knowing Salina might have to stay on the damp, eerie, wind-swept island in the middle of the bay. He shouldn't care what happened to her, but he was starting to. "What would you have me do now, sir?"

"Nothing more at present. I'll send for you when I need you," Duncan said distractedly.

"Very good, sir. Then I'll take my leave. I'm most interested to learn what your conversation with Miss Carey brings." Colby touched the brim of his cap in salute.

"Yes, you and me both." Duncan packed the items one by one into the wooden crate.

With a click of his heels Colby turned and walked out of the room, leaving Duncan alone to think a while longer on the things he had yet to do. He fidgeted with his gold wedding band again, pondering the fact that he was the husband of Annelise Spencer Hastings.

Matrimony had been the farthest thing from Duncan's mind. He was nearly forty years old, had never been married before, and was in the midst of a war. But wedlock became the only way to remove Annelise from the reach of the over-zealous Major Barnes.

John Barnes had never made a secret of his hatred for Garrett Hastings, though the foundation for the deep animosity was sketchy. In truth, Duncan had never given much thought as to why John Barnes hated Garrett Hastings, considering it of little import. It was becoming clear, however, that Barnes had turned his search for the Rebel captain from duty and orders into a personal vendetta. Since Hastings was dead and Major Barnes was unable to pursue the man beyond his grave, Barnes now set his sights on the rest of the Hastings family.

To Barnes's dismay, the son had joined the Rebel army under Stonewall Jackson, and the daughter had fled Virginia altogether. That left Hastings's widow, and Barnes became determined to hunt her down.

By providential chance, Duncan had seen with his own eyes the order to issue an arrest warrant bearing Annelise's name. He could not stomach the thought of Garrett's lovely wife incarcerated in a dark, dank prison cell. She'd been through too much in the last few months— a miscarriage, the death of her husband, and the seeming desertion of her children. Duncan wanted to remove her from the trouble at hand, so he'd married her. Then he took her out of Virginia altogether—north to Gettysburg, where no one knew her, to hide her in the shelter of his family in the small anonymous Pennsylvania farming town. He believed Annelise would be safe there, away from Major John Barnes or anyone else who might wish to do her harm in retaliation for the acts of her deceased husband. Garrett Hastings had his share of enemies, and war seemed to have strange effects on people. Besides, Shadowcreek had been destroyed, and there was nothing left for her but sadness.

Initially Annelise had balked at the idea of marrying Duncan. She listened to what he thought were all sound reasons for the match. He only wanted what was in her best interest, he had argued. He was trying to honor Garrett's memory by keeping his vow to protect her, not to defile his memory, as Annelise vehemently accused. At last Duncan had convinced Annelise that there was no better solution, and she surrendered, albeit reluctantly, to his proposal of marriage. She took Duncan's name and his ring, if not his love. He knew she failed to see the wisdom of marrying a Yankee like himself; but with her spirit waning, consent followed, and she mildly accepted her fate.

Duncan shook himself out of his reverie and quickly gathered together his papers and Salina's belongings. He smiled sadly. Duncan did not imagine for a minute that Salina would be as docile as her mother had been as far as the arrangement was concerned. How could he explain what had taken place to Garrett's daughter?

☆☆☆☆☆☆☆

"You're taking this too hard, Salina." Taylor Sue rocked back and forth, back and forth, with Salina in her arms, crying uncontrollably. "It's *not* your fault. You did the best you could do. No one can ask for more."

Salina wracked her tired brain for something that she could have done differently. "B-ut the cam-campaign f-failed b-because of m-me..."

"No, Salina, I don't believe that." Taylor Sue shook her russet head with determination. "I think the campaign failed because the Yankees finally got wise. It was only a matter of time before they caught up with us." Taylor Sue stroked Salina's dark head. "We prayed that God's will would be done. Perhaps it's His will that the Rebels don't invade California. We don't see things the same way He does, Salina. And He doesn't always answer our prayers with a *yes*. Perhaps what we think is the best course of action is not in His plan. We have to wait on Him, seek His ways and not our own. All things work together for good—His good. He's our Heavenly Father and He knows much better than we do what is right for us. It is a matter of trusting in Him."

"I kn-know," sobbed Salina. She was coughing again. Her head pounded and her chest felt as though an iron weight had been laid upon it, making breathing difficult. The tears continued to stream down her face even while Taylor Sue rocked in silent comfort.

The door of their room banged open, slamming against the wall, startling them both. It was Duncan. A frown creased his forehead as he looked at the two girls.

"Are you sick, Salina?" He shut the door behind him.

"I'll b-be f-fine, M-Major," Salina stammered.

"Lieutenant Colby has told me of your plunge into the ocean. And he believes that it was not an attempt to escape. Is that true?" Duncan cocked an eyebrow in question.

"It was an accident," Taylor Sue defended Salina. "Her heel caught on her hem, that's all."

"Salina?" Duncan expected an answer from Garrett's daughter.

"It w-was an accident, M-Major. If I h-had intended t-to attempt an escape," she coughed, "I'd n-not have ch-chosen the d-dock or a m-mile of water s-surrounding m-me."

Salina's saucy answer pleased him; it meant she hadn't given up fighting. "I'll send for Dr. Laurence to examine you again. We don't want pneumonia to develop."

Salina nodded, covering her mouth as another spasm of coughing shook her slight, shivering frame.

"Salina, I have something that I must tell you," Duncan's gray eyes were filled with concern for her. He didn't want to upset her, but she must be told. And he wanted to be the one to tell her. "Salina, I've married your mamma."

"What?" Salina coughed several times and her heart raced frantically. "You've done *what?*"

"I've married Annelise," he repeated, refusing to acknowledge the look of sheer horror in her eyes. "Now don't get all riled up. Just give me a chance to explain." Duncan methodically went through the whole order of things, step by step, point by point—the arrest warrant, Major Barnes's apparent obsession with her family, the desire to obey society's dictates. None of his practiced rationale, however, had prepared him for Salina's stormy reaction.

"Mamma'd only been a widow for two months! She hasn't even mourned Daddy properly, and you've gone and married her!" Salina exclaimed angrily. "How could you?" A fresh rush of tears streamed down her flushed face.

Duncan clamped his teeth tightly; the muscle along his jaw line twitched. "I'm not asking for your approval or understanding, Salina," he said lowly. "I merely wanted you to hear it from me first. I brought a letter from Annelise. She wanted me to give it to you when I saw you." He handed Salina the envelope. "That will explain that I didn't force her into it, but that she, too, saw the sense in it. I've given her my name, my ring, and a safe shelter. I've fulfilled my vow to your father."

"Do you love her?" Salina demanded.

The innocent question startled him. "I've known your mamma since long before you were born, Salina. I always told Garrett I thought he was a lucky man to have such a wife. She's a good woman, one whom I am genuinely fond of. She was deeply in love with your daddy, and still is. I understand that. Our marriage is not based on romantic love, but there is a bond between us that has grown over the years of our long acquaintance. When I first met her she was Garrett's girl, and a friend of his was always a friend of mine."

"You've never been married before," Salina remembered. Whenever Duncan visited Shadowcreek, never once had he brought a family with him.

"No." Duncan shook his chestnut head. "I was engaged to be married once, a long time ago. There was an accident at a skating party, and the girl I loved fell through a patch of thin ice. I couldn't get to her in time, and she drown. After that I busied myself with my family's business and farming—until the war came. And now that occupies all my time and energy." Duncan paused. A sad smile turned down the corners of his mouth. "Perhaps one day, when you and your mamma get over the fact that I am a Yankee soldier, we'll all learn to love one another. Until that time, she is legally my wife, and it is my duty to take care of her the best way I know how."

Salina blinked, completely taken aback. Duncan Grant was her stepfather—her *Yankee* stepfather. It was too much, too soon, and her head ached all the more. She moved to the window, hugging her quilt about her, and gazed out at water. She watched silently as the white fog rolled in, enshrouding the island on all sides, cutting them off from the mainland and San Francisco. She closed her eyes and leaned her dark head against the window frame. All she wanted was to go home to Virginia, to the way things used to be. Yet she knew wishing had little effect on changing the precarious situation she found herself in.

Well, that's done, Duncan thought uneasily as he watched Salina at the window. *It's best to have it out in the open. Or was it? Was marrying Annelise worth the pain he was inflicting on them—on himself?* Now was not the time to dwell on it. Duncan cleared his throat. "Miss Carey, I've come to ask you a few questions."

Taylor Sue nodded absently. She was just as disconcerted by what Duncan had divulged as Salina was. "What is it that you want to know, Major?"

Duncan regained his composure. "Miss Carey, did you assist Salina with any of her translating or sending messages?"

Taylor Sue cast a worried glance at Salina.

Sensing Taylor Sue's uncertainty, Salina nodded, encouraging her to tell Duncan the truth. Their predicament was quickly shifting into a paradoxical matter of trust.

Taylor Sue answered Duncan's query, "I helped her with transcription, but I never sent any messages."

"Among all those maps, the lists of names, and locations of supplies, arms and ammunition, and the mail and freight schedules, do you recall *anything* that might have seemed out of place in relationship to the Western Campaign?" inquired Duncan.

"No, I don't think so. I mean, all those items seemed to tie in together right down to the instructions as to when the campaign would be launched. It should have happened this morning, had things gone as planned," Taylor Sue confessed.

"Yes." Duncan sighed. "There was nothing else?"

"Well." Taylor Sue tipped her head to one side, pondering. "Come to think of it, there was *one* thing that was different." Again she looked to her friend. "Remember, Salina? There were several pages that weren't in your father's handwriting. The ones where only his notes were in the margins."

Salina nodded. For some reason, it hadn't seemed important at the time, but now it clicked into place.

"What?" Duncan asked anxiously. "What was it?"

"It was an assassination plot to kill Abraham Lincoln," Salina answered somberly. "It was mixed in with those documents Daddy took from your office at the War Department."

Certainty dawned on the Major. All those papers Garrett managed to steal from his office in Washington last September...Duncan slapped his knee. "That's it! I had a gut feeling something was missing. That's exactly what it is!"

"You knew of it?" Taylor Sue questioned. "It was downright evil."

"It was," Salina agreed, shivering. "Daddy didn't like it. He wrote that he couldn't bring himself to pass something like that on, even though he was a Rebel. He drew up the plans for the attempted Confederate invasion of the West, but I know he didn't plan something that wicked."

"Rest assured, Garrett wasn't involved in hatching that scheme." Duncan patted Salina's hand. "I know who is behind the assassination plot, and I am ashamed to confess that it is someone who works in the Capitol itself. He's what we call a mole. While he pretends to support the Union, he secretly sells information about the Union government and Federal troops to Confederate spies for tidy sums of money. He is a slippery fellow whose allegiance can be bought by the highest bidder, and he usually leaves no traces behind him. If I had those papers you've mentioned, I could go back to Washington and have him removed from his post and tried for treason against the United States. However, those pages were not with those that you left for Dr. Nichols to pick up."

Salina shook her head. "Like Daddy, I couldn't bring myself to pass them along either. The Southern sympathizers here did not know of the existence of the scheme."

"If you didn't pass the pages along, then where are they?" Duncan wanted to know.

"We tore them up," Taylor Sue answered simply. "Salina tossed them into the grate to be burned."

"In your room at the Dumont house?" Duncan was immediately on his feet, standing beside Salina at the window.

"Yes." Salina nodded. "I didn't want to be involved with that any more than Daddy did."

Duncan was out the door, hollering for Lieutenants Colby and Everett. He sent them immediately back to the mainland, in spite of the dark foggy night, with orders to search the ashes. Duncan could only hope and pray that he wasn't too late. He reentered Taylor Sue and Salina's room and declared confidentially, "If they can find anything, any little trace of proof, then I will have my basis for requesting your pardons."

"Pardons?" the two girls asked in unison, certain they had heard him incorrectly.

"Yes, pardons," Duncan repeated resolutely. "In my report to the President, I mean to rationalize that by destroying the pages which contained the assassination plot, you've done the Union a service by protecting Lincoln's life." His mind churned swiftly. "It's the only basis on which I can justify such a recommendation. I know I may be grabbing at straws, but I know of no other way to see that the two of you are set free."

Salina willed herself to believe what Duncan was implying. He evidently didn't waste the time to consider what might happen to all of them if he were discovered. "First, you risked helping Daddy try to escape. Now us."

"No—not an escape." Duncan's eyes flashed. "Not this time." Vivid memories of his last meeting with Garrett Hastings in a dark prison cell flooded his mind, and Duncan shook his head to clear them. "A pardon would be different, but that remains up to President Lincoln."

"What if there isn't anything left? What if the pages have all been burned up?" Salina asked. "If you have no proof, then what will they do to us?"

Duncan set his square jaw. "I gave my word of honor to your father that I would look after you. There has to be *something* left in that grate. There *must* be!"

Chapter Four

*A*fter Duncan left, the girls sat quietly together, without speaking aloud. The glances they exchanged, however, communicated what their words did not. The hope Duncan had planted with his talk of their pardons was mirrored in each of their eyes.

Dr. Laurence arrived within the hour to check on Salina's condition. His thermometer indicated that Salina's temperature was high. Then he listened to her chest and back through an instrument he called a stethoscope.

"Very congested, I'm afraid," Dr. Laurence murmured, clearly unhappy. "I will prepare a mustard poultice for you, and I have a tonic that has worked for some of the men here. It's not the tastiest stuff, but it should alleviate the coughing to a certain degree and help you sleep." He touched Salina's forehead. "The fever is very hot." He arranged for more blankets to be brought in and made sure that Salina was kept warm. The pneumonia was setting in, but the doctor hoped that treating her early would preclude a more severe case.

Salina was feeling worse and worse by the minute, and sleep sounded like a welcome respite. But her labored breathing made her chest and back ache painfully.

Taylor Sue squeezed her hand. "You rest, now, Salina. You've had a long day."

Salina nodded, closing her eyes. "I'm so thankful that you're with me, Taylor Sue," she whispered hoarsely. "I don't know that I could bear it all by myself."

"I know." Taylor Sue smoothed the hair back from Salina's face. "Hush for now. We'll talk later."

☆☆☆☆☆☆

Some hours later, Duncan Grant received a handful of paper fragments with charred edges from Lieutenants Everett and Colby. Duncan smiled, more pleased with the discovery than he knew he ought to be. He would show the girls at breakfast what Colby and Everett had found. It was more than what he had prayed it might be. He whistled on the way to his quarters, where he would complete his report for the President.

☆☆☆☆☆☆

Salina's breathing was shallow and her chest rattled with an alarming wheeze, Duncan noticed with concern. There was a high color in her cheeks and a feverish glaze in her eyes. She was huddled in the blankets, looking very fragile, very ill.

Duncan seated himself at Salina's bedside and triumphantly handed her the black-edged scraps of paper.

What little breath she had was very nearly taken away. Salina's eyes flew to Duncan's. "How? How can this be? I put these pages in the grate myself. I was *sure* they had been burned to ashes..."

Duncan smiled. "Perhaps you thought they were, but it seems that they weren't. Taylor Sue, what do you think?"

Taylor Sue sat silent, but opened-mouthed. She shuddered and rubbed her arms to stave off the chill prickling down the back of her neck. After the initial shock of disbelief, she found her voice. "I believe we are witnessing a miracle, Major Grant. No one but the Lord God could have saved those particular pieces from ruin. Salina and I burned dozens of pages—yet these scraps alone survived the flames? There is no other explanation except that of the work of God's hand."

Duncan nodded gravely, sharing her conviction. "I must agree with you on that point, Taylor Sue. Like you, I believe that He alone has the awesome power to answer prayers so completely. He moves in mysterious ways." Duncan retrieved the charred bits of paper from Salina's outstretched hands. "Colby will see to piecing the pages back together and recopying them. I'd like you each to take a look at it when he's finished just to make sure everything is in place."

Salina nodded. With her hands empty, she put one to her aching chest and the other to her mouth to cover a wracking cough.

Duncan watched with increasing anxiety as Salina leaned back against her pillows. Her breath was so ragged and uneven. *People die from pneumonia,* Duncan thought morbidly, but he quickly dismissed that line of thinking from his brain. Salina *could not* die. He needed her to help disclose the mole at the capitol in Washington. He needed her to vouch for his findings. And he had need of her and Taylor Sue to explain their side of the story in order to obtain pardons for them from President Lincoln. *No, Salina cannot die,* he willed firmly.

Another hacking cough wracked her slight frame. "Here," Taylor Sue offered a mug of hot tea, lemon, and honey. "Drink some of this if you can, Salina."

Salina made the effort to do so, but her head felt so heavy that she leaned back again as quickly as she could. "I admit...that I'm glad...about finding...those scraps of paper."

Duncan took her small hand in his own larger one. "I will do what I can." He nodded. "Trust me?"

"I have...no choice," Salina replied, her green eyes flashing.

"No, you don't," Duncan confirmed. He was pleased to see the flash of life in her eyes. "You rest, now, Salina." Duncan squeezed her hand.

Salina nodded, closing her eyes.

"I have things I must attend to at the Presidio. Watch over her, Taylor Sue." Duncan's whisper was still an order. "I'll be back as soon as I can."

Salina's feverish eyes flew open. "You're not leaving us...out here alone...on this island...are you?"

Duncan squeezed her hand. "I'll be back before dark," he promised. Like Salina, he was sensitive to the dismal atmosphere of this place. The gloom seemed to intensify once the sun had set. "You rest."

☆☆☆☆☆☆☆

Within hours of sending his telegram to the War Department, Duncan received a reply. His orders were clear and concise: He was to bring the young ladies in his custody back to the War Department as expediently as possible—no later than mid-December. The matter was to be tried and closed prior to the Christmas holidays. Upon the girls' arrival in Washington, an interview was to be scheduled—with President Lincoln himself.

Now that he knew what was expected of him, there was no time to lose. Duncan quickly left the Presidio and went to the wharves, where he located Rafe Montoya, captain of a sleek steamship called the *Consequence*.

The two men, one in impeccable military uniform and the other decked out in comfortable seafaring garb, sat at a back table in a shore-side saloon. Between them, they worked out the details of a charter.

"How soon can we sail?" Duncan inquired, urgency showing in his slate-gray eyes.

"Whenever you wish. I can be ready to sail on a moment's notice, *amigo*," Rafe assured Duncan, the unaffected demeanor of the suave Spaniard contrasting sharply to the Union officer's impatience. "I've nothing more pressing than to wait until you decide when you want to return east."

"I'm ready now." Duncan replied without hesitation. "Or I will be once I collect the people who will travel with me." Knowing men such as this Spanish *capitán* often proved to be most beneficial, Duncan knew. Rafe Montoya sailed where he pleased, whenever he pleased. To sail with the Spaniard eliminated delays imposed by strictly scheduled travel on commercial line steamships. Duncan was wise enough, however, not to question the legality or destination of whatever cargo was being transported.

"You'll arrange for a ship to meet us at Aspinwall?" asked Duncan.

"Sí—yes—it will be done, *amigo*. It will be the steamer called *Gypsy Rose*—the same vessel that brought you to Aspinwall from Alexandria on your journey here. Once we dock in Panama City, you and your *compañeros* will go on to ride the distance of the isthmus on the train which crosses the span of land between Pacific and Atlantic. It takes maybe—what? Half a day at the most?"

"It takes four hours," Duncan said precisely. "I kept careful track of the time on the way here."

Rafe grinned and asked, "How many passengers, *amigo*? I have need to know for the preparations which are to be made to ensure your comfort."

"There will be myself, my Lieutenant, and three prisoners—two of whom are ladies, so I'd very much appreciate you asking your crew to mind their manners. Try to impress upon them that they shouldn't act like the pirates they are." His tone held a slight but firm note of caution.

Rafe was amused and snapped a mock salute. "I will see to it, *amigo*. You will not be displeased. You will come *mañana*, no?"

"No. I will come before sunset," Duncan informed him. "I will have them readied to leave Alcatraz immediately, and we will spend the night on board the *Consequence*. I want to sail at first light."

"As you wish, amigo." Rafe smiled broadly, extending his hand. "*Hasta luego*."

"Yes." Duncan shook Rafe's hand to seal the agreement. "See you then."

☆☆☆☆☆☆☆

"I must be frank, Major. The poor girl should not be moved. The congestion in her lungs is deep and heavy. I've left Taylor Sue watching to make sure Salina doesn't stop breathing. Her fever has not abated, and I cannot recommend that she be taken from here before she has had a chance to get well," the staff physician said emphatically.

"I appreciate your concern, Dr. Laurence," Duncan said, nodding his understanding of the army physician's appraisal. "But we must be away from the fortress tonight. We will have another doctor on board with us who will see to her care."

"That Rebel, Nichols?" the staff physician asked incredulously.

"Yes, Nichols. He is certainly qualified. Besides, they are the same kind. He'll care for her," Duncan said with certainty. He'd already talked to the Southern doctor and was convinced that he would tend Salina to the very best of his ability. Duncan had made sure Nichols comprehended the fact that his life might well depend on hers. "Here is a list of the items he will need for the voyage to Washington. Will you see that it is granted, please."

"I'll see to it immediately, sir." The staff physician saluted.

"Bring the supplies to my office," Duncan ordered. "I'll go over every last detail before we depart."

"As you wish, Major," Dr. Laurence acquiesced.

The plans were set, the details arranged. Ben Nichols was already on his way to the *Consequence* with Colby to prepare a bed for Salina. Duncan found Taylor Sue sitting apprehensively at Salina's side, holding the sick girl's hand in her own. "She's doing rather poorly, Major. Dr. Laurence doesn't think she should be taken from here."

"I've already spoken with the doctor, Taylor Sue." Duncan patted her shoulder. "And I've spoken with Ben Nichols. He will attend to Salina during the journey. I have my orders, and we are expected in Washington no later than the fifteenth of December."

Taylor Sue nodded. When the Major had told her that the trip would take approximately three weeks, she was astonished. It had taken the girls six weeks by rail and by stagecoach to arrive in San Francisco. To go back by water sounded like a much easier trip—and for Salina's sake she prayed it would be. "What time do you want us ready?" she finally asked, knowing that the time had come to trust Duncan Grant.

"Now. The fog hasn't rolled in yet, but the sun is setting quickly. Let's go," Duncan prodded.

Taylor Sue wrapped herself in her cloak and then tucked the quilts securely around Salina once Duncan had lifted her into his strong arms. It took a minute or so for her to pack the scant belongings of her own and Salina's into the satchel. She nodded to Duncan that she was prepared to follow him.

Salina's head lolled against the front of Duncan's blue uniform coat, and he could hear the rattling wheeze from her chest as she struggled for each breath. It pained him greatly to see her like this. A coughing spasm shook her narrow shoulders, and Duncan laid his cheek on top of her head. "Ssshhhh, you're going to be all right, Salina Hastings. Everything's going to work out, you'll see."

Taylor Sue witnessed the Major's tenderness and concern as he cradled Salina close to his body. *Garrett Hastings himself could not have shown more gentleness*, she thought.

Salina barely opened her eyes as Duncan carried her down the incline that led from the Citadel to the sallyport and then to the landing. She hardly stirred when they boarded the small boat that rowed them from Alcatraz to the steamship owned by Rafe Montoya. Nor did she flinch in the least when, once aboard the *Consequence*, Duncan and Taylor Sue worked with Ben Nichols to settle her among the thick down-filled comforters in the wide bed of a warmed cabin below decks.

When he was at last satisfied that Salina was resting as comfortably as possible, Duncan sought out Rafe on the quarterdeck.

"Everything in order?" the captain of the *Consequence* inquired.

"Yes, as far as I can tell." Duncan nodded. "How long before you can get steam up, Rafe?"

"We'll be ready to sail at first light, just as you ordered, *amigo*," the swarthy Spaniard assured Duncan. "The pretty little dark-headed one—is she all right?" Rafe's concern was genuine.

"Time will tell. She's got pneumonia, but we've a doctor along with us for the journey," Duncan replied.

"Why is it she is one of your prisoners?" Rafe could not contain his curiosity.

Duncan answered grimly, "She's a Confederate agent."

Rafe Montoya whistled and shook his head in disbelief. "Well, she sure is one pretty little spy, eh?"

"She's also my stepdaughter, Rafe," Duncan confessed without knowing exactly why. "The other girl is her accomplice. You and your crew won't forget to mind your manners?"

"We'll behave for you, *amigo*. Don't think on it another minute. And rest assured, none of my men will ever repeat what they see or hear on this vessel. My crew is a select one—chosen for their willing blindness of eye and deafness of ear. You've nothing to worry about as far as military secrecy is concerned, for neither do they have wagging tongues," Rafe added seriously. Then he chuckled good-naturedly, turning to a lighter topic. "I've hired a wonderful cook. You'll join me for supper—you and your lieutenant?"

"Lieutenant Colby will have to stay on guard. I've already told him that the girls are not to be left unattended, so we will take shifts," Duncan said sternly. "But tonight, I would be delighted to join you."

"Very good, *amigo*." Rafe smiled. "We'll see that your mouth and your stomach are well cared for."

Duncan returned his friend's smile. "I'm counting on it." Over his shoulder he could see the clinging mists swirling around the steamship, obliterating the island, and he was unspeakably relieved to be away from it.

☆☆☆☆☆☆☆

"Jeremy?" Salina called ever so softly, and then the beloved name escaped from her dry lips again in a hoarse, throaty whisper, "Jeremy?" Her eyes felt gritty and sandy as she struggled to open them. For a brief instant she mistook the blond man sitting near her bed for Jeremy Barnes, but when he leaned closer in reply to her call, she recognized that it was not her Jeremy, but the Yankee Lieutenant

Lance Colby. Salina's eyes squinted in confusion. Glancing around the luxuriously appointed interior of the ship's cabin, she grew even more disoriented.

"Well, I am pleased to see you've decided to return to the land of the living." Colby's voice was accompanied by a gentle smile and compassionate eyes. "You're on board the *Consequence*, Salina. We're sailing back to Washington. Do you remember?"

Salina shook her head hesitantly, somewhat disconcerted by Colby's nearness, and she pulled the down-filled comforter up to her chin. Her voice was little more than a dry croak when she asked, "Where's...Taylor Sue?"

"In the adjoining cabin. She's been a little seasick. Dr. Nichols has had his hands full between the two of you," Colby answered. "Would you like something to eat or drink?"

"Drink...please," Salina rasped. Colby's touch was tender as he gently lifted her dark head and pressed a pewter mug to her lips.

"Better?" He smiled at her.

Salina nodded, whispering her thanks. "Where are we? Are we moving?"

"No, not exactly. We're docked at the port of San Diego. Major Grant had some business to take care of, and the captain of the ship is loading additional supplies on board. In a few hours we'll proceed on our way."

"The Major's business...is it concerning me?" Salina dared ask.

"Concerning your father," Colby clarified. "I don't know all the details for certain, but it might have to do with why Mrs. Hollis accused your father of being a murderer."

Salina shivered involuntarily. *Murderer.* "My daddy...wouldn't shoot...anyone in...the back."

"You mustn't dwell on it now." Colby did not confirm or deny Salina's statement. "How are you feeling?" he asked, putting a hand to her forehead, which was hot and sticky with fever.

"My chest feels...so tight...my back...hurts to breathe...when I cough...my insides feel...as if they will...rip right apart." Tears filled her eyes.

"Don't cry." Colby lightly patted her hand. "Major Grant will be back soon. I'll get Dr. Nichols."

Salina warily watched him cross to the door, giving an order to a sailor in the companionway. Colby's tenderness was rather disquieting. He was the same Yankee who'd arrested her, but she was puzzled as to what had happened to bring about such a noticeable change in his attitude. His unexpected kindness seemingly replaced the profound disdain and loathing he previously displayed—and Salina wasn't quite sure what to make of it.

The Rebel doctor was brought in, bound in iron handcuffs. He worked as best he could, applying a hot, thick poultice to Salina's back. "Don't quit fighting, Salina," Ben Nichols whispered. "You've got to want to get well. Don't you give up, you hear?"

"What of you?" she whispered so that only Ben would hear.

"Don't you worry none about me," was all that Ben would say. He winked at her, encouraging her again. "I'll be back later. You rest. It's the best thing for you."

"Ben...what...happened?" Salina asked.

Dr. Nichols' smile was tinged with sadness and regret. He whispered, "The Yankees followed me from Chin Li's Restaurant. They took me right outside the back entrance in the alleyway behind Madame Lucy's Boutique. There they confiscated all the documents you worked so hard to translate and deliver to us. The campaign was thwarted before it could begin. Lucy notified the others immediately, and I can only assume they managed to go into hiding. You did your best, Salina, and that's all you could have done. It's best to leave well enough alone."

Salina nodded, almost imperceptibly. A single tear made its way down her cheek.

☆☆☆☆☆☆☆

Salina was asleep when Duncan came to relieve Colby of his watch duty. The distinct odor of mustard assaulted his nose from the minute he opened the stateroom door.

Colby chuckled at the expression of distaste on Duncan's face. "Believe me, you get used to it."

"I'll have to take your word for it. How's she doing?" Duncan pulled up a second chair near Salina's bed, deliberately inhaling through his mouth rather than his nose.

"We talked some when she first came to, but not very much. Tired her out, I reckon."

"And Taylor Sue?"

"She managed to keep her dinner down today," Colby said optimistically. "Dr. Nichols thinks she's becoming accustomed to the ship's movement at long last. You know, I've been thinking—had I known I was going to have to play nursemaid, I might have reconsidered accepting this assignment."

"We all have duties that we don't particularly care for." Duncan ignored his lieutenant's attempted jest. He peered down at Salina's sleeping form. Her breathing seemed to come easier, and the wheezing that had plagued her for the past few days was silently absent. Duncan took that to be a good sign. He'd seen Dr. Nichols prior to coming to Salina's room, and the doctor's report had been favorable. Salina's fever was decreasing. From here it might well be just a matter of recovery. Duncan prayed she was over the worst of it.

Her dark hair spilled over the pillow and the crescent fringe of her lashes looked as black as charcoal against her wan, ivory cheeks, Duncan noticed. He returned his attention to Colby and saw that the expression on the lieutenant's face was more than a mere look of passing interest.

"Beware, Lieutenant," Duncan said with a note of caution, "she's still the enemy."

"Yes, I'm quite aware of that," Colby said stiffly, rather embarrassed that his superior officer could read his thoughts so plainly.

"Correct me if I'm mistaken, but could it be you've grown attached to her?" Duncan was not accusing, merely sympathetic. He tipped his chestnut-colored head to one side and quizzed, "Whatever became of that tintype portrait of her that I purchased from that Irish photographer near Ivywood?"

"It's in a safe place," Colby hedged. He wasn't about to admit that he carried it in his breast pocket.

Duncan grinned outright. "You're almost ten years older than she is, Colby."

"What does age matter?"

"Not a whit to some. However, it might matter to Jeremy Barnes," Duncan pointed out. "I'd back off, if I were you, Lieutenant. If she isn't already betrothed to him, she's the next best thing."

"Well, we'll see about Jeremy Barnes." A flicker of discomfort touched Colby's features.

Duncan guessed at the cause and asked, "Does she call out for him?"

"Yes." Colby nodded. "I must bear quite a remarkable resemblance to Barnes. When she first opened her eyes, she looked at me and was completely confused. In the very next moment she sensed that I wasn't him. She must love him very much." The admission was bitter and Colby swallowed hard. He was losing his heart to her, and she had no interest in any part of it.

"Salina is like her mother—loyal to a fault," Duncan said matter-of-factly. "She loves Jeremy Barnes, and she probably always will."

☆☆☆☆☆☆☆

Twenty-four hours passed before Salina stirred to wakefulness again, rubbing her eyes prior to hesitantly opening them. Duncan sat in the chair at her bedside.

"Hello." He nodded.

"Hello," she returned weakly. "What were you doing in San Diego?" Salina's question was a mere whisper.

Duncan smiled wryly. She reminded him so very much of Garrett. He answered, "Looking for some information."

"Did you find out what you wanted to know?"

Again Duncan nodded. "Yes. Perhaps when you're a bit better, I'll tell you what I've discovered."

Salina started to make another inquiry, but Duncan held up his hand to quiet her. "All right, all right, I'll tell you now. I was trying to clear your father's name."

"Why?" asked Salina, bewildered that he would interrupt their sailing schedule.

"I felt I owed it to him. Irene Hollis accusing Garrett of being a murderer didn't sit well with me. I was determined to find out why she said that. I knew Garrett very well. He was closer to me than my own brother. He was shot down as a traitor in the eyes of the United States government, but he wasn't a common murderer. His refusal to forward the assassination plot to the Southerners is proof enough of that. Yet the fact remains that Hollis's accusation stands on record. I intend to include my findings when I submit my final report, thus clearing Garrett once and for all."

"Please," Salina requested, "tell me what you found out."

Duncan tapped the edge of her nose with his finger. "I'll ring for some broth for you and some dinner for Colby, Taylor Sue, and myself. You think you're up to eating something?"

"Now that you mention it, I am a little hungry." Salina nodded. "Duncan?"

"Yes?" A dark eyebrow shot up in question.

"Thank you for caring so much about us, even when you shouldn't," Salina sighed.

"I'll remind you that you said that later." Duncan winked. "You're not out of the woods yet, you know."

"I know." Salina smiled. "But I mean it just the same."

☆☆☆☆☆☆☆

Lieutenant Colby brought a tray with four bowls of hot, fragrant chicken soup and four steaming mugs of cider stirred with cinnamon sticks. Duncan was thankful that Rafe's cook was a good one. Salina needed nourishment to regain her strength. All the better that the food was palatable.

Duncan distributed the bowls of soup and cut thick slices of bread. "It's a comfort to see that your color is better, Salina. At least you don't look like you're blending into the bed linens anymore."

"I've been very sick, haven't I?" Salina awkwardly stirred the contents of her bowl with the spoon. Her stomach grumbled as she inhaled the delicious aroma of the hot soup. Tiny pieces of chicken and rice floated in the golden broth.

"Yes, very sick," Duncan confirmed. "You had me quite worried. Dr. Nichols says you're on the mend, though, and given time you'll regain your strength. Just take it slow. You're not going anywhere, and there's plenty of time before we arrive in Washington."

Salina's emerald eyes clouded. She had been dreaming of things that might happen to her once she arrived in the Union capital. She envisioned herself locked up in the same cell Daddy had occupied at the Old Capital Prison when he'd been arrested and taken there prior to his death. She called to mind things that she had heard about other female Confederate spies: the two most renowned being Rose Greenhow and Belle Boyd. Neither had been sentenced to hang, but they had been deported to Richmond, with dire warnings of severe punishment should either of them again be caught behind enemy lines.

Taylor Sue caught Salina's eye but said nothing as they began to eat the evening meal. She certainly was glad to see Salina fully conscious again.

Salina's hand shook as she attempted to lift a spoonful of broth to her lips. After two unsuccessful tries, both of which resulted in soup dribbling down her chin, she relinquished the spoon to Duncan and allowed him to feed her as he spoke, describing his findings in San Diego.

"To say that Garrett Hastings had at least one Southern friend in every major town in the West is a vast understatement," Duncan began. "It's more likely he had two or three no matter where he went. He had friends who would introduce him to people in advantageous positions; he used his contacts well. His Southern friends were a tight-knit group, and while Garrett was the one out in the open, the others remained behind a carefully cultivated screen of anonymity.

"Garrett had a certain knack for making people trust him, and he was skilled in getting people to tell him things without it seeming that he had asked for the information. Most times he didn't have to ask outright. People simply told him because they thought it safe to do so. He was remarkably adept at making "friends." He even befriended loyal Unionists without their knowing it. There was such a man in San Diego—a merchant whose name is Judah Gilbert."

Duncan paused to take a sip of his cider before continuing his story. "Judah never suspected that the arms and ammunition he sold to your father were actually being delivered into the keeping of Confederates. Garrett had persuaded him into believing that all the rifles and cartridges were being shipped and resold in Mexico."

"When did this take place?" Salina asked, attempting to piece together the time frame.

"Sometime last July, roughly five months ago," Duncan replied. "One day Judah noticed that Garrett was being followed and, ironically, warned him to take care. Garrett learned that a man named Simon Hollis—Irene's husband—had been assigned to find out what business Garrett had in San Diego. What Garrett might not have known was that Judah and Simon Hollis were acquaintances. They had known each other prior to the war while living in Baltimore. So Hollis informed Judah of the rumors that Garrett was working for the Confederacy, but Judah was reluctant to believe him. Hollis tried to enlist Judah's aid in supplying information concerning anyone who was purchasing suspiciously large quantities of arms.

"Judah confronted your father, and shortly thereafter Garrett succeeded in moving the stash of guns and ammunition from a warehouse in town to a location somewhere in the hills beyond the mission. Jeremy Barnes was riding with your father then. The two had run into each other up in San Francisco, and Garrett invited Jeremy to work with him. Jeremy learned that Hollis was stirring trouble and gathering men for a raid—their primary objective being to seize the hidden Confederate armory—and Jeremy warned Garrett. Judah ineptly tried to press Garrett about where he had relocated the guns, but Garrett did not reveal their hiding place. Knowing Garrett and having seen his plans for the Western Campaign, I'd venture to guess the arms ended up somewhere near a place called Palomar Mountain, waiting only until it was deemed safe to ship them on to Santa Fe in New Mexico Territory, or Carson City in Nevada Territory. Garrett was acquainted with Southern sympathizers in Temecula and at Warner's Springs. They might have handled the shipments for him, but of that I have no formal proof.

"Garrett and Judah argued severely, but they reached a mutual truce, parted as polite friends, and went their separate ways. There were no further business dealings between them. After his falling out with Judah, Garrett decided it would be best to leave San Diego for a time. He was determined to get out of town before Hollis could expose who he really was. Jeremy was with him in front of the general store, just about to mount up, when Simon Hollis called Garrett out in broad daylight. Hollis swore at him, accusing him of Southern sympathies, and vowed that he would make Garrett pay for his disloyalty to the Union. The ruckus drew attention from the people along the streets who quickly hurried into whichever building was nearest them, peeking out from the windows to witness the scene between the two men.

"Hollis demanded a gunfight, right then and there, though Garrett tried calmly to talk him out of it. Jeremy caught a glint of brass in an upstairs hotel window across the square. He fired into the window and wounded a sharpshooter perched there, no doubt ordered to kill Garrett if Hollis missed. When Hollis drew on Garrett, Garrett dropped to one knee, leveled his pistol, and fired. Hollis's shot flew harmlessly over Garrett's head, but Hollis was dead before he hit the ground. Irene saw nothing except for the shooting that felled her husband. She ran from her hotel into the square, shrieking that Garrett had murdered Hollis. She called out to the local people, but they had seen the entire fight and elected to mind their own business.

"On their way north to Los Angeles, Garrett and Jeremy rode to Temecula, a crossroads town which was once a stage stop on the Butterfield Overland Route. They stayed only long enough to tie up any loose ends. It was mid-August by the time Garrett and Jeremy returned to Virginia."

Duncan paused to take another sip of cider. "Irene donned her widow's weeds, determined that she would take up where Hollis left off. When I was introduced to her in Los Angeles, she had already been working with the Army. In the years they had been married, Hollis had tutored Irene well in espionage and detective work. He taught her to use her feminine skills and acting abilities to ferret out details about people suspected of having Southern leanings. She is very good at her job. She has reported that there are many in southern California who, having come from Southern states, would be willing to throw in their lot if the Confederacy could muster a successful campaign for an invasion."

"But that won't happen now," Salina's voice faltered.

"At least not this time," Duncan conceded. "Irene Hollis will stay here in the West working as an agent for us. She knows what to look for, and she has kept us well-informed concerning Southerners and their activities. She will continue to do so, I'm sure."

"How did you learn all this?" Salina wondered.

"I spent the better part of the afternoon taking a deposition from Judah Gilbert. The incident will be added to my report of your father's case," Duncan told her.

Duncan's findings eased Salina's mind, proving that her father was not the murderer that the Widow Hollis accused him of being. And she took comfort, too, that Jeremy had been with him. If Jeremy had not been at Daddy's side, Garrett Hastings might have been dead long before his attempted escape from the Federals last September. If that had been the case, Daddy couldn't have come home to give Salina the doll for her birthday on the twentieth of August. He wouldn't have known that Ethan was turning into a fine doctor. And he would not have known about the baby Mamma carried at that time, but later lost. The Lord had kept him alive in San Diego, obviously to serve a purpose.

Salina was reminded of the words Jubilee, her mammy, used to say about the purpose for each life on the earth. "When dat purpose be a-filled up," Jubilee would say, "da good Lord, He done catch up His chillen ta come on home ta heaben ta be wid Him ferever an' ever." Salina was encouraged to think that the Lord must still have something else planned for her own life because the pneumonia had not killed her. She felt a peace about going to Washington now, believing that quite possibly it had been her purpose to destroy the assassination plot. But the verdict and her interview with President Lincoln remained ahead of her.

☆☆☆☆☆☆☆

At Panama City, Rafe Montoya wished Duncan well as he and his lieutenant prepared to escort their three prisoners across the Isthmus of Panama by rail to Aspinwall, where the *Gypsy Rose* would sail them northward on the Atlantic side of the continent. Duncan thanked his Spanish friend for his assistance and paid him handsomely.

"I will look forward to sailing with you again one day, *amigo*. You be sure to take care so that we can, eh?" Rafe grinned, happily jingling the leather pouch full of gold coins.

"You do the same, Rafe," Duncan admonished.

Bundled warmly in her quilts, Salina slept fitfully in the curve of Duncan's protective arm for the better part of the four-hour train ride across the expanse of land which divided the two oceans. Dr. Nichols shared Duncan's seat. Taylor Sue, with Lance Colby at her side, looked through the dirty window as best she could, taking mental notes and committing to memory details of the jungle around them. She had taken up the habit of penciling entries in Salina's journal while Salina was too sick to do so herself. When she had the chance, Taylor Sue would add this event into the journal, and she would read it to Salina when they were left alone.

None of them spoke, and time marched at a snail's pace. Only the continued jostling and the noisy, repetitious *clickety-clack, clickety-clack, clickety-clack* marked the train's progress until at last they reached Aspinwall. Shortly after disembarking from the train, they were rowed out to the north-bound steamship. The *Gypsy Rose* was a welcome sight, and this time, Taylor Sue was not overwhelmed by the seasickness she had experienced from San Francisco.

Chapter Five

*O*ver the next week, Salina's health improved rapidly. As quickly as the pneumonia had taken possession of her lungs it left her, and Dr. Nichols was immensely encouraged by her speedy recovery. She was eating more, but Salina was shocked at her frail appearance in the mirror the first morning she was strong enough to stand at the basin and make her own toilette without assistance. As she pulled the silver-handled hair brush through her dark curls, Salina noticed how big and luminous her eyes appeared to be in her sallow face. She looked so thin, almost bony. Her dress hung loosely on her skinny frame.

"You're up!" Taylor Sue smiled, pleased.

"You've been on deck!" Salina said grudgingly.

"Yes, but it's cold outside. You're to keep warm, and unfortunately that means staying here," Taylor Sue said in a motherly fashion. "Besides, there's no more to see out there than the same wavy water you can see through the porthole."

"I suppose," Salina sighed. "But these same four walls are beginning to seem as though they're inching closer and closer together. I feel trapped," she said and then laughed ruefully. "Perhaps because I am."

Giggling only slightly, yet compassionately, Taylor Sue was unable to dispute the truth of Salina's observation. Then the two girls laughed together, if merely in an effort to keep from crying.

"There's a sound I've longed to hear for quite some time." Lieutenant Colby stuck his head in the door. "Everything all right in here?"

"We're fine, Lieutenant," Salina was quick to assure him, but her laughter faded. "Is there something you wanted?"

Colby shook his head. "No, I was just checking on you. I understand your need for a moment of privacy, but Duncan will be here soon to sit with you again."

"Thank you for the warning," Salina said coolly, lowering her eyes in order to avoid his.

The cabin door closed, and Taylor Sue whispered, "In truth, I'm surprised they've left us alone for these five whole minutes. We've been under their watch all the way from Alcatraz."

"They don't want to take any chances that we might be conspiring," Salina said, a green glitter shining in her eyes.

Taylor Sue recognized that steely look of determination. It was identical to the one Ethan displayed when he had his mind set on something. "What are you thinking?"

Salina shrugged. "Lately, I've been trying not to, if you know what I mean."

Sighing softly, Taylor Sue replied, "Yes, I know exactly what you mean." She didn't want to think of what lay ahead in Washington any more than Salina did.

Salina fingered the silver brush which had been a birthday gift from Jeremy. "Taylor Sue?"

"Yes?"

"What kind of impression does Lance Colby make on you?"

"I have the distinct impression that he's falling for you, Salina," Taylor Sue said bluntly, relieved to have her suspicions out in the open. "You can almost see the battle he struggles inside himself. He knows you're a Southerner. He also knows you love someone else. But the affection he holds for you is plain enough to discern in his pale blue eyes."

Salina shuddered, wrapping a shawl around her to dispel the chill that overtook her. "I was afraid of that. You know that I've done nothing to encourage him."

"You wouldn't have had to," Taylor Sue said knowingly. "He carries a photograph of you, Salina, the one you had taken at Mary Edith's wedding. One day, when he was sitting with me while I was seasick, I saw him take it out of his pocket and glance at it when he believed I was asleep."

"I wish he would not grow too attached," Salina sighed. "Even if he is a Yankee, I suppose he might have feelings, and I've no wish to deliberately hurt them."

Taylor Sue nodded, understanding. "You've never made a secret of the condition of your heart, and Colby knows it."

Salina touched the golden locket that lay close to her heart and smiled wistfully, "I often dream of what it will be like to see Jeremy again."

Taylor Sue confided, "I've created scenes of a reunion with Ethan at least a hundred times in my head."

"Lord, grant us the strength to get us through the remainder of this ordeal and back into the arms of the boys we love," Salina whispered her prayer with a grin tugging at the corners of her mouth.

"Amen!" Taylor Sue readily agreed.

Duncan knocked but did not wait for a reply before entering the cabin. "Well, there's a bit of a surprise," he said, taking note that Salina was standing. "If you're up and about, perhaps you'll let me challenge one or both of you to a game of chess? The captain has allowed me to borrow his chessmen, and I thought it might be a way to pass the time."

Salina took him up on the offer but after losing to him twice in a row, she pleaded a headache and returned to the haven of the warm bed while Taylor Sue made an attempt to best the Major. It was no use, however, he was far too cunning for her feeble attempts at strategy.

"I give up!" Taylor Sue threw up her hands. "I'm certainly no match for you."

Duncan chuckled. "But you tried, and I respect you for that."

The three of them conversed idly, and eventually Salina maneuvered him into telling stories of the old days when Daddy was alive. She had heard most of the stories of West Point and some from the war with Mexico, and even those of the business ventures the two friends had entered into together. Daddy had been a wonderful storyteller, but this time the anecdotes were from Duncan's perspective, and that cast them in a somewhat different light.

Taylor Sue sat with her embroidery while Duncan told stories to Salina. As he talked, Salina realized it was difficult to dislike Duncan, especially because he continued to be kind to her, as he always had been, and she enjoyed his company very much. Somewhere along the way, Salina quit trying to hate him for being a Yankee, for capturing her, and for marrying Mamma. He went out of his way for the Hastings family, and Taylor Sue, and Salina knew that he risked his career for their sake. She also realized that if she felt this way toward Duncan, Mamma might feel something for him, too. And that didn't seem so terrible a prospect.

"Garrett had so many demerits that the rest of the cadets in our class at West Point were taking bets that he wouldn't last the term—let alone graduate," Duncan recalled. "But Garrett did, by the skin of his teeth. He was too good a soldier, and he took the dare of one of our fellow cadets that he could make higher marks than any of us if he truly applied himself. In the last term, Garrett finished with the highest marks, but because he hadn't applied himself a whit at the beginning, he still graduated second to last in our class.

"I remember one night when two fellow cadets convinced Garrett and me to sneak out to Benny Havens. We should have known better. Benny Havens was a local tavern, forbidden to the West Pointers but many went there regardless—some for the liquor, but some merely for a break in the routine of the cadet life. That night Garrett and I sat back to back and sipped ale. The innkeeper had told us if we did that, we could legitimately say that we hadn't *seen* each other drinking at his establishment. One tankard was plenty, and we settled at a table near the back door should we need a sudden escape route. There we were—young, inexperienced boys who tried so vainly to put on a show of being the men we were longing to be. We studied Napoleonic strategies of war, soldiering, and the tactics necessary to defend our country. We studied engineering, mathematics, science, topographics, artillery, swordsmanship, and a few other subjects I can't even remember anymore. We learned a code of honor, of bravery, and we were filled with untested courage. I asked Garrett what he imagined it might be like to kill another man. I had never done anything like that and was hard pressed to imagine that I ever really could. I was so naïve...and I was utterly astonished when Garrett confessed that he had killed someone."

"Daddy shot a man named Beau Jefferson in a duel when he was sixteen." Mamma had told Salina this story before, and she knew it well. "Mamma was only fourteen at the time, but Grandfather Spencer had promised her to be married to a neighboring planter who was much older than she was. Beau Jefferson was very wealthy but he was a brutish man, and Mamma did not want to marry him. She had her cap set for Daddy, and Daddy wasn't about to give Mamma up without a fight. When Jefferson called him out, he accepted the challenge."

"The incident sounds like a prelude to what happened in San Diego," Taylor Sue noted.

Duncan nodded, pondering, "In retrospect, it does, doesn't it?" He glanced at Salina. "Go on."

"Well, I guess everyone thought that Daddy was sure to be killed because Beau Jefferson was a very good shot and had a string of duels to his credit. But he underestimated Daddy. He practically dismissed him as an unworthy opponent due to his youth, and that was Beau Jefferson's undoing. The night before the duel, Jefferson prematurely celebrated his victory. With no sleep and the effects of a drinking spree, Jefferson was unprepared. After the ten paces were counted off, each turned to fire. Daddy's shot hit the mark, and Jefferson's went wide. Instead of hitting Daddy, Jefferson's bullet passed swiftly through Daddy's unbuttoned vest," Salina remarked. "Jefferson was dead. Daddy went away to West Point not long after the duel, and Mamma was whisked off to Fredericksburg to attend the Female Academy. But after his graduation from West Point, they were married."

"I was there." Duncan smiled at the fond memory. "I was Garrett's best man, and I stood up with him while he took his vows to love, honor, and cherish Annelise—'until death do you part,'" he added with a touch of sadness.

"You've done much for us, Duncan," Salina said quietly. "What have we Hastings given you in return but grief?"

"That I don't know." Duncan's smile, tinged with remorse, twisted his lips. "Someday we'll all sit down and figure it out. Maybe after the war is over."

"When do you think that will be?" asked Salina cautiously.

"God alone knows the answer to that. The longer the war continues, the more lives it takes. There are those who think it's a larger sin to keep the fighting going than to let the Southern states secede in peace. As for me, I think I'll most likely be in the thick of it until the Union is whole once more," Duncan said with keen determination.

There it was again: Union, secession—all the things that the fighting stood for. Salina closed her eyes. She had no wish to get back on that subject. It struck Salina again how much she truly liked spending time in Duncan's company. He was a good man, and his pre-war visits to the Hastings at Shadowcreek had always been pleasant ones. The more time she shared with him, the more the Yankee Major reminded her of Daddy. The two men were so very much alike in some ways, and it was with mild surprise that Salina admitted this to herself. When it came down to being a matter of trust, she felt sure she would be safe in placing her trust in Duncan.

☆☆☆☆☆☆☆

"You actually ate *mule* meat?" Taylor Sue wrinkled her freckled nose in disgust.

Duncan nodded. "Up there on that hill—Mule Hill we called it—when we had nothing left, we had little choice. We wanted to live. Both Garrett and I had been wounded, but not as badly as some of our comrades. Your Uncle Holden died up there on that hill, Salina. We fought outnumbered."

Duncan had been telling the girls about serving under General Stephen Kearny in California during the Mexican War. He had fought side by side with Garrett and Holden in the Battle of San Pasqual. Duncan and Garrett had survived, but Holden had not been so fortunate. "If the reinforcements hadn't come up from San Diego when they did, the *Californios* would have gotten us in the end. While the *Californios* dealt a severe blow to our force, Kearny's reports stated we were the victors as we remained while the *Californios* withdrew from the field of battle. It wasn't long after that Garrett and I got our orders to be transferred from San Diego to Vera Cruz."

Salina pondered silently. The Battle of Chantilly was similar in nature. The Yankees had battled the Rebels soundly, but the Rebels held the field. Antietam, too, had been a stalemate, yet claimed as a Yankee victory. She had heard it enough to know that possession of high ground was a key objective on a battlefield.

Duncan stood abruptly, stretching and stifling a yawn. The supper dishes had been cleared by Colby more than an hour ago. "I think you should both turn in and get some sleep," Duncan ordered softly. "Tomorrow we'll be in Alexandria."

"Tomorrow?" Salina's eyes opened wide.

"Yes, sometime in the afternoon the captain predicts," Duncan replied flatly. "Good night, girls. Anything you wish me to relay to Dr. Nichols for you when I see him?"

Salina shook her head. "No, but thank you. Just give him our best." They had seen less and less of Ben Nichols as Salina's health improved.

Duncan nodded and shut the cabin door behind him. Both of the girls heard the lock click into place.

"He expects us to trust him, but he won't trust us," Taylor Sue commented dryly. "What does he think, that we'll go overboard and try to swim for it? As if that were even a remote possibility."

"He's just being cautious. He knows that he underestimated Daddy, and Duncan's not a man to make the same mistake twice," Salina said reflectively. "Tomorrow."

"Yes, tomorrow," Taylor Sue repeated. She squeezed Salina's hand, then retreated through the connecting door which adjoined their two staterooms. Kneeling at the side of her bed, Taylor Sue whispered a fervent prayer, "Into Your hands we commit our spirits, and whatever may happen, we will not be moved, for You, Lord God, are our shield and our defense..."

☆☆☆☆☆☆☆

The next day, the girls kept to themselves, pensive and quiet. Colby sat with them in the morning and read to them from a Cooper novel, *Last of the Mohicans*. Salina hardly paid attention to the tale. Her thoughts drifted far away from the adventures of the character Hawkeye, beyond the confines of the cabin, the ship, the Yankee capital, to a cavalry camp she imagined might be located somewhere south between here and Fredericksburg.

Duncan appeared in the late afternoon in full military attire. He had left word when he went ashore that the girls were to be dressed and packed by the time he returned to fetch them. "I've sent word to your mother, Taylor Sue, and I've wired yours, Salina. Annelise will arrive in Washington on Thursday."

"What day is this?" Salina asked. The sameness of days on board the steamship had caused her to lose track of time.

"It's the ninth of December—Tuesday," Duncan replied. "Come, I've an ambulance wagon waiting at the dock."

"Where are we going?" Taylor Sue voiced the question.

"You're being taken to the Old Capitol Prison. You'll spend the night there, and then in the morning I'll come for you and escort you to your appointment with the President."

Salina nodded. "Oh," she said in a small voice.

Taylor Sue saw Salina square her shoulders and mimicked the action. "We're ready, Major."

Duncan turned sharply on his heel. Unwillingly, he admired these young Southern ladies and held a reserved appreciation for their tenacity, however misguided. He was required to fulfill his duty, and he decided to spend the night at Willard's Hotel rather than his apartment on the outskirts of the capital city, if only to be nearby.

To their great relief, the girls were not separated when they were incarcerated at the Old Capitol Prison. They were allowed to keep their quilts after the superintendent was assured there was nothing illegal or dangerous sewn into the linings. Duncan kept their satchel, promising to bring it with him in the morning, early enough so they would have a little time to prepare themselves to meet with Abraham Lincoln.

☆☆☆☆☆☆☆

Salina and Taylor Sue sat in the hall, just outside the President's second-story office in the east wing of the White House. Duncan was closeted with the Union's President for what seemed like forever, Salina thought, though in reality they had been sitting there less than twenty minutes. They waited under the vigilant eye of the man responsible for watching the upstairs corridor, until the time came for them to be presented to President Lincoln.

The President accepted appointments each day, generally between ten o'clock in the morning until one o'clock in the afternoon—but often those hours were stretched into longer periods of time. Multitudes of people came to the White House seeking favors or jobs or interviews with the Union leader. Some waited for hours or days on end. Some wrote instead of waiting. It was not often people were turned away. Salina wondered how many strings Duncan must have pulled to get her an appointment for a private audience with President Lincoln.

"Stop your fidgeting!" Taylor Sue snapped, her own nerves as taut as a drum.

Salina was startled. Evidently Taylor Sue didn't realize that she'd bitten all of her fingernails in nervous agitation. Salina was sympathetic, however, and did not take offense at her friend's burst of wrath. Her own stomach churned in tight knots and a light-headedness had been plaguing her since they'd left the Old Capitol Prison. She hadn't eaten the meager breakfast offered that morning and was now feeling the combined effects of both apprehension and an empty stomach.

In the back of her mind, Salina reviewed the details Duncan had briefed her on for at least the tenth time, and she remembered his command: "Whatever the President asks you, be sure you tell him nothing but the truth. He is a firm believer in honesty."

☆☆☆☆☆☆☆

Inside the President's office, Duncan finished going over Salina's file and submitted his report to the Commander-in-Chief of the Federal government.

"This recurring idea of capturing the West—the Southerners deserve some credit for trying to attempt to make good their dreams," Lincoln murmured ruefully. "That's twice we've been fortunate enough to keep them from making those dreams a reality. Twice that we know of, at least."

"Yes, sir." Duncan nodded.

"Who's to say they won't try again. Another time, perhaps another place? How many more times must we thwart them before they'll give up their fight?" the President lamented.

"I have no idea, sir," Duncan replied candidly.

The President nodded, slightly amused at Duncan's answer when he hadn't truly expected any sort of reply. He looked again at the handwritten pages which outlined the threat against his life. It was not the first time he'd learned that someone wanted him dead. He shrugged the matter aside and exhaled slowly. "Major Grant, I believe you've told me everything except *why* you seem to take such a personal interest in this little girl. Is she dear to you in some way?"

Duncan swallowed hard but acknowledged, "Yes, sir, she is. She's my stepdaughter." Then he added, "It would probably kill her mother if I don't bring her home safely for Christmas."

"I see." Lincoln decided he'd deliberated long enough over the report and evidence Major Duncan Grant had presented. "Well, bring the girl in and let's see what she has to say for herself."

"What about the other girl?" Duncan queried. "Are you wanting to see her as well?"

"Seems to me the other was only following your stepdaughter's lead," Lincoln pondered. "I'll see to the Hastings girl first."

Salina leapt to her feet the instant Duncan stepped into the corridor. He made an imposing figure, sporting his best dress uniform. He had the look of a man one should not cross. Salina's hand went to her throat, where a circling ribbon of black velvet suddenly seemed as constricting as a hangman's noose.

"Are you ready, Salina?" Duncan asked curtly.

Salina nodded wordlessly, her eyes as big as saucers.

Duncan was acutely aware of Salina's apprehension, but he said nothing to ease her mind. Her green eyes were huge in her still pale face, and they reflected a volume of fearful anticipation. Duncan had a vague notion of what the outcome of the meeting with Lincoln might be. He knew Lincoln had a soft spot in his heart for young ladies like Salina. Never having any daughters of his own, but four sons instead, Mr. Lincoln had a reported fondness for the fair creatures and had a habit of calling them "Little Sister."

"Breathe, Salina," Duncan reminded her one step from the office threshold. "Just tell him the truth."

Salina nodded her understanding of Duncan's words. He squeezed her hand firmly, a gesture which betrayed his otherwise carefully concealed support, then accompanied her into the President's office.

Once inside the office, Salina immediately sensed the absence of formality. The President of the United States stood, walked across the carpet, and stopped in front of Salina, towering over her. "How do you do, Little Sister?" He bent slightly at the waist, bringing him down a little from his six-foot, four-inch height. He extended his large hand towards her.

Salina put her hand in his and managed a shadow of a smile.

Duncan made the introductions. "Mr. President, may I present Miss Salina Hastings, of Shadowcreek, near Chantilly, Virginia. Miss Hastings, this is President Abraham Lincoln."

Salina curtsied politely. "Pleased to meet you, Mr. President."

"You have a seat, Sis." Lincoln pointed to one of the horsehair-covered sofas. "Shall I take your wrap or your bonnet?" the President offered. "And please, Mr. President is too formal. Mr. Lincoln will do."

Salina sat down and murmured a soft, "Thank you, Mr. Lincoln." He took her bonnet and her shawl, and then he dismissed Duncan.

"Unless, of course, you wish him to stay. You're not afraid of me, are you, Sis?" Lincoln's eyes met hers squarely.

"No, Mr. Lincoln, I am not afraid," Salina replied, delighted to discover that indeed she was not.

Mr. Lincoln nodded towards the door. Duncan took the dismissive gesture as his cue to leave.

Salina looked up into the Union President's dark eyes which were shadowed by his heavy, thick brows. He looked exhausted and very tired, but his face had a certain measure of gentleness in it. Salina had heard him sarcastically referred to as a "gorilla," but she instantly disregarded it as an inappropriate description. She was inexplicably drawn to him.

Mr. Lincoln sat at his desk, reached into one of the pigeonholes, and pulled out his spectacles. He fixed his glasses in place on the bridge of his angular nose and sifted through some papers. Looking at her over the rims of his spectacles, he said, "You are the daughter of Captain Garrett Hastings."

"Yes, I am," Salina said proudly. "I'm quite certain Major Grant has told you all about me."

"Hmmmm." Mr. Lincoln nodded. "Indeed he has. It appears that you are quite an intrepid little lady and have partaken in some rather daring escapades for one so young. It says here that you've even spent time in prison."

Salina did not flinch. "I was arrested for conspiracy."

"So I understand," Mr. Lincoln said gravely. "According to Major Grant's report, you've seen the inside of the Presidio, Fortress Alcatraz, *and* the Old Capitol Prison. Conspiracy is a serious offense. We do not take it lightly—which brings us back to your father." He stroked his bearded jaw and shuffled some more papers. "I know of your father by reputation only. I've glanced through his military records prior to his resignation from the Union Army. He was considered a brilliant officer. He might have had a glorious career in store for him, had it not been for his untimely death—or his service to the Confederacy. He nearly arranged for a complete capture of the western states and territories."

"This is true," Salina whispered.

"And you helped him?" Mr. Lincoln inquired.

"Yes, I did," Salina answered honestly. She couldn't help blurting out, "Will you have me executed as a spy?"

Mr. Lincoln was silent for a few moments, studying her face intently. "Is there any reason why I shouldn't issue an order for such a sentence?"

Salina's mind raced. She could think of no reason, save one. "Well, sir, I didn't exactly carry out all my spy duties to the letter. In truth, I failed to pass along all of the information that my daddy had."

"I'm afraid I don't understand, Sis," Mr. Lincoln said. "Would you care to enlighten me?"

Salina leaned forward on the edge of the sofa. "There were lots of pages, lots of different items on those pages. But there was something else..." She took a deep breath. "My daddy stumbled upon a plan—a plot to have you killed, Mr. Lincoln. He intentionally withheld it from the Southern sympathizers in San Francisco, and so did I. I did not forward it to those waiting for the plans of the Western Campaign. I destroyed it instead."

"Did you now?" Mr. Lincoln's interest was piqued. "And why would you do that? As long as you were aiding the Confederacy in its plans to annex the West, why not get me out of the way in the process?"

Salina shook her head, tears welling in her eyes. "I don't know. I just couldn't bring myself to do that, nor Daddy before me. Neither of us wanted to be a party to such a blatant crime."

"Do you know that there was a conspiracy against my life even before I took office?" Mr. Lincoln asked.

Salina nodded affirmatively. "Daddy told me once about your secret trip through Baltimore. You see, at that time, it was his job to know all about you."

"Yet the two of you didn't feel you could be party to plans for arranging my death," Mr. Lincoln reiterated. "I am curious as to the *why*. Can't you tell me?"

Salina looked away from his probing eyes. "Somehow assassination is...*different*. And, well, you're different, if you'll permit me to say so."

A thoughtful smile lifted the corners of his mouth, which further pronounced his high cheekbones. "Different," he murmured. "Yes, I reckon I am at that. But I must thank you, then, for thinking enough of me to destroy those plans. You saved my life, the way I see it."

"I suppose so," Salina agreed, turning her mind to his way of viewing the matter.

Mr. Lincoln crooked his finger and motioned for her to come over to his desk. Salina stood at his side as he pulled out a drawer which contained a large, thick envelope. "Do you know what's in there?"

"No." Salina shook her dark curls.

Mr. Lincoln took some of the papers out of the envelope and spread them on top of Salina's file, covering the contents. "These are threats, promises, what have you. Warnings that say I am in grave danger—nearly a hundred of them by last tally. I've lost count since then. And I suppose my secretaries screen the rest as best they're able." He collected the pages again and put them back in the envelope, returning it to the drawer. "I like to believe the Almighty has me here for a reason, for a purpose I do not even pretend to understand." He sighed. "All of those are threats on my life, yet the Good Lord has seen fit to protect me thus far. Perhaps even now you're taking the place of an angel, Little Sister. Your action has spared my life yet again, eh?"

Salina didn't know what to say, though it seemed he didn't really expect her to answer. He continued, "I believe that such behavior should not go unrewarded."

"Sir?" Now Salina *was* puzzled. "Forgive me, but I don't think I know what you mean."

"I'm not going to condemn you, Salina Hastings." He removed his spectacles and closed his eyes, gingerly squeezing the bridge of his nose. Then he straightened and said, "I intend to grant a request, providing you have one that is in my power to fulfill, in trade for your prevention of an assassination attempt on my life."

"I...I...well, I..." Salina stammered. "You're going to let me go?"

"Is that what you'd like? A pardon? I can arrange for that." Mr. Lincoln dipped a quill into the inkstand and penned a few lines that gave Salina her exemption from the charges that had been brought against her. "Satisfactory?" he arched a bushy eyebrow in question.

"Oh, yes." Salina breathed after reading his written command to the Attorney-General: *Please make out and send me a pardon in this case.* "Mr. Lincoln?" asked Salina.

"Yes?" he replied. "What else can I do for you? You'll have safe conduct back to Pennsylvania with the Major. I've been told he's gone and married your mother. Clever, that Duncan Grant."

"Well, yes, but..." Salina stared down at the document in her hand.

"But what, Sis?" Mr. Lincoln encouraged. "Speak up."

"I don't want to stay in the North, sir. I'd much rather return to Virginia," Salina admitted.

Mr. Lincoln again shuffled through the papers of Salina's file. "Says here your family's estate has been burned to the ground. Where will you go? How will you live?"

"I have family, and someone very dear to me there," Salina replied softly. "I will find a way to manage."

Mr. Lincoln seemed to weigh the possibility. "If you go home to Virginia, would you behave?"

"Behave, sir?" Salina wanted his clarification. Might this be where he insisted that she sign an Oath of Allegiance? She didn't believe she could do that.

"Behave," the President repeated firmly. "That means no more dragging one of my best scouts across the country, and no more plans to overthrow the Federal government out west. Is that agreed?"

"Agreed," Salina readily nodded. They shook on it—her hand all but disappearing inside Mr. Lincoln's large grasp.

He took up his pen again and this time wrote:

Allow the bearer, Miss Salina Hastings, to cross through the lines in order to return to her home in Fairfax County, Virginia. If she is found in breach of the agreement made on this tenth day of December in the year of our Lord, 1862, this pass and the privileges thereof will be considered null and void.

—A. Lincoln

Salina dared to bring up the fact that Taylor Sue was also being held prisoner, and the President assured her that everything had already been taken care of. Both the girls were free to go.

"Is something wrong, Little Sister?" he asked, seeing the disbelief and whole-hearted gratitude shining in her eyes.

"You asked me why I did what I did," Salina answered. "I'm wondering if you'll permit me to ask you: *Why?*"

"There are many people who come to see me for many different reasons. Sometimes, I am able to grant the petitions and requests, which pleases me a great deal. Other times my hands are tied and there is nothing I can do. This I could do something about, and I wanted to do so. It was my choice."

Salina offered a deep curtsy and bowed her dark head. "I am deeply grateful for this, Mr. Lincoln. It is a debt I shall never be able to repay."

He waved aside her thanks. Instead, he told her that it had been a pleasure to meet her. "I know you'll be on your best behavior," he stated firmly.

She smiled brightly at him. "Of course."

"Then God go with you, Little Sister." Mr. Lincoln squeezed her hand affectionately. "And may He save us all from ourselves!"

Lincoln's secretary came in to remind the President that he had an appointment to see a new invention. Duncan was summoned to take Salina away. She looked back once more and watched the President hand her closed file to the secretary. It was done. She was squeezing Duncan's hand again, anxious to see Taylor Sue and tell her all that had transpired in the President's office.

Duncan was speechless. Salina could have been locked up, if not hung at the gallows, and instead was granted a full pardon accompanied by a traveling pass that would get her safely to Chantilly. "Amazing," Duncan finally stated.

"Yes, he truly is," Salina agreed. "Duncan, I think I could like your President, if he wasn't a Northerner. He seems like a good man at heart."

"I like to think so." Duncan nodded, not bothering to point out that by being born in Kentucky, Abraham Lincoln better qualified as a Southerner. "In fact, I think Garrett might have liked him, too, under different circumstances than those we face at present."

"Daddy just might have." Salina smiled through misty tears. "Duncan, when can I go home?"

☆☆☆☆☆☆☆

The locomotive slowed on the rails, wheels screeching horrendously as the brakes were administered. A shrill whistle-blast and clanging bell sounded before the train came to a jarring halt at the Washington depot.

Annelise Spencer Hastings Grant used a gloved hand to wipe a circle in the moisture that filmed the window next to her seat. Down on the platform she could see the bustling crowds of people rushing to meet their loved ones or hurrying away to tend to their business concerns in the Union's capital city. Annelise sat back in the leather seat and sighed.

No one on the platform was there to meet her.

She reread Duncan's concise wire. His message had clearly specified which train he expected her to be aboard. Checking the small watch pinned to her blouse, Annelise saw that her train had arrived nearly ten minutes ahead of the timetable schedule. Knowing Duncan, he would no doubt appear on the platform at the precise minute when the train was due. He was never late, so Annelise had ten minutes of solitude before she would see him again. Curiously, her heart constricted. Perhaps she had missed him more than she first thought she might...or should.

Those same ten minutes would pass before she would be reunited with her beloved daughter. How she'd missed Salina over these last few months! The two of them had shared a loving, close relationship—until this past summer, when circumstances had formed a breach in their communication. The rift had since been patched, but nonetheless, their relationship had changed. Annelise had to remember that her daughter was growing up. Salina was an intelligent, spirited young lady of sixteen. She had a mind of her own and an earnest beau. She also had Garrett Hastings's sense of duty, of purpose. She was, indeed, her father's daughter.

Nervously, Annelise wondered what Salina's reaction had been to the news of her marriage to Duncan so soon following Garrett's death. Annelise felt fairly certain that Salina was old enough and mature enough to deal with the situation. It was not as if she had married a total stranger, after all, Annelise told herself. Duncan Grant was someone they had known for years. Annelise knew his impeccable character, knew what kind of a man he was. In fact, she had probably begun to care for Duncan the first time they ever danced together at the Officer's Ball on the night of his and Garrett's graduation from West Point. It had been simple for her to like him then, because he was Garrett's best friend. Garrett had wanted them to get along well.

If Garrett could see them now, Annelise mused, he'd probably approve wholeheartedly of the way things had worked out. In truth, she would not have put it past him to have already thought of it as sensible solution. Garrett had always trusted that Duncan would be there to take care of his family if something should happen to him.

The marriage, though a bit awkward on occasion, had a solid background. Yet Annelise's grief over Garrett's death often got in the way of this new alliance with Duncan. Their best hope, Annelise knew, was to build a lasting union on the foundation which started long before the war, to build on their feelings for each other—without Garrett in the middle.

Annelise easily spotted Duncan, weaving a deliberate path through the crowds. He stood nearly a head taller than most of those around him, and she could just make out the girls following in his wake. Annelise collected her reticule and her valise and made her way down the aisle to the door at the end of the train car. There the conductor assisted her in descending the stairs to the platform.

They hadn't spied her yet, and as Annelise's gaze settled on her daughter, she was struck anew by the strong resemblance she bore to Garrett. Salina had his dark hair, his flashing green eyes. But the strength Annelise detected in her daughter was a blend inherited from both herself and Garrett.

Garrett...

He'd been dead for over two months now, and her heart still ached wretchedly, knowing he would never again return to her.

As each day passed, Annelise's thoughts began to include Duncan Grant a little more, but he could never take the place of the man she'd married first. Duncan had vowed to Annelise that he would carve his *own* place in her heart.

At that instant, Duncan located Annelise and their eyes fused. He was pleased to see her there, waiting. She looked well, even though there was a touch of haunting sadness in her rich brown eyes. He knew she would come as instructed. She was his wife and would do what he requested of her.

For a moment his mind regressed back to the arguments they'd had when he'd first suggested their marriage. Annelise had raged and cried and vehemently insisted that he was dishonoring Garrett's memory. Quite clearly Duncan had explained that he would marry her in order to secure her safety and well-being from Major Barnes. She had reluctantly accepted his offer, realizing that she would be utterly lost without his protection. Once Duncan had succeeded in making Annelise see the sense in it, they had argued over other issues: where she would live, whether she would keep Jubilee with her, whether or not he possessed a single sensitive bone in his entire body...

"Hello, Mrs. Grant," Duncan greeted her formally, constraining a smile but not the merry look in his eyes.

"Duncan." Annelise did not miss his teasing glance. She moved out of their brief embrace and immediately turned her attention to her daughter, hugging her tightly to her breast. "Salina, my darling!"

"Mamma! Oh, Mamma, I'm back! *We're* back." Salina looked over her shoulder towards Taylor Sue.

Annelise caressed Taylor Sue's cheek fondly. "Ethan will be so relieved to know you both are safe."

Taylor Sue warmly hugged Salina's mamma. "Mrs. Hast...Mrs. Grant," she quickly amended. "It's wonderful to see you, to know that you are safe as well. How are you?"

"Well enough," was all Mamma would say for the moment. She could feel Duncan's eyes on her, intense and silently questioning. She prayed he would not discern that she wasn't quite telling the truth. She had a secret, a rather unexpected one, but before she would divulge it to another living soul she wanted to talk to him about it—alone.

Duncan's arm protectively encircled Annelise's waist as he ushered the three ladies to a waiting carriage. He instructed the driver to take them to Willard's Hotel. On the drive, Duncan made no attempt to keep up with their endless chattering as the three caught up on all that had transpired since their parting. Duncan merely listened, speaking only when spoken to.

☆☆☆☆☆☆☆

Much later that night, long after supper, and quite some time after Salina and Taylor Sue had retreated to the adjoining room, Duncan and Annelise found themselves alone together. The war had limited the occasions and the length of time they had spent together since their hasty wedding, and Annelise always felt as if they had to break the ice all over again whenever they were left to themselves.

She sat at the vanity table, brushing out her auburn tresses with long, repetitive strokes. The reflection in the mirror showed Duncan in a chair near the fireplace reading the daily newspaper. She gazed at him a moment. Silently, she sent up a prayer of thanks that it was he who had been able and willing to retrieve her daughter. If Duncan had not been there, there was no way of knowing what might have become of Salina and Taylor Sue.

Duncan's gray eyes found hers in the looking glass. He set the paper aside. "My apologies for ignoring you. I just wanted to see what the press had to say about our troops, about the general state of affairs in the winter encampments."

"I've heard rumors there will be another fight," Annelise relayed what she heard other passengers on the train saying.

"It's possible. We'll have to wait and see." He sighed. He crossed the room, sat down on the edge of the bed, and removed his boots. "How are you faring in Gettysburg?"

"I hate it." Annelise was frank. "You know the people there. They treat me like an outcast, snickering over my drawl, and murmuring about our sudden marriage. Even your family keeps their distance." Annelise sighed. "If I didn't have Jubilee with me, I don't know what I'd do." She paused. "Duncan, now that Salina's back..."

"I won't let you leave, Annelise. And you know the reasons why," Duncan stated firmly.

"Major Barnes." Annelise hung her head. "What of Salina, then? Is it really safe for her to go back to Virginia?"

"I heard you discussing her staying at Ivywood. I'm sure she'll be safe enough there," Duncan replied. "Don't worry, Annelise. I'll see that she's looked after."

"How can you do that? There must be a risk for you." Annelise looked back at him over her shoulder. "How can you be sure?"

"I have my ways. Don't ask too many questions," Duncan cautioned.

Just like Garrett! Annelise thought angrily. She knew she shouldn't compare him to Garrett—it wasn't fair to Duncan. But it was a hard habit to break.

"Aside from hating Gettysburg, are you getting along well enough otherwise?" Duncan interrupted her thoughts. "You must let me know if there's anything you want or need. I'll arrange for it. I don't know when I'll be back again, especially in light of this much-talked-of campaign around Fredericksburg."

"I'll be sure to let you know."

Duncan studied Annelise carefully for a few minutes. *Was it the candlelight that made her soft features glow so prettily?* "Blow out the lamp and come to bed, Annelise," he whispered the command. "It's been a long day and I, for one, am tried."

She blew out one of the candles. "Duncan, I..." Annelise stopped short. She took a deep breath and let it out.

The crackle of the fireplace was the only sound in the room. His glance was quizzical, but he remained silent, waiting for her to go on.

She nearly extinguished the second candle but thought better of it. She wanted very much to see his expression. "Duncan, you and I..."

"Yes?" he prodded.

She met his eyes square and smiled sheepishly, "Duncan, I'm going to have a baby. You're going to be a father."

"What?" he fairly bellowed, his jaw dropping open.

Annelise laughed out loud, seeing that his otherwise cool composure had completely deserted him. "You heard me."

He sputtered, "But I...But you...But we..."

She nodded. "Yes, I know."

Duncan stood behind her, staring hard at her in the mirror. He put his hands tenderly on her shoulders. "And how do you feel about that?" he finally managed to ask. "Tell me the truth."

"I was scared at first. Maybe a little ashamed. People might conjure up some nasty things to say about us, Duncan. We haven't been married all that long..." Annelise's voice trailed off.

He nodded slowly. He knew there were a handful of gossips in Gettysburg who would say just about anything, making up some unfounded lie about his relationship with Annelise prior to Garrett's death—that her pregnancy might well be the very reason they'd *had* to get married.

"Apart from what people *might* say about us, how do *you* feel about it?" he needed to know.

"Well, it is unexpected." she laughed lightly. "I mean...Oh, I'm sure you know my history as far as childbearing goes. I'm certain Garrett shared his disappointment with you whenever I miscarried or gave birth to a stillborn babe..." Her voice caught. How could she explain to him that she was scared to death to be pregnant again, yet exceedingly ecstatic at the same time? She was not as young as she used to be—she would celebrate her thirty-sixth birthday come February. Ethan and Salina were all she had for the eight times she'd been with child during her marriage to Garrett. After her last miscarriage, Annelise never imagined she'd have another baby, and she said so to Duncan.

"What's important to me is what you think, Duncan. How does such news set with you?" Annelise asked.

"Well, I don't know yet." Duncan squeezed her shoulders. "Don't take that to mean I'm not happy about it—I am happy. If you're happy about this, then I am. I just...I guess what I'm trying to say is that your life is important, and I don't want you to risk it to give me a child. I'd given up long ago any notion of having a child of my own. It didn't seem important anymore...but now..."

Annelise smiled timorously. "It will be worth any risk, Duncan. You'll make a very fine father."

Duncan dropped to one knee next to the vanity table stool and took both of Annelise's hands in his own. He studied the plain gold band on her finger. "A baby. Between the two of us, we've made a baby." He shook his chestnut head back and forth in awe. Then he chuckled. "How long do I have to wait?"

"Until July," Annelise replied. "This baby will likely be born on a hot, sweltering summer day."

Duncan smiled. "I can hardly wait for that day to come. We'll just have to pray that the Lord will see fit to bless you and the babe."

Annelise nodded, her fingers entwined with his. "This baby will be a blessing," she predicted. "Don't worry about me. Everything will be fine. I'm sure of it. Now, all we have to do is tell Salina."

Duncan snapped his head up, his eyes wide. "And I thought she took the news of our marriage hard! I can't even imagine what kind of reaction she'll have when she finds out about this baby."

☆☆☆☆☆☆☆

Much to the surprise of both Mamma and Duncan, Salina welcomed the news of a new sibling. After a joyful embrace, Salina asked, "Have you been sick this time or fainted at all?"

Mamma shook her head. "No fainting spells this time around, not even morning sickness in the least. I've never felt so well being pregnant."

"Praise God for that!" Salina was delighted. A baby for Mamma and Duncan. She could hardly believe it. A child might even strengthen the bonds of their marriage, she mused.

After the excitement died down, Duncan excused himself from breakfast, nobly making his apologies to the ladies about having to exchange their pleasant company for his work at the War Department.

When he had gone, Salina asked, "What's it like, Mamma, living in the North?"

"It's different from what I'm used to," Annelise hedged. She didn't want to burden Salina with her own misery. "I miss Shadowcreek, but thankfully, I have Jubilee. She sends you all her best and wishes she could see you."

"Does she like Gettysburg?" asked Taylor Sue.

Mamma shrugged. "Well enough. We're both surviving. Jubilee is accustomed to running an estate house almost single-handedly, so she insists that she's too idle. Noreen, Duncan's mother, has allowed her to take over the cooking, so that occupies a good portion of her time. She has also taken in some sewing and had gained quite a reputation through her needlework skills."

"Are Duncan's people treating you well?" Salina inquired.

Mamma smiled wistfully. "As well as can be expected, under the circumstances. I'm of the opinion that Noreen had quite given up on Duncan ever marrying and settling down, but when he brought me home with him—unexpected *and* unannounced—well, his family was a bit shocked. Noreen has tried to be friendly, and we do get along together." Mamma purposely failed to mention that it was Duncan's sisters, Felicia and Lydia, who haughtily rejected her attempts at friendship.

"It's a large house there on Oak Ridge," Mamma continued, "and whenever we tire of each other's company, there is space enough to retreat. Duncan's father is usually busy with tending to the farm, and his brother, Orrin, is a blacksmith with a thriving business. Orrin has two sons, Nathan and Jared, who have gone to fight with the Pennsylvania volunteers. Two sisters are married and have their own families elsewhere around town. Dulcie is the only sister who lives at home. As a matter of fact, she is engaged to be married to Lance Colby's older brother."

"I wish Lance Colby would find someone to get engaged to. Perhaps then he'd leave me in peace," Salina confided.

"Duncan mentioned that in a letter." Mamma nodded. "I seem to recall him referring to something about your winning Colby's heart without even trying."

"Colby knows I love someone else," Salina insisted, her fingers seeking her heart-shaped locket.

"And speaking of Jeremy," Mamma said knowingly, "he's the reason you won't come home to Gettysburg with me, isn't he?"

"Yes," Salina admitted. "I want to find him—and Ethan."

"The main house at Shadowcreek is gone. I'd prefer you stay at Ivywood for a time, where Priscilla and Mary Edith can keep an eye on you. They have plenty of food and lack for little else. You could rest there, get fully recovered." Mamma glanced at Salina. "Are you sure you're up to dealing with your cousin?"

Salina knew Mamma was referring to Lottie, not Mary Edith; wherever Lottie was, clash followed. There was nothing but strife between Salina and Lottie for assorted little reasons that had only compounded over the years of their growing up. As a general rule, Salina tried to avoid Lottie as best she could, but her cousin had a knack for making her angry. Once Daddy had remarked, "Those Armstrong twins should have been one person, but they were born equally divided, right down the middle. Mary Edith is everything sweet and good while Lottie is just the opposite— and got a double portion of disagreeability." Salina smiled at the recollection. It was something Daddy had often told her to comfort her in the aftermath of Lottie's many childhood pranks.

"I'll have to bear Lottie as best I can." Salina mentally prepared herself to brave the situation. After all, if she could endure being followed by Yankees, bear up under arrest and imprisonment for treason, fight to survive pneumonia, and get through an interview with President Lincoln, she ought to be able to handle her cousin.

Mamma could see evidence of her daughter's determination in the set of jaw and the squaring of her shoulders. "I'll write the necessary letters to your Aunt Priscilla, then. And by the way, I've already received a rather scathing epistle from Genevieve."

"Oh, I can imagine." Salina giggled. "She didn't care for anything about me, and I'm sure she was just as glad to wash her hands of us."

"Once the gossip dies down about your capture—right in her very own home, for goodness sake!—she'll survive." Mamma laughed, knowing well the temperament of her oldest sister. "She cares very much what other people might think. She dedicated two pages to her disapproval of my marrying so soon after your daddy's death. I've wrestled with that issue myself," Mamma admitted, "but there's no going back now. The Lord will not give us more than He knows we're able to bear. Keep that in mind when it comes to dealing with Lottie, hmmm?" Mamma lightly caressed Salina's shoulder.

Salina nodded. "I will."

"What do you think Duncan's family will say about the baby?" Taylor Sue asked, bringing the subject back to the original topic.

Mamma shrugged. "That remains to be seen."

☆☆☆☆☆☆☆

While Mamma wrote to Aunt Priscilla and Uncle Caleb at Ivy-wood, Salina made an entry in her journal. She jotted down the elation she had felt coming out of President Lincoln's office yesterday with a full pardon. He had given her a clean slate, and she intended to behave, as he directed. She would be content to return to Chantilly and stay put.

*Pardoned...clean slate...*It was somewhat similar to the way she felt when she'd given her life to Jesus Christ. God's forgiveness cleansed Salina, giving her a fresh start. By dying on the cross, Jesus' blood washed her whiter than snow, assuring her salvation and eternal life.

Salina smiled to herself. Taylor Sue frequently referred to the promise found in the twenty-eighth verse of Romans chapter eight: *And we know that all things work together for good to them that love God, to them who are the called according to His purpose.* In her heart, Salina rededicated her life to serving in God's will and not her own.

Later that morning Taylor Sue suggested that they do some shopping while in Washington. Mamma agreed that it would help pass the time. Duncan was working, and he had given them a generous allowance, ordering the three to purchase at least one frivolous thing apiece. Salina purchased a new bonnet, Taylor Sue a fur muff, and Mamma a bottle of *eau de cologne.* They bought a pair of warm gloves for Duncan as well as a muffler. Then they decided to spend the remainder of the money on practical things the girls would need for the return to Virginia.

All their purchases were delivered to their rooms at Willard's, and Salina took great care in packing them into her new traveling trunk. She had ten yards of thick flannel, a pair of leather work gloves, a canteen, a dozen skeins of woolen yarn, knitting needles, candles, matches, and a small medical kit which included several vials of laudanum and chloroform. She also had a volume of Dickens and one of Brontë, a pocketknife, and some pretty pink stationery in a small lapdesk with a quill and inkstand. Lastly, there was a small "house-wife," which was the equivalent of compact sewing kit.

"I can see the wheels turning in your head." Taylor Sue watched Salina packing.

"I'm just trying to think if there's anything else we might buy here that we can't get at home," Salina replied. "There aren't shortages here that we experience there. Maybe tomorrow we could get some more medicine, and more material for day dresses, and another pair of shoes each."

Taylor Sue nodded. "I'm sure my mama has some dress patterns she will let us use."

"You're a much better seamstress than I will ever be," Salina lamented.

"I'll help you," Taylor Sue assured her. "You can learn. I'm sure of it."

Duncan returned in time to escort them to the downstairs dining room for dinner. The clientele were all buzzing over some bit of news from the front.

"Has something happened today?" Salina wanted to know. "The armies are facing each other across the river at Fredericksburg. Has there been action?"

"General Burnside finally got his pontoon bridges in place across the Rappahannock River," Duncan replied darkly. "Our troops shelled Fredericksburg, which set much of the town on fire, and then went over and looted whatever was left."

Mamma gasped, disturbed by the news of the wreckage of the town where she had lived while attending finishing school as a girl. Fredericksburg was a strategic military target—a major rail link and riverside port—and it was located halfway to Richmond from Washington.

"And nothing was done by the Confederates?" Taylor Sue asked in disbelief.

Duncan shook his head. "Your General Lee has 75,000 men entrenched up in the heights across the river. He's just waiting. I'll wager he knows a more concentrated attack will come."

"When?" Salina wanted to know.

"I'm not sure," Duncan admitted. "It could be tomorrow, could be the next day. It's General Burnside's decision on what will happen next." Duncan withdrew a folded leather wallet from the breast pocket of his coat and handed it to Salina.

Gingerly she unfolded the wallet. It contained the official documents concerning her pardon. They were signed simply, *A. Lincoln*. Her eyes flew to meet Duncan's.

"All charges of treason have been dropped. The warrants for your arrests rescinded," Duncan said somberly.

"Thank you, Duncan, for what you've done for us." Salina quickly put her hand over his. "I'm sure you know how much this would mean to Daddy if he were alive, and I don't have the words to tell you what it means to me."

"Or me," Taylor Sue put in.

"Or me," Mamma added softly. "I, too, am more grateful than words can express."

Duncan nodded to his wife. He placed his hand on top of Salina's, giving it an assuring squeeze. "Those papers authenticating your pardon and your traveling pass from President Lincoln will serve you well when it comes to our government or army personnel. Your people will be another matter, one you will have to deal with on your own."

"We can deal with our own people," Taylor Sue said confidently. "Rest assured."

"I am quite certain the two of you can handle yourselves well. You've already proved that beyond the shadow of a doubt." Duncan picked up a menu, wanting to change the topic of discussion. "Anybody hungry? With all the activity at the War Department today, I skipped eating at noontime."

As the women talked about the dinner choices, dark thoughts plagued Duncan. He knew he shouldn't discuss the war with Salina and Taylor Sue. They were going back to Virginia, and he would not willingly send them through the lines with any information they might be able to use against him. They were pardoned, he reminded himself, and Salina had agreed to behave. He could only trust her word as she had come to trust his.

Chapter Six

*T*wo days passed, and the Federal attack on Marye's Heights commenced. The fighting on December 13 was a tragic Union defeat. Duncan had been at the War Department all day, waiting for news, orders, or both. On the evening of Sunday, December 14th, a steamer loaded with wounded officers and soldiers arrived in Washington from Aquia Creek. They told of the horrors of the fateful attacks against Fredericksburg.

Duncan returned to the suite at Willard's late on Monday evening. Salina had been reading *Jane Eyre* to Mamma and Taylor Sue, but she stopped when Duncan came in. He looked tired, emotionally drained.

He let out a long breath, then stated evenly, "I find it most providential that you went before the President prior to the battle at Fredericksburg, Salina. I doubt if he would be so generous now, in the wake of all that has transpired in the last few days."

She swallowed. "Yes, most providential. Has the attack been renewed?" she dared to inquire.

"No," Duncan answered curtly, unbuttoning his coat and tossing his new gloves on the desk. "The Army of the Potomac continues to straddle the Rappahannock River." He offered no more information as he shrugged out of his coat, and Salina sensed that now was not the time to ask too many questions.

Duncan braced his arms against the fireplace mantle, his broad back to the three ladies in the room. He announced bluntly, "I think now would be a good time for you to leave, Salina. I want you and Taylor Sue to get ready to go back to Virginia. The first of the wounded arrived in Washington today, and things aren't looking very bright for us here. You've expressed your desire to return to your home, and I believe you'd be better off doing that."

Mamma immediately protested, "But we've had such little time together, and Christmas is just ten days away."

Salina stood between Mamma and her stepfather. She understood that her and Taylor Sue's presence could be construed as a security risk for Duncan. "If you think it's best, Duncan, we'll do as you say. We had wanted to go shopping again, but we'll leave first thing in the morning."

"Thank you for trusting me, Salina." Duncan smiled sadly. "I suppose one more day will matter little, and then you can return to Chantilly."

"Very well." Salina nodded.

"It is also time for you to return to Gettysburg, Annelise," Duncan said to Mamma. "After the girls are gone, you can board a late afternoon train. I'll get a message to Orrin and request that he's there to meet you at the station."

Mamma acquiesced, knowing better than to protest further now that Duncan had consented to one additional day. She would do all she could to make the best of it.

☆☆☆☆☆☆☆

By the next morning, word around the Union capital was that Burnside's army had retreated under the cover of darkness, and the Rebels had been unable to pursue them across the river. Severe storms all through the night of December 15 crashed so loudly that the Confederates had not even heard the Union army abandon the town, pulling back to Falmouth. The casualties of the North were counted at over twelve-thousand men. The Rebels might have lost less than half as many, but a good number of those missing gray soldiers had slipped away to spend Christmas with their families.

"Aunt Ruby?" Salina approached a woman with a basket over her arm at the fish market. "Aunt Ruby!"

"Salina! My dear girl!" Ruby Tanner hugged her niece. She was Salina's aunt by marriage. She had been married to Daddy's brother, Holden, who died in California during the war with Mexico. Ruby had since remarried and was now the wife of Will Tanner, a newspaper editor in Union-occupied Alexandria. "Thank the Good Lord you're safe! When we heard you'd been captured...well, we sent up prayers quick—and plentiful! Glory be to God! Oh, Annelise and Taylor Sue!" Ruby hugged them each in turn.

Joining them in their shopping, Ruby told them all she knew of the recent battle. She relayed the heroic actions of the Gallant Pelham— the young commander of Stuart's Horse Artillery—and of an *aurora borealis* in the skies above Fredericksburg following the battle. She also told them of a South Carolina soldier named Robert Kirkland, who was so moved by the pathetic cries of the wounded on the opposite side of the stone wall that he obtained permission from his commanding officer to climb over and bring the suffering souls water to assuage their thirst. "They're calling him the Angel of Marye's Heights," Ruby reported.

When Ruby learned that the girls would be leaving Washington in the morning, she invited them to stay at her home for at least a night. They readily accepted her invitation. It was clear that Ruby was very guarded about what she was willing to say in public, and they knew she would be able to speak more freely in private.

While Taylor Sue and Salina were making their purchases elsewhere in the store, Ruby cornered Annelise. "So, you went and married the Yankee captain," she said with a sympathetic smile.

"Yes—and actually he's a Major now." Mamma proceeded to explain how her situation had come about.

Ruby's heart went out to Annelise. She knew what feelings the younger woman must be experiencing. Ruby had had to deal with the death of a husband and a second marriage herself. She confided, "I would have done exactly the same, Annelise, had I been in your place. Truth be known, I accepted Will Tanner's proposal of marriage because I had no other means to provide for myself and my children after Holden's death. It took some time, but the loving came later," she said knowingly. "Don't feel guilty, Annelise. Garrett Hastings was the kind of man who would want you to be happy and secure. Holden was the same. You need to make the best of your situation with this Yankee Major, if you can find it in your heart to do so. You could have done much worse, you know. At least he's someone you're fond of. And remember, if you ever need anything, you be sure to let me know. There's always a place for you here, if need be."

"Thank you, Ruby. I appreciate your understanding." Mamma nodded.

"Are you staying here in Washington, then?" Ruby asked.

Mamma shook her head. "No, I was here just to see the girls. Duncan's sending me back to Gettysburg tomorrow, after they are gone. It is a comfort to know that they will spend a night with you and Will."

"I wouldn't have it any other way." Ruby smiled. "What those two must have gone through. Well, I'll send off a message to Tabitha Wheeler directly. She'll notify Reverend Yates, and he'll make arrangements for them to get home."

"I shall miss Salina more than ever," Mamma admitted.

"Just be sure to make the most of the time you've still got with her," Ruby encouraged. "I'll keep you posted. It's probably easier for you and me to write letters than it will be for you and Salina to do so."

"You wouldn't mind slipping a message to her for me from time to time?"

"If it can be done, we'll find a way," Ruby assured her. "Don't fret over her, Annelise. Salina can take care of herself, and Taylor Sue will help keep her in line."

Duncan returned to Willard's at dusk, hours earlier than he had any other night during that week. He surprised the ladies with tickets to a melodrama at a theater nearby. He escorted them to a late supper after the performance, and then he gave them each an early Christmas gift. For Taylor Sue, a handsome sewing kit; for Salina, a book of English poetry; and for Mamma, a gold cameo brooch with matching earbobs.

The girls giggled together as they watched Duncan open their gift to him—a new case for his reading glasses—and he smiled warmly. "I lost mine on the train we took to cross the Isthmus of Panama," Duncan told Annelise. "I certainly did need a replacement."

"And here is my gift to you." Annelise smiled as she handed Duncan the package.

Duncan unwrapped a framed photograph of Annelise and Salina sitting together, a hint of smile on both their faces. He tried to speak, but the words didn't come.

Mamma quickly murmured, "Just a token to remember us by when you're out in the field somewhere." She gathered a bit of courage and added, "It will remind you that you're in our thoughts and prayers."

"I'll carry it with me wherever I go," Duncan managed a hoarse whisper, wishing he could express to them how much he treasured the knowledge that these Hastings women *did* care something for him after all.

☆☆☆☆☆☆☆

Rebel Field Hospital, Army of Northern Virginia
Behind Confederate Lines at Fredericksburg
December 16, 1862

Captain Ethan Hastings worked for three straight days following the Confederate victory at Fredericksburg. He was so drained and weary that he could barely stand, barely keep his eyes open. His head pounded each time a thought crossed his mind. He acted mechanically, and he could feel his awareness slipping. He was desperately in need of a break.

With an uncontrollable yawn, he went out into the freezing night air in search of a hot coffeepot. He poured the thick, strong, black brew into a chipped enamel mug, then took a long, scalding swallow. Outside the hospital tent, he could still hear the moans and cries of broken, wounded men. He took a deep breath, filling his lungs with the reviving cold air, and went back inside to the operating table that awaited him, heat and stench hovering on all sides.

Bodies kept coming in an uninterrupted stream. There seemed to be no end to the procession of hurt and pain. Wiping his hands on his blood-splattered apron, Ethan went to wash up and braced himself to continue working on his fallen comrades.

A very still, deathly pale form greeted him at his "operating table." The long planks, covered with oilcloth and threadbare blankets, were laid across sawhorses beneath the dim light of a suspended kerosene lantern. At a first glance, the patient seemed to be a corpse already, but Ethan never gave up on a man until he was certain he was dead. He never abandoned the hope that he could do something to save a life.

Major Lyndon Whitelaw, the surgeon to whom Ethan answered, was currently the doctor in charge. Whitelaw meandered through the hospital tent aimlessly, always ready to share a joke or a smoke with the men, but reluctant to perform any useful medical duties. Ethan silently believed the man incompetent and harbored suspicions that Whitelaw was far more fond of strong alcoholic spirits than he was of administering care to the wounded. Although Ethan had no solid proof as yet, he was convinced that Whitelaw was behind the recent increase of missing morphine supplies. Pain-killers were in great demand and short supply in the Southern medical corps. Dr. Shields, Whitelaw's commanding officer, had been very fortunate to acquire a supply from a captured medical wagon. The supply of medicines, however, did not last very long. It seemed to have dwindled rapidly until the time of the engagement in the plains below Marye's Heights. Since the battle, the medicine had all but disappeared.

Whitelaw approached the table where Ethan worked. As he came closer, Ethan detected the foul odor of stale brandy on the Major. Whitelaw took one passing glance at the immobile soldier on Ethan's operating table and pronounced him dead. "He's takin' up space. Get 'im outta 'ere," Whitelaw slurred.

"Sir, with all due respect," Ethan said formally, even though he held very little esteem for the surgeon, "this man is an officer and entitled to care."

The two stretcher-bearers nodded, agreeing with the young Dr. Hastings, who was gaining a reputation amid the ranks. His compassion and skill were spoken of very highly, and the field soldiers whispered among themselves, "If, and God forbid, I were to fall at the hands of the enemy, I'd want Captain Hastings to attend to me, not Major Whitelaw—and that's for sure and certain!" More men died on Whitelaw's operating table than any other in their unit, and if death were not the outcome, missing limbs were certainly the exchange for life.

Whitelaw glared with glassy, bloodshot eyes at Ethan. He swayed on his feet but remained upright. "He's a *dead* officer!" the Major roared. "Move 'im out—now!"

The stretcher-bearers glanced helplessly at Ethan. They had their orders and were bound to obey.

So tightly did Ethan clench his teeth to restrain his flaring temper that a nerve jumped restlessly all along his taut jaw. His hands balled into bloody fists at his sides as he struggled to maintain control of his tongue.

The stretcher-bearers took the body of the officer outside and laid it with the other corpses that would require the attention of burial detail come morning's light. In a matter of seconds, another bleeding solider arrived at Ethan's table. This one had a badly injured leg but he was conscious.

Whitelaw stood close to Ethan—too close. Ethan nearly wretched at the repulsive aroma that clung to the Confederate Major. "Hurry up. Cut if off," came Whitelaw's growled order. "You know what to do, Hastings. Get busy."

"No! Please, please don't cut it off," the frenzied soldier begged "There's just a lot of blood. The bullet passed clean through—no broken bone. Please, listen to me!"

"I request permission to fully examine the wound, sir," Ethan made his petition firmly.

"You waste too much time, Captain Hastings. You will perform the required amputation of the injured limb, or I will do it for you." Whitelaw grabbed a small bone saw from the cluttered instrument table.

"No! *No!*" the soldier raged. He clutched Ethan's arm. "For pity's sake, don't let him do it, Doc. Please, save my leg! *Please!*"

The ferocity of the soldier's grasp on Ethan's arm caused him to wince in pain. Then the soldier's anxious eyes rolled back into his head, and the grip on Ethan's arm went slack. The injured soldier went limp as he expelled his last breath and died on the table.

Ethan had witnessed such scenes on a number of occasions. The very thought of amputation so traumatized the victims that their hearts failed. He turned his head away after gently closing the dead soldier's eyelids. There was venom in Ethan's eyes when he glanced at Whitelaw across the operating table.

"You're dismissed, Captain Hastings," Major Whitelaw ground out between his teeth. "You are relieved of duty, effective immediately."

"But there's work to be done here, Major. More wounded are coming, and they need help," Ethan countered. "We're already short-handed as it is."

"This fine Southern boy died at your hands, Captain Hastings," Whitelaw sneered. "I repeat, you are relieved, sir."

"But," Ethan again began to protest.

Whitelaw called two sentries to remove Ethan from the hospital tent. "Confine him to quarters. That's an order!"

Ethan knew the two guards who escorted him to his quarters. He'd treated Timmy Paulson for diarrhea and Irwin Bailey for a bullet wound, and he knew they didn't have any choice other than to do as Whitelaw had commanded.

Just beyond the boundary of pale light given off by the kerosene lamps of the hospital tent, near where the dead soldiers lay, Ethan heard a hoarse cry for help.

Paulson and Bailey heard it, too. "Captain Hastings, you did hear what I heard, didn't you?" Paulson asked.

Ethan was already on his knees in the snow beside the soldier who'd been taken from his table.

"Captain Hastings, if Major Whitelaw were to come out here, we'd all be in a heap of trouble. We'd probably wind up in that pile ourselves," Bailey cautioned.

"If Bailey isn't right about that," Paulson added, "it would only be because Major Whitelaw would have us thrown into Castle Thunder or Castle Lightning instead."

Bailey shuddered, partly due to the cold, partly in fear of landing in one of Richmond's notorious prisons.

"All right," Ethan acquiesced. "Take me to my tent—then bring him to me. I'll treat him there, understood?"

"Yes, sir." Bailey and Paulson each nodded.

Three hours later, Ethan was exhausted, but in the end, he had managed to save the life of his fellow Captain.

"If you hadn't brought me here, I'd have died of exposure instead of from my wounds," the injured Captain commented dryly. "I'd have frozen to death out there."

"Most likely," Ethan agreed with a yawn. He picked up a round metal dish containing several bullets and miscellaneous bits of shot and shell.

"You took all that out of me?" the Captain asked hesitantly.

"Yep." Ethan nodded. "Care for a souvenir?"

"Thanks, no," the stitched-up Captain declined.

"Forgive me. Sometimes I get too morbid and say things that are uncalled for. It's not a laughing matter, and I do apologize," Ethan said solemnly.

"It proves you have retained your sense of humor, at least. Far too many people have lost theirs altogether—right along with their common sense." The Captain groaned when he tried to shift his position on the narrow cot.

"I wouldn't do that, if I were you," Ethan admonished. "You're going to have to lie perfectly still, or you'll undo my handiwork somewhere. I lost count of the stitches that are holding you together. You just rest. Somehow, I've got to find a way to get you on the next freight train heading south to Richmond." The tracks of the Richmond, Fredericksburg & Potomac Railroad were not far from the Rebel camp. "They'll most likely take you to Chimborazo or one of the other general hospitals in the capital."

"I owe you my life." The Captain breathed more evenly now.

"Give it to God," Ethan said simply. "He only used me to give you another chance at living."

Ethan's words hit home with the Captain. "How did you know I was running from God?"

"I didn't." Ethan shrugged. "But He knows." Ethan gently patted the Captain's shoulder. "He knows the state of our hearts, our thoughts before we can think them, our needs in our times of trouble. But most importantly, He loves us and sent His only begotten Son to die for us."

"His blood covers us and makes atonement," the Captain murmured. "You deal with death on a firsthand basis."

"We all do." Ethan stood and yawned, stretching his arms above his head and straightening his rounded shoulders into their customarily broad line. He retrieved some carefully hoarded laudanum from his medical case and set the bottle near the Captain's cot. "Having an uncle in the blockade-running business can be beneficial," he said by way of explanation. Uncle Caleb had come through by sending another small crate of the scarce medicinal supplies. "I'm Ethan Hastings. Call me if the pain gets too bad, and I'll give you another dose so you can rest. Right now, I need some sleep in a very desperate way. God only knows what will happen here next." Ethan paused, studying his patient closely. "By the way, Captain, what's your name?"

"Franklin Shields."

"Shields?" The name caught Ethan's attention.

"Yes." Franklin nodded. "While your uncle might be a blockade runner, mine is Colonel Donald Shields. Perhaps you know of him? I haven't had any luck in locating him since I arrived, just prior to the battle."

"No, I shouldn't imagine you've had any luck since your arrival— especially since you were nearly left for dead," Ethan remarked caustically. "You sleep now, too, Captain Shields. Your uncle is here in this camp. We'll find a way for you to see him before you take the train out of here."

"Thank you, again, Captain Hastings."

Ethan nodded, mentally accrediting the glory to God, not himself.

After two hours of sleep, Ethan was wide awake—not refreshed but able to function. He stepped out of his tent and immediately had his path blocked by Paulson and Bailey. "Okay, all right, I understand— confined to quarters." He held up his hands in resignation. "Here's what I need the two of you to do..."

By ten o'clock that morning, Colonel Donald Shields was seated at his camp desk, reviewing a copy of the report submitted by Major Lyndon Whitelaw. He was hard pressed to believe a whit of it. Whitelaw's report contradicted every thing that Shields had been able to compile on the young assistant surgeon—and Shields was aware of Whitelaw's bad reputation.

Shields sent for Captain Ethan Hastings. He wanted to hear his version of what happened at the hospital tent the previous night.

Ethan exploded as Shields read the list of charges Whitelaw brought against him. "Including," the Colonel stated, "but not limited to disobeying orders, sluggish performance of duties, challenging the judgment of a superior officer, theft of medication from hospital supply stores, and practicing without proper certification."

"This translates into a court-martial." Ethan correctly interpreted the next step.

Colonel Shields nodded. "That's why I expect a truthful answer out of you, Captain Hastings. What *did* happen last night?" The Colonel sat patiently, listening attentively, jotting down notes from time to time. At the conclusion of Ethan's testimony, he leaned one elbow against the arm of his chair and tapped his temple with his index finger, deep in thought. After a few moments, he spoke, "Bailey and Paulson are denying that they know anything about the incident. Have you any other witnesses besides the two dead soldiers involved?"

"The first one *wasn't* dead, sir. He's alive, hiding in my quarters, and he can vouch for most of what happened last night."

"Does this living corpse have a name?" Shields dipped his quill into the inkstand, ready to make another notation.

"He says his name is Franklin Shields, and he's been looking for you, Colonel," Ethan replied.

Colonel Shields was instantly on his feet. "Franklin is here? Captain, I order you to take me to him!"

Franklin Shields verified the details of Ethan's story, but the original court-martial order was already on its way to the War Department in Richmond. The Colonel could do nothing to stop it.

"You'll have to appear before a commission," Colonel Shields told Ethan. "No date has been set as of yet, but I'll let you know when it is decided. Until that time, you are to be confined to quarters whenever you're not working. The Confederacy has too few doctors as it is, and this unit needs your medical skills desperately. We can't afford to have you locked up until your case is tried. I'll detail someone else besides Paulson and Bailey to stand guard—a more reliable sort, I can assure you." He took out his dispatch book and penned an order, handing a copy to Ethan. "I have one avenue of recourse, Captain, which I hope you'll consider in the good will in which it is intended. I'm ordering a transfer for you from Whitelaw's command into mine."

"Thank you, sir." Ethan saluted. "If you'll permit me to say so, I accept the change of reporting duty as a blessing."

"Yes, well," the Colonel replied, "it will allow me to keep an eye on you as well, Doctor."

Later that day, Franklin Shields was sent on to Richmond. As the doctor examined his patient one last time prior to his departure, Franklin let Ethan know that he intended to begin working on Ethan's defense just as quickly as possible. There was a good chance that the case would not be heard until after the New Year. Franklin was a lawyer before the war, and he had studied law long enough to know how to prepare a good foundation on which to build a most convincing case.

☆☆☆☆☆☆☆

Willard's Hotel, Washington
December 17, 1862

Two traveling trunks, a worn satchel, and a hatbox were stowed in the back of Will Tanner's wagon. He stood aside, waiting for the good-byes to be said.

"You behave." Mamma hugged Salina tightly. "Write me when you can. And please, try to stay out of Lottie's way. I know how she can be, but try to endure."

"If things don't work out at Ivywood, Taylor Sue's already invited me to stay at Carillon," Salina informed Mamma. "But I'll try to be good. Who knows? Maybe Lottie's changed?"

"I doubt it, sweetheart." Mamma shook her head sadly. "If things get too rough, and Carillon doesn't work out either, remember you've got Ruby and Will, or Reverend and Mrs. Yates, or even Tabitha Wheeler."

"I know." Salina nodded. In truth, she had spent the night contriving alternatives if life became unbearable with cousin Lottie. But she prayed that the Lord would give her the fortitude to try to stay at Ivywood as Mamma wished—at least until Christmas. "Good-bye, Mamma, and I will write. I love you!"

"I love you, too, darling. If you do get to see your brother, tell him I love him dearly. How I pray he won't turn against me when he finds out about Duncan and the baby." Mamma swallowed hard. "I'll expect a full report from you when he and Taylor Sue are married. I don't expect Duncan will allow me to come to Virginia for the event. He's still very suspicious of what Major Barnes might do. So you be careful."

"Yes, I know he is, and I will be careful," Salina said coolly. She had argued with Duncan just after breakfast about Jeremy's uncle. Duncan had firmly suggested that Salina change her name to his, but she obstinately clung to Hastings. "I am your stepdaughter," she had insisted emphatically, "but that's all. I'll keep my daddy's name until a husband comes along to change it."

"Salina, be reasonable! Can't you see that I'm only trying to protect you?" Duncan had insisted. "There's no telling what John Barnes might do when he learns of your return."

"I'm not afraid of him," Salina had replied.

"Then you should be!" Duncan had answered hotly. "He's a dangerous, disturbed man. He has already shown an obsession towards your family. If you won't take my name, then don't do anything to draw unnecessary attention to your whereabouts. There's still a Union garrison near Centreville and an outpost at Chantilly."

Now, Duncan stood only a few feet away, anxious concern showing in his storm-gray eyes. He put an arm around Mamma's shoulders, an offering of warmth to ward away the bite of the December morning air. They both waved as Will clucked to the team of horses and began the journey to Alexandria.

"Godspeed!" Duncan called after them.

Salina turned and waved, and she saw that Mamma held onto Duncan for support. With tears in her eyes, she faced forward again. It was the first time in her life she would not be with her family to celebrate Christmas. Last year, Daddy had managed to slip home on Christmas Eve, though he had been gone again before first light of Christmas Day. The longer the war continued, the more separations it caused—either temporarily by distance or permanently by death.

That night Ruby tucked Salina and Taylor Sue into bed in the attic room at the top of the stairs.

"Here we are," Salina murmured. "We've come full circle since we left for California."

Ruby nodded with a smile, but she remained subdued. They had spent the afternoon talking about the girls' adventure to San Francisco and back, including the miraclulous pardon from Lincoln. Ruby had listened intently and had shared some information, but she had seemed a bit reserved.

"Salina," Ruby now asked quietly, "what happened to that Southern doctor?"

"I had to pester Duncan for the answer," Salina replied, "but he finally told me. Ben Nichols signed an Oath of Allegiance, and enlisted in the Union Army. Duncan had him sent to Tennessee, out in the western theater where they might not have heard of him or his background. Duncan says doctors are in high demand, and Dr. Nichols was content enough to be given the opportunity to save lives. He says that's the important thing. It ceased to matter to him what color uniform his patients were wearing."

"Did *you* sign an Oath, Salina?" Ruby asked hesitantly. "Is that how you received your pardon?"

"No!" Salina was quick to reply. "I wouldn't have signed, and Duncan knows that."

Ruby was obvioiusly relieved. "Well, you two get some rest. Reverend Yates will be here come morning to take you back to Chantilly. Sleep well, girls."

"Good night, Aunt Ruby," they returned simultaneously.

Taylor Sue was asleep almost instantly after Ruby had gone back downstairs. Salina, however, stared into the blackness of the darkened room. She now realized that Ruby's reserve had been because she thought Salina had signed an Oath of Allegiance in order to obtain her pardon.

Could that be the reason why Ruby had said relatively nothing about Jeremy or Ethan? Salina wondered further. In the past, Ruby had always volunteered any information she had concerning the boys. Salina pondered where her brother and her beloved might be. She expected Reverend Yates would be able to bring some news of them. Would he bring letters? She could only hope. How had the boys fared during the battle at Fredericksburg?

Dear God, I pray that our boys have come through the fighting unscathed. We're so close to being home, Lord. Help us—myself specifically—to not lose sight of You amidst the longing for a reunion with Ethan and Jeremy. Be with them and comfort them, wherever they might be. I ask these things in Your name, Jesus. Amen.

Chapter Seven

We're waiting to see if we'll be attacked again," the letter began. Actually, the letter opened with the familiar greeting "My Darling Salina," but Lottie Armstrong chose to skim past those particular words. Jeremy started all of his letters in that fashion—at least the three letters Lottie had intercepted each began the same way.

> Last night was the most incredible sight—the sky above was red and blue and looked as though the heavens were filled with glowing streamers of fire from here to Washington. I've never seen anything like it before in my life. Our soldiers boasted that God Himself was celebrating with His own brand of fireworks over our victory here at Fredericksburg.

Lottie checked the date of the letter—the fourteenth of December By now it was common knowledge that the Yankees had not renewed the fight on the second day. After fourteen unsuccessful attacks, General Ambrose Burnside's subordinates had pleaded with him to let the Rebels alone. General Robert E. Lee's troops were too well entrenched in their diggings along Marye's Heights. The Federals suffered tremendous casualties, the Confederates relatively few by comparison. But then, how could anyone consider some five thousand dead and wounded a *few*? Lottie kept reading Jeremy's bold handwriting.

> *The worst part has been the cold—that and being able to hear the cries of the wounded on the battlefield. In the darkness, the haunting voices sound very near, begging for water and for mercy. Genl. Longstreet's artillery mowed down wave after wave of the Union lines that attempted to cross the plain up the slope in front of the stone wall that borders the Sunken Road. Our sharpshooters let some of the Yankees advance to as close as 25 paces and then opened fire on them. Early this morning, at first light, the battlefield had a strange appearance. It seemed to have white splotches here and there. It was not snow, however; it was dead Yankees whose clothing had been stripped from their bodies.*

Lottie set the letter aside, shivering with revulsion. How could Jeremy write about such horrid things? She inhaled deeply and continued reading.

> *The fog is thick, and we can't really see where they are over there on Stafford Heights. We can hear them, though. Every now and then, on the shift of the breeze, we can hear their movements, their music, their men coughing. We know they're still there and wonder if they will be so foolish as to attempt another attack. Yesterday was a dreadful loss of life for them. The burial details will not lack work to keep them busy for quite some time—especially since the ground is frozen.*
> *The cavalry has been held in reserve for the most part. Our orders were to guard Genl. Jackson's right flank. But Maj. Pelham, of the Stuart Horse Artillery, wreaked absolute havoc on the Union left. He must have*

had fifty batteries at his disposal, and he put up quite a show with heavy enfilade fire against the Yankees, who crumbled and withered in front of Pelham's guns. Jackson warned Pelham to keep out of destruction's way because he had lost men, horses, and several cannon, but Pelham stayed anyway. He is being touted as "the Gallant Pelham," and we cheered him for his bravery under fire.

Genl. Jackson sported the fine new coat Genl. Stuart gave to him, and Genl. Lee told Genl. Longstreet that it is well that war is such a horrible thing, otherwise men might grow too fond of it. Genl. Stuart, as usual, was right in the thick of things—probably less than 300 yards from enemy infantry fire. In my mind, he made too ready a target sitting up on his horse in that red, fur-collared cape his wife made for him. There are whisperings that he has grown even more reckless since word reached him that his little daughter, five-year-old Flora, died at the beginning of November. Twice when I've approached his tent at headquarters, I've found him leaning over his desk, head buried in his arms, his shoulders shaking uncontrollably. But he continues on, day in and day out, for he says duty is the call we all must answer.

Bored with Jeremy's stories of cavalry life and the atrocities of the recent battle, Lottie scanned the lines until finally she came to the closing paragraph.

Forgive me for rambling on, Salina. I hope you don't grow weary of it. Sharing things with you eases the burden of carrying them in my mind. I doubt very much whether I will be able to attain leave for Christmas, if you should happen to be home by that time. I watch continually for a reply, but none comes, and I can't help but worry. Be sure to have Rev. Yates or Tabitha let me know if you are returned to Virginia safely. I think about you constantly and love you more each day that passes, dreaming of the time when I can hold you in my arms again. I pray that the Lord will bring us together very soon.

Your devoted Horse Soldier,
Lt. Jeremy Barnes, Stuart's Cavalry
Confederate States of America

"Your devoted Horse Soldier," Lottie mimicked in the silence of her bedroom. "You're making a terrible mistake, Jeremy Barnes. Salina Hastings is *not* the girl for you—*I am.* But you won't give me a fair chance to prove it." Lottie laughed, realizing that it did little good to talk to herself about the handsome, sandy-haired cavalier whom her goody-goody cousin had wrapped around her little finger. But she did feel better.

Lottie sat down at the dressing table, staring into the looking glass. A line from a fairy tale came to mind: *Mirror, Mirror on the wall, who's the fairest of them all?* In her own eyes, as blue as cornflowers, she viewed herself much prettier than Salina would ever be—and much more clever. Lottie twirled one of her golden ringlets around her finger, sulking. She knew she would fetch a handsome dowry. Her father was becoming a *very* wealthy man due to his involvement with several blockade runners. Her father held partial ownership in two Confederate steamer ships, especially designed for sneaking past the Union Navy's guard ships. Salina, on the other hand, was without funds and without an estate. And since her father's death, the Shadowcreek land most likely belonged to Ethan now. Salina would bring Jeremy no possessions or inheritance. Lottie imagined herself a much better match, and if Jeremy wouldn't look at Lottie voluntarily, she'd just have to come up with a way to capture his attention.

Recalling the day that the battle had broken out near Ox Hill last September, Lottie smiled wickedly. She had literally thrown herself into Jeremy's unsuspecting arms. And she'd kissed him soundly —right in front of Salina. Lottie closed her eyes and sighed. It had been such a pleasant kiss at first, but then Jeremy had become so angry, ordering her to stay away from both Salina and himself.

"Just wait, Jeremy Barnes, until you find out what you're missing," Lottie told the mirror confidently. "I'll win you over yet."

She folded the pages of his letter and slipped them back into the envelope. Lottie hid it, along with two others. "I'm her cousin," Lottie had told the postmaster. "I'll be sure she gets them." Lottie knew that the irregularity of mail service was the best cover she had. Salina would never suspect. Besides, with a Federal outpost at Chantilly and the provost marshal's office at Fairfax Court House, it was safe to conclude that no one would make public inquiries about missing mail from a Rebel cavalryman who stole through enemy lines at every opportunity. She embraced the adage, "All's fair in love and war," and resolved to test the truth of it.

At a young age a rivalry had developed between the two cousins, and Lottie had taken great pains to cultivate the differences between them. Salina never had to *make* people like her, Lottie pondered ruefully. They simply did. Salina was always so nice, generally proper, and positively good-natured. It galled Lottie that Salina, without even trying, could usurp everyone's attention, leaving Lottie with none. Lottie had vowed that was going to change.

In the weeks following Salina's flight from Virginia, Lottie had planned and schemed. When word reached Ivywood that the Yankees had captured Salina and Taylor Sue in San Francisco, Lottie almost found herself rejoicing. She knew that if Salina were out of the way, she could charm Jeremy into taking a romantic interest in her instead. She wanted him for herself—if only to take him away from Salina.

☆☆☆☆☆☆

"You have a caller." Mary Edith, blond and bubbly, appeared in Salina's guest room door.

"A caller?" Salina worked to confine her dark curls with a black satin ribbon. "Who is it?"

"Well, I didn't hear him state his name or rank, but he's wearing a Union soldier's uniform. And he obviously knows you—and that you're here," Mary Edith whispered.

Salina glanced up in the vanity mirror, catching the reflection of Mary Edith's wide, blue eyes. A shiver of alarm raced along Salina's spine. Duncan's warning about John Barnes struck a raw nerve. It couldn't be him. He'd not be so polite, Salina was sure, and Mary Edith should have recognized him. Salina asked, "Is he a lieutenant? Blond, rather tall—sort of looks like Jeremy?"

"Yes! That's him! You do know him!" Mary Edith exclaimed. "Who is he to you, Salina?"

"He works for Duncan Grant," Salina half-explained. *What was Lance Colby doing at Ivywood?* "Would you tell him that I'll be down shortly, please?"

Mary Edith nodded and waddled out of the room. Though only four months along in her pregnancy, her abdomen protruded quite noticeably, and Aunt Priscilla adamantly predicted that there must be two babies growing in there. Mary Edith was very pleased with the prospect of being a first-time mother, and both Aunt Priscilla and Uncle Caleb were happy about the prospect of a new grandchild, if not two. They doted on Mary Edith continually, and she loved to bask in their tender attention.

Salina, slowly and deliberately, pinned her watch to the black fabric of her dress. She had no liking for dark colors, but she was socially required to observe mourning rituals in remembrance of Daddy. She studied her reflection for a moment and then took a deep breath. Why on earth would Lance Colby visit her here?

"Good morning, Miss Hastings." Lieutenant Colby was on his feet, hat in hand, the moment he saw her descending the wide staircase. "I hope you'll forgive the intrusion of a call so early in the day."

Salina nodded, saying nothing as Colby courteously lifted her fingers to his lips for a brief, unnerving instant. Finally she said, "It's a surprise to see you, Lieutenant."

"Didn't Major Grant tell you that I'm stationed near here?" Colby inquired. "I'm detailed in Fairfax."

"It must have slipped his mind." Salina shrugged. "He was so busy at the Union War Department." She cleared her throat and politely asked, "How are you?"

"Fine, just fine." Colby smiled. "And you? I see you've gotten over the effects of the pneumonia." He thought her a trifle too thin but he tactfully made no mention of it.

"I am much better," Salina agreed. Interminable minutes dragged by. "I'm sorry, Lieutenant, but was there a reason you've sought me out?" She was feeling a bit awkward. "Is there something I can do for you?"

Colby suddenly wondered why he had come over at all. He knew she had been back for two days, but just this morning he decided to ride over to see her for himself. What had he hoped to gain from it? "I learned that you had arrived home safely and wished to pay my respects, that's all."

"I do appreciate your concern. But in truth, there's no need for it. I'm quite all right, Lieutenant," Salina assured him.

"So I see." Colby nodded. "Well, if you ever come into Fairfax Court House, or if you need anything, please don't hesitate to call on me."

"I appreciate that, Lieutenant." Salina smiled slightly.

Colby bowed to her then departed in haste. He went directly to the stables and retrieved his horse from where the groom held the animal. He had intended to ask Salina if she cared to go for a ride, but her cool behavior toward him had squelched any such thoughts. He was angry at himself for playing the fool. He knew full well she was in love with that Rebel Jeremy Barnes.

Riding into the bright sunlight from the shade of the stable, his eyes did not adjust quickly enough. In his moment of temporary blindness, he nearly ran headlong into an approaching rider.

"Why don't you watch where you're going!" an outraged female voice scolded.

"Beg your pardon, miss." Colby raised a gloved hand to his brow, shading his eyes. The young lady looked at him for a quick instant, eyes round with surprise, while she quieted her circling horse. "Are you hurt?" he inquired.

"No, no," the young woman said, her surprise fading. "I just...well, for a moment I thought you were a dear friend of mine, and I couldn't imagine what he would be doing here."

"Let me guess." The blue-clad officer tipped his head to one side. "Might this friend's name be Jeremy Barnes?"

"Why, yes. How did you know?" she demanded.

Bowing at the waist, Colby introduced himself. "Lieutenant Lance Colby, United States Army, at your service, miss. I've been informed on a number of occasions that I bear a striking resemblance to the elusive Rebel."

Lottie was amazed. At first glance, and certainly at a distance, this Yankee lieutenant *did* look like Jeremy. The blue uniform, however, should have immediately indicated otherwise. Jeremy would never don Union blue. The longer Lottie studied Colby, the less he resembled the object of her desire.

Recovering herself, Lottie smiled mischievously. Befriending *this* Yankee might prove interesting, she reckoned, and she slipped effortlessly into her sweet Southern-belle charm. "Where are my manners?" she asked aloud. "I'm Lottie Armstrong." She held out her hand, and he took it in his, kissing it briefly.

"Pleasure to meet you, Miss Armstrong." Colby's eyes took in every detail—her blond curls, her blue eyes, her saucy smile, her pleasantly-plump and well-curved figure. She had an aristocratic haughtiness about her. "Have you already been riding, Miss Armstrong, or would you care for some company?"

Lottie batted her eyes at him. "I'd adore some company, Lieutenant. I'll race you to the edge of the run and back."

Colby saw where the stream cut through the pasture, a half-mile away. "You're on, Miss Armstrong." He whirled his horse in the direction of the gurgling water. In the back of his mind, he decided it might be advantageous to allow this Southern Miss to flirt with him. She might have useful information. His comrades at the outpost had told him that some of the girls in the neighborhood were friendly to

Union soldiers. Today, he would play her game until he could discover if she knew anything about Rebel cavalry movements—or other tidbits that might be useful.

He allowed her to beat him to the water's edge, listening to her airy, gilded laughter. "I demand a rematch," Colby teased.

"Come back tomorrow morning. You can take me to church and then we'll race again," Lottie baited him. "Say eight o'clock?"

"Say half-past seven and invite me for breakfast," Colby challenged.

"You're on, Lieutenant." Lottie bestowed a feline grin. "Half-past seven, Sunday morn. See you then."

"See you then, Miss Armstrong," Colby echoed, disregarding the warning bells in his head.

☆☆☆☆☆☆☆

"He just showed up yesterday, unexpected?" Taylor Sue inquired.

"And then today he had the audacity to appear just in time for breakfast," Salina added, glancing covertly around the clapboard sanctuary. "Apparently Lottie invited him but failed to mention the fact to anyone—including the cook. Aunt Priscilla and Maraiah were in a dither, muttering something about social convention and good Southern hospitality. Oh, why won't he leave me alone?"

Taylor Sue grinned impertinently. "Probably for the very same reason Charlie Graham used to turn up at Shadowcreek from time to time. They have a decided interest in you, Salina, in case you hadn't noticed."

"Well, I'm not interested in them!" Salina retorted sharply. "Sorry, I didn't mean to snap. Living under the same roof with Lottie is enough to stretch almost anyone's nerves to the breaking point."

"Giving you a bad time, is she?" Taylor Sue was sympathetic. "I've told you, Salina, you're more than welcome to come to Carillon. Papa has been asking about you. Paying him a visit would be a good excuse for you to get out of that house."

"That's just it—I'm supposed to be in mourning. I'm not supposed to be receiving or paying calls. I'm supposed to dress in unrelieved black and become a hermit! I had doubts this morning that I would be allowed to come to Sunday service, but after all, it is church." Salina shrugged distractedly.

After the service, Tabitha Wheeler greeted the two girls, giving them each a wide, toothless grin. The old woman's keen eyes scanned their faces. "Returned at last—glory be! I hope you don't mind, Miss

Salina, but I've taken the liberty of sending a message through the Remnant along to that beau of yours, telling him that you've arrived. Knowing him, I'll wager he'll be here just as quickly as he can manage!"

Salina's green eyes sparkled happily. "Oh, thank you, Tabitha! Thank you so much!" She hugged the stoop-shouldered old woman. "What of my brother? Have you any news of him?"

"Yes, what of Ethan?" Taylor Sue asked eagerly.

"Aye, there's news. The Remnant keeps tabs on what's happening to its own," Tabitha said a bit mysteriously.

"Tabitha, what is the 'Remnant'?" Salina wanted to know.

The old woman put a gnarled finger to her lips. "Come." She led the girls away from the steps of the church. "I'll tell you all you need to know."

Reverend Yates stood at the door of the church, shaking each hand of the congregation members that trickled outside and down the steps. Inconspicuously, he stole several anxious glances at the threesome standing in the shade of a tree beside where a fence used to stand—the wooden rails having long since been used as army firewood. When the last of the congregation was gone, Reverend Yates quickly crossed the churchyard to join Tabitha, Salina, and Taylor Sue.

"The Remnant is all that remains of the Network your father had established," Tabitha explained to Salina. "Since your capture, the Network had ceased operations and had been dissolved for the most part. The local sources, however, resumed their communication lines, which stretch the ninety-some miles to the Confederate capital. This Remnant, who dares to keep the smaller version of the Network running, continues to gather information that might be useful to Rebel scouts. The only 'Northern' contacts now are Will and Ruby Tanner."

"I've had a letter from Hank and Joetta Warner," Tabitha mentioned. "When the plans for the Western Campaign were not fulfilled, they left Virginia City. He's working for the railroad now, and they've settled down in their new home with Austin."

Hank Warner had been another of the Network's contacts. His wife, Joetta, and son, Austin, had accompanied the girls by train from Washington to St. Joseph, and then by stagecoach from St. Joseph to Virginia City in Nevada Territory. "I'm glad that they are safe," Salina murmured.

Knowing that Aunt Priscilla and Uncle Caleb would begin to wonder about her, Salina pressed Tabitha for the news of Ethan. "Do you know where my brother is? Was he at Fredericksburg?"

"Yes, yes." Tabitha nodded. "But he's in a bit of a scrape..."

"What do you mean? A bit of a scrape?" Taylor Sue's eyes grew round with terror. "Is...Is he hurt?"

"No, no, not hurt," Tabitha assured Taylor Sue. "Court-martialed."

"What?" Taylor Sue and Salina screeched.

Reverend Yates saw that the Yankee lieutenant was making his way toward them. "It's too dangerous to talk here. Better to discuss this somewhere in private," he said in a hushed tone.

"The boarding house?" Salina asked.

"Oh, no—too many blue-bellied officers around now. The only thing they're good for is paying their rent in advance and for their meals in gold or greenbacks," Tabitha huffed.

"What about the old schoolhouse," Taylor Sue suggested. "It's fairly centrally located to each of us. Can you tell me if Ethan's in prison?"

Reverend Yates patted her shoulder. "No, he's not in prison. Ethan's merely confined to quarters when he's not working in the hospital. Medical officers are treated somewhat differently due to their scarcity. Meet at the old schoolhouse at nine o'clock. We'll discuss matters then."

☆☆☆☆☆☆☆

"Thank You, Lord!" Salina breathed a prayer of gratitude. In the armoire in her room, hanging on hooks on the back wall, were a pair of forgotten trousers and a Jefferson-style blouse, which she believed were a divine provision. "It'll be just as before—when I used to go sneaking out of the main house in Ethan's old clothes to meet Daddy." She smiled to herself and pulled the suspenders over her shoulders. She snatched up her boots and went down the back stairs in her stocking feet. Uncle Caleb's coat was in the drawing room, and Salina took the liberty of borrowing it along with the woolen gloves in the pocket. She paused on the veranda only long enough to pull on her boots, then slipped undetected into the shadows. It was twenty minutes until nine.

Salina had pleaded a headache after supper and declined an invitation to listen to Lottie play Mozart on the harpsichord. Lottie played beautifully, which was something Salina could not do. Conversely, Salina could sing, but Lottie couldn't carry a tune in a bushel basket. Their varied musical talent was only another item on the long list of differences between the cousins.

Salina could hear the melodious strains of Lottie's recital halfway to the old schoolhouse, which was located on the border land between

Shadowcreek and Ivywood. It served as a well-taken reminder that sound carried easily on the crystal-cold night air. Salina was the first to arrive, and Tabitha joined her a few moments later.

"Knew you'd come early." Tabitha nodded sagely. "Here. This is for you. It's old news now, but I'm certain the sentiment it contains will be welcome to you."

Salina eagerly opened the letter from Jeremy. Its contents were similar to the telegram Drake brought her the night before her capture in San Francisco. This letter, however, was longer, with additional details concerning the Chambersburg Raid. "This is dated October. Has not written since that time?"

Tabitha waved away what she considered an insignificant detail. "Don't take that to mean much. Mail's not so reliable as it used to be. Sometimes it comes, sometimes it don't. Chantilly's post office shut down early on in this war, but the mail still comes to Fairfax with frequent irregularity. Every now and then, something one might believe would never arrive suddenly does." Tabitha shrugged. "It's just the way of it for now. I can tell you that I have seen Master Barnes—or shall I say *Lieutenant* Barnes—since he was promoted not long after that letter was penned. You can rest assured, you are continually on that young lad's mind whether there's a letter to say it or no."

"Lieutenant?" Salina asked with a proud grin. "He's earned a lieutenant's rank already?"

"Evidently General Stuart's quite pleased with Jeremy's performance under fire, as it were, and recommended the promotion," Tabitha confirmed.

Salina was warmed by Tabitha's encouraging news. "This is a copy of a poem he wrote." Salina's eyes scanned the familiar lines.

"Read it to me," Tabitha requested. "Come over here, closer to the candlelight."

Salina sat down by Tabitha, cleared her throat, and read Jeremy's *Poem of a Cavalier.*

> *Confederate hoofbeats muffled by sucking mud*
> *As a cold autumn night grows even colder still*
> *Beneath the eerie gray light of a distant moon.*
> *Hunger growls in the pit of every comrade's gut*
> *   threaten*
> *To drown the hushed whispers of leaves overhead;*
> *We ride with orders to hasten our pace to reach our*
> *   target by noon.*

No warmth of a campfire will ward off the cutting chill
That penetrates our tattered uniforms and threadbare
    blankets
While some try in vain to use rags to replace
    the lack of shoes.
Miles begat more silent miles while we go
    trotting along
Not a one dare sing for fear of certain discovery
    by enemy pickets;
Others give their mounts their heads and in
    their saddles snooze.

Thoughts of home far away and those of loved
    ones missed
Tend to dampen the spirits of many a brave
    and gallant man
Who in days have not chanced to taste the
    thrill of a good fight.
Risky is our mission: circling the perimeter of
    the Yankee forces
That are oft too slow in following when we strike,
    and thankfully
They seem unwilling or unable to give us chase
    in the dead of night.

"Well, it seems our Master—*Lieutenant*," Tabitha corrected herself, "—Barnes is a bit of a poet—though to look at him, one might not know it!" She chuckled and Salina couldn't help but join in.

Tabitha pointed to the closing of Jeremy's letter. "See here. He was still signing as a private. This was written before his promotion."

"Is he officially attached to General Stuart's staff, then?" Salina inquired, her pride in Jeremy's accomplishment quite evident in her eyes.

"Not really. He's there voluntarily. He assists in a capacity much like your father did, serving wherever they need him most. Stuart uses him as a courier and a scout, more often than not. At times, however, when sent with dispatches, Jeremy stays to serve the staff he's been sent to until required to return to Stuart with a reply or new orders from the high command. Most frequently he's with Stuart, unless assigned miles away on some other errand of military importance," Tabitha explained. "He has been detailed to escort prisoners to Richmond while carrying dispatches, but I think he likes reconnaissance the best."

"That's because reconnaissance is the most dangerous," Salina said matter-of-factly. "I know him well. Jeremy's not happy unless he's in the thick of things, and he always opts for the challenge wherever he might find it."

"Yes, I reckon you know your young lieutenant quite well." Tabitha winked.

Salina hugged her arms tightly. "It's been so long since I've seen him. His face is still vivid in my memory, but I want to be with him, spend some time with him, even just talk to him for a few minutes. The last time I saw him was in that prison hospital in Washington—Harewood, it was called. The war doesn't allow much time for romantic inclinations or courtship, does it?"

"No, Miss Salina, it don't," Tabitha confirmed the obvious. "I expect he'll come by as soon as he can."

"I do hope so." Salina nodded eagerly. "Listen..."

Tabitha strained to hear what Salina did. "Reverend Yates and Taylor Sue?" she whispered.

Salina heard their voices and then nodded. "Yes, it's them."

When all were present, Tabitha wasted no time telling what she had learned of Ethan's predicament, the sketchy details of the incidents at the field hospital following the Battle of Fredericksburg.

"Ethan's run into a bit of a conflict as far as his superior officer is concerned. Lyndon Whitelaw knows Ethan is a better doctor than he is, so he don't want the fact made public. That opinion is my own, but I'm not alone in thinking so." Tabitha nodded.

"So, Franklin Shields will work to defend Ethan." Salina was pacing the schoolhouse floor with her hands clasped tightly behind her back. "It sounds as though this Colonel Shields might even investigate Whitelaw himself—especially after Whitelaw left Franklin for dead. We must pray that Ethan gets a panel sympathetic to his case. If Whitelaw has any friends in high places, he'll be working on having them appointed to the committee, wouldn't you think?"

"As you said, Salina," Reverend Yates agreed, "we'll have to pray for the best where Ethan is concerned."

"But hasn't there been any word of when he'll go before the committee?" Taylor Sue's eyes were wide and brimming with tears. She nervously twisted her diamond engagement ring around her finger.

"Just as soon as I find out anything else, I'll let you know directly," Tabitha assured her. "Don't you worry."

☆☆☆☆☆☆☆

Salina stood in the doorway of her bedroom, holding a pearl-handled pistol aimed directly at Lottie. Lottie was caught, and she knew it—but so was Salina.

"What on earth do you think you're doing?" Salina demanded. She uncocked the hammer of the gun and refastened the safety catch.

"I might ask the same of you." Lottie's ice-blue eyes scanned Salina from head to foot. "What are you doing in those clothes, and why are you sneaking back into this house? I ought to tell my papa that I want you out of here for threatening me at gunpoint!"

"Be my guest," Salina muttered. "Uncle Caleb won't throw me out, and you know it. I'm kin and, like it or not, you're quite aware that your mother takes care of her own flesh and blood. If you say one word to them about my being out or holding a gun on you—which was simply a natural reaction when I thought a burglar was in my room—I'll tell them I found *you* snooping through my private things."

"You have no right..." Lottie began.

Salina interrupted, "No, Lottie—it's you who haven't got the right. You have no right to go poking and pawing through my things. They are none of your concern. Now get out!"

Lottie rose from her knees and closed the lid of the traveling trunk. She hadn't found anything of particular interest, but perhaps another time she might. If Salina was so adamant in protecting her personal things, she figured, it might well mean she was hiding something. Haughtily, Lottie crossed the floor and went down the hall to her own room.

"And stay out," Salina called softly after her. "I mean it, Lottie. Do you understand?"

Lottie glared at her cousin, but didn't reply. She just shut the door to her own room.

Salina sat on her bed, her heart pounding. Lottie had been very close to discovering the leather wallet containing the pardon and traveling pass from President Lincoln. Then Salina noticed that her journal was not in the drawer where she had left it, but on top of the desk instead. *How much had Lottie read?* she wondered. There was no way of knowing for sure.

Salina quickly got out of her borrowed clothes, replacing them where she'd found them in the armoire, and wriggled into her long flannel night dress. She pulled her sleeping cap down over her ears and climbed under the thick quilts. *I can't stay here,* she thought, but she knew Lottie would see herself as the victor in driving Salina away if she were to leave at this point. She had promised Mamma that she would stay with Aunt Priscilla and Uncle Caleb until at least Christmas, and Salina was determined to honor her word. That way, she could keep Lottie in check—at least inside the house. When Lottie was in town or out with Colby, there was little she could do to observe her cousin's actions.

☆☆☆☆☆☆☆

If she didn't think it would wake the entire household, Lottie would have slammed her bedroom door shut in furious rage. Instead, she threw herself into the middle of the huge, four-poster bed, harmlessly kicking and pounding her fists into the plump mattress. She wanted to scream. But then she stilled, thinking. She rolled onto her back and stretched like a cat, staring up at the moulding pattern on the twelve-foot high ceiling. She'd only skimmed some of the entries in Salina's journal, but it had been enough to provide glimpses of what had happened to Salina and Taylor Sue in San Francisco, and more importantly, what had happened after Salina's interview with the Union's president.

Jeremy Barnes would positively recoil in a panic if he were to learn that Salina's Yankee stepfather had secured a presidential pardon. He would abhor the fact that Salina owed her life to the enemy. And what if Jeremy were told that Salina was rumored to be spying for the Union now in payment for her freedom, instead of remaining true to The Cause? That might create the breach between them that Lottie needed to draw Jeremy's attention away from Salina. "But how?" she whispered into the empty room. "There *must* be a way."

Lottie hugged a down-filled pillow closely and giggled wickedly to herself. She would do whatever it took to make it work.

Chapter Eight

Much to Salina's discomfort, Lieutenant Colby had accepted Lottie's invitation to the Armstrongs' Christmas Day dinner. The Armstrongs had hosted other Union officers from time to time, friends of friends they knew and Lottie was cunning enough to figure that her father would not voice any displeasure at having this Federal in the house. Caleb Armstrong counted on his reputation of friendliness toward the Union soldiers occupying Fairfax and the outposts to keep them from prying into his Confederate activities. It was a delicate balance, working the two sides, but there was profit to be made from each, and so Caleb played along. Besides, there was a degree of safety to be gained by making friends with the Yankees. They sometimes offered protection from those bent on confiscation or destruction of private property. He did not want to lose Ivywood on account of the war.

Lottie made such a fuss over Lieutenant Colby that even Mary Edith was rolling her eyes in utter disbelief. She had difficulty accepting the fact that her twin would take such pleasure in entertaining a Yankee soldier. But then, Lottie was known for her whims. Mary Edith said nothing, knowing Lottie would only be encouraged and fuss over him all the more if she knew what she was doing wasn't appreciated. Mary Edith knew her sister better than anyone, yet she was at a loss to comprehend how Lottie got her mile-wide mean streak.

The main house at Ivywood was filled to capacity, with a good many of Uncle Caleb's side of the family arriving from Fredericksburg. With so many people about, Salina did not have to work to make conversation. She merely ate and watched the activities all around. Shortly after dinner, Salina made her excuses. She had promised to pay a call on the Careys and was planning to spend the night at Carillon. Aunt Priscilla had not been able to talk Salina out of it, and Uncle Caleb thought it might be a well-earned respite. The tension at Ivywood between Salina and Lottie did not go unnoticed by the other inhabitants.

Lieutenant Colby accompanied Salina to the stable claiming he had to get back to Fairfax Court House.

"You've been avoiding me," Colby lightly accused, taking the saddle blanket from her hands. He knew Salina was capable of saddling her own horse, but he would not allow her refusal of his assistance.

"I thought I had made it clear that I have no wish to share your company, Lieutenant. I don't mean to sound cruel or harsh, but I will state it as plainly as I can—leave me in peace," Salina implored.

"All right," Colby agreed with a sigh. "You can't fault a man for trying."

"You are trying," Salina had to agree, and then she giggled. "*Very* trying!"

Colby smiled wistfully. "I guess I've taken it upon myself to look after you since Duncan isn't around to do so himself. Have you heard from him?"

"No," Salina answered. "I don't expect to. He knows how to find me if need be."

"I suppose you're right about that," Colby remarked candidly. "On the other hand, if you ever have need to reach him for any reason, I hope you know you can rely on me to get a message through our lines to him."

Salina merely shrugged, unwilling to give him too much hope of another chance to see her again. "We'll have to wait and see what happens."

"Then in the meantime, might I suggest that we remain friends?" Colby asked tentatively. "I promise I'll not attach any more importance to our relationship than that. Allow me that small comfort?"

"All right," Salina hesitantly complied. Had Colby forgotten, or chosen to disregard, that she was his enemy? What sort of an ally could he possibly be?

"Thank you." He nodded, quite obviously pleased. "It took me a long time to see you as the lady you are, Miss Salina," he confessed. "For all the miles I chased you across the country, I tried to picture you as nothing more than a Rebel who deserved to be punished. I know I shouldn't have been glad that you were awarded a pardon, but I was. It pained me to think that you might be locked up or possibly executed for your part in the conspiracy." Lieutenant Colby took a deep breath. "Somewhere along the line, I started to care about what might happen to you. I admire your spirit and your determination. Your intelligence and cleverness are to be commended. You are a very pretty lady, Miss Hastings, and I envy Jeremy Barnes a great deal. Should the two of you end up as man and wife, I believe you will be a great credit to him."

Salina didn't know what to say, and her voice faltered. "Lieutenant Colby..."

"Don't say anything. It's not necessary. As I said, we will continue from this point on as merely friends," Colby resolved. "Good-bye for now." He touched the brim of his hat and mounted his own steed. "Merry Christmas to you, Salina."

"Merry Christmas, Lieutenant." Salina watched him go. She climbed into her horse's side-saddle, thankful Uncle Caleb had been willing to keep Starfire for her while she had been away.

As Salina began to ride in the direction of Centreville, she suddenly slowed and turned back to the Armstrongs' stable. She checked the stalls, but no one was present, and she forced herself to shake the feeling that someone had been there—watching—listening. She shrugged and again rode off.

☆☆☆☆☆☆

Lottie let out a pent-up breath of relief. She was laying face down on the floor of the hayloft, hiding behind a bale for cover. Salina had *almost* found her when she had returned to the stable. Lottie smiled at her own cleverness. She was pleased beyond words with her latest discovery. Lance Colby was in love with Salina, even though he insisted they maintain a polite friendship. And Salina had truly been pardoned. "I do wonder if she had to sign an Oath," Lottie muttered to no one. "That would tear Jeremy apart. It could well destroy his trust in her." She thought for a moment or two, then sat up. "It wouldn't matter if she had signed an Oath or not. All that would matter was if Jeremy *believed* that she had." Lottie nearly purred as she scurried back to the house. Salina's visit to Carillon would provide another opportunity to inspect the items in her cousin's room without her knowledge.

But Lottie was disappointed. The door of Salina's room was locked, and only Salina had the key.

☆☆☆☆☆☆☆

Dawn of December 29 broke over the rolling hills of what was left of Shadowcreek. The lands were still in tact, but the main house and barn were piles of burned rubble. Salina picked her way through the ashes, here and there uncovering something that had survived the vicious flames. The charred ruins depressed her. She wandered about aimlessly until she found herself at the little family cemetery. She opened the wrought-iron gate and passed quietly through the mute gravestones.

In the gray morning light, Salina stood shivering in front of the monument that had been erected as a memorial to Captain Garrett Hastings. He wasn't actually buried there. Duncan had seen that his best friend's body had been interred in Pennsylvania. Salina, however, spoke as if her daddy were right beside her.

"I feel like I'm lost, Daddy. I don't know what to do. I've refused to go to Gettysburg with Mamma, but I can't tolerate staying under the same roof as Lottie. She has become more vindictive than ever. I know Jesus said to turn the other cheek, but she goes too far. I pray every day that the Lord would give me the strength to deal with the circumstance, but I am very weak and lose my temper quite often when it comes to her. She is so unlike Mary Edith, sometimes it's frightening."

Upon the iron fence near Grandma Glenna's headstone, Salina spied a climbing rosebush. To her delight, she found that there were rosebuds blossoming in spite of the winter season. She plucked one of the buds and laid it tenderly at the base of her father's marker, reading the epitaph again:

> *Garrett Daniel Hastings*
> *b. December 31, 1822*
> *d. September 21, 1862*
> *Faithful in love, courageous in duty*

His word was his honor.
The beloved ones he left behind
will always remember him
as a good and gallant man,
one much missed and still loved well.

Thundering hoofbeats pounded the ground, and in the blink of an eye the small cemetery was circled by a half-dozen armed riders. There was no time or place for Salina to run, but she quickly saw that their uniforms were not blue but gray. Her rapid heartbeat slowed as relief washed through her.

"What are you doing here, Miss? Are you alone?" a Rebel horseman inquired, his suspicious eyes darting beyond her.

"Yes, I am alone," Salina answered trustingly, though anxiously curling her fingers around the pistol in the pocket of her voluminous black skirt.

"You from these parts?" he asked.

"This was my home, and this is my daddy's grave. The Yankees are responsible for the destruction and for killing him as well," Salina answered evenly.

The gray-clad officer dismounted and leaned over the fence to read the inscription. Recognition dawned on him. "You're the daughter of Captain Garrett Hastings?"

"I am," Salina answered without the slightest reservation.

"Stay put," the officer ordered. "I know someone who's going to want to see you."

The riders disappeared as quickly as they had come. Then one solitary rider approached, reigning up on the opposite side of the iron fence. Salina exited the gate and stood, pulling her shawl tightly around her. In the blink of an eye, the other riders thundered back, halting abruptly in a crescent-shaped line around the little graveyard.

The leader dismounted and approached Salina. He wore high boots and a flowing red cape; his plumed slouch hat perched at a jaunty angle on his brow; and he sported a full, long beard of cinnamon-colored whiskers. The cavalier rested one gloved hand on the hilt of his sabre, taking her fingers in his other hand and pressing them to his lips. "Major General Jeb Stuart, at your service, Miss."

Jeb Stuart! Here was the South's own heralded cavalry leader. Salina giggled nervously beneath the attention of his vivid blue eyes, and she smiled prettily. Stuart released Salina's hand, and she curtsied before him. "It is an honor and pleasure to make your acquaintance, General."

"The pleasure is mine," Stuart assured her. "You're the last person I expected to find out here at this time of the day, but I'm glad 'twas you and not some Yankee patrol. Please, accept my condolences over the loss of your father. He was a courageous scout, and we miss his skills sorely. You must always remember that he died in the name of Virginia's honor. If this war is to take my life, 'tis the way I would want it as well."

"I appreciate your kind remarks, General." Salina nodded. "I, too, miss my daddy very much."

"It is my understanding that you were of great assistance in some of the work your father accomplished," Stuart said. "Is this the truth?"

"Yes, I did some work for him," Salina admitted. "How do you know this?"

Stuart laughed, a hearty, jolly sound. "Your father spoke of you often. He was very proud of you and your brother, who I've heard is a very capable assistant surgeon. But aside from that, there is a certain lieutenant currently serving with my staff who might have mentioned your name from time to time."

Salina's cheeks blazed a rosy pink. "I should think the General has more important items to discuss than me," she stammered shyly.

"We've had a lively camp this fall, and once daily duties are tended to, I am afforded a little time to get to know my officers better. I singled out your lieutenant and got him talking one night by the light of a campfire and the strains of Sweeney's banjo. Your young lieutenant is a fine soldier, to be sure," General Stuart pointed out. "He has spoken of you only because I have questioned him. He's usually as closed-mouthed as a clam, that one. But it's not a bad trait. He is reliable and can be trusted. I value those qualities in a man very highly—and in young ladies, too."

"You wouldn't happen to know where this particular lieutenant might be, would you, General?" Salina dared ask.

"As a matter of fact, I do." A merry twinkle shone in Stuart's eyes. "You are familiar with the Sully Plantation?"

"Yes," Salina replied. "It's just down the Little River Turnpike a ways."

"That's where we're headed—for breakfast. If you care to join us there, I'll see what I can do about arranging a meeting. You see, Lieutenant Barnes has been rather glum as of late, and I would like to see a smile on his face for a change. I imagine laying eyes on you could bring that about in an instant," Stuart predicted with a wink.

"I'll be there." Salina was determined. "Are you headed that way now?"

"Directly," Stuart confirmed. "Will you ride with us?"

"If you'll permit me, General, I'd like to freshen up and change. I won't be long, I promise," Salina added. "You don't know how much this means..."

"I have an idea." Stuart grinned. "There are times when I miss my own wife very much indeed, and wish I could have more time to spend with her and my son." His voice faltered slightly, but he masked his pain with another hearty, if hollow, chuckle. "Be at Sully as soon as possible—and wear anything but black," he ordered. "I don't tolerate melancholy in my ranks. When you arrive, tell the sentries on guard that I sent for you."

"Yes, sir." Salina curtsied once more, smiling brightly. "And thank you, General Stuart."

Stuart brushed aside Salina's words. He deliberately snapped a rosebud from the bush entwined among the iron gate posts, gallantly presenting it to Salina. He bowed ceremoniously. "A pleasure to be at your service, Miss Hastings." General Stuart kissed Salina's hand again and made haste to depart. He reared his horse, waved his plumed hat in salute, then wheeled and galloped away.

"General Jeb Stuart." Salina smiled, watching him go. She twirled the stem of the rose between her thumb and forefinger and hummed the tune of *Riding a Raid*, a song of tribute to the flamboyant cavalier. "I'm going to see Jeremy!" She yanked Starfire's reins from where they were tied to the iron fence and raced like the wind back to Ivywood.

☆☆☆☆☆☆☆

"Forgive me, Daddy," Salina whispered aloud to her reflection as she discarded her black mourning dress and hastily donned a navy blue brocaded satin frock which was new from Washington. The dress was her best, and she did want to look precisely that. She fastened a matching ribbon round her slender neck, centering the small ivory cameo. In the looking glass, she still appeared thin, but her face had lost its sickly pallor and her excitement lent a healthy flush to her cheeks. She dabbed a bit of perfume on her wrists and throat. Her heart beat wildly, her eyes flashing with green fire.

It was not much past seven, and the household of Ivywood was still sleeping when Salina crept down the stairs. She left a note for Uncle Caleb and Aunt Priscilla, telling them she'd gone out for an early-morning ride.

Salina pushed Starfire hard, and in record time she arrived at the Sully Plantation. "Please, sir, can you tell me where I might find General Stuart?"

Two sentries looked up from their coffee cups, exchanging a glance between them. The one on Salina's left asked, "And what might you be wanting with the General, miss?"

"I'm to meet him here," Salina said. "I have an appointment to see him."

"All right, if you say so." The sentry on the right merely nodded. General Stuart often had visitors in his encampments, both military and civilian. "I'm sure he'll want to deal with you himself. If you'll follow me, I'll take you to the General."

As they approached, Stuart was pouring himself another cup of coffee. He looked up at the sentry and the pretty young woman who stopped in front of him. He smiled broadly. "Thank you, Corporal, you're dismissed. Miss Hastings, right this way. I know exactly where your young lieutenant is."

Stuart offered her his arm and escorted Salina away from the encampment to the barn. "Now, you go on in there, and you'll surely give him a surprise."

Salina peeked inside. Jeremy had his back to the door. He looked tall and lean. His sandy-blond hair just brushed his broad shoulders, and many days of not shaving was evident along the angles of his cheeks and jaw. Suspenders kept his gray pants in place, and the sleeves of his faded, red plaid flannel shirt were rolled up, uncovering his tanned forearms. He held a canvas bag of oats up to Comet's greedy mouth and was muttering softly to the horse.

Salina hesitated just inside the door, saying nothing. She looked over her shoulder back to where Stuart was standing, and he motioned for her proceed. "Go on," he encouraged with a back-handed wave, a bright, mischievous smile splitting his cinnamon-colored whiskers.

She halted in her steps. All the things she had rehearsed to say on the ride over suddenly deserted her, and her tongue seemed glued to the roof of her mouth.

Stuart took charge of the situation. "Excuse me, Lieutenant?"

"Yes, General!" Jeremy spun around at attention, but his eyes rested on Salina. He never quite saw his commanding officer, and he dropped the bag of oats.

They ran to one another, clasping each other in a swift embrace. Salina's laughter rippled through the air, and Stuart clapped his hands, chuckling as he witnessed the reunion. The General slipped out, unnoticed, and returned to his coffee by the campfire.

Jeremy impulsively kissed Salina, and then he held her close. He couldn't believe she was right here, with him, at last. He wasn't about to let her go.

Salina's pulse quickened just being in his arms again. "Jeremy...Jeremy...Jeremy...*Jeremy*!" she laughed and giggled, and he swung her around twice, her feet dangling inches above the barn floor.

"Oh!" he sighed in contentment, setting her feet back down on the straw-covered ground. "God has answered my prayers and brought you back to me." His smile held a trace of impertinence, and in the next instant he bent his sandy-blond head until his lips met hers in a second kiss. "My darlin' Salina!" he murmured in her ear, then simply stared down at her, as if memorizing her face anew.

She touched his whiskered cheeks, admiring his recently-grown beard. "And what, Jeremy Barnes," she asked with a sly grin, "are you all doing here?"

"General Stuart decided to pay the residents of Sully a visit." Jeremy pulled her beside him as he took a seat on a hay bale. "He sent one of the other scouts ahead, who came and talked with one of the two women who've remained on here. The sympathies of the Barlow and Haight families lie with the Union. The menfolk have long since disappeared from here, knowing they risked capture if they'd stayed. I'd not be surprised if we discovered that the men have joined up to fight for the Yankees. In fact, when our scout asked Maria Barlow if her husband was home, she said not presently. And when asked if she'd seen any Rebels about, she made no reply. Our scout told her she would see Rebels, and plenty of them, in short order. So, here we are. I think it was General Wade Hampton who ordered them to make coffee for us—and the staff officers are now having breakfast. Our horses have already been fed from the corncribs." Jeremy tipped his head to one side. "You almost have to admire Maria Barlow and Phoebe Haight for their hospitality this morning. I heard they went to General Beauregard early on in the war, when his army was camped here, for protection from foragers. They've been known to sell goods to the armies— milk, corn, oats, livestock, whatever they've got. Think they'll take this near-worthless Confederate scrip in payment for some fresh milk?"

Salina shrugged. "Who can say? But enough about the Barlows and the Haights. What about you? How long are you going to stay? Where have you been? What are you doing? Were you at Fredericksburg?" Salina had a hundred questions.

Jeremy answered her impatient inquires. "We won't be here long. We've been on a raid—some of us to Dumfries, the others to Occuquon. We've picked up supplies and prisoners along the way, cut telegraph wires, burned bridges. Much on the same order as the Chambersburg Raid last October, but not so grand a scale. We've been riding since the twenty-sixth. When we stopped at Burke's Station, General Stuart caught a telegraph operator who was in the process of wiring our whereabouts to Washington. General Stuart waited only long enough to capture the reply describing the Yankee movements concerning us. Then he replaced the Yankee telegraph operator with one of our own and had him fire off a telegram addressed to Meigs, the Union Quartermaster-General. In the telegram, General Stuart complained of the poor quality of the mules we had recently acquired, stating they didn't move the wagons we captured in a satisfactory manner. As soon as the telegram was sent, General Stuart cut the line."

Salina laughed at the cavalry leader's bold audacity. "The very idea of complaining about the quality of confiscated mules! I'm sure Washington was in an uproar over that! Can you imagine the look on the Quartermaster-General's face as he read that telegram from Stuart?"

"It certainly was amusing on *our* end of the line." Jeremy chuckled triumphantly. The merriment in his eyes faded, though, when he answered another of her questions: "And, yes, I was there at Fredericksburg. Didn't you get my letters?" He raised an eyebrow in question.

"I got one—the one with the poem in it, right after you'd been to Chambersburg. Were there more?" Salina asked.

"I've sent three *since* Fredericksburg," Jeremy said, puzzled, but then he shrugged. "Well, at least that explains why you haven't replied. I was beginning to think you'd forgotten about me," he accused teasingly. He echoed Tabitha, "The mail is not always dependable. The letters will probably arrive eventually.

"We were at Fredericksburg in case we were needed, held in reserve," Jeremy told Salina. "It was frightening to watch wave after wave of Northern soldiers get mown down by our sharpshooters entrenched all along the wall bordering the Sunken Road. The Yankees just kept coming and coming—and we watched them, sometimes even cheered them. It was like watching a grand parade. They all marched in rank and file, and then our artillery and infantry on Marye's Heights opened up on them. Huge, gaping holes, filled themselves with fresh bodies again and again. It was the most eerie thing I've ever seen. And that night the skies were filled with the Northern Lights. It's the closest thing I can imagine to holy fire..." Sometimes he relived the scenes in his head at night. No need to repeat the nightmares in the daylight, too. He changed the subject. "Obviously you're back, but how? They told me you had been captured. Then I got word from Tabitha you'd come home, but she didn't give me any details in between."

"I've written, but you haven't gotten my letters either, it seems," Salina deducted. "I was imprisoned at Fort Alcatraz for three days and interrogated about my involvement with the Western Campaign." A chill stole down her spine at the unwanted memory of it, and she shuddered. "A spooky place, that island out in the middle of the bay. I have served my time and hopefully I'll never have to do that again. Ever."

"Wait. Start from the part where you got captured." Jeremy wanted to know her entire story.

Salina began to fill in the details, but her happiness at being with him got the better of her, and she kept getting off-track and asking him more questions, which he patiently kept answering. Salina's story came out piecemeal, fragmented and frequently out of order. "Oh, I fell overboard and I was sick for a long time."

"That's plain to see. You're so skinny." Jeremy's eyes inspected her figure. "You're a little thin," he amended, not wanting to hurt her feelings. "By the look in your eyes you don't appear very strong." He touched the side of her cheek with his hand in a gentle caress. "You look more like a little scarecrow," he said tenderly, with love in his sapphire eyes. "We'll have to work on getting you some good, nourishing food so can so you can get healthy again."

"You're thin, too," she pointed out. "The dark shadows beneath your eyes show you haven't had much sleep lately."

"No time, always on the move. I'm usually out with the advance scouts. We ride out first to reconnoiter, then report back any findings—enemy troop positions, sizes, you know, things of that nature." Jeremy shrugged. "Sometimes, I lose track of the time."

"Oh!" At the mention of time, Salina suddenly remembered the gift she brought with her. "I intended this for your birthday, but I don't know if we'll be together then. Here." She put the watch case into Jeremy's hands. "Now you'll have no excuse for losing track of time."

"Salina, this is beautiful." Jeremy grinned when he'd unwrapped her gift. He popped the stem and the pocket watch snapped open. He read the words engraved on the watch aloud: "To J.B. from S.H., All my love to my own Horse Soldier. January 15, 1863."

She slowly looked up to meet his dancing eyes. "You like it?"

"Very much. Thank you, Salina." He nodded affirmatively, squeezing her hand and brushing her cheek with a light kiss in gratitude. They were quiet for a moment. "What happened after you fell overboard?" he finally asked.

"I had a mild case of pneumonia—at least that's what the doctors called it. It didn't feel so mild to me." She told of the Widow Hollis's accusations against her father, and what she learned from Duncan after his visit to Judah Gilbert in San Diego.

"I was with your father in San Diego," Jeremy confirmed. "It wasn't cold-blooded murder, Salina. Honest, it wasn't. It was a fair fight, once I took care of the sniper in the hotel window, and Simon Hollis lost."

"That's what Duncan told me," Salina said. "He also told me that the Widow's determination reminded him much of the determination your uncle had to pursue my daddy...and to find you."

"That's not altogether surprising, Salina," Jeremy commented off-handedly. "The Widow Hollis—Irene is her first name—she's Uncle John's half-sister."

"What? They're related?" Salina asked incredulously.

"Yeah." Jeremy nodded his sandy-blond head. "You know, it's starting to fit together. That duel between Garrett and Jefferson over your mamma all those years ago...supposedly Irene was heartbroken over Jefferson's death, so I reckon Uncle John must have felt justified in vowing his revenge. No wonder he was so adamant to get rid of your father. It was his attempt to settle the score over his sister's lost love. It's festered inside Uncle John for over twenty years."

"But that doesn't excuse anything—his meanness and cruelty, or his relentless beatings while you were growing up," Salina argued.

"I'm not saying it excuses his behavior, but it certainly brings some of the pieces into perspective, don't you think?" Jeremy queried.

"Do you think that's why he wanted to arrest Mamma? To punish her for her part in it all, even though she didn't know she'd played a part?" Salina wondered.

"Salina, whatever happened to your mamma? After you girls left, she disappeared," Jeremy said. "I tried to make inquiries, but it was too difficult for me to learn what became of her."

Salina hesitated for a minute, sure his reaction to the news of Mamma's marriage to Duncan would be much like her own had been. She disliked keeping things from him, but for the moment she didn't want him to be fierce or angry. She chose her words carefully. She would give him a full explanation when there was more time to make him see the reasons clearly. "Duncan took Mamma out of the way.

She's safe, but she's not around Chantilly at all. Duncan sent her North, someplace where your uncle won't know to look for her."

"North." Jeremy mused. "Your poor mamma...but if she's safe, I suppose that's all that truly matters."

"Excuse me, Lieutenant?" a voice belonging to one of the other cavaliers interrupted their conversation.

"Yeah, Jake?" Jeremy called.

"Well, sir, it's your breakfast. It's getting cold, sir. And if you didn't want it, I was wondering if you mind if we divide it up between us," the rider said, nodding politely toward Salina.

"Go ahead, Jake. I'm not hungry for breakfast just now," Jeremy answered.

"Thank you, sir!" Jake grinned and quickly left.

Salina smiled. "One of your men?"

"I ride with nine fellows who I've met since I joined up. That one was Jake Landon. I've known Weston Bentley since my time at Harewood—he was involved in the prisoner exchange with me—and then there's Pepper Markham, Curlie Hawkins, Cutter Montgomery, Boone Hunter, Browne Williams, Harrison Claibourne, and Kidd Carney. They're good men. Dependable and dedicated," Jeremy praised them. "We all get along, but more importantly we work well together when it comes to carrying out our assignments. For whatever personal reasons, they've decided to follow me. They've proved their reliability, and I don't ask many questions. We each have our own motives for fighting. General Stuart has let me have them as my command."

Salina and Jeremy talked for a good long while—about the war, about each other, about the days ahead. At a few minutes past eleven, according to Jeremy's new watch, they were interrupted again when the barn door swung open.

"Corporal Weston Bentley, at your service." He put a rough hand to his forehead and tipped his kepi, winking at her. "You're not listening to his lies, are you, miss?"

Salina looked up at Jeremy and smiled, then returned her attention to Bentley. "I'm afraid you have me at a disadvantage, Corporal Bentley. While I get the distinct impression that you know me, we've yet to be properly introduced." She rested her head comfortably against Jeremy's shoulder, glorying in the feel of his protective arm around her waist.

"Oh, yes, I know you, miss—in a manner of speaking." Weston chuckled. "You're the one who's had our young lieutenant so tied up in knots. Why ever since Chambersburg..."

"That's enough, Bentley," Jeremy muttered uncomfortably.

Salina laughed softly, quite pleased. She tilted her head back, looking askance at Jeremy. "Tied up in knots? Shall I take that to mean that you have been missing me as much as I've been missing you?"

"More," was Jeremy's grave reply. "Was there something specific you came in for, Bentley?"

"We're moving, sir. Get that horse of yours saddled up. General Stuart has given orders that we're to scout on ahead. He knows about all this though." Bentley hinted at the *tête-à-tête* between the reunited pair. "He'll probably understand why you left a little late, but I'd still get a move on, if I were you. The General must sense somethin' and wants to be away from this place quick like."

"Where are the boys?" Jeremy asked.

"Curlie, Harrison, Pepper, Browne, and Jake have already gone," Bentley reported. "Cutter, Carney, and Boone are here with me. Boone's still shinin' his new boots. You know how delighted he was to find such a big pair on that dead Yankee we buried at Fredericksburg." Bentley belatedly saw that Salina frowned in consternation. "Pardon me, miss. It's just that Boone has very large feet compared to most, and it's taken him quite some time to find replacements for the pair he'd worn out. That Yankee didn't need 'em no more, so Boone captured them boots. They're a right good fit, too."

"Bentley, if you're quite finished," Jeremy interrupted, shaking his head.

Bentley took the hint. "My apologies, miss. We'll wait for you outside, Lieutenant. But you might want to hurry things up here, just the same."

She needed more time—time to properly explain everything and to tell him how she felt, tell him why she'd longed to come back to Virginia. "Do you have to leave now?" Salina's disappointment shone in her emerald eyes.

"I'm afraid so." Jeremy was as disappointed as she was. "Duty calls. General Stuart is wary about staying in one place for too long. Too many Yankees in the area, too much chance for getting caught. We've been behind enemy lines for three days now—we could practically see Alexandria, we've been so far north. And we've been fighting Yankees along the way. We don't need another skirmish. Are you staying with Tabitha?"

"No, I was staying at Ivywood," answered Salina.

"Stay with Tabitha instead," Jeremy ordered softly. "There's a chance we'll pass through Fairfax Court House, possibly as soon as tomorrow. I want to see you again, if time permits. Do as I say?"

"Yes." Salina nodded. "I'll leave for Fairfax this afternoon."

"Fine. Then we'll pick up your story where we left off. I know there's got to be more than we've had time to discuss. I'll see you as soon as I can." Jeremy held her to him, reluctant to release her from the circle of his arms. Quickly and quietly they prayed, thanking God for what little time they had had together.

"And thank God for General Stuart," Salina added with a grin.

"Yes, indeed." Jeremy chuckled. "I'm grateful he found you and brought you to me. I love you, Salina," he whispered earnestly.

"And I love you, my Lieutenant Horse Soldier." She beamed. "God willing, I'll see you again soon."

Silently, she stood nearby as Jeremy finished cinching Comet's saddle. Feet in the stirrups, he rode out of the barn, Salina walking beside him. There in the yard, heedless of Bentley, Carney, Boone, and Cutter watching, Jeremy leaned down from the saddle and kissed Salina good-bye. She stood on tiptoe to meet his lips. He whispered a hasty farewell.

"Good-bye." She wiped her eyes with a lace handkerchief. "Be careful, all of you!" She included the other gray-uniformed riders who accompanied their lieutenant.

Jeremy squeezed her hand firmly and nodded. He relieved Salina of the lace handkerchief, flashing an incorrigible grin. He tucked the pilfered token into his jacket pocket before riding off.

Salina turned her back on the Sully Plantation as she mounted Starfire and headed for Ivywood. As she rode, thinking only of Jeremy, she wished he could take her with him as easily as he'd taken her handkerchief. She smiled, recalling a similar instance when he had once filched a yellow ribbon from her hair as a keepsake reminder. Jeremy certainly had a penchant for collecting sentimental treasures from her, but Salina didn't mind in the least. She was touched by it.

When the last of Jeb Stuart's gray cavalry moved off the plantation grounds, one of the women who occupied Sully, Maria Barlow, was left the enormous chore of hauling countless buckets of water from the covered well. The troopers under Stuart's command had abandoned hundreds of campfires, and it took the lone woman over an hour to extinguish the flames left burning in their wake.

Chapter Nine

*L*ottie held the reins of her horse loosely as the lathered animal drank from the gurgling creek to quench its thirst. She smiled smugly as Lieutenant Lance Colby approached. "You look disappointed."

"How so?" Colby asked. "I found what I came for."

"Liar." Lottie smiled coquettishly. "You were looking for *her*, only *she* isn't here anymore. She left for Fairfax Court House earlier today, and I'm glad of it. I didn't want her to stay here in the first place—but unfortunately, she's kin. I have no say."

"What if I told you, in all honesty, that I came out here looking for you, Lottie?" Colby watched her expression change from haughty disdain to one of guarded surprise.

"I'd be hard pressed to believe you. I happen to know how you feel about her." Lottie patted her horse's neck. "Besides, why would you be looking for me?"

"I thought we might share another ride, or better yet, another race," Colby suggested.

Through her lashes, Lottie coyly observed Colby. He was handsome, in his own way, and he was a Yankee. That alone made the rest of her family angry. It would do well enough for an excuse to spend time with him. "I'd be delighted, Lieutenant."

Their bantering was light, meaningless conversation as they rode the hills and trails together for the better part of an hour. After racing for over a mile, Lottie had again bested him, honestly this time.

She laughed gaily as she sat down on the blanket Colby spread out next to a thick-trunked tree. "You need a faster mount, Lieutenant, unless you merely intend to chase the Rebels!" She took a sip of cool water from the canteen he offered, but she refused the salty jerky. "No, thank you. I'm not in the army. I prefer regular, home-cooked meals."

"Sure you won't try it? I'll wager it's better than what they've got to eat in the Rebel cavalry sometimes," Colby said, a trifle snidely.

"How would you know? You Yankees are usually too slow or too clueless to know where the Rebel cavalrymen are or what they're doing, let alone what they're eating," Lottie taunted. "Especially if all the Federal horses are as slow as yours!"

"Really? Am I to understand that *you* know what they're doing these days?" Colby queried.

"Careful. Are you asking me to spy for you?" Lottie chided. "Well, you've got the wrong cousin. Ask Salina if you're into spying!" Cross and irritable, Lottie scrambled to her feet and immediately brushed away the blades of dead grass from the skirt of her riding habit.

Colby was at her side in an instant, his curiosity getting the better of him. He couldn't help but ask, "What did she ever do to you, Lottie? What causes you to dislike Salina Hastings so strongly?"

"You wouldn't understand," Lottie muttered, pulling her arm free of his grasp, attempting to mount her horse. "No one does!"

"Try me," Colby coaxed persuasively.

Lottie took her foot from the stirrup and stomped it on the ground. She opened her mouth to speak but snapped it shut again and crossed her arms defensively over her chest. Her cornflower eyes blazed furiously.

"Well?" Colby persisted.

"Salina's got what I want," Lottie admitted grudgingly, toying with the end of one of her golden curls.

Colby knew Salina had little. It was Lottie who had the riches and the wealth. "What does she have?" he wondered aloud. "It can't be lands or possessions."

"No, it's nothing like that. Though you're right, she hasn't got much to her name. No, it's...it's Jeremy Barnes," Lottie pouted.

The blue-clad Lieutenant pondered her answer a moment before speaking. "Ah, Jeremy Barnes. He is the bane of my existence as of late," he admitted before he could stop himself. "But you only want him because Salina's got him," he continued quickly. "If she loved someone else, my guess is you'd want the other man instead. Correct?"

"No," Lottie maintained, "no, I would still want Barnes."

"Now, who's the liar?" Colby lifted her chin, studying her eyes. "From where I stand, it appears that you simply don't like Salina—period. You probably never have liked her because she's competition, and you don't like that. You'd rather just collect all you think is your due rather than share anything, no matter how small, with the likes of your cousin. It's plain enough to see that. Why not just forget about her and live your own life?"

"Oh, that's quite easy for you to say!" Lottie retorted hotly. "You don't have to live with *Salina did this* or *Salina did that*. She can sing, and she can cook, and she's so pretty, and she's so clever, and she's so loyal, and she's such a good nurse, and she's so nice. Everyone positively *adores* Salina."

"Haven't you ever heard that one can catch more flies with honey than with vinegar?" Colby challenged.

She disregarded his comment. "Oh, but now it's beyond the little things. Now it's Salina and the spy ring, or Salina in prison, or Salina and Jeremy. I'm heartily sick of her, and I wish she'd never come back!"

"You're jealous of her," Colby stated the underlying issue. "Well, you shouldn't be. You've no need."

Lottie turned away, not wanting to share another moment of his company.

Yet he halted her with his next words. "You're a beautiful woman, Lottie Armstrong. Well-educated, financially secure—you have much to offer." He turned her face back toward his and lightly caressed her flushed cheek. "When you find the right man, someone who'll love you for being you, you'll sweep him off his feet. In the meantime, put the rift between you and Salina out of your head. Concentrate on the things you do well and make your own way. Envy can be deadly—it'll eat you up inside."

Lottie's eyes grew cold. "I'm not jealous of her," she insisted. "And for as making my own way—I intend to! I'm going to win Jeremy's love if I have to fight her every step of the way." She tipped her head to one side, looking up to meet Colby's eyes. "And you..."

"What about me?" Colby could see her cunning mind was working fast and furious, and he was almost afraid to know what she might be thinking.

"Why, you're just the person who could help me." She smiled ever so sweetly.

Colby, anticipating her scheme, said, "You think our relationship could prove to be beneficial because I could help you come between them."

Lottie feigned shock at such a notion. "Me? Come between them?"

"You're not as innocent as you pretend to be," Colby said knowingly. Lottie was a chameleon—she changed her colors to suit her purpose without thinking twice about it. She would befriend him—Yankee or no—so long as she got what she wanted in the end. War was a game to her, and she was willing to overlook the fact that soldiers chose sides. Lottie didn't choose between the blue and the gray; she chose them both. She had no loyalties to either cause. Hers were purely selfish motives, and Colby sensed that she was used to getting her own way.

Lottie's smile was practiced. "Do you have any fondness for me at all, Lieutenant Colby?"

"If I didn't, I wouldn't be here," Colby clarified, his pale blue eyes narrowing in scrutiny. It was a true enough statement. She intrigued him for some reason. He quizzed her, "What is it that you want me to do?"

"Help me drive them apart," Lottie answered, direct and to the point. "Plant a seed of doubt, cast an implication that there might be someone else, possibly even hint that one of them might not be true to their cause. You're an intelligent man, Lieutenant, use your imagination," Lottie dared.

"What's in it for me?" Colby wanted to know. "You get him and I get her? It's not that simple, Lottie."

"Of course, it's that simple," Lottie insisted. "It can't be that difficult if we can pull it off right."

"Lottie, you're dealing with emotions and feelings of other people. It will never be simple," Colby added.

Lottie didn't want to hear it. "I know that if we do this right, she'll turn to you, he'll turn to me, and we both get what we want." She took a step closer to him. "You can't deny that you care for her."

"Well, I wouldn't want to do anything to hurt her," Colby confessed.

Lottie's smile was malicious. "Don't let her know you're behind any of it, and then all you have to do is be sure you're there to comfort her when she needs you most."

"How do you suggest I do that?" The idea was ludicrous, but if Jeremy was out of the way, he would have at least a chance with Salina.

Judging by the look in his eyes, Lottie knew Colby was beginning to see things her way. "Help me, Lieutenant," she purred. "It'll all work out. You'll see."

☆☆☆☆☆☆☆

Jeremy returned, halting Comet next to Stuart's mount. He saluted his commander and presented his report. "Too many Yankees, General. We were fired on as soon as we were spotted. In my estimation, they outnumber us too strongly for an attack on our part to be successful."

"Yes, that's similar to what the others had reported. Thank you, Lieutenant." General Stuart dismissed Jeremy Barnes with a nod.

"My compliments, sir." Jeremy left the General's side to allow him to formulate their next move. If Stuart needed him, he'd send for him. Jeremy rejoined Bentley, Jake, Boone, and the others among the ranks.

"What took you so long to get back? Curlie and Browne have been back for nearly thirty minutes." Bentley raised an eyebrow in question. "Did you get too close to Fairfax Court House?"

"I didn't get to talk to her, if that what's you're hinting at, Bentley." Jeremy's tone was brusque. He had seen Salina, but he hadn't liked the scene. And he liked even less what he'd been told...

Jeremy had gone to Tabitha's boardinghouse and gotten as far as the back door of the kitchen. He was anxious for even five minutes to see Salina alone, but he'd employed caution and peeked into the window before barging in. Through the window, he witnessed Salina sitting at the table across from Lance Colby as he ate, engaged in what appeared to be a most congenial conversation. Unable to clearly see Salina's face, Jeremy saw the Yankee's face plain enough—and the expression on the Union officer's face as he glanced at Salina didn't sit well with Jeremy in the least. That blue-bellied lieutenant was smitten with her. It was evident in his eyes.

He'd ridden away from the boardinghouse unnoticed, his jaw set in an uneasy line. Not half a mile down the turnpike, Jeremy had been surprised to discover Lottie Armstrong out in the cold night.

"I followed you," she admitted, breathing white puffs of steam, which circled her hooded blond head. "I came to warn you not to go into Fairfax, but you were too fast and I couldn't catch up. The Yankees are waiting. They're hoping to catch General Stuart."

"How do you know that?" Jeremy cautiously queried.

"I tricked someone into divulging the information," Lottie confided. "Recently I have acquired the...friendship...of a certain lieutenant stationed at the outpost. He's staying at a boardinghouse in Fairfax, and he's in a position to know of certain troop movements and orders. His name is Colby, and he tells me all sorts of things without even realizing what he says," Lottie added lightly. "From what I've been able to detect from some of our conversations, he seems to know Salina quite well. Perhaps she gets information out of him, too. I'm not sure, but I do know they are acquainted."

Jeremy's eyes narrowed at her remarks. Lottie's information about the troops in Fairfax was correct. "Why are you telling me about the Federal troops?"

"I didn't know what to do at first." Lottie shrugged. "But then I thought you of all people would know best what to do with such information. That's why I followed you, to warn you." She lowered her eyes. "I don't want anything to happen to you. I thought I could help in some way."

Jeremy was puzzled. Lottie actually seemed sincere. "What else can you tell me about Colby?"

"Before his current assignment," Lottie replied, "Colby worked for a man named Duncan Grant. He was assigned to follow Salina all the way to California, and she was under his guard when they brought her back to Washington."

"Has he mentioned anything about Salina's return?" Jeremy demanded, his curiosity piqued. In the barn at Sully yesterday, Salina hadn't quite finished sharing *all* the details of her trip with him. The more he thought about it, the more questions he had.

"Have you seen her since she's come back?" Lottie tried to glean information of her own.

"Yes," Jeremy answered but did not elaborate.

"So, then, you know about the pardon and all she had to go through just to get it. And I imagine she was deported back here to Virginia." Lottie watched Jeremy's face for a reaction. "I was rather surprised that she came back instead of staying up North with her mamma."

"Where is Mrs. Hastings exactly?" inquired Jeremy.

"Oh, she's not *Mrs. Hastings* anymore." Lottie pounced on Jeremy's ignorance of the situation concerning Salina's mother.

"Aunt Annelise has gone and married that Duncan Grant. I wouldn't wonder if Salina *refused* to live with his Yankee relatives. But I reckon Aunt Annelise would have to go where her new husband sends her. Why, Jeremy, didn't Salina tell you any of this?"

Jeremy reluctantly shook his head. "No." There *were* gaps in Salina's story. *In addition to her mother's marriage, what else hasn't she told me?* He pulled his jacket closer around him, yet the cold seeped into his bones. His fingers idly closed over the square of lace in his pocket while his thoughts continued to drift. *Salina was pardoned for her part in delivering the plans for the Western Campaign? What had been required in exchange for her release?* Jeremy questioned silently, afraid of the answer. To the best of his knowledge, an Oath of Allegiance to the Union played a vital role in such cases, but certainly Salina wouldn't sign such a document as that—would she?

He recalled Salina talking with that Yankee lieutenant at Tabitha's. *Was she spying for their side?* That was absurd, he chided himself. Salina wouldn't spy against him. She was a Hastings, and she was in love with him. But why hadn't she mentioned her mother's marriage? Jeremy let out a long sigh. Garrett Hastings must be rolling over in his grave. Jeremy wondered if Ethan was aware of any of this. As soon as they returned to camp, Jeremy was determined to find out.

"Thank you, Lottie. You've been quite helpful. I appreciate the risk," Jeremy said before he rode away.

She watched him go and a delighted smile curved her lips. She felt giddy. She was sure he believed what she had said. It was a start.

☆☆☆☆☆☆☆

Dipping her quill into the inkstand, Salina hurriedly penned a brief note. Stuffing it into the pocket of her cape, she left the boardinghouse. Brooding in her thoughts, she failed to notice she was being followed.

Jeremy hadn't come to see her yesterday, and her disappointment had carried through the night. Somewhere in her dreams, the notion had come to her to put a note for him in the same hollow oak tree where Daddy used to leave messages for him. Salina had no way of knowing when the next time Jeremy might be in the area, or even if he would bother to make a stop at the tree, but it was worth a chance.

On her ride, Salina crossed the Shadowcreek lands. She rode down by the footbridge, and the old slave quarters came into view. Before she was born, Shadowcreek's farmland had been worked by two dozen slaves, and the main house had a handful of servants as well. After Grandpa Henry's death, Daddy had let their slaves work off the price for which they had been purchased. Some had stayed on, earning wages, but some had left without looking back. Once they were freed, he had not replaced them. Daddy had unpopular ideas for the times, but he didn't care. He didn't believe that one race should be forced to serve another simply because of the difference in skin color.

Like Jubilee, Peter Tom had stayed on even after the war began, but now Salina knew why he had chosen to do so. Peter Tom had been playing the role of a double agent—spying for Duncan as well as for Daddy. Jubilee had stayed out of her loyalty to Mamma and her love for Salina and Ethan. Salina reined Starfire in front of the brick and whitewashed cabin, and she stayed there for quite some time, just thinking. She could almost hear their voices: Peter Tom's deep bass; Jubilee's clucking alto. *"Chile, ah's only wants da best fer ya,"* Jubilee frequently used to say. Salina smiled wistfully, remembering her mammy fondly.

Was the Southern way of life really worth dying for? Not everyone in Virginia owned slaves, but many of the old, aristocratic families did. Salina had heard it said that this conflict was a rich man's fight, but a poor man's war. Even Duncan had asked her what she herself was fighting for. Salina mentally shrugged and rode on towards Carillon.

Taylor Sue was extremely pleased to see Salina. "We've wonderful news!" she exclaimed. "Papa's been reassigned. Now that he's well again, he's been summoned to Richmond. He isn't able to serve in the field because of his disability, but they've found an office job for him in the War Department. He's a very good tactician, at least that's what his orders said. He read them to us as soon as they were delivered."

"What does your mama think?" Salina inquired, shocked at the unexpected news. "And your little sister?"

"Papa's taking Mama and Jennilee with him to live in Richmond," Taylor Sue explained. "Mama's in a panic, trying to get everything packed away. The Yankees who commandeered our house before the Battle at Chantilly were kind to Carillon. We were spared the damage that some of the other houses have suffered. But Papa doesn't think the old house could be so lucky twice. If Yankees again use it for shelter, or Confederates for that matter, there's a chance the place might not survive. Mama plans on leaving little for anyone to have the opportunity to destroy."

"What of you?" Salina queried, a lump forming in her throat. "Are you moving to Richmond as well?" She did not like to think of not having Taylor Sue nearby.

"I'm going to go with them. But if I can find Ethan and we can be married, I'll go where I can be near him," Taylor Sue said firmly. "I have been meaning to ride over to Tabitha's and tell you about this. I want you to come with us to Richmond. Papa has already said you're more than welcome. Besides, you promised you would stand up with me when I become your brother's wife."

"Richmond? I thought Reverend Yates was going to marry the two of you," Salina reminded her.

"I wanted him to." Taylor Sue nodded. "But what if Ethan can't get enough leave to travel all the way here? I'm going to ask Reverend Yates if he can recommend a minister in Richmond. Surely he must know someone who would be willing to perform our ceremony."

"I should think so," Salina agreed. "When are you planning to leave?"

"Papa says we'll be leaving within the week. Please say you'll come, Salina," Taylor Sue implored.

Salina hesitated. What if Jeremy were to come to Fairfax Court House looking for her? "I suppose I could get a message to Jeremy and tell him..."

"Of course." Taylor Sue's golden eyes lit with a smile. "And you could leave word with Tabitha and Reverend Yates as well, if that would make you feel better about going."

"I do want to see Ethan." Salina only at that moment realized how much she missed her older brother. Her thoughts had been so consumed with Jeremy that thoughts of her brother dimmed by comparison. "I'll go with you, if you're sure your parents don't mind my tagging along."

"Not at all," Taylor Sue assured her. "Come on, let's go tell them."

Both Colonel and Mrs. Carey were more than happy to learn Salina had accepted the invitation to travel with them. Jennilee was pleased, too. "Just think," Taylor Sue's younger sister said, "how exciting it must be in Richmond."

Salina wondered at that. She had seen the Yankees' capital city—its crowds, noise, and filth. She imagined that Richmond, like Washington, would resemble an armed camp, filled with soldiers and wounded men and refugees. Wisely, she held her tongue. Jennilee was young, barely thirteen. She ought to be allowed to have something to look forward to.

On her way back to Tabitha's boardinghouse, Salina paused only long enough to hide another note to Jeremy in the tree, this one telling him she was going to Richmond. She expressed her wish that he would join them there, if he could manage to do so. She urged Starfire to increase their pace as they galloped to Fairfax.

☆☆☆☆☆☆☆

Lieutenant Colby read Salina's note prior to handing it over to Lottie.

"You've done well, Lieutenant." Lottie smiled wickedly. "Very well indeed!" Recklessly, she kissed his cheek. "I do thank you!"

☆☆☆☆☆☆

All the next day Salina worked diligently to help Tabitha make sure that things at the boardinghouse were in running order.

"I am grateful for all you do around here, Salina." The old woman repeatedly patted her hand. "But I'll get my chores done without you, you know. I'm not the invalid you seem to believe I am."

"I just want you to take it easy. You fell hard when you missed that bottom step in the cellar the other day, and you should rest," Salina said in her most mothering tone. "If you didn't have so many boarders at the moment, I wouldn't worry about you so much while I'm away."

"Stuff and nonsense," Tabitha countered. "There's some real nice ladies staying here—wives or sisters of Union officers—who've offered to lend a hand if I need it. If I take them up on their kindness, who knows? It just might be I can get them to talk to me, if you know what I mean."

Salina grinned. Tabitha was always working for the Remnant and her information was always reliable. "You be careful, then. I don't know when I'll be back."

"No matter." Tabitha hugged Salina. "You know there's a room for you here whenever you need it."

"Yes, I do. Thank you." Salina nodded. "I need to stop by Ivywood to tell Aunt Priscilla where I'm going in case Mamma should write asking about me."

"Yes, you do," Tabitha agreed. "And I'll get word to Ruby Tanner. And don't you fret. If Lieutenant Barnes comes around, I'll be sure to let him know he can find you somewhere in the capital."

Salina packed her things and hauled her carpetbag down the stairs. *Off on another adventure,* she thought. She had been reading in the Psalms earlier that morning, and one of the verses came to mind: *Thy word is a lamp unto my feet, and a light unto my path.* She had the confidence and the experience to know that God would guide her where He would lead.

"You're leaving?" Lieutenant Colby's voice came from the landing at the bottom of the stairwell.

"Yes," was Salina's reply, purposely not disclosing her destination to him.

"Well, then, I'm glad I caught you. Duncan has forwarded a letter from your mother. Here you are." Colby handed her the envelope.

"Thank you, Lieutenant." Salina was eager to hear how Mamma was faring up north in Gettysburg.

"Will you want to send a reply before you go? Duncan's in Washington, and I can make sure it is delivered into his hand," Colby offered.

"Thank you just the same, but I haven't time at the moment," Salina declined. "I'm in a bit of a hurry."

"Then I won't keep you." Colby nodded. "Good-bye, Salina."

She smiled tentatively. "Good-bye, Lieutenant."

As he watched her go, Colby felt a certain disgust with himself rise within. His alliance with Lottie Armstrong would come to no good if he wasn't careful. Each time he caught a glimpse of Salina, he felt guilty for betraying her. With Salina away for a time, Lottie would be forced to let her manipulations fall idle. *And perhaps I should reevaluate the circumstance I've voluntarily embroiled myself in,* he thought bitterly.

☆☆☆☆☆☆☆

At Ivywood, Salina was greeted by Mary Edith. Her belly was growing more pronounced than ever, though she still had four months until the birth. She was sorry to learn that Salina and the Careys were heading south, but she wished them all the best, as did Uncle Caleb and Aunt Priscilla.

Lottie appeared just as Salina was ready to depart, and the two cousins stared each other down. "Where are you off to?" Lottie finally demanded, knowing Salina's departure meant she would have nothing to hold over Lance Colby.

"Nice of you to be concerned, Lottie, but it's none of your affair." Salina brushed passed her and fairly skipped across the veranda and down the stairs.

Later that same evening, in Taylor Sue's room at Carillon, Salina opened the letter from Mamma. Annelise had written to make sure Salina was well and still on the mend from her bout with pneumonia. She reassured Salina that things were much the same in Gettysburg, and that she was still feeling well, with no morning sickness whatsoever. A brief description on how Christmas had been celebrated was punctuated with the bewilderment and shock Duncan's family had suffered when she announced to them she was having a baby.

Taylor Sue sighed. "Your mamma is a very brave woman, Salina."

"Yes, I think so, too," Salina murmured. "She always says that the Lord will not give us more than we can bear. He knows the limits to how strong she is, and He knows that with His love and strength she can bear her load."

"The Lord deals with each of us individually, at our own level, in His own time," Taylor Sue added. "I'm curious, Salina. How did Jeremy take it when you told him that your mamma had married Duncan?"

Salina fidgeted uncomfortably. "There wasn't time to explain to him that day in the barn at Sully. But I remember how hard I took the news, so I'm guessing Jeremy's feelings will be at least double that."

"Do you think Jeremy will come to Richmond to look for you?" Taylor Sue asked.

"If he gets my notes, I hope he will. I've so much to tell him. We never did quite get around to the interview with Lincoln, or the pardon, or any of that. I kept asking him about Fredericksburg, riding with General Stuart, and then one of his men came in..." She trailed off, remembering. "We've got to talk, the sooner the better. But I have no idea when that will be," Salina said sadly. She held his locket in the palm of her hand. "He was pleased with the watch I gave him, especially since the Yankees stole his old one from him when they took him prisoner. Perhaps we'll see each other in Richmond, somehow, and we can talk then."

Taylor Sue glanced down at her engagement ring. "I've got to find Ethan just as soon as I can. Papa says they will hold his court-martial in Richmond, so hopefully we'll get there in time for his hearing."

"Have you found out when he's to be tried?" Salina asked eagerly.

"No." Taylor Sue shook her russet head. "But I intend to once we arrive, rest assured."

☆☆☆☆☆☆☆

Harrison Claibourne, Weston Bentley, Kidd Carney, and Boone Hunter waited at a distance as Jeremy approached a stone cottage. The four men kept watch, talking quietly among themselves. Their lieutenant had been acting rather strangely the past few days. Bentley claimed Barnes was all tied up in knots again—only now it was even worse since he'd seen his dark-haired beauty after the Christmas raid on Dumfries.

Mary Edith Armstrong Baxter was surprised but pleased to have Jeremy visit her at the cottage called Little Ivy. Visitors were few and far between. She had only recently returned from her holiday stay at Ivywood. The arrival of two dozen cousins and aunts and uncles on her father's side made her savor the peace and solitude of her snug little home. "Are you on a scouting mission, then?" Mary Edith asked, offering Jeremy tea and some fresh muffins she had baked.

Jeremy politely declined the offer of food, though his stomach growled. "In a manner of speaking, I guess you could say I am on a scouting patrol," he answered. "I can't seem to find Salina anywhere. She's not at Ivywood, or Carillon, or in Fairfax—which is where I saw her last."

"Well, that's odd. I thought she would have told you. She's gone, Jeremy," Mary Edith said simply.

"Gone?" Jeremy queried, raising a dark eyebrow in question.

"Why, yes. She went with the Careys to Richmond. They're hoping to find Ethan so that he and Taylor Sue can be married. Colonel Carey has a new position, and he'll be living there with Jennilee and Mrs. Carey probably for the duration of the war."

"Richmond," Jeremy echoed. He had to report back to camp, but then he would devise the means to ride south to the Confederate capital. Perhaps one of the generals in the field would need to send a messenger to President Davis for some reason or another.

Mary Edith was a bit puzzled. "Jeremy, I'm truly surprised Salina didn't let you know."

"Maybe she didn't know where to find me." Jeremy tried to give Salina the benefit of the doubt, even when his mind taunted, *Maybe she didn't want to find me...*

"She was so happy the morning she was finally able to see you again, Jeremy, if you'll permit me to say so. Promise me you won't tell her I told you, but she positively glowed with love for you. She had been so sick coming back from California. I think it was her resolve to be with you that gave her the strength to get well. After that ordeal in Washington—all the questions, and that interview with Lincoln..."

"Interview with *Lincoln*?" The question crossed Jeremy's lips before he could stop it.

"Well, of course. How else do you think she was allowed to come back to Virginia?" Mary Edith replied with a question. "She obtained her pardon from the Union President after she promised that she would behave if he would let her return." Mary Edith saw the expression on Jeremy's face and suddenly wondered if she had divulged something

Salina had yet to tell him herself. "Jeremy, I just assumed that you and Salina had talked..."

"We did, but evidently not quite enough," he said tightly. "If you hear from her, you tell her I'll track her down."

Mary Edith swallowed, glancing away from the hard look in Jeremy's blue eyes. A brief shudder of apprehension for Salina's sake trickled down her spine. "I'll let her know." Mary Edith nodded.

"Have you heard from your husband?" Jeremy inquired.

"Randle's last letter was posted from Nassau. His ship was preparing to depart for England with a hold full of cotton," Mary Edith answered. "He promised to bring something back from London for the babies." She patted her well-rounded belly, agreeing with her mother's idea that she was carrying twins. "Are you sure you won't have something to eat?"

"Well, it's not just myself," Jeremy clarified. "I've got my men waiting, too, and we've got to move on."

"It'll just take a minute for me to bag these muffins, and you all can take them with you," Mary Edith offered. "Did you fill your canteens from the well?"

"We will." Jeremy's nod reflected his gratitude. "Thank you for your time, Mary Edith, and your food."

"Certainly." She smiled up at this uniformed Confederate officer. "Do be careful, Jeremy."

"I will." Jeremy bowed slightly and took his leave. "Come on," he barked to his companions. He gave no indication as to why they had stopped at this particular cottage, and the other four riders knew better than to ask. They wordlessly distributed the contents of the bag among themselves.

"Happy New Year!" Mary Edith called after them, but Jeremy merely waved in return.

A cloud of hurt and disappointment covered Jeremy. *Why is Salina deliberately keeping things from me? What else hasn't she seen fit to tell me?* he wondered. His stomach churned as he thought of something else that had been gnawing at the dark corners of his mind. The night he'd gone into Fairfax and found Salina sharing the kitchen table with that Yankee Colby, they had been talking together. Jeremy had told Salina the day *before* he would be in Fairfax. Could it be that Salina's pardon might be predicated on promising to help capture him in return? No, he *couldn't* believe that. He *wouldn't*. But the idea was there, in his mind. He was one of Stuart's scouts and couriers, and Salina knew he oftentimes carried dispatches that could prove costly if they should fall into the wrong hands.

The bitter taste in his mouth threatened to choke him. There had to be a way to arrange for a journey to Richmond. He considered it his duty to go find out for himself what on earth Salina was up to—and why!

Chapter Ten

"Lieutenant Barnes?" Kidd Carney stood outside of Jeremy's tent two days after they had returned to what General Stuart called "Camp No Camp."

"Come in, Carney," Jeremy answered. "What is it?"

"Orders, sir. You're being summoned to Richmond." Kidd Carney attempted to conceal a grin. He'd learned that was where the elusive Miss Hastings had gone, and now Lieutenant Barnes was being presented with the perfect excuse for being there as well.

"Richmond?" Jeremy's brow arched in question. He read the subpoena, issued by a military commission, ordering his appearance as a character witness in the court-martial of Captain Ethan Hastings, Assistant Surgeon, Second Corps under Stonewall Jackson, C.S.A. "Court-martial?" *Where have I been that I haven't heard of this absurdity?* he asked himself silently, but he didn't probe too deeply for an answer. His mind had been on Salina. "Carney, where is Captain Hastings now?"

"Confined to quarters at Stonewall Jackson's encampment, sir. He'll stay there until they send him to Richmond under guard," Kidd Carney replied.

Jeremy shook his head. "I'll secure permission to see him. Get Bentley and Boone. Tell them we'll ride in an hour if I can arrange it."

"Very good, sir." Kidd Carney saluted. "And the others?"

"Tell them stay put unless ordered out to picket duty. And tell them to keep their eyes and ears open," Jeremy ordered.

Before the day was out Jeremy was granted entrance by the guards on either side of the door to Ethan's quarters. "My compliments to the Captain," he said, finding Ethan at his desk, elbow-deep in a mountain of paperwork and endless forms required by the medical department on a daily basis.

"Well, Lieutenant Barnes, this is indeed a welcome visit." Ethan grinned. "I'm surprised you were allowed to see me at all."

"It took some doing, but I persuaded your colonel that it was a matter of medical importance." Jeremy grimaced. "Though I don't know if even you have a cure for a wounded heart."

"A wounded heart? What's the matter with you? And why do I get the distinct impression that my sister has something to do with this black mood you're in? Haven't received any letters from Salina in awhile?" Ethan jabbed.

"Have you heard anything from Salina? Or from your mamma for that matter?" inquired Jeremy.

"Twice I've gotten messages from Reverend Yates, but other than that, nothing," Ethan replied.

"Brace yourself," Jeremy warned. "What I've got to tell you won't set well."

Ethan was pacing the tent much like a caged circus tiger by the time Jeremy finished telling him the sketchy details of his mother's marriage, the girls' return, and what Jeremy knew of Salina's pardon.

"Amazing," Ethan breathed.

"I've seen Salina only once since she's been back," Jeremy said.

"Who told you all this? How did you find out about Mamma and Salina's pardon?" Ethan asked.

"Some from Mary Edith, some from Lottie. They're both in a position to know." Jeremy shrugged in temporary resignation. "But I didn't come here to talk to you about your sister." The bruises on his heart would have to heal themselves, and he knew that. "I came to find out who Franklin Shields is."

"He is handling my defense," Ethan clarified. "It was his life I saved on the night I am accused of having disobeyed direct orders. Had

I followed the orders of my superior officer at the time, Franklin would have died. He's representing me out of gratitude—my life for his."

"He's summoned me to be a witness. What did you do, tell him that you've patched me up in the past?" Jeremy asked. Ethan had treated the wounds Jeremy had sustained near Groveton, following a run to Cedar Mountain last August.

"Yes, and you lived though my ministrations to fight another day," Ethan commented. "Part of the list of charges declares that I have no proper certification other than signed verification from Dr. Phillips, which states I served as his apprentice and have passed both his oral and written examinations. No one questioned it when I first enlisted. Only now they are going through my records with a fine-toothed comb. When they discovered that I am not yet twenty—assistant surgeons are preferably at least twenty-one—that put another wrinkle in my case. Franklin's doing his best. That's why he's called on you."

Ethan went on to tell Jeremy of all that followed the Battle of Fredericksburg. Jeremy shook his head. "I've been out scouting so much I hadn't heard of any of this."

"When's the last time you were up Chantilly way?" asked Ethan. "The day you saw Salina?"

"No." Jeremy shook his head. "It was the day I found out she'd left again. She's moved south to Richmond with the Careys. In all probability, they'll be in Richmond on the date of your trial. I reckon they'll stay at the Spottswood Hotel."

"Doesn't everybody who's anybody?" Ethan jested. Though he'd never been there himself, it was said that the Spottswood was the place to see and be seen. On a serious note Ethan added, "If I come through this, and Franklin can prove that Whitelaw's charges against me have no grounds, will you stick around long enough to stand up as my best man?"

"You're still planning to go through with it, then?" Jeremy knew there was no reason to ask such a question, but he did anyway. "Getting married?"

"Of course! I am a man of my word. I promised Taylor Sue that we'd be married when she returned from the West. Besides that, I love her dearly, and I want very much to make her my wife." The depth of his emotion was audible in his voice.

"I pray you won't make her a widow," Jeremy said caustically.

Ethan cast a curious glance across the narrow tent to where Jeremy sat on a low camp stool. "There's a morbid thought. I don't know if I like this dark side of you I'm seeing. And it grieves me to think my little sister is the cause."

"I'm finding I can't bring myself to trust her like I did." Jeremy swallowed. It pained to put his doubts into words. "The work I do for Stuart behind enemy lines is risky, dangerous, and highly confidential. How do I know she wouldn't tell Colby if she finds out anything that might be of value to the Yankees? How do I know that wasn't part of the agreement in exchange for her release?"

"You can't actually give credence to such nonsense. Listen to yourself! This is my little sister we're talking about!" Ethan exclaimed. He resumed his agitated pacing. "How can you possibly think such things of someone who has risked as much as she has? You must be mad, Barnes!"

"She's not the same, Ethan. I can't afford to be wrong." Jeremy's voice was monotone.

"Then you've got to ask her!" Ethan insisted. "Mary Edith would tell the truth, but I, for one, can't fathom why you would take the word of Lottie over that of Salina. You know how Lottie schemes, and we both know she's still got her sights set on you. I reckon Lottie would do just about anything to drive a wedge between you and Salina. My cousin considers herself a woman spurned by you. I know Lottie all too well. She would do whatever she can to inflict revenge, so watch your back," Ethan cautioned.

Jeremy recognized the soundness of the advice, but doubt prevailed. "Salina's changed. You haven't seen her. You wouldn't know."

"You changed, too, while you were in California, remember?" Ethan prodded. "You must allow that my little sister has been through some experiences that have forced her to grow up. Even before serving time in prison, she worked in the field hospital near Chantilly and worked with you as a translator for the Network. These things aren't commonplace events for most girls her age. And the two of you have been apart for quite some time. Give her a chance, Jeremy. I know that Salina cares very deeply for you. She's been in love with you since she was a young girl. Love like that doesn't go away in times of adversity. It grows stronger if it's genuine. Perfect love bears all things, believes all things, hopes all things, and endures all things. Love never fails." He stopped pacing and stood directly in front of his friend. "I told you once before, you'll answer to me if you ever trifle with her affections. I meant it. If you hurt her, you'll regret it."

Jeremy held his tongue, his eyes clashing with Ethan's. After a few long moments he finally muttered, "I'll see you in Richmond."

"Give *both* girls my best," Ethan requested. "And tell Taylor Sue I love her."

"As you wish, Captain." Jeremy's salute held a hint of mockery. "I'll follow your orders to the letter."

☆☆☆☆☆☆☆

A Richmond newspaper ran an acrimonious editorial concerning Lincoln's Emancipation Proclamation. The Proclamation, effective as of January 1, 1863, was considered evil by some Southerners, absurd by others. In the edict, Lincoln claimed to have freed all the slaves in each state which had seceded from the Union. According to the Confederate government, Lincoln had no jurisdiction in their country, and many wondered that the Union's President made no effort to abolish slavery in the Northern or Border States. Salina's confusion over the issue only increased. There was already one law for whites and one for blacks. And now it appeared there was one for the North and one for the South.

Another point in case was western Virginia, where the citizens were staunchly loyal to the United States. A part of Virginia beyond the Allegheny Mountains had seceded in order to return to the Union and would soon be recognized as the new and separate state of West Virginia. If secession *from* the Union was not recognized as the right of each sovereign state, then why was secession *into* the Union acceptable? Salina had no clear-cut answer in her mind. She wondered if even Daddy could have explained such circumstances in a way that she would understand.

And then there was another recent battle that reminded Salina of the stalemate outcomes of Chantilly and Sharpsburg. According to the newspaper, the battle near Murfreesboro, Tennessee, at Stones River, on the day before and again on the day after New Year's Day, was said to be a "tactical victory" for the South. The soldiers under General Braxton Bragg, however, had not succeeded in forcing the Yankees from the field, and many alluded to the fact that Stones River was instead a "strategic defeat" for the Confederacy.

The news of Stones River put a slight damper on the holiday mood in Richmond, whose inhabitants were still clinging to the glorious victory over the Federals at Fredericksburg. Hope was high for the New Year of 1863. The Confederates yearned for this to be the year when they would win their independence and be recognized as a separate nation.

Salina sighed and looked up from the newspaper. Taylor Sue sat across the room, rocking steadily, knitting needles clicking at a rapid pace. Colonel and Mrs. Carey were occupied with efforts to find a house to rent, and they had taken young Jennilee with them. Restlessly, Salina glanced out the window, down four stories to the street below in front of the Spottswood Hotel.

In the four days since her arrival in Richmond, Salina had observed the severe crowding, the noise, and the shortages. Inflation was outrageous. The cost of a bonnet, if one could be had, was $500. More essential goods, such as flour, sugar, meat, soap, and the like, were all sold for exorbitant prices. Housing was scarce, and horses and carriages belonged only to those who could afford to keep them. By now the majority of the citizens were becoming veterans of the war, like the soldiers who passed through on their way to and from the front, and they grew accustomed to the emergency crises and the threats of invasion. Thousands of refugees flocked to the capital city, thinking it to be the safest place in the Confederacy. To Salina, there seemed a sense of raw excitement—a sense of expectancy. Richmond was just waiting for *something* to happen...

"How long before we hear from Ethan?" Salina asked, already knowing Taylor Sue hadn't any more idea than she had herself.

"Papa said he would see what he could find out. When he learns something, I'm sure he'll let us know," Taylor Sue said calmly.

Salina sighed again. She felt helpless and useless and restless and bored.

Taylor Sue grinned. "Come over here, Salina. I want you to read to me while I knit."

"What would you like me to read?" Salina sat in straight-backed chair next to Taylor Sue's rocker.

"Just open the Bible, let your eyes fall on a page, and begin there," Taylor Sue suggested, praying that the Holy Spirit would impart some sort of comfort to Salina. Taylor Sue had noticed that Salina was increasingly agitated, and while she may not admit it, she was growing more afraid each day.

Salina opened the Bible. Her eyes rested on the twenty-sixth chapter of Isaiah. She began to read: "Thou wilt keep him in perfect peace, whose mind is stayed on thee: because he trusteth in thee. Trust ye in the Lord for ever: for in the Lord Jehovah is everlasting strength."

"Trust in the Lord forever," Taylor Sue echoed when Salina finished the passage. "This is a continuation of the lesson we were being taught on the journey from San Francisco—to trust in Him, not in ourselves. He gives us the strength to endure when we are weak."

Salina nodded. She had been feeling weak, and in silent prayer she gave her situation over to the Lord, placing it in His hands, to do with it as He would. She prayed, too, for the strength of acceptance, and she felt the peace she sought.

A few hours later, Colonel Carey, Mrs. Carey, and Jennilee returned to find Taylor Sue and Salina huddled over their knitting. "I'm pleased to see you two have not been wasting the afternoon away," Mrs. Carey commended. "We can be industrious here in Richmond, even as we were with the Ladies' Assistance Guild back at home. There are many soldiers' aid and relief societies here in Richmond, I dare say."

"Many," Colonel Carey affirmed. "Good news on two accounts. Which would you have? The first account or the second?" he asked Taylor Sue specifically.

Taylor Sue looked up, her golden-brown eyes filled with hope. "Um...the second account."

Colonel Carey proceeded, "We've taken a house, in Linden Row on Franklin Street."

"It's lovely, Taylor Sue," Jennilee assured her sister. "Colonial brick with a columned porch, three stories in height, a basement, with an ironwork fence out in front, and a courtyard in the rear. The gardens will be beautiful in the spring. The wisteria vines will be a cascade of purple!"

"We can settle in first thing tomorrow morning. How's that?" Colonel Carey asked.

"That's nice, Papa, if Mama is pleased with it." Taylor Sue glanced at her mother.

"It's perfectly lovely, as Jennilee said, and very nicely, if sparsely, furnished." Mrs. Carey smiled graciously. "I intend to set up house-keeping as quickly as we're all moved in. There are enough spare bedrooms for each of you girls to have your own. I think we shall be content there—thankful at least for a roof over our heads."

"Papa, if the house was the second account of news, what is the first?" Taylor Sue inquired.

"Ah, the first account." Colonel Carey made a fuss over lighting his pipe and pretended to ponder the matter quite seriously. "The first account," he said between puffs.

"You said it was good news," Salina said anxiously. "Please, Colonel, don't keep us in suspense. Is there word of my brother?"

"As a matter of fact, yes. I've been told Captain Hastings will be in Richmond this very evening." Colonel Carey's answer was directed as his eldest daughter. "He'll be taken to Castle Lightning or Castle Thunder until his hearing, tomorrow afternoon." Colonel Carey put his tobacco pouch into his breast pocket and withdrew a small envelope. "I've secured permission for you to visit him tomorrow—but only after you've helped your mama move us from here at the hotel to our new home, understood?"

"Oh, yes, Papa, and thank you!" Taylor Sue hugged her father tightly. Her eyes danced with delight. "Salina may come along as well, can't she, Papa?"

"Of course." Colonel Carey nodded. He withdrew another envelope from his breast pocket. "Dear me—I'd nearly forgotten all about this. I suppose this would be considered a *third* account of good news."

Taylor Sue anxiously opened the envelope and read from the printed lines on the card, "...cordially invited...reception at the White House...President and Mrs. Davis hosting... "

Colonel Carey nodded. "The First Lady and President Davis hold levees, receptions, if you will, each fortnight. It's Richmond society at its peak, I'm told. When it was known that I have a lovely daughter, and she a lovely sister-in-law-to-be, it was suggested I should bring them round so that they may shine in the company of the other Richmond belles. Your mama and I will bring Jennilee and act as chaperones to keep the numerous gray soldiers who are bound to be in attendance at bay."

"Music and dancing?" Jennilee was excited. "May I really come along?"

Mrs. Carey took the invitation from Taylor Sue's fingers. "You may, Jennilee," she acquiesced. "But as your Papa has stated, you will accompany us. You're still too young for such events, but you will get to see Richmond and her high society."

"Very well, Mama." Jennilee nodded, only partially disappointed. She didn't mind as much that she didn't get to participate so long as she was allowed to watch.

☆☆☆☆☆☆☆

Lieutenant Jeremy Barnes stood on the platform at the Richmond, Fredericksburg & Potomac Railroad Depot, waiting for the passengers on the late afternoon train to disembark. At last came a Rebel, cuffed and under guard.

Jeremy sauntered over to where Ethan was being held. "Hello, Ethan—Captain Hastings," he amended, adding a salute. "How are you?"

"As well as can be expected. Thank you for asking." Ethan nodded. "I've not heard yet—is it Castle Lightning or Castle Thunder?"

"Lightning, I'm told, but I've heard one's as bad as the other," Jeremy answered brusquely. "Here come the orders now."

A uniformed officer brought orders to Ethan's guardsmen. They were to take him to Castle Lightning, a brick warehouse-turned-prison where citizens of questionable loyalty, serious offenders, deserters, and suspected spies were locked up. Ethan would remain there until guards came to deliver him to the Federal Court House, a building now occupied by the offices of the Confederate government, where the court-martial proceedings would take place.

"It's only one night in prison, two at the most," Ethan said optimistically. Both men knew that his statement was true only if Ethan was not convicted of the charges being leveled against him. Then Ethan started to chuckle at the irony of the situation. "The only one in my immediate family who has yet to serve any time in prison is my mamma. Must be some sort of mocking twist of destiny..."

"Makes it sound as if you Hastings are all a bunch of scoundrels," Jeremy attempted to joke with Ethan, but Ethan's observation was true. Garrett Hastings, Salina, and Ethan had all been to prison, for one reason or another, within the past year. "You're the only one who's served your time below the Mason-Dixon Line, though."

"Yes, as a matter of fact." Ethan nodded and scratched his dark head. "It would almost make it seem more honorable had I been in a Yankee prison like Daddy or Salina was."

Jeremy failed to see the humor, and he neglected to take Ethan's bait in bringing up Salina. Instead he said, "I'm staying at the Powhatan House. I'll be over to visit you in the morning. Take care, my friend."

"And you, too." Ethan nodded. "I'll see you tomorrow."

The next day, Ethan had visitors at Castle Lightning even before Jeremy arrived. It did his heart good to see both his intended and his little sister, and the meeting brought tears to his eyes.

"You're beautiful," he whispered in Taylor Sue's ear while holding her close in a tight embrace. He then glanced over her head to see where Salina stood a short distance away.

"Captain Hastings." Salina smiled timorously. "You've never resembled Daddy more so than you do right now—rank and all."

"Come here, you," Ethan beckoned with an outstretched hand. He stood for a long moment with his arms around his two favorite young ladies.

Salina and Taylor Sue gave him a detailed account of their journey to San Francisco. When they finished, Ethan felt he understood why they had done what they did, and he firmly believed Salina was quite innocent of any further involvement with the Yankees. And while the fact that Mamma and Duncan had wed and were to have a child made him feel uneasy, he could rationalize the reasons behind the marriage as far as Jeremy's uncle was concerned. "Have you told Jeremy all this?"

"Parts of it," Salina allowed, "but mainly in disjointed pieces. There hasn't been time to sit down with him and tell him the whole of it."

"You're going to have to make the time, Salina. It's imperative that you make Jeremy understand the same way you made me understand," Ethan admonished sternly. "Promise me, you'll see to it just as soon as you possibly can."

She was taken aback a bit by her brother's sharp insistence. "I don't know when I'll see him again. I missed him at Fairfax before we came to Richmond, but I will tell him, Ethan," Salina vowed.

"And speaking of promises," Taylor Sue interrupted, "we've met with a friend of Reverend Yates, a minister here in town. He can arrange for us to use St. James Church, and he said he will be more than happy to perform our marriage ceremony, just as soon as you are released from this awful place."

Ethan touched Taylor Sue's cheek in a gentle caress. "I admire your optimism, darlin', and I covet your prayers. We should know one way or the other by this afternoon, I reckon. Tell your minister friend to be ready. If I get out of here this afternoon, I'll marry you this very night!"

"You'll have to talk that one over with Papa." Taylor Sue colored slightly. "You've yet to ask him formally for my hand, you know."

Ethan grinned. "Asking your father will be the easy part. It was asking your mama that terrified me."

The three laughed together for an instant, recalling the stormy afternoon on which the battle near Chantilly had disrupted the announcement of their engagement. Ethan kissed Taylor Sue intensely and murmured, "I'm afraid for you to come to the courthouse, but I can't help wanting you there. Knowing you're outside waiting will be a comfort to me."

"Then I shall be there, if only for moral support," Taylor Sue promised. "Won't we be, Salina?"

"Of course, we'll be there for you, Ethan." Salina nodded her dark head. "And Taylor Sue is very good in giving moral support. I wouldn't have made it through without her. Once the two of you are married, Ethan, you'll have all the moral support you could ever hope for." She grinned.

Jeremy arrived just a few minutes after Taylor Sue and Salina had gone. "What news? Have you heard anything yet?"

"The time of my hearing has been moved up by an hour," Ethan replied. "You just missed the girls, though. Did you know they were here?"

Jeremy nodded in acknowledgment, but he said nothing.

Ethan continued, "I've prepared myself. I'm ready to stand trial before the commission. Franklin Shields was here last night to review his latest findings. My trial will be shortly followed by one of Whitelaw's own."

"I should like to see that." Jeremy was skeptical, but he clapped a hand on Ethan's shoulder. "We're going to celebrate tonight, when the verdict of your innocence is pronounced."

"Yes, at my wedding," Ethan confirmed. "If the charges are dismissed this afternoon, I'll be a married man by tonight."

"Name the time and the place," Jeremy chuckled. "I'll be there. You can count on it."

"Taylor Sue has been arranging the details, so I'll let you know just as soon as I find out myself." Ethan's smile faded, and his voice took on a serious tone. "I've taken the liberty of telling Salina to speak with you at the first chance that presents itself. I've heard her story, from beginning to end. You're going to need to hear it from her, my friend, in its entirety. I think you'll be most interested in what she has to say."

"I've heard all she's cared to tell me," Jeremy muttered doggedly. "It's gone beyond what I feel. It's honor and duty. My first responsibility is to Stuart."

"Just give her a chance, Barnes," Ethan softly commanded. "Don't make me pull rank on you, Lieutenant, and order you to do so."

Jeremy took the threat lightly. "If and when I see your sister again, Captain, I'll listen to her."

Ethan had little course of action other than to take Jeremy at his word.

Chapter Eleven

*T*he girls sat on the edge of their seats, waiting in the corridor. Each time a door opened or an officer passed by, they jumped and clung apprehensively to each other's hands. The hours dragged with interminable slowness, until the proceedings came to an end. The committee, at last, had finished listening to the testimony given in Ethan's behalf.

Taylor Sue snatched a brief moment with Ethan before he was escorted away, still under guard. "What?" she asked anxiously. "What did they say?"

"The committee will deliberate, and then they'll submit their verdict tomorrow morning," Ethan answered, pressing his forehead to hers. "One more night at Castle Lightning, then back here tomorrow. Meet me right here?"

"Yes, of course." Taylor Sue nodded, squeezing both his hands in hers.

Ethan kissed her tenderly before his captors prodded him along. "Come with us, please, Captain. With all due respect, Miss." The two guards touched the bills of their caps in deference to Taylor Sue. She waved, mustering a smile.

"Let's go." Salina put an arm around her friend in silent comfort. "There's nothing more we can do here today." Involuntarily, she looked back over her shoulder, her eyes searching the crowded area for Jeremy's tall form. His glance settled on her, cool and guarded. Her breath caught.

"Go talk to him," Taylor Sue encouraged, having spied Salina's handsome, gray-uniformed lieutenant standing just a few yards away. "You need to restore the communication between you. Now's as good a time as any to make an attempt."

Salina hesitated for a moment, and when she met Jeremy's eyes a second time, she offered a tremulous smile. She took a step toward him to decrease the distance between them. She did want to talk with him, and not only because Ethan told her she should. She missed him so.

Jeremy stuffed his hands deep into his jacket pockets, bringing his broad shoulders into a partial shrug. The fingers of his left hand closed around her lace handkerchief. Hope shone brilliantly in Salina's eyes and he was reminded of his promise to Ethan—to at least listen to whatever she had to say. "Hello, Salina."

She swallowed nervously, returning the greeting, "Hello, Jeremy." He chivalrously took her hand and pressed her fingers to his lips. Salina noted that his eyes harbored a guarded expression. "You look well," she complimented.

"As do you." He nodded, perhaps holding her hand for a slight instant longer than was necessary.

Salina was painfully aware that small talk wasn't going to get them far, but they had to start somewhere. "How have you been?" she asked tentatively.

"Busy," Jeremy replied coolly. He was distracted for a moment when he saw Kidd Carney a little ways off, beckoning toward him. "My apologies, but it seems my presence is required elsewhere." He tipped his hat in a stiff, polite gesture. "If you'll pardon me." Jeremy brushed past her, quick steps leading him to where Carney waited.

Salina felt a certain smarting sensation. *Quite obviously I don't rank high enough to hold his attention,* she mused silently. She knew personal matters were of little import compared to those of military significance, but it didn't make her feel any better. She ignored the indignant heat which accompanied the rush of color in her cheeks, and wordlessly she followed Taylor Sue home.

Jeremy, while hearing what Carney was saying, covertly watched Salina's departure. Mentally he scolded himself, for he'd given his word to Ethan that he'd try to talk to her, and he hadn't followed through. But there were too many other people about, too much activity pressing. Another time, when they would have the luxury of each other's undivided attention, they would talk it out, he felt sure. His shifted his weight from one foot to the other, unexpectedly hopeful that their next meeting might be sooner rather than later.

Early the next morning, Taylor Sue, Salina, and Colonel Carey left the house on Franklin Street, arriving at the Court House even before Ethan had been brought there from Castle Lightning. By this time, the military commission had reached their verdict.

When Ethan emerged from the committee chamber at the close of the session, there were no guards flanking him, only Captain Franklin Shields and his uncle, Colonel Donald Shields. Introductions were made all around, but Salina sadly noted that there was no sign of Jeremy. It took a concentrated effort on her part to refrain from asking her brother about him. Jeremy knew where to find her should he desire to continue their interrupted discussion from the previous day. She would let him seek her out whenever his busy schedule might allow.

Franklin announced to the girls and Colonel Carey that Ethan had been acquitted of all charges leveled against him, but the verdict was tempered with stipulation. "He's got to go before the medical examining board and the Surgeon General. If Ethan can pass the required tests, they'll reinstate him as an assistant surgeon, even though he's only eighteen. He has his good reputation to thank for that. However, if he does not pass the exams, he'll forfeit his captaincy for the time being and return to orderly status. But I'm confident that he'll pass."

"I've got lots of studying to do." Ethan squeezed Taylor Sue's ringed hand, his eyes silently begging for her support and understanding. "I have until the end of this month. The examinations will be given on or about the first of February."

"That means you'll have a few days off for a honeymoon." Salina winked. "Afterwards you can seclude yourself away with those medical textbooks."

Ethan hugged Taylor Sue with one arm. "Yes, a honeymoon. But first, our wedding. Colonel Carey, sir, with your permission, I should like to take your daughter to wife."

"Carry on, Captain Hastings," Colonel Carey granted. "And with my blessing, son."

That same evening, Taylor Sue Carey and Ethan Garrett Hastings were joined in holy matrimony at St. James Church. Jeremy, as best man, dutifully produced a gold band which Ethan added to the diamond engagement ring on Taylor Sue's left hand. Taylor Sue also had a golden ring for Ethan. The promises of love were spoken, communion solemnly partaken, and then the minister pronounced them man and wife. A loving kiss sealed the marriage service and commenced the celebration.

Mrs. Carey doused her handkerchief with tears of joy. Colonel Carey welcomed Ethan into the family as the son he'd never had. Jennilee taunted her older sister, "Mrs. Ethan Hastings, an old married lady!"

The sixteen-year-old bride was all smiles and laughter. "Yes, at long last, I'm an old married lady." Taylor Sue happily gazed into Ethan's deep blue eyes, plainly seeing the smoldering fire there in their depths.

The reception was not an overly frivolous affair, for the Careys knew but a handful of people in Richmond. In addition to the wedding cake, there was a watery punch and a plateful of small, thin sandwiches. Good wishes showered the newlyweds, and the hired musicians played for their first dance in the middle of the parlour floor.

While Salina was with her brother, Jeremy chanced to notice her handbag lying forgotten on the polished wooden floor, having accidentally fallen from her lap when she stood to accept Ethan's invitation to dance. Without drawing attention to himself, he reached for the handbag, merely intending to place it on the chair next to his own. If Salina would sit down long enough, he wanted her to explain. A small leather wallet fell from her handbag, and a folded document slid a few inches across the glossy floorboards. Jeremy retrieved the document, and his curiosity got the better of him. He read the conditions of the traveling pass and the contents of the pardon—both signed by Abraham Lincoln.

So, what Lottie had said *was* true. He held the proof in his own two hands. Blind rage caused him to see red, and he hastily stuffed the documents back into the wallet, and then into the handbag. Quickly Jeremy sought out Ethan and Taylor Sue, bidding them a hasty farewell. "I've a long ride ahead of me, and I'd just as soon begin tonight," he weakly explained. "I must return to camp, see what my men have been up to in my absence. If General Stuart plans another raid, I don't want to miss out on the fun."

"We appreciate your kindness, Jeremy." Taylor Sue stood on tiptoe to kiss his whisker-roughened cheek. "You've done so much for Ethan, and I thank you for it."

"My pleasure, Mrs. Hastings," Jeremy said fondly. He glanced around, relieved that Salina was not present at the moment. "Bid Salina good-bye for me, would you? I really must be off. God bless you both." He lightly kissed Taylor Sue's cheek and squeezed Ethan's shoulder. "Take care, you two."

Ethan sighed, instinctively knowing his friend and his sister were still at odds. Maybe he should tell Salina what Jeremy had told him. Perhaps it would soften the blow. He knew Salina didn't have an inkling as to the depths of Jeremy's distrust. On the other hand, it was not his place to interfere. He prayed they would make amends soon, before a wall was built up that would take a fair amount of time to break through.

When Salina returned from the necessary, she discovered Jeremy had disappeared without a word, a smile of affection, or an attempt to speak with her. He'd not even bothered to say good-bye. They had stood up together for Ethan and Taylor Sue, yet Jeremy had barely given her any indication that he noticed she was there at all. And now he was gone again. Her heart was heavy, and tears brimmed her eyes when she saw the happiness and love radiating between her brother and his new wife. At the rate things were going, there was little to sustain the hope that Jeremy might ever look at her that way again.

Salina was so involved in her own misery that she failed to notice Ethan spiriting Taylor Sue away from the house in Linden Row. She was talking to Franklin Shields, who was again assuring her that Ethan's pending medical examinations were little more than a formality.

"My uncle is quite impressed with your brother," Franklin was saying, "and will in fact be taking him to visit several of the hospitals here in Richmond. Chimborazo is the largest facility, boasting of a hundred wards spread out over forty acres on the outskirts of town. But there are many additional hospitals in churches and warehouses all over the city as well."

Salina nodded, only half-listening to what the Confederate captain was telling her. Once the remainder of the guests discovered the newlyweds were missing, the reception drew to a close. Salina retreated to the solitude of her room, where she cried herself to sleep.

☆☆☆☆☆☆☆

Colonel Carey had done what he could to occupy the days following Taylor Sue and Ethan's wedding. He could see that Salina was lonely and Jennilee bored, so he took pains to see that they were entertained. He took them on buggy rides while Mrs. Carey was at her soldier's aid and relief gatherings. Colonel Carey drove Salina and Jennilee to see Capitol Square, the impressive statue of George Washington that had been crafted in England, and the Bell Tower.

"Not only does the tower proclaim the hour of day, it announces important events," Colonel Carey explained. "It also will send a warning tocsin out if the capital is in danger of being seized. Three short strokes, a pause, and then three more strokes is the call to arms for the militia. An emergency call filled the hearts of Richmond's citizens with fear one Sunday in April of 1861. A false alarm foretold of a Union warship sailing up the James River, certain to destroy our capital. The ship, thankfully, never arrived."

One afternoon, the Colonel took Salina and Jennilee to the Confederate Reading Room, not far from Capitol Square. There, soldiers who paid the ten-cent entrance fee could get newspapers from their home states and even Northern papers when they could be had. There were rumors that Ambrose Burnside was to be relieved of command of the Army of the Potomac, and Colonel Carey was curious to find out who the next candidate for commanding General would be.

Within the week, the Colonel was required to report to his new position at the War Department just a few blocks away in Mechanic's Hall. Jennilee was enrolled at Mrs. Pegram's School for young ladies, and Salina was left to her own devices.

Salina wanted to do something, anything. Cooped up in the house left her with too much time to think about Jeremy. Accompanied by the Careys' driver, Salina went to General Hospital No. 5, the old Kent and Paine Dry Goods Warehouse, located on the south side of Eleventh Street and Main. She found the matron and respectfully requested that she be put to work as a nurse.

"You're a bit young," the matron noted, a tad skeptically. "Have you done this type of service before?"

"Yes, I have." Salina nodded. She told the matron about her experiences working in a temporary field hospital following the battle near Chantilly.

The matron agreed to give Salina a trial period. If she was able to bear up under the strain and successfully deal with wounded and dying soldiers, then she would be more than welcome.

Salina was not at the brick house in Linden Row when Ethan and Taylor Sue returned from their brief honeymoon. The Careys' housekeeper, Pansy, explained that Miss Salina had taken to spending her days at the warehouse hospital, and Ethan went out to find her.

Upon his arrival at General Hospital No. 5, Ethan simply observed from a distance as Salina read quietly to a wounded soldier with bandaged eyes, lying still in his cot, hanging on her every word. Salina's voice was sweet and low, and she had a skill for reading aloud. But Ethan liked it better when she sang. After making his presence known, he insisted that she sing for the men, prior to his taking her home. With resounding encouragement on all sides, Salina hesitantly complied.

A blush stained her cheeks, but even with all eyes upon her, her voice did not waver as she sang several tunes, including *The Bonnie Blue Flag, Southern Soldier Boy,* and *The Yellow Rose of Texas.* Upon request, she sang *Lorena* and *When This Cruel War Is Over,* causing many a tear. From that point on, Salina sang for at least fifteen minutes before she was allowed to go home after the end of each long day.

Taylor Sue was back—the same, but somehow different. Being married agreed with her immensely, but Salina sensed a change about her sister-in-law that she couldn't quite put her finger on. What was it that made a woman different—other than a gold ring and a few uttered words of love? Salina suspected it was the man. She'd never seen her brother happier. And while it pleased her to share in their contentment, she felt like a third wheel at best.

As Taylor Sue fussed over Salina's hair and dress the night of the reception at the Davis's, Salina was most reminded of her old friend. They giggled together as they readied themselves for their "debut" into Richmond society.

The drive was not long from the Careys' to the house on the corner of Twelfth and Clay Streets. The Executive Mansion not only served as the home of the Confederacy's President and his family, but it also played a role in official functions and was the center of social and political life in Richmond.

They were greeted warmly by President Jefferson Davis and First Lady Varina Davis. Ethan spied some friends from his unit with the Second Corps and took Taylor Sue to meet them. Colonel Carey also got caught up in introducing his wife and younger daughter to his acquaintances, and Salina was again inadvertently left to fend for herself.

Mrs. Davis kindly took notice of this and chatted amiably with Salina until the two were comfortably acquainted with each other. Mrs. Davis glanced through the crowded center parlor and the adjoining drawing room until her flashing dark eyes rested upon a young, blond lieutenant leaning against the fireplace mantle.

"I do enjoy making matches," Varina Davis confided to Salina. "The soldiers come here to meet the belles, and the belles to meet the soldiers, so I do what I can to see that introductions are arranged. I even take credit for a few of the recent marriages. Allow me to introduce you to this fine-looking lieutenant over this way." Mrs. Davis guided Salina by the elbow through the assemblage of officers in dress uniforms, enlisted men in their dyed butternut uniforms, and ladies in dresses of every imaginable fabric and color, including plain home-spun. It was quite a mixed gathering, a "social jumbalaya," as someone called it.

"Mrs. Davis," the sandy-blond lieutenant bowed formally. "My compliments to you and President Davis. How can I be of service?"

The President's wife smiled. "I present to you Miss Salina Hastings, Lieutenant. I should be pleased to enlist your service to lead her in a reel or two—perhaps a waltz?"

"Your wish is my command, Mrs. Davis," the lieutenant murmured. He held out his arm in an overly-chivalrous manner. "Miss Hastings, would you do me the honor?"

"Why, yes, Lieutenant Barnes." Salina curtsied politely, her heart pounding so loudly she was certain he would hear. "It would be my pleasure."

Mrs. Davis was decidedly amused. "Hmmm...I see someone has beaten me to the introductions. Very well. Carry on, Lieutenant Barnes."

After a few minutes of initial uneasiness, their awkward movements became fluid and graceful. They whirled as one on the dance floor. A long time had passed since the two of them danced together, and for now they opted to simply enjoy the music. The musicians performed a rendition of *The Cavalier's Waltz*. Jeremy held Salina tight as he led her in the steps.

"You're angry with me," Salina said below his ear.

"Shouldn't I be?" Jeremy bit back a more harsh rejoinder. "I'm not the one withholding information."

"Someone has told you about my mamma and Duncan," Salina supposed correctly. "And what else?"

"Are you spying for the Yankees? Is that how you convinced Lincoln to give you such a gracious pardon? Were you plotting an ambush with Colby at Fairfax?" Jeremy demanded, his eyes blazed with open hostility. "Did you think you could waltz right into the Confederate capital, into the White House itself, and then report back to Duncan Grant upon your return to Northern Virginia? Just because you weren't hung as a spy in the North doesn't mean that you wouldn't swing if your actions were discovered here in the South."

Salina's eyes grew round in disbelief, and her jaw dropped. "Oh!" she cried indignantly. If she were a man, she would have challenged him to a duel for slinging such nasty accusations. Or at the very least, punched his smug face!

Jeremy curled his forefinger beneath her chin. "Not a very pretty expression, Salina. Close your mouth. People will think you look like a fish."

"First it was a scarecrow, now a fish!" Salina returned hotly. "When will you see me as myself for a change?"

"When are you going to tell me the truth?" Jeremy challenged, his sapphire eyes full of reproach.

Salina glanced up at him. In that hurtful moment, she realized that in his present mindset Jeremy wasn't about to believe a thing she told him. Deeply she regretted not telling him everything that morning in the barn at Sully, but Salina could not undo what had been done.

"Excuse me, Lieutenant," an officer cut in. "Your presence is required by those gathering in the dining room."

Jeremy handed Salina over to the young officer. "This is not finished yet, Salina," he warned her. "Far from it."

Salina did not lack in dance partners, and Jeremy did not seek her out on his own. Finally she begged one dancing partner for a rest and went looking for Jeremy. She found him outside on the piazza. Taking a deep, cleansing breath, she approached him cautiously. She laid her gloved hand upon his arm and tipped her head back to look up at him. "May we sit down together, please?" she requested.

Jeremy silently seated himself on the bench next to her and waited, his arms folded across his broad chest. He simply sat there, saying nothing, refusing to look anywhere except at the ground. Salina struggled to keep up her end of the one-sided conversation, but she plodded along determinedly.

"I didn't want to accept Mamma's marriage at first, and I felt so bad letting her go back to Gettysburg alone. But Jeremy, I honestly did not want to go North. I wanted to come find you and to see my brother marry my best friend. I want to continue to be of service here in the South." Salina tried her best to make him understand.

"But you must have signed an Oath to obtain those documents that Lincoln gave you," Jeremy ground between clenched teeth. "Your father went to his death because he wouldn't give up his beliefs..."

"You assume I signed an Oath of Allegiance?" Salina interrupted, her green eyes glittering dangerously. "How dare you? How can you possibly think that after what I went through to get the information concerning the Western Campaign to San Francisco?"

"The campaign failed," Jeremy said flatly. "You were taken prisoner. Then graciously—miraculously—you were pardoned for your part in the plans. You don't just obtain freedom without something being required in return."

"I'm *not* spying for them, Jeremy. You've got to believe me," Salina implored. "Don't you trust me?"

"I used to," Jeremy said coldly. "But I don't anymore. I've seen you with Colby. The two of you talk far too easily for my liking."

"He and Duncan, along with Taylor Sue and Dr. Nichols, cared for me while I was sick. I was confined to a ship's cabin, with no one else to talk to except for them," Salina tried to explain.

"How do I know what you might have already told Duncan and Colby? How can I be sure what you're telling me now isn't lies?" Jeremy questioned her.

"When have I ever lied to you?" Salina queried.

"At Sully, you didn't exactly lie, but you didn't tell me all of the truth, either," Jeremy accused. "That's too suspicious. If half the people inside knew that you carried a traveling pass and a signed pardon from Lincoln with you, they'd have you thrown out of here in no time."

Salina lifted her chin to a defiant angle. "How do you know that I carry such items with me? Have you been spying on me? You would know that only if you had been prying in my handbag."

"I do what I deem necessary," Jeremy hedged.

"The same as I." Salina nodded. "I did what I thought was right. Duncan had a hand in the process, I'm sure, but only because he was determined to honor a vow he made to Daddy to watch over us. That's why he married Mamma—to protect her from your uncle." Salina could see that her words were having no effect on him. He already admitted he didn't trust her. "Oh, why am I wasting my breath?" she wondered aloud.

Jeremy stood and shrugged. "Tell it to someone else, Salina. They might believe you."

Salina dissolved into tears as Jeremy's boots thudded heavily across the piazza. She put her hands over her face and cried. *Dear Lord, what am I to do? He must hate me. He thinks I'm a traitor...*

Unaware of how long she sat alone in the cold darkness, Salina nearly jumped out of her skin when a hearty voice boomed, "Well, hello, Miss Salina! Why are you out here all alone and not with that young lieutenant of yours? I know he's here in Richmond somewhere. Shall I send a search detail out to bring him here for you?"

"N-o, G-General St-Stuart, but thank you just the same." Salina hurriedly wiped at her tears with the backs of her hand.

"What is this about now?" Stuart sat down next to her, tossing his scarlet-lined cape over his shoulder. He wiped a tear from her cheek with a gloved thumb and inquired, "What business do tears have falling from such eyes as yours?"

Without meaning to burden the cavalry leader, Salina poured forth the entire story. Stuart allowed her to carry on, most interested to hear all she had to say. She concluded by showing him the documents from Lincoln and asked him with a trembling chin, "Do you think I'm a traitor to the South, General?"

Stuart stroked his cinnamon-colored beard and his blue eyes glowed with intensity. He didn't think much of people who did not embrace the Confederate cause—as was the case of his own father-in-law, who served with the Union forces. And over the long months of the war, Stuart had captured a number of Northern spies, but Miss Salina did not seem to be one of those. He finally said, "I have knowledge of this Major Grant. I also had the privilege of working with your father when he was alive. He would never have entrusted so much to you if he didn't believe your heart was true. I believe in your sincerity. You're a Virginian. You did the best you could, and no one can require more. You followed your instructions and paid the price. No, Miss Salina, I do not consider you a traitor. Come with me." Jeb Stuart took her by the hand and led her into the drawing room.

The General was greeted with cheers and shouts, and he gloried in the adoration. Mrs. Davis came to welcome the dashing cavalry leader, and he whispered to the First Lady, "If you'd be so kind to accompany Miss Hastings and myself to a quiet place where we can conduct a piece of business, I promise I'll play whatever part you see fit to assign me in the charades later on."

Varina Davis smiled, pleased. "Right this way, General Stuart. Is your wife with you on this trip?"

"No, I'm afraid Mrs. Stuart will be staying near Fredericksburg for a few more days before she joins me," the General replied. "I'll mention that you asked after her in my next letter."

"Do give her my best." Mrs. Davis nodded. She led them upstairs to the small linen-closet-turned-office that belonged to President Davis's secretary. "No one will disturb our conversation here in Harrison's office."

Stuart sat at the marble-topped table and explained the situation to Mrs. Davis. "Well, I am deeply sorry about this whole mess, my dear," Mrs. Davis said to Salina. "I saw your young lieutenant gather his coat, hat, and gloves not long ago. I believe he has left the reception."

"No matter. He won't listen to what I've said." Salina's tears threatened again.

Stuart took a piece of writing paper, pen, and quill from the desk. He spoke aloud as he wrote: *"Let it be known that from this day forward, I, J. E. B. Stuart, do hereby endorse the unwavering loyalty of Miss Salina..."* He paused to ask, "What is your second name, please?"

"Rose. I am Salina Rose Hastings," she answered with a slight smile.

"Salina Rose Hastings." Stuart nodded and went on. *"Miss Hastings has performed service, to the best of her ability, in the name of Virginia and her country, and will continue to do so if called upon and willingly accepts such an assignment."* He dipped the quill in the inkstand. *"She is to be treated with respect and revered as a true Southern Lady ought to be. My hat is off to her for her bravery and courage in carrying out deeds past. Anyone who doubts her sincerity is welcome to see me directly concerning the matter."* He signed the paper, *Maj. Gen. J. E. B. Stuart, Richmond, Virginia,* and then added the date. He allowed the ink to dry fully, then folded the paper and handed it to Salina. "You keep that, and the next time you have the opportunity to see Lieutenant Barnes, you show it to him."

"I will, General, and thank you!" Impulsively, she hugged Stuart fiercely and then caught herself. "Beg your pardon, General. I did forget myself for a minute."

Stuart laughed heartily and then nodded to Mrs. Davis. "I suppose it's time for the charades to begin."

"I dare say it is at that, General." Mrs. Davis smiled. "Miss Salina, will you sing for us? I'm told you have quite a lovely voice."

After the charades were concluded, Salina did sing—a duet with Stuart. The parlour and drawing room were filled with thunderous applause even before the last strains of *The Girl I Left Behind Me* had dwindled. Stuart held Salina's gloved hand as she took her bows and smiled warmly at the crowd. He said, for her ears alone, "I do much prefer laughter to tears, and I expect you will do more laughing than crying, is it agreed?"

"I'll do my best, General." Salina smiled at the cavalier.

"That is all I ask." He chuckled. His blue eyes snapped intensely, and he added, "It is what I require."

Chapter Twelve

*P*ositively everyone's talking about you, Salina—about how General Stuart was doting on you at the Davis's reception." Taylor Sue chattered. "I've heard it said he's devoted to Hetty Cary, one of Richmond's most beautiful and well-known belles, but that duet the two of you sang together certainly made an impression in your favor. Mrs. Stuart is coming to the city soon. Evidently she spends her time between here and a friend's house near Fredericksburg. They've only their son, now, since their little daughter died..."

"Yes, I know," Salina replied. "Jeremy wrote about the death of Little Flora in a letter once."

"And they're talking about the wonderful work you're doing for the wounded soldiers at General Hospital No. 5," Taylor Sue added. She finally noticed that Salina was donning her cape and tying a bonnet ribbon beneath her chin. "Are you going out again now?"

"Yes." Salina nodded. "Ethan has a few hours free from his studies, and he's taking me somewhere. He didn't say exactly. I'm rather hoping it's to Pizzini's for strawberry ice cream, and then to Vannerson's studio to sit for a photograph. I want to send one of myself to Mamma along with the one you and Ethan had made for her."

"Oh, yes, I do remember him mentioning that now." Taylor Sue was disappointed that her husband hadn't extended the invitation to include her. Yet she was wise enough to note he and his sister had spent very little time together here in Richmond, and she wanted them to be able to do so. How she dreaded the day when the war would take Ethan from her again! She was determined that they make the most of his time away from the front, because there was no way of knowing when they'd be able to spend time together again.

Taylor Sue read for part of the afternoon and took up her knitting again when she grew tired of her book. At half past three, the Careys' black-skinned housekeeper appeared at the door to the back parlor. "Gots a visitor, Liddle Missus."

"Who is it, Pansy?" Taylor Sue asked, smiling. Ever since the wedding, Pansy referred to Taylor Sue as "Liddle Missus" while she continued to call Mrs. Carey "Miz Rachel."

"It'd be dat young lieutenant Missy Salina fancies so much. Ah done tole 'im she weren't 'ere, so 'e be askin' fer ya instead," answered Pansy.

"This is a pleasant surprise," Taylor Sue said as she entered the front parlor. Jeremy stood with his broad back to her, staring out a tall, narrow window that reached from the floorboards to the vaulted ceiling. He held a round, golden object in his palm. When he heard her approach, he turned his attention to Taylor Sue. She smiled wistfully up at him. "I'm sorry that Salina is not at home at present, but shall I tell her that you'll call again?"

"Don't bother." Jeremy shook his sandy-blond head. "I apologize for disturbing you at all, Mrs. Hastings." He intentionally addressed her by her married name.

Taylor Sue detected a playful twinkle in his eyes, though it disappeared all too quickly, replaced by a sad expression that dimmed their blue glow. "Why, Jeremy Barnes, certainly you know that you are welcome here. Your presence is never a bother but rather something to cherish as we see you so seldom these days." She sat down on the horsehair sofa. "Will you take refreshment? I'll have Pansy bring some tea or raspberry shrub. Of course, we have a good supply of 'stone wine,' if that would suit you better," she made reference to a euphemism for water.

Jeremy nodded ruefully. The citizenry of Richmond had no choice but to continue daily living in spite of shortages of pre-war niceties. Before the hostilities, a guest would never be offered mere water. Times changed. Hospitality did what it could to adapt. Another popular term for water, which he had heard previously at the President's house, was "Jeff Davis Punch." "I'll take a little of the raspberry shrub, if it's not too much trouble."

Taylor Sue scolded mildly, "I've already told you, it's not a bother. Now, come sit down." She rang for Pansy, and in a few minutes the housekeeper produced a bottle of raspberry shrub and two crystal glasses.

Abashed, Pansy admitted, "Ain't got no liddle round cakes baked fresh, Liddle Missus. Twernt 'spectin' no callers today."

"No matter, Pansy," Taylor Sue assured her with a whisper. "I have the impression Lieutenant Barnes won't be staying long."

Jeremy still stood by the window, staring absently down at the ticking pocket watch.

"That's the watch Salina gave you, isn't it?" Taylor Sue inquired conversationally.

Jeremy's eyes narrowed. "She gave it to me all right. Are you sure she didn't intend to give this to Colby instead?" His question was cutting.

Taylor Sue was taken off-guard at his sharp retort. She countered, "Read the inscription again, Jeremy. What do you see?"

He reread the engraving, "To J.B. from S.H., All my love to my own Horse Soldier."

"Hardly the type of thing Colby would appreciate, I'm certain of that," Taylor Sue said pointedly. "What has happened that you're being so hard on Salina?"

"She isn't the same girl I knew before," he said obstinately. He started to say something more but caught himself, saying instead, "By rights, I shouldn't trust you any more than I can trust her—which I don't. I'm having a difficult time reconciling her sudden affiliation with the Yankees."

Without saying so directly, it was clear he was implying Duncan Grant and Lieutenant Lance Colby. "Aren't you being a little unfair, Jeremy? She's tried to explain, and you're deliberately shutting her out. You've been so mean to her, I wonder that you don't drive her straight into the arms of that Yankee lieutenant. At least he's admitted to feeling something for her. You—you seem to shun her at every turn. You accuse her of lying, and you refuse to try to understand what she's saying. I was there, Jeremy. I know what she did. I know where she was. And I know that you have nothing to fear from her! She followed Garrett Hastings's instructions to the letter, and she delivered the documents as she was told to do. It was the contact who was followed, and while the information was in *his* possession—not hers—it was confiscated by Colby and his Yankees."

Jeremy pondered Taylor Sue's outburst. Then he said coolly, "Her interview with Lincoln—she has passes with his signature authorizing travel wherever she might please to go. He *pardoned* her."

"Yes, he pardoned her, and as a result, myself as well. His basis for that pardon was *not* founded on her signing an Oath, but on the fact that she saved his life, in a manner of speaking." Taylor Sue saw that Jeremy still struggled with what she was telling him. "Ask her. She'll tell you everything."

"I've already heard all I need to." Jeremy shook his head. "From her, you, Ethan..."

"Then are you implying that we're *all* telling lies?" Taylor Sue wanted to know. "In my mind, three separate sources bearing out the same facts would serve as verification. When you're assigned to reconnaissance, aren't there usually two or three of you who'll go out together? And when you report your findings to General Stuart, and you all can validate the same bit of information, does he doubt you? Or does he trust your word and act upon it?" Perhaps, she fervently hoped, putting it into his own terms would cause it to make some sense to him.

Jeremy remained silent, a muscle working tensely along his jawline.

"Why are you being so stubborn, so determined she's wrong?" Taylor Sue wondered. "Why not seek her out, talk to her? Be nice to her—like you used to be."

"How do you know if she'd listen to me at this point?" asked Jeremy, tardy in realizing the truth in Taylor Sue's illustration. He grappled with his insecurity and doubts. What if he was driving Salina away?

Taylor Sue shrugged. "I'm not sure that she will listen. I wouldn't blame her if she didn't. A person can only stand so much rejection. There's been enough deceit between you. Try a little truth."

Jeremy nodded. "I'll think about it."

"Oh, that's gracious of you," Taylor Sue said sarcastically. "You claim Salina's changed, but let me tell you something, Lieutenant Barnes, so have you. It might be due to the war, and the danger you are constantly subjected to. But she loves you, in spite of the changes, Jeremy. And the way you've been treating her is breaking her heart. I'll not stand by and let her be hurt by the likes you. She's too dear to me, even if she no longer holds a place in your affections. You used to trust her with your very life."

"She's broken that trust by consorting with those people..." He didn't finish his sentence.

"She hasn't really." Taylor Sue shook her head in argument. "At least not the way you think. I know trust doesn't come easy for you, but I know Salina *is* trustworthy. I dare you to let her prove it to you. Give her a fair chance."

Jeremy felt, and rightly so, that he'd been knocked down a peg or two. "I owe her at least that, I reckon. Taylor Sue, you're a good friend to have. Ethan's a lucky man."

She smiled. "I'm the lucky one. And you'd be blessed, too, providing you can patch things up with Salina."

Jeremy nodded. He squeezed the pocket watch tightly in his fist. "I'll give her a fair chance, but unfortunately it won't be today or even tomorrow. I've orders and I don't know when I'll be back."

"She's not going anywhere," Taylor Sue told him. "She'll be right here, waiting, I dare say. If I were you, I'd make peace with her as quickly as possible. Who can tell? Mrs. Davis might try to introduce her to some *other* soldier at the next levee, hmmm?"

Jeremy's sapphire eyes blazed. "I'll be back, Taylor Sue. Don't let anyone steal her away in the meantime."

Taylor Sue fanned herself coquettishly. "I'll see what I can do, but as you saw for yourself, the boys do buzz 'round her as if she were a pot of sweet honey." She saw the look of discomfort on Jeremy's face and threw up her hands. "Oh, when will you get it through your thick skull that she has eyes for no one else? Her cap is set for you alone, Jeremy, honest."

Jeremy nodded, properly contrite. Taylor Sue's words matched most of what Ethan had already told him. Ethan was right. He should have known better than to believe Lottie Armstrong in the first place.

☆☆☆☆☆☆

Because the first day of February in 1863 fell on a Sunday, Ethan's examination date was set back to Monday, the second. He kissed Taylor Sue and his sister good-bye that morning, not returning until late in the evening.

"How did you do?" Taylor Sue asked, taking his coat from him, planting a kiss on his unshaven cheek.

Ethan squared his exhausted shoulders and rubbed his tired eyes. "I'm not close to being finished. There must be least two more days to go." He dropped into bed immediately after supper and woke early the next morning. He slipped downstairs to the drawing room for a brief time of quiet devotions and some last minute studying. "Into Your hands, Father God, I commit my medical future."

Four days later, Colonel Shields and Franklin were dinner guests at the Careys' house in Linden Row. Colonel Shields brought with him the news that Ethan had passed every phase of the medical examination with flying colors.

"You've done well, Captain Hastings, so well, that I'm here to offer you your new commission." Colonel Shields smiled, handing him a sealed document. "It's a position with Stonewall Jackson's own medical staff. You'll report to Dr. McGuire, when the time comes. It's not official yet. It might take awhile for your assignment to be processed. In the interim, I intend to enlist your services as my assistant here in Richmond. I could certainly use your help."

Ethan read the commission aloud:

> *Confederate States of America*
> *War Department*
> *Richmond, Virginia—February 1863*
>
> *For: You are hereby informed that the President has appointed you Assistant Surgeon in the Provisional Army in the service of the Confederate States: to rank as such from the first day of March, one thousand eight hundred and sixty-three. Should the Senate, at their next session, advise and consent thereto, you will be commissioned accordingly.*
>
> *Immediately upon receipt thereof, please communicate to this Department through the Adjutant and Inspector General's Office, your acceptance or non-acceptance of said appointment, and with your letter of acceptance, return to the Adjutant and Inspector General the OATH, herewith enclosed, properly filled up, SUBSCRIBED and ATTESTED reporting at the same time your AGE, RESIDENCE, when appointed, and the STATE in which you were BORN.*

> *Should you accept, you will report for duty to the*
> *Head Surgeon, at the Headquarters of Genl. Thomas*
> *Jonathan Jackson, Second Corps, Army of Northern Vir-*
> *ginia.*

James A. Seddon
Secretary of War

Ethan Garrett Hastings
Captain, Medical Corps, A.N.V.

Ethan winked at his wife, thankful to be granted more time in her company. "I accept," he said with a grin. "Assistant Surgeon. I couldn't have done it without your help, Colonel Shields."

"I must admit that it was for selfish reasons that I secured your commission. You're a very good doctor, Ethan. Unfortunately, men of your caliber are all too few. The Confederate army is sorely in need of your exceptional skills. I do look forward to working with you in caring for our wounded. If there is anything else that I may do to be of service to you, please let me know," Colonel Shields ordered.

"Now that you mention it," Ethan spoke up, "Salina's been working at General Hospital No. 5, but I'm trying to convince her that the Robertson Hospital would be better for her."

"I'd be happy to speak to Miss Sally Tompkins on your sister's behalf," Colonel Shields offered. "Miss Tompkins has a very fine reputation for caring for the soldiers. President Davis commissioned her a captain, you know, so she could keep her hospital open even after the government took over the other private hospitals scattered throughout the city last year. I'm sure Captain Sally could use another experienced volunteer. I'll look into the situation first thing tomorrow."

"I appreciate that, Colonel, very much." Ethan nodded his thanks. Sally Tompkins's hospital had a very good reputation for returning wounded soldiers to the field. Few died there, as Captain Sally only had twenty-two patients at any given time. Officers begged to have their men placed in her facility, because they knew their men would receive personal attention and qualified care under her watchful eye.

"Tell them about the theater," Franklin encouraged his uncle.

"Oh, yes. I'd be remiss in my social duties if I didn't share that." Colonel Shields dabbed at his mouth with a linen napkin. He reached inside his breast pocket and withdrew eight tickets to the Richmond Theater. "I'd be honored to invite all of you to accompany Franklin and myself. Alas, these are not for opening night, as the theater is completely sold out then, but if the next week is open for you, we'd love to have you join us."

Taylor Sue and Salina pored over the tickets. "Shakespeare," they said in unison, enormously pleased.

"We'd be delighted," Colonel Carey accepted for all of them.

A week later, Salina stood on the porch, leaning against one of the columns, gazing into the cold night sky. Above her, the stars of the constellation Orion shone brightly. If Salina remembered correctly, Orion was the son of Poseidon and a mortal mother, and was the most handsome man who ever lived. According to legend, Orion was a hero, a warrior, and a great hunter. He was blinded by the jealous father of his intended bride, and he eventually regained his sight by looking into the sunrise. Aurora, the goddess of dawn and Apollo's sister, became Orion's lover.

The constellation's stars winked and glittered like diamonds against rich black velvet, and another handsome warrior came to mind. *"Lord Jesus, please, keep my Horse Soldier in Your hand wherever he may be this night, and please, soften his heart towards me..."*

"What are doing out here in the cold?" Ethan joined her on the top step of the porch. "Or need I guess?"

"No need to guess. You already know. I was merely dreaming a bit." Salina flashed a wavering smile.

Ethan took in his younger sister's striking appearance. "You're quite the belle, Salina, even in dark mourning dresses. I'm glad you haven't made a hermit of yourself for Daddy's sake. He wouldn't have wanted that."

"He wouldn't have wanted tears, only remembrances of laughter." Salina nodded. "I miss him."

"You're not alone." Ethan squeezed her shoulders. "I miss Mamma, too, and the way our lives used to be. But those times are gone forever, Salina. We must pick up the shattered pieces and bravely carry on."

"I know." Salina sighed. She turned and studied Ethan. He looked so gallant and dashing, proudly wearing his new military attire. Taylor Sue had painstakingly sewed the uniform for him, as prescribed in the army regulations manual. The tunic was cadet gray, with black facings on the standup collar. Black trim lined the outside seams of his dark blue trousers, the legs tucked into his boots. He wore white gloves and a sash of green silk net about his waist. On his cap the letters M.S., for Medical Service, were embroidered in gold.

Salina touched the gold star on the collar of his tunic and smiled. "You do look fine, Captain Hastings. If only Mamma could see you now."

"I wish she had been at our wedding," Ethan lamented. "It makes me sad to think of her so far away up North."

"I wonder how she is faring. At least she has Jubilee," Salina added. "I didn't want to hurt her by not going with her, but I think she understands why I had to come back to Virginia."

"I'm sure she does," Ethan comforted. "Come now, we mustn't be so melancholy tonight. Taylor Sue is very much looking forward to this visit to the theater. She told me about the play Duncan took you all to in Washington. She has made several comparisons between the two opposing capitals."

"There are some," Salina agreed. "More than one might imagine. Here's Taylor Sue now."

Salina's sister-in-law was dressed beautifully in a gown of burgundy brocade. "The two of you are a picture," Salina complimented Taylor Sue and Ethan. "Whenever I think of the both of you, this is what you'll look like in my mind's eye."

The reopening of the rebuilt theater had been heralded for a long time in the local newspapers. The old theater burned down the year before and was finally reconstructed. The pillared facade was impressive, Salina noted as they entered the lobby of the theater from Broad Street. Colonel Shields escorted all of them to the second level, to one of the tiered boxes on either side of the stage.

The play, Shakespeare's comedy *As You Like It*, was in progress when the clatter of hoofs combined with shouts and commands interrupted the performance. The audience buzzed with confusion and excitement as gray-clad troopers sauntered down the aisles, their sabers clanking and spurs jangling noisily.

Salina placed her hand on the box railing, glancing down into the aisle below. From her vantage point she saw the cavalrymen arrest a handful of like soldiers and began to escort them out. One of the cavaliers turned abruptly, looking up to where Salina sat watching the scene. Her emerald eyes grew round as saucers, and her heart skipped rapidly as she identified Lieutenant Jeremy Barnes. His eyes were expressionless, void of anything other than scant recognition. He touched the brim of his plumed hat in mute acknowledgment, but Salina leaned back and hid herself from sight behind the drapery.

The lieutenant's telling gesture was not lost on Taylor Sue, Ethan, and Franklin—or a dozen or more other patrons who noticed the bold motion as well. Several curious glances lifted toward the box, but they could not see the young lady's flushed face due to her retreat into the shadows.

"He must have felt you watching him and looked up to see for sure." Taylor Sue prodded Salina, "Why didn't you at least smile at him?"

Ethan leaned closer to his wife in order to catch his sister's dull reply, "It would have hurt too much if he refused to smile back," Salina murmured, lowering her eyes and fidgeting with the fringe trim of her handbag.

Two days later the girls, along with the general population of Richmond, learned what the incident at the theater was all about. Jeb Stuart's troopers were camped near the capital, and on a whim a few of them decided to take in a play at the theater. They neglected to obtain sufficient permission from their commander; so they were absent without leave, and Stuart had ordered for their arrests and immediate return to the cavalry headquarters.

Richmond's provost marshal, General John H. Winder—a man much disliked for his harsh and arbitrary rule in the city—determined that Stuart should not be allowed to use such force under his jurisdiction. General Winder sent off a brusque note to General Stuart, in which Winder threatened to have Stuart arrested if he continued such unauthorized raids inside the city limits. Stuart's reply was prompt. He would patrol the streets with 30 of his men in search of any absentees from his command, and Winder was more than welcome to make an attempt to arrest Stuart himself—if he was able.

Salina peeked from her window that night, hearing the racket of hoofbeats, clanking sabers, and ringing spurs echo through the empty streets. She caught a glimpse of the daring cavalry troops, unmistakably led by General Jeb Stuart, and she sensed that Jeremy was with him. There was no sign whatsoever of either the militia or of General Winder's men. Winder's threat of arresting Stuart was proved to be just that, and nothing more was made of the event.

☆☆☆☆☆☆☆

"Ethan, I've decided that I want to go home." Salina paced the polished wooden floor of her second-story room, wringing her hands anxiously as she rehearsed the speech she intended to present to her brother later on this afternoon. As far as she knew, he was out at Chimborazo with Colonel Shields, as had become his custom. Salina's voice was low, but just loud enough so she could hear how she thought her argument should be delivered. "Ethan, I can't stay here in Richmond any longer..." She paused and started again. "Ethan, I have a strong desire to return to Chantilly because...because..."

Salina sighed and hung her head, closing her eyes. "Oh, how can I explain to him how jealous I've become each time I see the happiness he and Taylor Sue share? How can I tell him that my heart aches at being a witness to his abiding love for his new wife when my own dreams of sharing such a love with Jeremy are dwindling so rapidly? How can I make Ethan understand how I feel?"

"Well, you might try telling me about it, little sister, face to face." Ethan casually leaned against the doorjamb. "I'm not as unapproachable as you seem to think, you know. And I can sympathize with how you must feel. I should have been more sensitive to the pain you've been going through, Salina. But at the same time, I admit that it would give me great pleasure to wring both your stubborn necks just seeing you at odds against each other." He smiled belatedly. "I've already promised Taylor Sue that I'll stand aside and let you and Jeremy work out your own affairs. It's not my place to meddle, however much I might like to."

Salina swallowed, not meeting his intense gaze. She was quite aware that her feelings and thoughts more often than not made their appearance in her expressive green eyes, and Ethan was an expert at reading her like a book. "You've skirted the subject of my returning to Chantilly. You're not going to let me go, are you?"

Ethan crossed the floor and stopped directly in front of his sister, resting his large hands on her shoulders. "I know you've been restless, more so since the night we went to the theater. The glance you and Jeremy so briefly exchanged spoke volumes, whether you realize it or not. I know how much you love him, Salina. I think he does, too. That might be why he's so obviously avoiding coming back here to Richmond. Jeremy knows you're here, but he doesn't know how to deal with you. All you can do is wait for him to come around."

"He doesn't come to Richmond because he doesn't trust me. He thinks I'm spying for Duncan." Salina stomped her foot angrily. "I don't even know where to begin anymore to make him see reason. He must think me horrible..."

Ethan squeezed her shoulders lovingly. "Then maybe now is as good a time as any for you to leave Richmond. I've had a hunch the day would come, Salina. In truth, I'm surprised it's taken this long for you to voice your discontent. Your timing, however, in my opinion, is most providential. I even have a traveling companion waiting in the wings."

Was Ethan really letting her go without a fight? She knew her brother well enough to know that there had to be an ulterior motive, or he'd make a loud and distinct fuss over her wanting to go. "Traveling companion?" Salina asked, puzzled.

"Yes, traveling companion. Certainly you don't think I'd let you go alone, do you?" Ethan queried.

"No, I know better." Salina nodded. "You'd insist there be someone on hand to see to my protection."

"Very astute, little sister." Ethan tapped the end of her nose with his finger.

"What sort of plan do you have in mind?" Salina wanted to know.

Ethan grinned. "You leave the details to me," he evaded. "I'll even go so far as to break the news of your eminent departure to Taylor Sue myself."

Salina was suspicious. "You're taking this awfully well."

Again Ethan grinned. "You just leave it all up to me. You pack."

"Ethan..." Salina touched his arm but hesitated.

"Out with it." Ethan could see in her eyes there was something she needed to ask him.

Salina bit her lip. "I was wondering why you want me to go away."

Ethan laughed heartily. "You were so sure I was going to protest that now you're disappointed because I'm helping you do what you wanted from the first. This is what you want, right?"

"Yes." Salina quickly nodded.

"Good, because I have my reasons for wanting you back home. There's a north-bound train heading out of Richmond late tonight. Can you be ready?" asked Ethan.

"Well, yes." Salina quickly eyed the room. "It won't take long to gather my things. What reasons?"

"I'll tell you later," her brother promised.

"Will you at least tell me who it is I'll be traveling with?" Salina prodded.

"Charlie Graham," Ethan replied, waiting for his sister's reaction. Charlie was once a suitor of Salina's—until Jeremy Barnes returned from California last summer. With Jeremy around, none of the remaining beaux ever stood a chance as far as Salina was concerned, and Charlie knew it. He'd even gone so far as to challenge Jeremy to a duel at Mary Edith's wedding reception, but Uncle Caleb had been quick to diffuse the situation before it came to pistols on Salina's account.

"Charlie Graham?" Salina raised an eyebrow in askance. "He's here in Richmond?"

"Has been since shortly after the battle at Stones River near Murfreesboro. He's lost a leg, Salina, and he's been mustered out of the service, medically discharged. He's very, very disheartened and understandably bitter about the situation. I'd appreciate it greatly if you'd serve in the capacity as nurse for him on the journey back to Chantilly. Is that acceptable to you?" Ethan wanted to make sure Salina would not object. "You've worked on hundreds of wounded soldiers. Could you help Charlie as well?"

"I'd be glad to help him," Salina assured Ethan. "Poor Charlie."

"Pity is the last thing he needs," Ethan cautioned. "He's been wallowing in it for weeks. He needs someone who'll teach him how to be strong again, to snap out of his black moods. Are you up to the challenge?"

"I am." Salina squared her shoulders and lifted her chin, accepting her brother's thinly veiled dare.

The last of Ethan's doubts were settled. He hoped that some of Salina's determination might rub off on Charlie while he was under her care. Ethan knew well how Salina enjoyed a good challenge, and already her spirits seemed revived. He had watched over the past few weeks as she wilted in Richmond's high society. The work she did first at General Hospital No. 5 and then at the Robertson Hospital had been her sole outlet. He touched Salina's cheek. "You belong at Shadowcreek."

"There's not much left since the fire, but maybe I can find something salvageable." Salina shrugged. "Who knows?"

Ethan gathered Salina into the protective circle of his arms. "I'll miss you. We'll both miss you, but I know it will be for the best."

"You're a good brother, Ethan." Salina escaped his embrace, gathered her shawl and cape, and began to search for her gloves.

"You're going out?" Ethan asked, thinking she would begin her packing immediately.

"Well, yes. I want to see Captain Sally and tell her good-bye. I don't want her to think that I'm deserting my work at the hospital without reason. And I wanted to tell Mrs. Davis I was leaving. She's tried so very hard to introduce me to some other soldier she thinks might turn my head, but I believe she knows there's only one Horse Soldier for me."

Ethan nodded, handing Salina her gloves from off her dresser. "Yes, Taylor Sue told me she'd handpicked at least a half dozen other suitable lieutenants, but you're just not interested."

"No, I'm not," Salina confirmed. She pulled on her gloves. "Thank you, Ethan."

"For what?" he asked.

"For your understanding." She nodded, flashing him a beguiling smile. She fairly skipped down the stairs, leaving him standing in the room alone.

"Oh, Salina." Ethan sighed and shook his dark head, a deep, throaty laugh rumbling in his chest. His little sister never ceased to amaze him.

☆☆☆☆☆☆☆

"What's *she* doing here?" Charlie Graham sneered caustically.

Ethan maneuvered Charlie's wheelchair up the ramp to the platform. "*She's* going to be your nurse, so get used to the idea."

"Why'd you have to get *her* involved? I don't want her to see me like this," Charlie ground out angrily. "I'm a cripple, for Pete's sake!"

"She's seen men in worse condition, Charlie. Salina's become an accomplished nurse. I trust her skill," Ethan said coolly. "I hope you'll mind your manners in her company." It was a thinly concealed threat at best.

"I don't want her help. I don't want her near me," Charlie argued bitterly.

"That's not for you to decide," Ethan said brusquely. "She needs to get home, and you need someone to look after you. Think of it as doing each other a favor—nothing more, nothing less."

Charlie's eyes flashed dangerously. "Hastings, I swear, I'll..."

"You'll be so grateful to get back home. And you'll appreciate the fact that you're in Salina's fine care to change the dressing and make sure your fever doesn't go up again," Ethan cut him off. "When you're through being so peevish, you really ought to thank God for sparing your life, Charlie."

"I wish I'd died out there," Charlie hissed, venom in his eyes. "At least there's honor in the dying for your country and your cause. There's no honor in returning home half a man."

"You're only missing a leg, Charlie," Ethan pointed out, then added sarcastically, "If you're counting by limbs, that's three-quarters remaining, not a half."

"You know what I mean, Hastings!" Charlie raged. "How would you feel if you only had one leg?"

"I'd thank God that He'd not taken something else in it's place. That He'd left my hands, my sight, my hearing, my manhood, my life. It's only a leg, Charlie—a peg can replace that. You can ride a horse and won't notice the difference that it's gone. You can live without it. But the life that follows will be your choice. Choose wisely," Ethan recommended, though more harshly than he'd intended. He'd grown weary of Charlie's attitude and refused to sugar-coat reality any longer. He left Charlie in the porter's attention and turned to Salina, who joined him on the platform.

"I couldn't help but hear," Salina said, looking past Ethan to where Charlie was being carried into the train car. "You were a little rough on him, don't you think?"

"It's up to you whether you want to treat him with kindness—which he'll resent—or with indifference—in which case he'll do anything to goad you into a flash of temper. Or you can deal with him honestly, and let him deal with you in return. He's not rational. He's in pain, and he's too proud to accept assistance graciously. You're sure you're up to this?" Ethan questioned again. "You can still change your mind. You don't have to go through with it, if you don't want to."

"Am I to interpret that as though you've changed your mind? You don't want me to go home, really, and you're using Charlie to discourage me?" Salina returned.

"No, no, on the contrary. I need you to go home, Salina," Ethan assured her. "Earlier, when we discussed this, I told you I had reasons for wanting you back at Shadowcreek. Helping Charlie was one reason. The other reason, I admit, is of a selfish nature."

"Which is what?" asked Salina.

"I want to know that Taylor Sue will have a place to stay. I don't want her to remain in Richmond after I've gone back to the front," Ethan admitted. "With you near Chantilly, I feel better about bringing her back there. For a long time, it plagued me to think about the two of you alone while I'm away. But I think the two of you are capable enough. It took me awhile, but I have to accept the fact that there are women all over the South who are having to survive without their men around. You and Taylor Sue are certainly strong enough to endure. Look at what you've come through so far."

"I'm glad you believe in me." Salina stood on tiptoe to kiss her brother's cheek. She looked up to the train window, meeting Charlie's ill-tempered grimace. "Well, it looks like Charlie's anxious to be underway."

"God bless you, Salina." Ethan grinned.

"And you, Ethan. When do you have to rejoin the Corps?" she asked.

"A week from now, by March first," Ethan answered. "I've got permission from Colonel Shields to have leave. During that time, I'll bring Taylor Sue to Northern Virginia myself."

"That's dangerous for you," Salina reminded him unnecessarily.

"We'll be careful." Ethan nodded with a wink. "See you in a week."

"I'll have a place for us to live by then," Salina said confidently. She'd ruled out Ivywood, for the sake of her own sanity and to avoid Lottie. She also ruled out Tabitha's boardinghouse, for Jeremy's sake, and Carillon, which was too far away if they were to need help from anyone. As a temporary measure, Salina planned to accept Mary Edith's standing invitation. But by the time Taylor Sue arrived, Salina was determined they would have a place to call their own, on Shadowcreek land if she could manage.

The porter cupped his hands round his mouth and yelled, *"ALL A-BOOAAARRDDD!"*

"I must go, Ethan." Salina squeezed his hand. "I'll give Charlie your best."

"By all means." her brother grinned. "You do that!"

It was the longest train ride Salina could remember ever having to withstand. Charlie was a horrible patient, and Salina's tolerance was worn thin within the first hour after their departure from Richmond. By the time they stopped at Fredericksburg, Salina was overjoyed they had reached the halfway mark. After the delays at Fredericksburg, the train pushed on, and she didn't think she had ever been so glad as when they pulled into Fairfax Station late the next morning. At the depot, she met Charlie's grandfather and two sisters.

"Charlie's sleeping at the moment," Salina explained to them. "As soon as the porter can retrieve Charlie's wheelchair, he and the conductor will bring him down."

Charlie was sullen and bad-tempered as his sisters fussed over him. He glowered at Salina while she tucked the lap robe under one leg and neatly folded the other half of the blanket. It rested limply where his other leg should have been.

Salina touched his shoulder. "Good-bye, Charlie. I hope you'll come visit when you're up to it."

"Don't be absurd, Salina. I hardly think I could wheel this blasted chair over any great distance," Charlie sneered.

"I heard my brother mention horseback riding, and I recall you being a very fine horseman. I shall look forward to the day you show up for tea," Salina said lightly. "Until then, I'll be praying for you, Charlie, that the Lord will heal not only your wounds, but your frame of mind as well."

"Go on with you," Charlie grated between his teeth. "You're just like Ethan, so pious and holier than thou!"

Salina's eyes widened, but then she simply smiled. "The invitation for tea still stands, Charlie, no matter what your bitter anger provokes you to say. Good day to you." Salina took her leave to find the porter, missing the vehement glare Charlie shot at her back.

Charlie seethed inside. *She'd react differently if something happened to her precious Jeremy...*

Salina found the porter at the far end of the platform. "Excuse me, sir, would it be possible to have this trunk taken to Little Ivy, near Fairfax Court House?"

"Aye, miss. I know of the place. I'll send it over straight away." The porter touched his cap.

"Salina?" a familiar voice called her name. "Miss Salina Hastings."

Salina inwardly cringed. She hadn't been back for a full five minutes before running smack into Lottie Armstrong.

Chapter Thirteen

Jeremy's head broke the surface of the icy-cold water, and he let out a shout that reverberated through the woods surrounding the pond.

He'd known quite well that the water would be freezing even before he dove in. Long, sure, swift strokes carried him to the edge, and he climbed up the bank to where he'd left his uniform spread out along the hedge. He dried himself with the towel, exchanged his wet longjohns for a dry pair, and hurriedly pulled on his wool britches. He tucked his shirt in and pulled his suspenders over his broad shoulders while his teeth chattered. As he pulled his boots on, Harrison Claibourne, Weston Bentley, and Kidd Carney rode up alongside the mill pond at Carillon.

Bentley scratched his head, shaking it slowly from side to side. "What kind of fool goes diving into a half-frozen pond in the middle of winter?"

"I needed a bath," Jeremy said tersely.

"You got something against *hot* baths, Lieutenant?" Harrison asked with a chuckle.

Bentley answered before Jeremy could comment, "Maybe he just needed some ice water to cool that anger burnin' in his gut. Ever since Richmond, you've been drivin' yourself—and the rest of us—like a man possessed. If I thought Miss Salina's absence had you tied up in knots—her presence has done worse!"

Jeremy cast a scathing glance at all three of his friends, but more specifically at Bentley. "It's got nothing to do with her."

"You don't lie well, Lieutenant, anybody ever told you that?" Bentley grinned. "It's your face. You're too honest. And your eyes— they surely give you away."

"If you asked me, Lieutenant, I think you shoulda gone up to the second floor of that theater in Richmond an' snatched her right outta that fancy, high-falutin' box she was sittin' in." Kidd Carney grinned good-naturedly. "It woulda been a sight to see you kiss her right there in front of such an upstanding audience."

Jeremy poked his arms through his vest. "I didn't ask, Carney, and that's enough. I'll not have you talk about her like that."

"Rushing to the damsel's defense," Harrison guffawed. "Could it be that she has somehow restored herself in your esteem, Lieutenant? I thought she was out of favor there for awhile."

Jeremy's eyes narrowed. "I do not see this a fit subject for jesting," he said firmly. "I'll admit, I had my suspicions about Miss Hastings's loyalty and the motive for her return, but it appears that I stand corrected." Jeremy had been given a rather large dose of General Stuart's unasked-for advice on the matter, and he had been commanded, just short of an official order, to apply it accordingly.

"But you still don't trust her," Bentley surmised. "You're just waiting for her to do something—either to slip up or to prove her worth. Isn't that right, Lieutenant?"

"Yes, I suppose that's hitting the nail on the head," Jeremy conceded. "Now, I'm going to ask you all just once—which one of you is hiding my jacket?"

"None of us, sir," Harrison said, speaking for each of the three subordinates.

Kidd Carney held his hands up, and Bentley did the same.

"Look, I left it right here, with all my other clothes, and now it's missing," Jeremy insisted. "I'm running out of patience with all of you."

"Honest, Lieutenant," Bentley piped up. "You're welcome to search."

"None of us has dismounted, Lieutenant," Kidd Carney reminded Jeremy. "Especially because we'd rather have hot baths, not cold ones."

Jeremy didn't care that his men were laughing at him. He knew his friends, and they were very much capable of staging a practical joke. Jeremy shook his head and shrugged into his cape. "Ah, well, that jacket needed mending anyway. There's still a hole in one sleeve, the seam under one of the arms is out, and it's missing a couple of buttons." He searched the nearby hedge again, but the jacket was indeed gone. "Now I'll have to hire a tailor to fit a new one for me, I reckon." He chose not to elaborate on the fact that it wasn't so much the jacket itself he'd miss most but the delicate lace handkerchief stored in the pocket.

The four riders continued on to Carillon's mill. No one had been near the place for ages, and it certainly hadn't been used for its true purpose any time recently. The mill probably hadn't seen any activity since Colonel Carey had gone to join the war effort in spring of 1861. Jeremy, Harrison, Kidd Carney, and Bentley took inventory of the stone structure.

"This might work, Lieutenant. There're plenty of hiding places here," Kidd Carney noted.

"There're enough nooks and crannies to stash supplies without having to leave them in the open," Harrison added.

Jeremy agreed with their assessment. With any luck, the Careys would never have to know that their property was used as an ordnance warehouse—the Yankees either. "All right, then. We'll go ahead with the plans to stash the arms here for now, and later the ammunition. Harrison, ride out and tell Boone and Curlie we've found a place for storage. We'll be along directly to help move the wagons up."

Harrison saluted. "Yes, sir."

Kidd Carney ascended the narrow stairwell, while Jeremy and Bentley attempted to see through the dirty glass windows. "This will work quite nicely," Jeremy gave voice to his growing confidence.

"Will you tell her about it?" Bentley dared ask.

"No." Jeremy shook his sandy-blond head. There was a time when Jeremy used to tell Salina every secret, every plan, every anticipated move. But that was then. "She's still in Richmond, by last report. She still hasn't answered any of my letters. I've sent two more since the night of the arrests we made at the theater."

"Don't give up. There's a good number of reasons why your letters might not have reached her. We are operating behind enemy lines anyway. I am surprised you risk sending them at all," Bentley ventured.

"Lottie promised she'd post them for me, and she's vowed to keep my whereabouts a secret," Jeremy said, but doubt plagued him. He belatedly regretted his decision to allow Lottie to post his mail. She had too willingly volunteered. Giving the letters to her had probably been a mistake, but there was nothing he could do to recall them at this point. Looking up the stairwell, Jeremy shouted, "Come on down, Carney. Let's go meet the wagons."

☆☆☆☆☆☆☆

"Good morning, Salina," Lottie purred condescendingly. "Why, I had no idea you were coming back to this area. I thought you'd be staying in Richmond with the Careys."

Salina smiled ever so sweetly. "I grew rather weary of the various receptions, concerts, plays. The social activity there is a continuous whirl. But that was just at night. During the day I worked in the hospitals. That's where so many of our boys in gray end up, you know, in the Richmond hospitals."

Lottie wrinkled her nose in disgust. "Oh, Salina, you never have been afraid to get your hands dirty, have you?" she remarked snidely, trying to disguise her envy over Salina's extended visit to the Confederate capital.

"How's your sister?" Salina asked politely.

"Why, she's just as big as a house," Lottie exclaimed. "Mary Edith looks like she expands every time I see her. Those twins are bound to be a handful once they finally come. I don't know how she can bear it." Lottie shuddered. The very notion of childbearing was distasteful and grotesque to her. She tossed her blond locks. "I'm going to drop off some things for Mary Edith. Mrs. Yates has made some delicious apple butter and some heavenly peach jam. I just love it on fresh biscuits. I'm headed to Little Ivy. I suppose I should be neighborly and offer you a ride?"

Salina eyed Lottie warily. How much harm was there in accepting a ride to the cottage where Mary Edith lived? "Thank you, Lottie. It's very kind of you."

A stony silence fell between the two cousins as Lottie drove the carriage away from the depot. Salina grew more unsettled—as though waiting for the other shoe to drop.

She hadn't long to wait. Salina's eyes fell on the basket at her feet which apparently belonged to Lottie. The item on top was made of gray flannel wool and was distinctly familiar.

Lottie saw that Salina's attention was focused on the gray lieutenant's jacket. "Isn't that a ragged old thing? I just can't believe he goes around wearing clothes that are so worn out and practically threadbare. I promised Jeremy I'd mend it for him so he'd look at least halfway presentable. He's an officer, for pity's sake!"

Salina's eyes snapped to Lottie's face, her eyes trying to penetrate her cousin's demure facade. *Jeremy's jacket.* Salina shifted uncomfortably on her side of the seat.

Lottie kept the horse at an even trot. She was smugly pleased, sensing Salina's evident discomfort. It would never do to laugh aloud, no matter how badly Lottie wanted to at that very moment. From then on, she kept up a steady stream of idle chatter about the recent weather, the local gossip, and finally turned to another subject, Lieutenant Lance Colby.

Salina bit her tongue, refusing to rise to Lottie's obvious baiting. She would not allow her cousin to know how deeply the things she said affected her. She answered Lottie only when necessary, which was not often. Lottie's incessant monologue had few pauses. The ride, which Salina regretted accepting, seemed interminable. She was much relieved when Lottie reined the carriage in front of the stone cottage.

Mary Edith was so delighted to have Salina stay with her at Little Ivy that when a local boy brought Salina's trunk from the station, she insisted on paying him a handsome tip in Salina's behalf.

The three girls endured a long afternoon of mending and knitting together. Lottie's perpetual prattle more than made up for Salina's lack of conversation. Mary Edith did what she could to speed up Lottie's departure, but she knew Lottie would not leave until she was good and ready to do so.

Mary Edith leaned on the door once she'd closed it behind Lottie. "Hope to see you again *real* soon, Salina," she mimicked her sister's farewell.

"Mary Edith, why do I have such a difficult time dealing with her?" Salina questioned. "Her greatest skill is knowing just how to aggravate me."

"She works very hard at making you miserable, and she takes such pleasure in watching you squirm, Salina," Mary Edith said truthfully. "I wish she wasn't so black-hearted. Lottie is just so—Lottie!"

The two girls laughed together in the truth of the absurd statement. Mary Edith added, "No doubt she's just saying it's Jeremy's jacket she's mending specifically to get your back up. I must say it worked."

"That *is* Jeremy's jacket," Salina clarified. "Lottie wasn't teasing about that."

Mary Edith blinked. "Well, now where would she get his jacket from?"

"Probably from Jeremy himself," Salina mused.

"Well, if it's any consolation to you, I know she's been seeing quite a lot of that Yankee Colby since you've been gone. They're a pair: riding, dining, dancing. He takes her everywhere and anywhere she wants to go when he's not on duty at the outpost. If Jeremy's truly around these parts, it could only be within the last few days." Mary Edith confided, "I just can't fathom why Lottie flirts so unmercifully with the enemy."

"For the mere thrill of it," Salina supposed. "Lottie enjoys inflicting hurt on people. Why not the blue-bellies as well?"

"She must have a reason for entertaining Colby's company. You know as well as I do that Lottie does nothing without an underlying motive," Mary Edith pointed out.

"Yes, I know that." Salina nodded, dropping her stilled knitting needles in her lap. "All too well."

✰✰✰✰✰✰✰

Caleb Armstrong opened the barn door cautiously. He'd heard noises, and he'd brought his shotgun in case he came upon whatever foragers might have taken shelter on his property. "I know someone's out here. You might as well show yourself!" He held the lantern at arm's length, peering into the wavering shadows. All was silent. But then he heard a noise up in the loft, and he saw the quick movement of a light-haired head. A gray garment was knocked from the loft to the first floor as a result of the scuffling above.

Caleb picked up the Confederate jacket and hung it on a nail next to the corncrib. "You young Reb soldiers! If you'd have come up to the house, we'd have fed you a decent meal. But if it's just a safe place to sleep for the night, you're welcome to it. Just be gone by morning. Don't want no trouble here, understand?"

"Yes, sir. Thank ya, sir," came the boyish reply in a thick Southern drawl.

"G'night then." Caleb retreated back to Ivywood's main house.

Peeking through a knothole, Lottie only removed her hand from Colby's mouth when she was certain her father had gone back into the main house. "Your Yankee accent would have given us away for sure if you'd made so much as a peep!" she snapped in a harsh whisper.

Colby rolled onto one elbow. "Nice touch, Lottie, kicking the jacket to the floor below. He didn't make the connection, though, did he?"

"Maybe not tonight, but he will. Papa's a shrewd man. He'll piece it together, you just wait and see." Lottie's eyes burned intently. "It's merely a matter of showing him each specific piece at the proper time."

Dim moonlight pouring through the hayloft window cast enough illumination to allow a glimpse of the expression on Lottie's face. For a long, eerie moment, Colby studied the beautiful, calculating young woman next to him. She was lethal, and he should discontinue the alliance between them. If he didn't, what was there to prevent him from ending up as the next victim of her malicious manipulations?

☆☆☆☆☆☆☆

Driven by a determined sense of urgency, Salina hurried along the bank of the stream with a fixed purpose. She buried her gloved hands in the pockets of her coat; her boots crunched the leaves beneath her every step. In the distance, she saw the footbridge, but that was not her goal. It was the clearing beyond that she was anxious to reach. And more specifically, the ivy-covered cabin that stood on the other side.

Arriving at the overgrown, whitewashed structure, she nodded satisfactorily and took the stone steps two at a time. The porch railing was broken, but that could be fixed. She turned the porcelain door handle and, with a rusty scream of the hinges, the door opened wide. Salina could not make out much in the darkness of the cabin's interior. She fished in her pocket for the candle and matches she'd had the foresight to bring along.

The candle's flickering glow revealed the cause of the absence of light—all the windows were boarded over. Using all her strength, Salina struggled to pry the boards from the sills to let the light shine through. Two slivers later, she used a wad of discarded mosquito netting to wipe away the grime on the glass panes of one of the windows.

The room wasn't the shambles she'd expected to find. In fact, everything was neat, though covered with a thick layer of gritty dust and cobweb wisps. A good cleaning would make the cabin inhabitable. It was quite clear that Peter Tom had not used this place for the better part of a year.

This cabin, one in a string of five like structures, was once part of Shadowcreek's slave quarters. This and only one other were fit to use as shelter, but this particular cabin was located nearest the stream and the footbridge. From the top of the front steps, Salina could just make out the brick chimneys which stood as silent sentinels guarding the remains of the main house, roughly two hundred yards away. It was common knowledge that Shadowcreek had been burned out, and no one frequented the estate—of that Salina was reasonably sure.

The stream gurgled off to the left. To the right, down the hill, was the cemetery. Salina hugged her elbows, a smile curving her lips at her recollection of when General Stuart presented her with a winter rose.

Inside the cabin, she stood with her hands on her hips, taking mental notes of what must be done prior to Ethan and Taylor Sue's arrival. Salina had dreamed of this place last night, and now she thanked the Lord for His provision of a place to call home. In Salina's mind, the cabin was perfect. Due to the screen of trees and shrubs, it was invisible from the turnpike, yet near enough to the stream that hauling water would not be a major chore. It was also surrounded by good ground for spring garden planting and less than a mile from Mary Edith's stone cottage.

Salina sat down on the hearth of the huge brick fireplace, propping her elbows on her knees, chin in her hands. She needed a broom, mop, bucket and a scrub brush to start, and candles, kerosene, lanterns, canned goods...

Salina sprang to her feet. The ruins would be the place to begin digging. Mamma had been clever in her planning. When she hid items to keep them from being confiscated by the Yankee patrols, she never put everything together in one place. Mamma distributed the supplies evenly in the attic, the root cellar, and the barn. The attic and the barn were gone, but the root cellar might have enough for her immediate needs. Mary Edith had volunteered to help as best she could in spite of her protruding belly, and Salina decided that she would pay a visit to Tabitha Wheeler as well. She could use some advice from the old woman about how to store certain items to make them last.

She went to the porch again, gingerly testing her weight on the wooden swing before sitting firmly down upon it. The old ropes creaked in protest as she moved back and forth, back and forth. This would do, and quite nicely. There were several pieces of furniture—a table, chairs, a dresser, and a bedstead with drawers underneath and shelving above. Later on she'd explore the loft.

When planting season came, she could put in a vegetable garden, like Mamma and Jubilee used to do near the main house. And of course she would have to have roses. Salina closed her eyes and envisioned the house cleaned up in her imagination. She saw a fire burning cheerfully, Mary Edith rocking before the hearth, and the cabin filled with tunes from a feisty fiddle and a rollicking harmonica. Braided rag rugs adorned the floor, boots stomped in time to the lively music, and she herself was being twirled in a waltz in Jeremy's arms...

Salina opened her eyes. The bright daylight assaulted her vision. For tiny instant she had *seen* the faces of the others in the room—Ethan, Taylor Sue, Boone, Curlie, Jake, Harrison, Charlie Graham, herself, and Jeremy. How very vivid the scene behind her closed eyelids had been! Salina shivered, rubbing her arms to ward away the brisk chill that stole down her spine.

That night at supper, Salina shared her plans for the cabin with Mary Edith. Mary Edith was disappointed that Salina did not want to stay with her at Little Ivy, but she was pleased that they would be such close neighbors. "I'll go see Papa tomorrow and ask him if I can have some of the old dishes and draperies that I know are in storage and not being used anymore. My mother might protest, but Papa will generally let me have whatever it is my heart desires. He'll let us borrow the handcart, I'm sure. In fact, why don't you come with me? You'll need to get Starfire from the barn, and Daphne, too."

"I could bring the horses home. I'll turn the other cabin into a stable for them." Salina nodded. "Mary Edith, this just might work. I want to have it all done by the time Ethan brings Taylor Sue."

"That's ambitious. It sounds like there's a good deal of work to do to make it presentable." Mary Edith smiled.

"Well, at least that's the goal to aim for." Salina returned with a smile of her own. "I'll go with you to Ivywood, and on the way I'll brace myself for the next run-in with your sister."

"Lottie rarely gets out of bed that early in the morning. She was out somewhere with Colby again last night, I'll wager," Mary Edith whispered knowingly. "If we leave here at dawn, we can be on our way home before she even knows we were there."

✩✩✩✩✩✩✩

"Look, just leave me be! I've had enough! I don't want to be involved in this anymore!"

Mary Edith was startled when Lieutenant Lance Colby barged through Ivywood's barn door as if he owned the place. His tirade continued before she could speak, but then she decided that perhaps the best thing to do would be to keep silent. Maybe she could glean some useful information from his angry outburst.

"I'm heartily sick of this! I refuse to be party to your twisted vendetta against Salina Hastings anymore. You've used me the way you wanted to. You've accomplished what you set out to do. I'm leaving here. I've been assigned another post, and I am leaving," he repeated emphatically. "You're on your own, Lottie."

He thinks I'm my sister. Mary Edith, mindful to keep the wall dividing the two stalls between them so her distended abdomen would not give her away, tried to form an expression that she thought her twin might have used at a time such as this.

"Don't look at me like that!" Colby exploded. "I should have seen that you were trouble from the start. In truth, I did, but I was foolish enough to believe I might have begun to make a difference to you. I must have suffered a mental lapse, and if I don't watch my step, they'll be committing me to the insane asylum! The only person you care for is yourself. And I know you'll never care for me in return."

Mary Edith crossed her arms over her chest. "Anything else?" she asked piquantly.

"Yes. Leave Jeremy Barnes alone. I don't care if he is a Rebel. He does have a heart, and he's got a lot more integrity than you give him credit for. Interesting when you study your adversary—you get to know the kind of person he truly is. He's not a bad sort, but thanks to you, you've really gotten to him. He doesn't know what to believe anymore where Salina's concerned. Deep down, I think he still knows that he loves Salina, but you've succeeded in driving a wedge between them, and he doesn't know what to do about it."

With angry, jerky movements, Colby threw the saddle blanket on his horse's back and the saddle immediately followed. His fingers worked the cinch buckle, and in a moment he had his boot in the stirrup, swinging himself up onto the horse's back. "I should *never* have agreed to that scene in the loft. It was for your father's benefit, but that was a little much—trying to get him to believe it was Barnes who was up there with you. I regret it now. I regret *all* of my dealings with you. I wish I'd never laid eyes on you." Colby adjusted his saddlebag over the pommel of his saddle and went on. "If I *ever* lay eyes on you again, you'll be the one who regrets it! I allowed you to use me to play out your manipulations, and I am well aware of that." A wicked smile crossed his face. "In return, however, you did serve a purpose for me—though proper young ladies don't discuss such sinful antics in the daylight or mixed company. It would be better off for both of us if we make a clean break from each other. I'm willing to forget that there was any sort of relationship between us, and it might be in your best interest to do likewise."

"Are you quite finished?" Mary Edith inquired saucily.

Colby slipped his hand inside his jacket pocket. "I want you to take this letter to be delivered to Salina. It's from him. I should not have stood by and let you intercept their letters. It's not right. None of this is right. I suddenly remembered I do have a conscience, and it's been bothering me tremendously. I'll have to answer for my actions, I know that much. And you will answer for yours. Leave them both be. You've hurt them long enough." He rode away before she could form a reply.

Mary Edith was stunned. She stooped to retrieve the letter Colby had flung down onto the stack of hay bales near the door. Bold, slanted handwriting comprised the address: *Miss Salina Hastings, c/o Tabitha Wheeler, Fairfax Court House, Northern Virginia.* How many letters had Salina and Jeremy mailed to each other, which had never gotten any farther than into Lottie's clutches? Mary Edith's heart sank. She felt such pity for Lottie, who was consumed with such hatred. It pained Mary Edith greatly to uncover the extent of her twin's evil deeds.

"I'll find their letters and return them—I mean *deliver* them," Mary Edith determined. "I'll give his to her, and hers to him. I'll try to help build a bridge over the chasm Lottie created. I can do at least that much, I'm sure of it."

☆☆☆☆☆☆☆

Salina sat on her heels, dumped the scrub brush into the bucket of sudsy water with a *ker-plop* and a splash. She wiped her forehead against her sleeve and dried her work-roughened hands on her apron. She was tired. She'd been working on the cabin for the last four days with very little sleep between chores. At the end of the week Ethan would bring Taylor Sue, and Salina was determined that the place should have some resemblance of a home.

Glancing around the room, she could see that her efforts were beginning to show. The winter sun streamed through the clean windowpanes. Fire burned warmly in the black cast iron pot-bellied stove and in the fireplace. And the paneled walls smelled of lemon and beeswax. Salina smiled to herself. When she'd first decided to undertake the task of refurbishing the little cabin, she hadn't known where to begin or what to do first. It was a pleasant surprise to be able to draw from memory the myriad of things Jubilee used to do at the main house to keep everything looking sparkled and polished. "Jubilee would be proud." Salina nodded in satisfaction. She rubbed the tense muscles at the base of her neck, then plunged one hand into the bucket in search of the scrub brush. "And Mamma, too, I think."

The floor needed a good polish, but she thought she could hide the badly scarred planks if she had some rugs. She added the item to a growing mental list of all the things she didn't already possess and didn't have enough money to buy. She'd used a good portion of her money to purchase oats and hay from Uncle Caleb to keep Starfire and Daphne fed. But she had the feeling things would work out. The Lord was faithful, and He would provide whatever else she had need of, Salina was certain. From her reading in the book of Romans she was learning that without faith, it is impossible to please God. She desired to live her life pleasing to Him, and she made up her mind that she wanted to be a godly woman, like the one described in Proverbs 31. Salina longed to be a woman whose "value was more than rubies." She quoted softly, "Favor is deceitful, and beauty is vain: but a woman that feareth the Lord, she shall be praised." She smiled and took up scrubbing with a renewed vigor.

An inviting fire glowed in the red brick fireplace. Salina hung a kettle of water from the iron crane and adjusted its arm so that the kettle hung over the flames. Mary Edith had given her some cleaned poultry, and Salina intended to put it to use by making chicken soup.

The fireplace dominated one side of the room. It was nearly as large as the one Jubilee used to have in the kitchen house, except this one was not so deep. It should have been, though. The edge of the hearth protruded a good four feet into the room. Salina sensed that *something* about it was not quite as it might seem, yet she couldn't put her finger on what it was.

A loud knock caused Salina to turn toward the door. Mary Edith was early.

"Oh, Salina, look what you've done!" Mary Edith exclaimed. "You've managed a miracle here!"

"I've much more work to do, though." Salina shrugged with a grin. "What's in the wagon?"

Mary Edith smiled. "A housewarming gift. Come on, I'll show you."

The two cousins walked down the steps arm in arm. "Papa brought those things from the attic I mentioned to you, things Mama doesn't use anymore. Look—there's some old china dishes, a clock, and some old tapestry draperies we can cut to size for the windows. They're very thick and will conceal candlelight well," Mary Edith said purposefully. "Papa made sure that I had such curtains on my windows. If any riders were to see lights, they might come calling. Just a precautionary measure."

Salina fingered the heavy woven tapestry lined with black taffeta silk. "These'll work quite well."

"I've some lace, too. It will let in the light by day and add a homey touch." Mary Edith smiled. "Mother sent you three sacks of flour and one of brown sugar. There should be a jug of molasses in that crate with the dishes."

Salina hugged Mary Edith. "You're so good to me! You go sit down inside, and I'll unload the wagon."

By the time Salina finished bringing in Mary Edith's generous gifts, Mary Edith had taken stock of Salina's little home. "I can't believe how much you were able to salvage from the ruins. All this food was in the root cellar?"

"Yes." Salina nodded. "And the supply of candles and kerosene was more than I expected. It's a wonder it didn't all go up in smoke." She shook her head, dispelling the haunting vision of the horrific flames that had devoured what used to be her home.

Late that afternoon, the girls finished hanging curtains at all four windows, two flanking the front door and one on either end. The ticking of the pendulum clock accompanied their laughter, and after each had eaten her fill of chicken soup and biscuits, Mary Edith declared it was time to head back to Little Ivy.

As she settled herself in the driver's seat of the wagon, Mary Edith said, "I've asked Papa to find a dog for me. In fact, I asked him to find two—one for each of us. He said he'd look into it. Oh, and here." She held out a crumpled wad of Union greenback bills. "Papa said he can't take your money. The feed was already paid for. If there's anything else you have need of, you're to let me know, and I'll tell him."

"I can't live off of your family's charity." Salina unconsciously raised her chin. "You've been more than kind already."

Mary Edith divulged a secret. "I wasn't supposed to know, and you aren't supposed to either, Salina, but I've found out that Duncan Grant sends Papa a monthly check—has done so since December. His instructions are that you are to be taken care of—half the amount is Papa's to keep, half to use as he sees fit in securing your well-being." Mary Edith saw Salina's eyes grow round in surprise. "As your stepfather, he feels obligated to provide what your own daddy might have. But Major Grant doesn't want you to know, and Papa will not admit to it. So don't ever let on that you have an idea. Understand?" Mary Edith questioned. "Not a word, Salina."

"Not a word," Salina agreed. She felt odd about taking Duncan's money, but a voice in her head reiterated what she'd been thinking before Mary Edith arrived: *The Lord is faithful and He will provide...*

Chapter Fourteen

"Whoa, there." Lieutenant Lance Colby reigned his bay, dismounted, and patted the horse's thick black mane. He carelessly flung the reins around the porch railing then advanced toward the stone steps with caution. Salina had made it quite clear that she did not require, nor did she request, his company. But he felt he had to see her before he rejoined Duncan in Washington. "Hello, cabin! Anybody home?"

Salina heard the call. Recognizing the owner of the voice, she sighed, but then she decided it was ill-mannered of her to be so unfriendly. Colby had agreed to her terms of friendship and, until this unexpected visit, had kept his end of the bargain by keeping his distance. She tucked an errant curl into the loose chignon at the base of her neck and wiped her floury hands on her apron. As she walked across the room to the door, she felt the reassuring weight of the pistol in her pocket as it bounced lightly against her thigh.

A brisk knock on the door was followed by, "Salina, are you home? I can smell you're baking something..." Colby stopped mid-sentence when the door swung open. He removed his hat and bowed slightly. "Miss Hastings, it is a pleasure to see you again."

"How did you know I was here?" she wanted to know.

"It's my job to keep up on the happenings in this area," Colby replied lightly. "But no longer. I'm here to bid you farewell. May I come in?"

Salina halfway smiled. "Please forgive my lack of manners. Do come in, Lieutenant. Would you care for a cup of mint tea?"

"Certainly," Colby seated himself at the table. "You intend to stay here all by yourself?"

Salina eyed him warily. She had no intention of giving him anymore information than necessary. "My sister-in-law will be joining me shortly."

"You should really have a dog," Colby murmured. "I think it would be safer for you."

"It is a matter that is under consideration, Lieutenant. Thank you for your concern." She set a nicked china teacup and saucer before him, pouring the steaming liquid from the copper kettle.

Colby intently studied the teacup's delicate rose print pattern. Salina was much like a rose—beautiful to behold, yet at the same time a bit thorny if not approached with the utmost care.

"Do you take sugar?" she inquired politely. "I have no lumps, just plain brown, but you're welcome to have some if you wish."

"I'd prefer honey, if you have it," Colby said candidly.

"Very well." Salina turned to fetch the sweetener. When she returned to the table, the Yankee lieutenant was grinning at her. "What is so amusing, might I ask?"

"You don't look a bit like the defiant Rebel spy I arrested in San Francisco last November," he answered honestly. "You look like a dutiful little housewife—complete with ruffled apron and a smudge of flour on your cheek." He leaned across the table and brushed the white powder from her face.

Salina felt a blush creep up from her neck clear out to her ears and end at her hairline. "Was there a specific reason for the honor of this visit, Lieutenant?" she stammered, flustered.

Colby withdrew his hand and lifted the teacup to his lips. He sipped the mint tea and nodded. "I've been reassigned. Duncan and I will be working together in Washington again. You remember that Duncan had hoped to catch the mole with the assassination plans he'd discovered in your possession?"

"Yes." Salina nodded. "Was he successful?"

"No." Colby shook his fair blond head. "The mole got wise and burrowed deep. Recently, however, he's reared his ugly head again, and this time Duncan's not going to give up the chase."

"Best wishes to you. It sounds a little dangerous."

"Duncan thrives on the danger," Colby said with a chuckle. "Besides, he says I still have much to learn about being a good agent. And he'll use this assignment to hone the skills I have and to teach me more."

"I see," Salina said. "How is Duncan? Have you heard anything from him aside from your orders?"

"I brought this—it came to me with his last letter. He sends his best and wanted me to remind you that if you ever change your mind about living in Virginia, or if you need anything at all, that you're to let him know immediately. Here is an address and the name of a contact, if you should ever need him." Colby slid the pieces of paper across the table.

Salina looked at the card with the name and address. "I'll keep it, but I don't anticipate having to use it," she informed him. The second piece of paper was a note from Mamma.

"Well, I'll be on my way. I merely came to say good-bye and deliver those things to you. I know my being here makes you uncomfortable." Colby did not beat around the bush. "Think on the dog, Salina. Whoever is my replacement patrolling this area might be curious, and I wouldn't want anything amiss to transpire. Do you understand?"

"You're telling me that all Yankees are not as easily persuaded by Southern charm as you?" Salina goaded.

A wistful smile played on Colby's mouth. "In a manner of speaking, yes. You hit the mark squarely." He met her gaze evenly. "I'll admit I am intrigued by the belles in this part of the country."

"So I've heard," Salina replied knowingly. "I'm sure my cousin will be quite lonely when you're not here any longer to squire her around."

"Lottie will waste little time on tears for me," Colby said coolly. "In fact, our relationship broke off rather abruptly, and not in the best of circumstances, I am sorry to say."

"Well." Salina tilted her head to one side, digesting this revelation. She smiled at him. "I'm sure you'll find some nice, deserving, Yankee girl to spend time with instead once you reach Washington."

"We'll see." Colby shrugged. "Unless I miss my guess, Major Grant will have me too busy working to pay any heed to romantic inclinations." He gathered his coat and put on his hat. A low rumble of thunder sounded in the distance. "If I leave now, I might be able to ride ahead of the storm. Good-bye, Salina." He kissed the back of her hand. "You take care of yourself. Perhaps one day, our paths may cross again."

"Perhaps," was all Salina would allow.

"Don't forget to use the name of Major Grant's contact if you should need to," Colby reminded her.

"Good day, Lieutenant." Salina held the door for him.

Colby nodded briefly. *Good-bye, sweet Rebel...*

Salina stood on the porch and watched him ride away. Once more she was disturbed by the uncanny resemblance Colby bore to Jeremy from this distance. If the two of them had been fighting on the same side, one would be hard-pressed to tell them apart. And if Colby had known where she was, then why hadn't Jeremy been able to find her yet? The thick clouds and cold breeze gave no answer to her question. She sighed and returned to her baking.

☆☆☆☆☆☆☆

Not ten minutes passed after Lieutenant Colby's departure when Salina heard a scratching noise at the bottom of the front door, sounding like an animal of some sort. The rain was coming down steadily, and whatever the poor creature was, it wanted to be inside in the warmth rather than left to the elements. Pulling back the drapery, Salina peeked out through the windowpane. It was a dog—a breed Salina had never seen before. As she marched to the door, her temper rose. It was one thing for Colby to *suggest* a dog, but to drop a huge beast like that on her front doorstep was something else altogether. She yanked open the door and yelled into the thick, wet twilight, "Colby! I said I'd *think* about getting a dog! Who do you think you are depositing this...this..." Salina looked down at the rain-drenched creature. Its hair was wet and matted and hanging in its trusting brown eyes. The dog was shivering, as she herself was. Her rage dissolved into tenderness. "...this creature on my porch. You poor, bedraggled dog..." She bent over slightly and put her hand out, palm up. The dog sensed she was trying to be calm and licked her hand happily. "You look like someone tried to drown you in the stream," she said aloud and lightly petted the dog's head.

The dog nudged into her touch, inviting her to rub its ear, which Salina obligingly did. She knelt down in front of the odd-looking dog and managed to brush some of the hair away from its eyes. The dog's winsome expression earned a smile from Salina. She looked around the edge of the clearing, but there was no sign of Colby. "Where did you come from, hmmm?"

Jeremy pressed his back into the tree until the bark bit his shoulder blades through his cape. He held his tongue, preventing the torrent of angry thoughts from spilling into words. *Colby!* From Salina's tone, it sounded as though the Yankee lieutenant had been paying a call to the little whitewashed cabin—a rather recent call. The jealousy that rose in his throat tasted unpleasantly bitter. *Put it out of your head,* he told himself harshly. *You certainly can't let her believe that Colby left the dog for her, no sir-ee! Just march up those stairs and set her straight about that huge furball! And while you're setting her straight on that subject, might as well try to set her straight on a few others...*

He gathered his courage around him like a frail, invisible cloak. A churning deep in the pit of his stomach did not aid what he hoped was a calm facade. He rapped lightly on the cabin door. No answer. He knocked harder, and this time the door opened a mere crack. The barrel of a silver pistol greeted him. "I am comforted to see you haven't thrown all caution to the wind, Salina," he said smoothly. "It makes me feel much better to know you remember the shooting lessons Ethan and I taught you."

A ripple of distressed delight darted down Salina's spine. "You?" She uncocked the gun's hammer and employed the safety lock, slipping the gun back into her apron pocket. Her eyes were riveted on Jeremy as she stood aside, opening the door to allow him admittance.

"Were you expecting someone else?" Jeremy inquired in a gravely voice.

Salina closed her eyes and sighed. "You heard me call Colby's name a few minutes ago."

"Quite obviously," Jeremy replied tersely. "Is he a frequent visitor?"

"No," Salina said quickly, then added bravely, "but I wish you were."

Jeremy cleared his throat, deliberately ignoring her comment. "I see you've found your new watchdog. She doesn't look like much all wet, but when her coat dries, she'll be as fluffy as all get out. She's quite adorable when she's brushed and combed."

"*You* brought the dog?" asked Salina.

Jeremy nodded. "I stopped by Little Ivy to see you, but Mary Edith told me you'd moved out here. Caleb was there as well and had just brought the two dogs with him. I volunteered to bring yours out to you."

Salina lowered her eyes, feeling the need to clarify the situation. "Let me explain. Colby was here to say good-bye, to tell me he was being transferred back to Washington. He brought a letter Duncan forwarded to me from Mamma. He was insistent that I should look into getting a dog for protection. I just thought that..."

Again Jeremy nodded. "You thought Colby brought the dog."

Salina swallowed. "Well...yes." She glanced at the hairy creature who appeared to be quite at home, lying contentedly in front of the fire. "What sort of dog is that? It certainly hasn't got much of a tail to wag."

"It's a bobtail—a sheepdog—or so I'm told. Your uncle got her from one of his English blockade runners. Mary Edith has one, too, only hers isn't full-grown yet. This one's name is Duchess, and she's supposed to be a good watchdog—very loyal and devoted. Admirable qualities, wouldn't you say?"

Salina bristled at his implication. Shutting the door behind Jeremy, she took a deep, calming breath and forced a pleasant smile up at him. "Please, come in. It's awfully wet and cold out there. I've a good fire, and you're welcome to warm up by the hearth. I've only just started to fix some supper. Do you have time to stay?" she invited.

"I came to talk. But more than that, to listen," Jeremy informed her brusquely, pulling his gloves from his hands. He rubbed them together rapidly for warmth. His eyes darted about the cozy little cabin which Salina now called home. His sapphire blue eyes burned intensely, and he said lowly, "The last time we saw each other left us little opportunity to speak—with words anyway."

Salina, too, remembered quite clearly. Not a sound had been uttered between them that night at the theater in Richmond, but the glance they had exchanged had been nothing less than potent. "Are you going to hear me out and not jump to conclusions? I can explain..."

"So I've been informed by your brother, Taylor Sue, even General Stuart," Jeremy said, not without a hint of sarcasm. He hung his damp cape from a hook on the back of the door and set his hat on the settee under the window, its wet plume drooping over the brim. "Let's get this straight right from the start. I'm not leaving until I get all the explanations I'm looking for. I don't care if it takes all night. I was avoiding you in Richmond, but we need to get this straightened out once and for all. I expect nothing of you, Salina, but the truth."

"You'll listen to what I have to say, without passing judgment, without condemning or accusing me?" she inquired, lifting her chin in challenge.

"I promise I'll do my darndest to keep my temper in check and to give you a fair chance." Jeremy plainly saw the wariness in Salina's emerald eyes, and knowing he was responsible for putting that expression there tugged at his insides. He cupped the side of her pretty face in his hand, gently caressing her cheek with his thumb. "Something wouldn't let me give you a chance before, Salina. Pride, stubbornness, stupidity—take your pick. I'm here now because I want to give you a chance. Give me one in return?"

Salina's eyes glowed, and she cupped her hand over his, nodding her assent. Her fingertips lightly skimmed the ring he wore on his pinkie finger—it was her ring. Taking his hand in her own, she gingerly touched the flashing emerald stone set in a gold filigree band. "You wear it still."

"You asked me to," he needlessly reminded her. "I'll not take it off 'til you tell me to do so," he vowed.

She squeezed his hands, whispering a soft command, "Then keep wearing it for me." He'd sought her out. They were together again—of that she was glad—but she wanted some explanations of her own from him.

Neither of them knew how long they stood holding hands in the center of the room, staring at one another. But when Salina smelled supper burning in the kettle, she left him and hurried to the hearth. Stirring the thick stew with a large ladle she asked, "Are you hungry?"

"A bowl of stew would be nice." His sapphire eyes continued to survey her. "Corn bread?"

"Corn bread!" Salina yanked the oven door open. The corn bread was golden brown, not scorched as she had feared. "Yes." She smiled brightly, much relieved. She took the pan from the oven, placing it on a trivet on the table. "We have corn bread. I have honey or apple butter—you choose."

"Apple butter." Jeremy lit the candles in the middle of the table while Salina set chipped rose-patterned china dishes down and added utensils of well-worn silver. Linen napkins, only slightly frayed at the edges, and pewter mugs that might have dated back to colonial times and the Revolution, completed each place setting.

"Mary Edith brought some milk over yesterday. Would you care for some?" Salina asked nervously, the butterflies in her stomach all but chasing her appetite away.

"Yes, please." He nodded. He could see her apprehension in the way her hands trembled. "Sit down, Salina," he ordered gently. "Let's eat before it gets cold."

Salina folded her hands and prayed in earnest, "Father God, thank You for Your bountiful blessings. Thank You for my new dog, who should protect me from any intruders, and thank You that Jeremy was able to bring Duchess to me himself. Thank You, Lord, too, that he appears to be in one piece, healthy and whole. I pray that You will bless this meal, and our unexpected but welcome time together. In Jesus' precious name, amen."

The first few spoonfuls of the hearty stew were eaten in silence, until Jeremy initiated the conversation. "I think I know the story, Salina. General Stuart was the one who set the record straight. Ethan didn't want to interfere, and Taylor Sue wanted to tell me but figured I should hear it from you. Mary Edith knows the majority of the facts, but Lottie has twisted the details until they suited her brand of truth. Start at the beginning, Salina. This time I want to hear it all. *Every* detail. Don't leave anything out—right up to how all this came about." His gesture encompassed the cabin's cozy interior.

"All right." Salina took a deep breath, but she didn't look at him. She couldn't. She didn't want him to see all the way to her very soul through her eyes. She toyed with a carrot floating in her bowl, avoiding the probing intensity of his dark blue gaze. "I wanted to tell you everything that morning in the barn at Sully, but it didn't turn out like I planned. I didn't have enough time to make you understand certain things..." She proceeded to tell Jeremy all he wanted to know—in every detail, holding nothing back. She recounted, chronologically this time, all of the events that had transpired: of being arrested in San Francisco; of Drake's vow to come back and rescue them; falling overboard at Alcatraz followed by her illness; learning of Mamma's hasty marriage to Duncan Grant; what she could recall of the return trip aboard the steamships by way of Panama; of her interview with Abraham Lincoln; of her miraculous release. She told him she was going to have a new baby brother or sister come summer, and then she told him of her stay with the Careys in Richmond, and of her continuing difficulties with Lottie. Lastly, she showed to him the traveling pass and pardon authorized by Lincoln, as well as the letter of endorsement from General Stuart.

"General Stuart says he believes that I did all I could, to the best of my ability. He understands that my 'connections,' so to speak, were able to deliver me from my predicament. It was Duncan who pulled the necessary strings. I *did not* sign an Oath of Allegiance. I did, however, make a promise to behave. Lincoln's definition of behaving was that I not lead one of his best scouts on any more cross-country adventures. I have no intentions of doing that, and so I fulfill my promise." Salina carefully folded each document and put them away. "General Stuart wrote that endorsement for me the night Mrs. Davis tried to introduce us. He fairly ordered me to show it to you! Jeremy, if he can accept what's been done and doesn't condemn me as a traitor or a Yankee spy, then why can't you?" she demanded, tears brimming her eyes.

Jeremy leaned back in his chair, studying her, weighing her testimony. "I accept it, Salina. Better late than never, hmmm? If I wasn't willing to try, you know I wouldn't be here."

Salina nodded, then she described how Ethan arranged for her to travel to Northern Virginia as Charlie Graham's nurse, and how she and Mary Edith had worked to turn the cabin into suitable living quarters. "Ethan plans to bring Taylor Sue here before rejoining the medical corps in their winter quarters."

"Yes, I know. He should be here with Taylor Sue tomorrow or the next day," Jeremy said matter-of-factly. He sat, arms folded and elbows on the table, watching her intently. She appeared so vulnerable, so forlorn. The candlelight flickered between them, and he saw the tears collecting in her eyes. "What, Salina? Why are you crying?"

Teardrops spilled past her thick lashes, rolling unchecked down her cheeks. Each salty tear that dripped from her chin was absorbed into the gingham tablecloth. Absently she traced the squared pattern with her fingernail. She found her voice. "It hurts more than I can tell to know you don't trust me...that you considered me a traitor...but mostly that you took Lottie's word above my own. I've been at my wit's end trying to come up with *something* I could do to prove to you that I am still trustworthy. I was almost ready to quit making an effort. I figured that if you wouldn't listen to my words, why would my actions make any difference?"

"I am listening now, Salina," Jeremy assured her.

"Are you?" she wanted to know. "Are you *really* listening? More importantly, are you believing?"

"Yes," he answered firmly. "You said Colby came here to deliver a letter from your Mamma, upon Duncan's request. I do believe you."

Salina, wanting to dispel any further doubts Jeremy might harbor, stated once and for all, "I have *no* feelings for him, Jeremy. I never have. Colby knows you are the man I love. I can't even imagine how uncomfortable it must have been for him to sit by my sickbed day in and day out on the steamship, knowing that I continued to call out your name, never his—no matter how he might have wished otherwise. I never meant to hurt Colby, but inadvertently I have. Then when I finally get back, I ended up hurting you, too, breaking your trust without even realizing it..."

Jeremy reached across the table, interlacing his fingers with hers. The heart-shaped locket, his gift to her, glinted in the golden candlelight. The fireplace was at his back, the dancing flames reflected in her dark pupils. "We've hurt each other, and I am deeply sorry for that, Salina. Can you love me still?" he asked in a throaty whisper, wiping her tears with his handkerchief.

"I never stopped," she insisted, but faltered slightly before daring to ask him, "Do you love me at all?"

His tender, flashing smile quickened her heart. He answered softly, "Yes, I love you."

"Then where do we go from here?" she asked. "We've both changed, but we're the same, aren't we?"

Jeremy shrugged. "I reckon for the most part we are. I understand now why you did what you did, and I can see how you arrived at the conclusions to the choices you faced. I admire your spirit and determination, Salina. Your resolve to follow your father's instructions, at the risk of your own life, amazes me. I admit I was wrong to jump to hasty conclusions before getting all the facts straight. I know I said things that I shouldn't have, leveled false accusations and cutting remarks. Words can do irreparable damage. Yet on the other hand, words can soothe, heal, rebuild, and encourage. I pray my love can mend the verbal wounds I've inflicted."

She wanted to be able to forgive him immediately, but her head heeded the caution whispered by her wounded heart. "The war too often puts time and distance between us. It can be a blessing or a curse," Salina murmured.

"Then we must use them to our advantage," Jeremy declared. "Providing you're willing. Shall we try?"

Salina nodded.

Jeremy sensed her reserve. "It might not be easy," he pointed out.

"I don't expect it to be," Salina countered. "Life isn't easy. It's hard work. Relationships must be nurtured and handled gingerly. I will show you that I can be trusted. I love you, Jeremy, and I trust you. I believe in you. I..." She shrugged, emitting a sigh of resignation. "I just wanted you to know."

"I do know it." Jeremy stood and walked around the table to stand behind her. He caught the scent of rose-water as he kneaded the taut muscles bunched in knots in her shoulders and neck. Her skin was smooth and pliant beneath his soothing touch. "Lottie's played me for a fool, and I should have been wiser than to believe her lies. I want to do whatever I must to make amends, Salina."

"When all is said and done, it comes down to the matter of trust that stands between us," Salina whispered.

"Indeed." He nodded. Trust was something earned and oftentimes difficult to repair when broken. It was a bitter pill to swallow in admitting that it was he who fostered the notion of broken trust, based not on solid evidence, but on Lottie's insinuations. Silently he upbraided himself. He should have known better. He knew Salina was raised with a code of honor, a sense of duty, and more than her share of stubborn pride. She adhered tenaciously to her beliefs, as her upbringing dictated, only wanting to do what she believed right.

Momentarily, Jeremy thought of his new orders. A few months ago, he wouldn't have thought twice about Salina becoming involved. But for now he decided against telling her about the cache of arms, ammunitions, and supplies stashed away at Carillon's mill. Jeremy decided instead to wait and watch. The lives of his men were involved, and that was more than he was willing to risk at this point. What Salina did not know might not hold the potential to harm her.

Jeremy's fingers loosened the tense knots in Salina's neck and shoulders. Her chin rested against her chest, and her head lolled from side to side. "What did your mamma say in her letter?" he asked quietly.

Salina replied, "Mamma wrote about how she'd celebrated Christmas with Duncan's family in Gettysburg, and how much she misses Ethan and me. She wanted to know if my darling brother had managed to get married yet. She said that so far her health has been exceptional. The baby is growing, and she has had no problems during this pregnancy." Salina smiled wistfully. "The poor little thing will be half-Rebel and half-Yankee. What do you make of that?"

"How do you feel about your mamma having Duncan's baby?" Jeremy asked cautiously.

Salina shrugged. "You mean so soon after Daddy's death? I can only be happy for them. Things like that happen between married people..."

"You don't feel threatened, or angry, or even a little resentful?"

"No," Salina said simply. "In fact, I think this baby will do Mamma a world of good, providing the pregnancy doesn't risk her life or the life of the child. What a sense of humor the good Lord has! It is almost comic when you think about it. Duncan, never having been married, is suddenly bound in wedlock to his dead friend's widow, inheriting two grown children and about to become a father in his own right for the very first time. It's quite ironic, don't you think?"

Jeremy didn't quite see the humor. "Ironic? More aptly a shock for everyone involved! Half-Reb, half-Yank—as you said, Salina, poor little thing."

"In my mind, I imagine that the Lord takes each of our lives like a single thread and then weaves us all together in His perfect tapestry,"

Salina commented, her voice low and melodic. "We might see bits of the pattern now and again, because we can see the under side of the work. But sometimes He allows us a glimpse of His intentions, and we try to envision what the front side might look like when it's all complete. He works on the tapestry in His own good time, until He weaves the pattern exactly the way He sees fit. In the end, I believe it will be worth the wait to see the finished work—His design in our lives, to realize how we each blend into the tapestry of His will. Perhaps this baby of Mamma and Duncan's will bring a special blessing. Who's to say? God alone knows the future plans He has in store for each us."

Jeremy nodded, noting the wisdom in what Salina was saying. "You're taking all of this rather well."

"I can do little else when the decisions are not mine to make and the outcome is beyond my control. Fighting the inevitable is useless," Salina remarked. "Each morning I ask the Lord to give me the strength to deal with what is happening in my own life—one day at a time. I am accountable for what I do. I want to affect those around me for His glory. He is faithful, He strengthens my faith, and He helps me to accept what I can do nothing about. His ways are higher than ours."

"This is very true," Jeremy agreed. He smiled tenderly at her.

Salina suddenly said, "You know, I have something else of interest to show you. I'll be right back." She ducked behind the quilts hanging on a clothesline strung from one wall to the other at the far end of the cabin. The quilts divided the sleeping quarters from the main room, concealing the bed, a washstand, and a small bureau. At the foot of the bedstead stood Salina's humpbacked traveling trunk. Opening the lid, Salina took but a minute to locate the letter Mary Edith brought over three days ago. "Here it is!"

Jeremy studied the envelope addressed to Salina—in his own handwriting. The letter was dated nearly a month ago. He tapped the envelope against his palm. "I meant to ask you: Why did you never write back to me? I've sent at least a dozen letters to you since October..."

"Jeremy, that letter you're holding was never posted. Mary Edith happened upon that letter, which was in Lottie's possession. How do you suppose Lottie might get her hands on my letter?"

"She's been *intercepting* my letters to you," Jeremy said, abashed.

"And probably mine to you as well." Salina shared an example. "Mary Edith told me you visited Little Ivy shortly after I departed for Richmond with the Careys. You didn't even know that I had gone, because you never got the note I left for you in the hollow oak tree near the old schoolhouse."

"No, I never received any messages from you in that oak tree." A nervous tic worked along Jeremy's jawline. "Nothing since your father died."

"Precisely." Salina nodded. "But I've left messages for you there on several occasions—none of which have been found. If Lottie was following me, which now seems more likely than not, she either confiscated those letters or destroyed them so you wouldn't find them."

"Do you have any proof?" Jeremy queried.

"No, but Mary Edith thinks that Lottie might have more. It's merely a matter of where she has them hidden," Salina replied. "Lottie has been rather cordial with the Yankee soldiers stationed at Fairfax—especially Lance Colby. Mary Edith says Lottie has no true loyalty for one side or the other. She merely goes along with whoever will best benefit herself at any given time."

Jeremy nodded slowly, seeing the pieces fall together. "Lottie took letters from me, promising she'd mail them off to you—we were moving fast and riding hard—and I was gullible enough to believe she would." Jeremy's stomach churned with loathing. *What on earth had possessed me to trust Lottie over Salina in the first place?* He had no answer, save his own obstinate folly. But he had learned a hard lesson and was determined not to repeat it.

"Did you ask Lottie to mend your jacket?" Salina prodded, almost dreading his answer.

"My lieutenant's jacket?" Jeremy questioned. "No, I never asked her to mend it—though the shabby old thing could have used a good dose of repair. I lost it about a week ago. I thought I hung it over a hedgerow, and it mysteriously disappeared while I was taking a bath..."

"Lottie has it, Jeremy. I've seen it myself," Salina said evenly. "The day I arrived with Charlie Graham at Fairfax Station, his family was there to take him home. For whatever reason, Lottie was there and offered me a ride, which I hesitantly accepted. I fell right into her trap. She went to great lengths to point out to me what a favor she was doing by mending your jacket, supposedly at your request."

Jeremy shook his sandy head. "She's been playing us against each other at every turn."

Salina nodded her dark head affirmatively. "And she's dragged Colby right in the middle of it, too."

"What has she done to us? What have *I* done to us?" Jeremy ran a hand through his hair. "Because I believed her, you've had to suffer.

I've made us both suffer because I misplaced my trust. Can you forgive me for that?"

"We'll work at it together. In time, we can repair the damage." Salina touched his arm tenderly.

Jeremy took her face in his hands. "We can start fresh..."

"All right," Salina agreed. "I'm willing to give it a try if you are."

"I love you, Salina." The grin he flashed at her held just a trace of rascality.

Salina framed his jaw with her hands and brought his head down to meet her mouth. "I love you, too, Lieutenant Barnes," she murmured against his lips. Too soon time and distance would part them again, but at last things were in the open between them. The mending of hearts had begun.

Chapter Fifteen

*H*e sat on the floor in front of the crackling fire, leaning his back against the hearth, watching Salina make quick work of cleaning up their supper dishes. Jeremy's long legs were stretched out in front of him, his stomach full and content from the hearty meal. A man would not go hungry in her kitchen. He'd had Jubilee's stew countless times, but he liked Salina's even better. He heard her humming, and he could see the thin sheen of perspiration beading her forehead as she worked so near the heat-emanating stove. Several of her curls had escaped the knot at the nape of her neck, and they hung down in wisps in front of her ears. Color was high on her cheekbones, and she exuded a sense of comfort to him. Whether she knew it or not, Salina was like her mamma, and the inherent hospitality made the little cabin a welcome haven, as Shadowcreek had always been for him, a safe refuge in times of troubles past. Absently, he scratched the ears of the big furry dog at his side. Duchess had eaten, too, and seemed satisfied with her new surroundings.

"That's done," Salina said more to herself than to Jeremy. She brushed her hands together and discarded her apron.

Jeremy noted the dark black of her dress and regretfully was reminded of the reason she was in mourning. He met her eyes, and he flashed a most disarming smile at her. "Come, sit down by me," he said, extending his left arm in invitation.

Salina's head rested in the hollow between his shoulder and his jaw, and she savored the feel of his protective arm around her shoulders. Her hand rested on his chest, and beneath her fingertips she felt the steady beat of his heart. "Jeremy?"

"Mmmm?" he replied.

"Will you sing for me?" she requested.

"What do you want to hear?"

"Whatever you sing when you're out riding a raid," she whispered.

"Well, sometimes we sing just that, *Riding a Raid*. It was written after Stuart's first ride around McClellan," he told her.

Duchess's ears perked up as Jeremy's sang in a clear, rich voice:

> 'Tis Stonewall, the Rebel, that leans on his sword,
> And while we are mounting, prays low to the Lord:
> "Now each cavalier that loves Honor and Right,
> Let him follow the feather of Stuart tonight."
> Come tighten your girth and slacken your rein;
> Come buckle your blanket and holster again;
> Try the click of your trigger and balance your blade,
> For he must ride sure that goes Riding a Raid!

Three other verses followed, and then Jeremy changed his tune to that of *The Girl I Left Behind Me*:

> The hour was sad I left the maid,
> A ling'ring farewell taking;
> Her sighs and tears my steps delayed,
> I thought her heart was breaking;
> In hurried words her name I blessed,
> I breath'd the vows that bind me,
> And to my heart in anguish pressed
> The girl I left behind me.

A small smile lifted the corners of Salina's mouth. "Sing some more," she encouraged.

Jeremy glanced down at her. She was nearly asleep. "Join me. I hear you know this song quite well."

Salina's smiled widened. "Who told you that?"

"Why, I believe it was the good General himself." Jeremy threaded his fingers in her curls, stroking her head in a slow, lazy motion. "I understand the duet you two sang got a standing ovation at the White House levee. I should have stayed to hear it. Sing the rest with me."

Salina complied, mingling her sweet soprano with his deeper baritone:

> *The hope of final victory,*
> *Within my bosom burning,*
> *Is mingling with sweet thoughts of thee,*
> *And of my fond returning;*
> *But should I ne'er return again,*
> *Still worth my love thou'lt find me,*
> *Dishonor's breath shall never stain*
> *The name I'll leave behind me.*

Salina snuggled into the crook of his arm, and the two sat for a long time in the reassuring quietness of the little cabin, with only the sound of crackling fire snapping in their ears. Jeremy's lips tarried near her brow. He felt much better than he had in weeks, and he thanked God for supplying the courage to come here tonight to make peace with Salina. The love he felt for her swelled his heart, and he wondered what it would be like to really come home to a place like this, knowing full well that she was the one he wanted to come home to. He determined that one day he'd marry her, if she would have him. But not now. With the war still raging, he had no desire to make a widow of her at such a young age. The South had far too many widows and orphans already, and inevitably there would be more to come.

Jeremy effortlessly scooped Salina's sleeping form into his arms. He thought she was still too thin. He carried her to the bed behind the curtain of quilts. Salina stirred to half-awareness as Jeremy covered her with the goose-down comforter. She tried to sit upright. "Are you leaving me? Don't go without saying good-bye."

"Sssshhh, little scarecrow. I'm not leaving yet," he assured her. He caressed her shoulder. "You sleep now, and dream of me."

Her thick, dark curls fanned out over the pillow, her lashes dark crescents against her cheeks. "I usually do," she murmured sleepily.

Jeremy grinned. He sat at the table for over an hour, the solitude offering him a chance to write up his reports of the past few days' accomplishments. He looked up when Duchess crossed the floor and went to the door. "You want to go out?" he asked.

The big, fluffy dog growled a warning when his hand touched the porcelain doorknob.

Salina heard it and woke up in an instant. Rubbing her eyes with one hand, she pushed the hanging quilt aside.

Jeremy touched the doorknob a second time, and Duchess growled louder. He saw Salina and said with a shrug. "She must not want me to go outside."

An icy finger sent a chill down Salina's spine. Her green eyes were wide and filled with apprehension. "No, don't go outside. Someone's out there. I can feel it."

Glancing around the tiny cabin, Jeremy discovered there was no back door. If he should have to leave for any reason—namely a Yankee patrol—his only route of escape would be to break out through one of the windows. "Odd," he murmured. "The cabin behind this one, where the horses are stabled, has two doors. I wonder why this cabin has only one. One way in, one way out..." He didn't like feeling trapped.

Salina listened closely, watching Duchess pace to and fro in front of the door. She heard horses whinny and nicker, and there was no denying the sound of muffled voices floating on the cold night air—voices in close proximity. *Colby had said something about the Yankees knowing she was here...*

Jeremy heard them as well. "Get your gun," he commanded softly. "Put on a coat. If I have to leave here, I'm not leaving you behind."

"Don't be ridiculous. You'd travel much faster without me," she returned firmly. "But you're not going anywhere. I think whoever was out there has decided we're not worth the bother."

Jeremy strained to listen for any sound that might give a clue as to who or what was out there in the darkness. But there was nothing. Try as he might, though, he couldn't get his heart to stop its wild pounding or shake the uncanny feeling that he and Salina had just passed through an extremely dangerous moment. He hugged her to him fiercely, holding her and rocking her in his arms.

☆☆☆☆☆☆☆

"How many horses, Farnham?" a Yankee major demanded.

"Three, Major," the soldier reported. "What do you make of that?"

"The little lass has some company, that's what I make of it. I figured as soon as she'd come back, he'd not be long in followin'." The Major leaned to one side and spat out a stream of tobacco juice. "I figured it were jist a matter of time. In fact, this could work to our advantage if we play it right."

"How so?" Farnham asked for clarification. "You think this has something to do with the missing supply wagons we're supposed to recover?"

"Could be. According to my sister, he's been into guns before, down San Diego way." The Major continued to inspect the scene. "But I've got him now," the blue-clad commander hissed. "I'll get to him."

"Sir?" The soldier again looked askance at his commanding officer.

"We get her, we get him. We get him, we get the arms and ammunition. It's that easy." The Major nodded slowly, a plan brewing behind his fierce eyes. "How many horses did you say?"

"Three, but only one of cavalry caliber," the soldier replied. "Do you want me to round them up?"

"No, we ain't gonna steal them horses tonight, but I'll keep the notion in mind." The Major nodded. "For now we'll just watch. Got to make plans. Then we'll lay the trap and spring it on him. Then he's dead."

"Who's dead?" Farnham wasn't quite following the Major's train of thought.

John Barnes's eyes narrowed into angry slits, his jaw clamped tightly. "My Rebel nephew."

✰✩✩✩✩✩✩

"Papa, please. You've got to listen to me!" Mary Edith tugged repeatedly on her father's elbow. Caleb Armstrong had a hard look in his eyes as he glanced down at his daughter. She continued, great tears balancing on the fringes of her sable lashes, "I know Jeremy Barnes is *not* responsible for what Lottie claims!"

Mary Edith turned on her sister with censure in her voice. "Lottie, you are lying! I *know* you are! A Confederate lieutenant's jacket proves nothing!"

Caleb crossed his arms over his chest, his square jaw set firmly. "I heard the noises myself in the loft not a fortnight ago—and not for the first time, either, mind you. I mistook it as soldiers searching for a place to rest. Lottie has confessed to me that it was she who was up there, and that it was she who accidentally knocked the jacket from the loft to the barn floor. She was not alone."

"I have no doubt that Lottie was in the loft, Papa, or that she was not alone. But I'm certain that it wasn't Jeremy who was with her." Mary Edith's blue eyes implored her father to relent. "You know how friendly Lottie was with that Yankee Lieutenant Lance Colby. She spent lots of time with him—hours on end—all those long rides and the parties at General Stoughton's headquarters in Fairfax."

Lottie flashed a cutting glance at her twin sister, and it did not go unnoticed by Caleb. He lifted Lottie's chin and studied her cornflower blue eyes intently. "Could that be it, Lottie? Could the baby you profess to be carrying have a Yankee lieutenant as its sire and not a Confederate one?"

Lottie jerked free of her father's hold without reply. Contrived teardrops rolled down her pale cheeks.

Caleb hunkered down in front of the bench Lottie rigidly sat upon. He took her by the shoulders and forced her to look at him. He said determinedly, "Listen to me, Miss Charlotte Virginia Armstrong. It matters not to me *which* color his jacket might be. I'll hunt him down and see that he makes an honest woman of you. Rest assured!"

Mary Edith wiped the tears that threatened to fall, and she sighed heavily. At the very least she had succeeded in putting doubt in her father's mind. Mary Edith knew that Lottie would do anything to come between Jeremy and Salina. Yet never had Mary Edith dreamed that her own sister could be so malicious. She recalled the day when Lance Colby had mistaken her for Lottie. Mary Edith was convinced that it was Colby who had assisted Lottie in this predicament. However, Mary Edith had no means of proving that Colby was responsible. The Yankee lieutenant had returned to Washington, but surely there must be some way to get word to him. If anyone could find him, Salina would be the one, of that Mary Edith was certain.

Mary Edith caught up with her father just before he reached the barn. "Where are you going, Papa?" Her breath hung like a misty halo in the cold night air.

"I'm going to search out Jeremy Barnes," Caleb answered tightly. "I'll see Salina first. She'd know best where that scoundrel can be found."

"Papa, no, please!" Mary Edith entreated. "Give me a chance. I can find Colby and you can question him. Spare me a week's time? Just don't say anything to anyone about all this yet."

"What makes you so certain that it's not Jeremy? I was under the impression that he and Salina had a falling out. Who's to say he wouldn't seek Lottie's company?" Caleb demanded.

Mary Edith told him plainly, "Papa, Jeremy was in Richmond at the time of Lottie's claimed indiscretion. Salina was staying with the Careys, and Jeremy was there in the capital. Colby, on the other hand, has been stationed here ever since Fredericksburg. He has been a regular visitor to Ivywood, and you know as well as I do that Colby bears a resemblance to Jeremy. You say you saw a blond head—they're both blond." She told him of the day the Yankee lieutenant mistook her for Lottie. "I don't believe Jeremy would put himself into such a compromising position."

"Jeremy Barnes is no saint, Mary Edith. I'm sure he's just as hot-blooded as any of the other beaux in the county. Boys will be boys." Caleb cleared his throat. "I'll grant you forty-eight hours. If you can manage to find Lieutenant Colby, I'll question him."

"You'd force Jeremy Barnes into wedlock at the muzzle end of a shotgun quick enough—no questions asked—yet you'd take time to quiz Lance Colby? Shotguns don't apply to Yankees, Papa?" Mary Edith queried snippily, her eyes narrowing in distaste at her father's double standard.

"Don't press me, daughter," Caleb Armstrong warned. "Another word out of you, and I'll rescind the offer of time to find that blue-bellied lieutenant. Understood?"

Mary Edith nodded. "Thank you, Papa," she whispered fervently. She allowed him to help her ascend into the buggy, and she drove herself back to Little Ivy.

First thing the next morning, she headed to Shadowcreek. Mary Edith wanted to be the one to talk to Salina. She didn't want her to learn of the nightmarish scenario from Lottie!

It was Jeremy Barnes who answered the knock on the cabin door. "Mornin', Mary Edith."

"What are you doing here?" Mary Edith asked nervously, quite surprised to see him.

"Patching things up with Salina." Jeremy's grin was lopsided. "She's fixing breakfast. Would you care to come in?"

Mary Edith crossed the threshold into the little cabin and found half a dozen other gray-uniformed cavalrymen already seated around the small kitchen table. Salina was cooking up flapjacks, stirring oatmeal porridge, and frying up bacon while the coffee pot boiled. Duchess rarely left Salina's side and paced back and forth with her between the counter and the pantry shelves.

Jeremy, serving up Salina's breakfast to his fellow riders, introduced Mary Edith to Curlie Hawkins, Kidd Carney, Cutter Montgomery, Pepper Markham, Jake Landon, and Browne Williams.

Cutter vacated his chair and offered the seat to Mary Edith. "Ma'am?"

"No, but thank you," Mary Edith politely declined. "I've eaten already. You all sit down and enjoy. Salina's a good cook."

"Amen!" Browne acclaimed. "The biscuits are as light and flaky as like my mammy's used to be."

Salina smiled as she heard this and other complimentary remarks Jeremy's riders made. She glanced over her shoulder and caught Mary Edith's troubled eyes. "Is something wrong?" Salina asked. A feeling of strong trepidation washed over her.

"I need to talk to you—and Jeremy, too, since he's here." Mary Edith nodded. "It's rather important."

"Jeremy, please take Mary Edith down to the footbridge. I'll be along directly," Salina assured them. She sensed the matter of urgency in Mary Edith's tone, and she hurried to finish frying up the last of the pancake batter.

Pepper confiscated the spatula from Salina's hand. "You go on, Miss Salina. We'll manage breakfast."

"Thank you, Pepper." Salina wiped her hands on her apron. She shrugged into her coat and let Duchess follow her out into the clearing. Mary Edith and Jeremy were already talking between themselves when she arrived. "What? What is it?"

Jeremy hung his head, absently kicking the base of the bridge with his right boot. "Seems Lottie is still up to her tricks."

Salina looked at him, then at Mary Edith. "Meaning?"

"Lottie's told Papa that she's with child—Jeremy's child," Mary Edith said gravely.

"She's lying!" Salina returned without hesitation. She looked back to Jeremy, but she could not read the expression in his eyes.

A few long moments of near-silence passed, and finally Jeremy met Salina's flashing green eyes. "You believe I'm innocent of what Lottie claims?" Jeremy asked. He needed reassurance of Salina's trust in him.

"Yes, I believe you're innocent. I think it's preposterous! We both know how she's tried to divide us," Salina pointed out, clutching Jeremy's sleeve. "It hasn't worked, and now she's grabbing at straws."

Jeremy's pride welled inside of him. Salina hadn't questioned him. She trusted him implicitly. She had never doubted him. She only continued to believe in him, and for that he was grateful—however unworthy of her enduring confidence he might feel. He took Salina into the circle of his arms and hugged her tightly to him, wordlessly thanking her for her unwavering support. They'd suffered enough deceit.

Salina rested her head against Jeremy's shoulder, intertwining her fingers with his. "Mary Edith, what do you propose we do about this situation?"

"Wire Colby. Tell him you need him to come back—immediately," Mary Edith instructed. "He'll do what you ask, Salina. We all know that."

"And if he is the one responsible?" Salina raised an eyebrow in question.

"Then Papa will see that he quickly inherits a wife," Mary Edith said matter-of-factly. "Colby, even though a Yankee, seems the type of man who would stand by his honor, wouldn't you agree?"

Salina nodded. She glanced up at Jeremy. "Shall I wire him?"

"In order to get all of this cleared up—yes, by all means," Jeremy answered.

☆☆☆☆☆☆☆

Salina was at Tabitha's boarding house when the wire was delivered bearing Colby's reply:

> *Miss Salina Hastings*
> *c/o Tabitha Wheeler*
> *Fairfax Court House, Virginia*
>
> *I am in receipt of your telegram. I stand guilty as charged and will honorably accept responsibility for said actions. A three-day pass in process of approval. I'll be there and be done with it as quickly as possible to spare the Armstrongs any further embarrassment. Regards to my future wife, sincerest apologies to her family.*
> *— Lieutenant Lance Colby*
> *United States Army*

Necessity along with the brevity of Colby's granted leave dictated all due haste. Lottie Armstrong unwillingly became the wife of her Yankee lieutenant before the week was out. Reverend Yates dutifully conducted the rites, pronounced them man and wife, and in that moment Lottie truly felt ill. She hated Colby, silently vowing that she always would. If Colby hadn't been so truthful, honorable, and gallant, Lottie's scheming might have worked. But now it was all for naught.

She glanced at the solid gold band circling her finger, and then she lifted her eyes to meet Colby's.

"Cheer up, Mrs. Colby," he said harshly, in a tone for her ears only. "There's a war on. There's always the chance you could end up a widow."

"If I could be so lucky!" Lottie hissed coldly. She turned from him, only to encounter Salina Hastings and Jeremy Barnes standing with Mary Edith and her parents. Lottie exited the church before anyone could detect that her facade was crumbling. To admit she was getting her just reward for her treacherous scheming would be to own up to defeat. That she would not do. She viewed her marriage as a temporary setback. When she got her head straight and gave it some more thought, she'd design a way to use it to her best advantage.

Jeremy gave Salina's hand a squeeze. She looked up at him. "You're going to confront her, aren't you?"

"I think I have the right." Jeremy nodded. "Stay here. This should only take a minute," he said and followed Lottie outside. Once and for all he was going to cut through the charades.

He didn't have far to go before he found her. Jeremy said coolly, "I have to hand it to Colby. I didn't think he'd voluntarily go through with the wedding."

"He doesn't care about me," Lottie retorted icily. "He's in love with your precious Salina. But he knows she'll not have him, so perhaps by marrying into the family he can somehow manage to be near her."

Jeremy shook his head. He could see clearly now that Lottie was still trying to build a barrier between himself and Salina. But Lottie's plotting had blown up in her face. He knew it, and so did she. "I have to respect your new husband, for evidently he knows you quite well. Yet amazingly enough, he was still willing to atone for your mistake. I'm sorry for you, Lottie—and for Colby. I truly am."

"Well, don't be. I don't want your pity!" Lottie seethed.

"I know. You wanted me instead," Jeremy replied. "I'm out of your reach. You'll never have me, Lottie. Ever. My heart belongs to Salina, my soul to the Lord. Nothing you can say or do will change that."

Lottie took a swing in blind fury. Her hand collided with the side of Jeremy's face. "I don't know what I ever saw in you! You're just a filthy son of a wretched gambler! You're nothing but a low-down, sneaking..."

A severe blue glare stifled her string of insults. Jeremy exercised his jaw and rubbed the place where her stinging slap had connected. He remarked sardonically, "For a pretty lady, you certainly have an ugly way about you, Lottie."

Jeremy strode purposefully away from her and Lottie dissolved into genuine tears.

In the next instant, Colby towered over Lottie. He was smartly dressed in his blue uniform, boasting yellow piping and shiny brass buttons. He lifted Lottie's quivering chin and wiped away her salty tears with a gloved finger. "Come, come, my dear," he said sarcastically. "I realize your tears aren't those of happiness or joy, but we must learn to make the best of a disagreeable situation. We have made our bed, Mrs. Colby, and must now lie in it."

A few yards away, Caleb Armstrong was approached by a blue-clad officer but both stayed in the shadows behind the church. "Major Grant," Caleb acknowledged.

"Well, at least that's settled." Duncan nodded toward the newly-weds. "All's well that ends well?"

"Lottie will make your lieutenant miserable, I suspect. How is *your* wife?" Caleb quickly shifted from the subject of his daughter's hasty marriage to the Major's own.

"Annelise is well and sends her best to you and Priscilla. I have here a bank draft and a letter for Salina. Would you mind delivering the letter to her in a few days? I'd prefer that she didn't learn that I'd come here today, but I didn't want to let Lieutenant Colby down. He's a good man, in spite of the situation he and Lottie have gotten themselves mixed up in."

"According to my Mary Edith, your lieutenant isn't fully to blame. I've turned a blind eye for years. I love both my twins dearly, but I'm beginning to see clearly that Lottie certainly has ways of manipulating people and events to suit her needs," Caleb acquiesced.

"She used her beauty and charm to sweep Colby off his feet, and it worked too well," Duncan affirmed. "Well, I suppose I must thank you for not shooting him outright. Colby might not have fared so well with another girl's father. He's a valuable man to me, and to the service of the Union."

"Then I may rely on your honor, sir, to see that he proves himself as good a husband as the separations of war will allow," Caleb asserted. "Lottie is free to stay with us at Ivywood until such a time as Colby might call her to Washington."

"If you ever venture to Washington, Caleb, be sure to let me know. I'll arrange for you have the finest accommodations at your disposal," Duncan promised. "You've been a great source of help to me."

"I'm fond of Annelise, and of Salina," Caleb admitted. "As long as your generous financial support and protection continues, Salina will not lack in basic necessities."

Duncan saluted. "I thank you for that. She still doesn't know where the money comes from?"

"She'll not hear it from me, rest assured, Major Grant." Caleb winked.

"Thank you, Caleb." Duncan slipped back into the shadows and watched Salina and Jeremy Barnes from a distance. He was a little surprised that the Rebel lieutenant would risk appearing in so public a place, but then Duncan spied the six men under his command waiting at the outskirts of the churchyard. Together, they presented a tough, rugged front—a small force, but one to be reckoned with.

Duncan had other things to do as far as the war was concerned, but one day he supposed he would be reassigned to tracking down the Rebel lieutenant. The Western Campaign had failed, but Duncan suspected that Jeremy Barnes would find other ways to aggravate the Yankees.

Duncan's thoughts turned to the Rebel lieutenant's uncle. There had been no word of him in the past few weeks, almost as if he'd disappeared, but Duncan knew John Barnes would resurface from whatever hole he was hiding out in eventually. And when he did, there was no telling what degree of retribution Barnes was capable of inflicting. Garrett Hastings was dead. Annelise was safe in Gettysburg. Ethan was well behind Confederate lines. And Salina had Lincoln's signature on her papers. But Duncan wondered how much protection that really afforded Salina should John Barnes choose to willfully overlook it. And if Major Barnes ever got a hold of Jeremy, there would be no way for Duncan to intervene. Jeremy was beyond his assistance.

Shivering in part to the cold and in part to the dislike he felt for John Barnes, Duncan wheeled his horse and headed for the headquarters of General Stoughton, near the court house. Once he delivered the bundle of dispatches he carried, Duncan would return to the Union capital. In Washington he'd do a bit of undercover tracking to locate Jeremy's uncle. It might take some doing, but Duncan was sure he could find out precisely what Barnes's recent orders contained.

☆☆☆☆☆☆☆

Ethan and Taylor Sue were waiting outside the cabin when Salina arrived with Jeremy. Duchess had growled at them each time they attempted to approach the porch. She would not let them any closer than the front stairs.

"Good girl, Duchess." Salina petted her dog's head affectionately. "But these are friends, and they are welcome. Come on, let me introduce them to you. This is my brother, Ethan, and his wife, Taylor Sue." Salina gave each of them a hug with Duchess looking on intently.

Taylor Sue and Ethan held their hands out to the skeptical guard dog. "So you have a protector." Ethan chuckled. "Good. I'll worry a little less about you and Taylor Sue out here alone now that I know you've got Duchess to look after you."

Salina hugged Taylor Sue again. "I'm so pleased you're here!"

Ethan and Jeremy exchanged speaking glances. "Back on speaking terms, are we?" Ethan nodded, indicating the obvious change in the relationship between his best friend and his sister.

"We've come to an agreement." Jeremy smiled. "I love her."

"Yes, well, tell me something I don't already know," Ethan clapped a hand on Jeremy's shoulder.

"All right, how about this? You missed the wedding," Jeremy said simply.

"Wedding?" Ethan exploded. "You've gone and married my sister without asking me for her hand?"

Jeremy cast a quick glance back at the girls, thankful that they hadn't overheard Ethan's outburst. "No, no. I know better than that." He shook his sandy-blond head and put a finger to his lips. "Sssshhh..."

"Explain yourself." Ethan's eyes flashed.

"Your cousin Lottie was the bride earlier today," Jeremy whispered roughly.

"Lottie? Who'd marry her?" Ethan inquired incredulously.

"Maybe you'd better sit down," Jeremy quipped. "Come on inside. We'll get you some coffee."

"What kind of substitute are you using for coffee beans?" Ethan wanted to know. "Chicory? Peanuts?"

Jeremy shook his head. "Real coffee—the genuine article. We acquired some on a raid not long ago," he told Ethan. Once everyone was indoors, coffee was poured while the girls prepared supper for all.

Curlie and Jake fell asleep near the fire. Kidd Carney played softly on a harmonica. Pepper whittled away at a chunk of wood, and Cutter and Browne wrote up reports on their little band's recent activities in the surrounding area. Jeremy and Ethan sipped the aromatic black brew from tin coffee mugs and talked between themselves.

"So she tried to pawn a baby off on you." Ethan was astonished. "That conniving bit of baggage."

"Salina wired Colby in Washington, told him what Lottie was up to. He got leave as soon as he was able, and this morning they were wed." Jeremy nodded solemnly.

"How'd Colby convince Uncle Caleb that you weren't the man and he was?" Ethan wondered.

"I didn't ask, but evidently he had the requisite proof, thank goodness. Remember your court-martial?" Jeremy tipped his head to one side and lifted an eyebrow in askance.

"Yes, rather vividly," Ethan returned. "What's that got to do with anything?"

"I felt just like I was going before a panel," Jeremy confided. "Your uncle was the sole committee member, and Lottie was the defendant while I stood accused. Caleb asked me a single question: Had I compromised Lottie's virtue? I replied that I had not. Then he interrogated Colby, relentlessly, and he listened to what Salina and Mary Edith told him. When that was finished, he said he wanted time to think about it. But Colby never left him alone. The two of them went behind closed doors. I suspect Colby confessed to more than what was proper to discuss in front of your sister. When they came out of the study, it was decided that Colby and Lottie would be expediently married."

"Whew." Ethan shook his head. "Must've taken some nerve on Colby's part to face up to Uncle Caleb."

"Must have," Jeremy agreed. "Your uncle made his apologies for jumping to conclusions without pursuing the facts. Then he invited me to the wedding. Lottie turned such a pale color she was nearly white as the snow on the lawn, and she's been cursing me ever since."

"So, she's married to a Yankee." Ethan shook his head. "Curious...I wonder if Colby will have any success in keeping Lottie in line."

"I seriously doubt that." Jeremy chuckled softly. "Ethan, if Colby hadn't been man enough to reply to Salina's telegram..." He ran a hand through his tousled blond hair. "I don't even like to think about what might have happened otherwise..."

Ethan nodded. "So, are you asking me for my sister's hand?"

Jeremy's blue eyes fastened on Salina, working in the kitchen. "I'm not sure."

"Not sure that she loves you?" Ethan rolled his expressive eyes. "You know that she does."

"I don't doubt her anymore, I doubt myself," Jeremy admitted.

"But you love her. You told me you did," Ethan countered.

"It's something else." Jeremy shrugged.

"A matter of trust?" Ethan inquired.

"No, not anymore." Jeremy sighed. "I know she's trustworthy. I just haven't wanted to tell her what I've been up to because I know she'll worry."

"What *have* you been up to, Barnes?" Ethan was curious. "You know I've been studying and working at Chimborazo, but tell me— how is it that you're here?"

Jeremy's voice was scarcely audible. "We're gathering arms, ammunition, explosives. It's all captured supplies from the Yankees. We have a secret depot in this area, a few miles away. We collect inventory and then redistribute as necessary."

"How are you getting past the patrols?" Ethan asked. "We had our hands full trying to ditch the Yankees on our way here."

"There's a gap in the picket lines between the Federal outposts at Centreville and Chantilly," Jeremy explained. "That Yankee General Stoughton has been so busy carrying on his social life with extravagant parties and soirees that he pays little heed to the business of war at hand. Another of Stuart's scouts, John Mosby, led a successful mission not long ago. Miss Antonia Ford supplied him with certain intelligence that made it work."

"Antonia Ford—her father's a merchant in Fairfax," Ethan recalled.

Jeremy nodded. "Yes. She's a friend of Mosby's and of Stuart's. She forwards vital information—much along the same lines as Salina used to do. Though I'm not sure if she's using secret codes or not."

"Southern women can be dangerous." Ethan grinned. "Their loyalties are oftentimes stronger than any chains ever forged."

"So much so," Jeremy confirmed, "that this General Stoughton reportedly wanted to send all loyal Rebel women behind our lines, or make them sign an Oath of Allegiance to the Union, so as not to be a threat to their lines of defense or the security of their capital."

Ethan absorbed the meaning of Jeremy's remark. "How safe is it for Salina and Taylor Sue to be here?"

"Not very, but you know how stubborn they are," Jeremy acknowledged. "I've felt somewhat better about the situation since the arrival of Duchess, but still." He shrugged. "Last night, Duchess alerted us to something. I didn't get a good look, but we heard somebody outside the cabin."

"I don't want them to stay here alone," Ethan said firmly.

Jeremy put a restraining hand on his friend's forearm. "If you object too loudly, it will only serve to strengthen their resolve to live here. I try to look at it realistically. There are hundreds of women living alone while their men are off fighting. Take the women over at Sully as an example. I'm just hoping that once the novelty of having her own place wears off, Salina might see reason and move in with Mary Edith, taking Taylor Sue with her. There's plenty of room for the three of them at Little Ivy. For now, I'll have to content myself with the fact that I'll be in the area and can check up on them every few days."

"But you've said nothing to Salina of this?" questioned Ethan.

"No." Jeremy shook his head. "It has to be done so she thinks it's her idea."

Ethan chuckled. "You know my sister well—which brings me back to my initial question. Are you going to ask me for her hand?"

"All in good time." Jeremy winked. "When I think she's ready."

"You mean when *you're* ready. What's stopping you?" Ethan wondered.

Images from Jeremy's past flashed through his mind. There were lots of things that made him hesitate. "I'd rather just give it time," he said, evading Ethan's question. "I'll know when the timing's right."

Following supper, Pepper and Kidd Carney moved the kitchen table aside, and Curlie and Browne rolled up the scattered rugs. With the floor bare, they had ample room to dance. Kidd Carney played his harmonica and Cutter was on the fiddle, and they had only just started into a lively rendition of *Dixie* when they were interrupted by Duchess barking at boots stomping across the porch.

Ethan shot Jeremy a look, as if to say, *Better some protection than none...*

Jeremy pulled his LeMat revolver from his holster and stalked toward the door. "Expecting company, Salina?"

"No," she answered in an anxious whisper.

From inside, they could hear the voices outside. "This has to be it—Lieutenant Barnes said she lived near the ruins." It was Weston Bentley, and upon recognizing that fact, Jeremy threw open the door.

"You could have given us some warning," Jeremy cautioned. "Sneaking around like that might get you boys hurt." He returned his revolver to its holster.

Bentley saluted, as did Harrison Claibourne and Boone Hunter. "Will do better next time, sir." They willingly gave up their coats to

Salina and Taylor Sue once they were inside and hurried to the fireplace to warm themselves.

Bentley made a show of rubbing his fingers together and closed his eyes as if enjoying some great ecstasy.

"You all right, Bentley?" Jeremy inquired solicitously.

"Yes, sir, thank you for asking. I don't suppose that you've forgotten how cold it can get out there when you're on reconnaissance duty, have you, Lieutenant?"

Jeremy took the prodding good-naturedly. "If you're implying that we've spent all day holed up in this nice, toasty warm cabin, you're wrong. If you all are hungry, there's some supper leftover."

"Thank you, ma'am," Harrison remarked when Taylor Sue provided a bowl of stew. "Hey, Boone, move your feet, would you? They're taking up all the room under the table."

Boone Hunter grinned sheepishly as Salina set a plate of hot food before him. "I'll keep my big feet out of your way, too, miss."

"They're not in my way, Boone. Don't worry." Salina returned the smile.

Jeremy clapped. "Let them eat, and let's get on with the dance."

Sweet laughter mingled with heartier chuckles amidst the music. Jeremy commanded Kidd Carney and Cutter to play the *Palmyra Schottische*, which was Salina's favorite tune to dance to. Bentley had the audacity to cut in on him.

Salina giggled, her nose crinkling merrily and green eyes glittering happily. This was one of those nights she'd contentedly write about in her journal at a later time. It pleased her to see the mild displeasure in Jeremy's stern expression as she was handed from Bentley's embrace, to Ethan's, to Harrison's, and then to Jake's. Each took turns swirling Salina and then Taylor Sue around and around and around. By the time Cutter and Kidd Carney played the *Cavalier's Waltz*, Salina was back in Jeremy's arms—until Boone cut in.

"Hunter!" Jeremy voiced his complaint, "I order you to give her back to me!"

"You may give orders in the field, Lieutenant." Salina smiled sweetly. "But tonight we're dispensing with rank here in our ballroom."

Boone was shaking with mirth and not quite paying attention to where he was putting his big feet, and he accidentally stepped on Salina's toes.

"Ouch!" she squealed. She quickly assured Boone that she was fine so as not to hurt his feelings. The other riders gave him enough grief about having feet so large; she didn't mean to offend him further.

Self-consciously, Boone backed away, careful not to step on Salina a second time. For all his care, his still managed to inadvertently kick the side of the fireplace.

"Boone!" Salina exclaimed.

"I apologize, Miss Salina! Honest, I didn't mean to hurt ya!" Boone's face flushed scarlet. "Here, Lieutenant. I'd better let you take care of your lady."

Salina, however, did not remain in Jeremy's arms this time. She moved to the fireplace, where an opening appeared directly behind the bricks. "Look! I *knew* there was something odd about the size of the hearth—see here!" She knelt down and glanced cautiously inside the yawning hole. Boone's inadvertent kick had sprung the release on a sliding panel.

"It's stairs leading downward." Ethan snatched the lantern from the table. He and Jeremy descended into the darkness, taking the light with them.

"It's a secret passageway, isn't it? Like the one that used to be in my room in the main house before the fire?" Salina called after them.

"Stay put, Salina," came Jeremy's order. "Don't come down until I tell you it's safe."

The ticking of the pendulum clock became absolutely annoying in the twenty minutes that passed with no sound from down below. Finally, Jeremy and Ethan returned, and they were covered with dust and cobwebs.

"It leads to the barn," Ethan told Salina. "When I think back to all the times Peter Tom seemed to move so quickly from place to place, he must have been traveling the distances underground. This passage has a tunnel that branches off and joins up with what used to be the tunnel coming from your room, and there's another that leads to the dairy. They're all connected."

"How bizarre," Salina whispered, the excitement of the discovery evident.

Jeremy was on his knees and Boone was beside him. "Boone, can you show me exactly where you think you kicked the bricks?"

Boone pointed. Jeremy touched the place, and the panel slid closed just as easily as it had moved open. Jeremy looked up at Salina. "You know what this means?" He settled back on his heels and wiped his palms on this thighs. "It means we could leave our horses out in the old corral in the woods beyond the dairy and come inside here without ever having to approach the cabin. We could also leave in a hurry, if need be."

"All these tunnels," Salina murmured, "like a maze beneath the surface."

Ethan's mind was still working fast and furious. "I'd be willing to wager that Peter Tom had used the passageways for years. In fact, I would even go so far as to say it would have made an excellent station for the Underground Railroad."

Salina's eyes locked with her brother's. It wasn't so far-fetched as to be unbelievable. "Jubilee must have known about it. One of her daughters escaped north, remember?"

"You were too young to remember that, Salina," Ethan argued.

"But Jubilee told me about it," Salina insisted.

"There is a room down there, not a big one, but space enough to hide a handful of people. Who's to say they weren't escaped slaves?" Jeremy shrugged.

Salina turned to Boone. "Your feet made this discovery possible. You realize that, don't you, Boone?"

"Well." Boone grinned shyly. "At least they're good for somethin'." Everyone had a good laugh.

Late that night, after they all had bedded down on the floor or up in the loft, Salina crept stealthily from behind the quilt that divided her room from the rest of the cabin.

"Where do you think you're going?" a throaty whisper growled.

"Jeremy?" She couldn't see him in the darkness, but she felt that he was close by. "Someone's out there again tonight."

"I know," Jeremy said lowly. "I don't have my field glasses, but I'd swear it's my uncle out there."

An icy finger trailed a sudden chill down Salina's spine. "Your uncle?"

"God is good, Salina. Tonight, He used Boone's big feet to reveal our exit route," Jeremy reflected.

"Yes, God is good," she repeated into the stillness. "Jeremy, do you think your uncle's followed you, or do you think he's just guessing because I'm here?"

"Hard to say," Jeremy dodged. "Go back to bed, Salina. As far as I can tell, he hasn't got enough men to make an attack."

"Maybe not tonight, but what about another time?" She spoke Jeremy's own thoughts aloud.

"We'll deal with that when we come to it," Jeremy said more gruffly than he meant to. "Go back to bed, I said." Thankfully, she did not argue with him. He scarcely heard her bare feet pad across the floor, though he heard the soft crunch of straw ticking as her weight pressed into the mattress followed by the whisper of the quilts as she snuggled beneath them. "Dream of me," he whispered, knowing full well she couldn't hear him. He resumed watching the woods from the window.

To avoid the risk of capture, all the men—including Ethan—slipped through the newly-discovered secret passage, disappearing long before first light.

Chapter Sixteen

*R*everend! Reverend Yates!" Lottie Armstrong Colby called out to the minister, out of breath.

"Lottie, what on earth?" Reverend Yates turned and came back to where she had stopped in front of the cooper's shop. "Is everything all right? Has something happened to your husband?"

"No, no, Lance is fine." Lottie was still panting, her countenance as white as a sheet. "It's..." She looked over her shoulder. "Reverend, can we go someplace where I can talk to you?"

"I'm off to the parsonage. Would you care to join my wife and me for our noontime meal?" he asked.

Lottie hesitated but then acquiesced. What she had to say to the Reverend could be shared with his wife as well. Mrs. Yates wouldn't say a word to anyone, Lottie was sure.

Reverend Yates waited until the meal was on the table and the three of them had held hands while he said grace before asking gently, "Now, then, what is it that has upset you so?"

Lottie wrung her hands together. "It's Jeremy's uncle—Major Barnes."

"Have you seen him?" Reverend Yates tried to hide his surprise.

"Yes." Lottie nodded, her cornflower blue eyes wide. "He nearly frightened the life out of me!"

"Where did you see him, dear?" Mrs. Yates passed her a plate stacked with fresh biscuits and a small dish of homemade peach preserves.

"He was in the barn at Ivywood. I don't know where he came from, or where he went, but he scared me." Lottie's voice trembled. "He knew that I had been at the gala in Fairfax with Lance last night at General Stoughton's headquarters. I didn't see him, but he had to be there, or how would he have seen me?"

"Go on, Lottie," Reverend Yates encouraged. "What did Major Barnes want with you?"

"He held a knife to my throat." Lottie's hand shook as her own fingers circled her neck. "He asked me if I'd given any information to a man named Mosby. I told him I hadn't, but he shook me and asked me what I knew. I..." She lowered her eyes, unable to meet the Reverend's curious glance. "I'm afraid I've done something quite dreadful."

Reverend Yates exchanged a glance with his wife.

"What is it dear?" Mrs. Yates patted Lottie's hand soothingly. "You've had a fright. Will it help you feel better to tell us the rest?"

"Oh, Mrs. Yates, I told Major Barnes he had the wrong cousin. If he was looking for spies or secret Rebel information, I said he ought to be dealing with Salina, not me." Lottie looked into the compassionate eyes of the minister's wife. "I shouldn't have said it, but I just couldn't help myself. What if he's gone after her? What if..."

Reverend Yates's tone was calm. "If what you say is true, then Salina may be in grave danger."

"I know I've lied about lots of things, Reverend." Lottie was chagrined. "You know I'm not a very nice person. I've hurt others, I'm selfish, and I don't like Salina much... but this is different."

"Then why not go to Shadowcreek to warn her?" Reverend Yates asked out of curiosity. "Why did you come here?"

Lottie shrugged. "I didn't know what to do! If I'd gone to Shadowcreek, Salina probably wouldn't have believed me anyhow. Oh, Reverend, I was terrified—I still am. I spoke without thinking of the consequences. If I've put her in trouble, I didn't intend to. I know if anyone can help her, you can. Can't you?"

In the back of his mind, Reverend Yates wondered what new ploy Lottie was maneuvering this time. But she was right. Salina probably wouldn't trust a word Lottie said. "You and Salina have generally been at odds against each other." The Reverend nodded his head gravely. "Why are you concerned about helping her now?"

"I admit I don't like her, but I don't want her dead," Lottie said emphatically. "That was the look I saw in Major Barnes's eyes—*murderous*." She shuddered uncontrollably.

"There, there." Mrs. Yates put an arm around Lottie's shoulders. "Come, finish your lunch, and I'll drive you home. I'm sure being back in familiar surroundings will help calm you. Such excitement isn't good for a baby, dear."

Mention of the baby caused tears to fall down Lottie's cheeks. "No, I suppose it isn't. Maybe I will feel better when I get home. But you don't have to go out of your way to take me. I'll just go over to the camp and see if Lance is there. He'll take me back to Ivywood."

"If you're quite sure," Mrs. Yates said. "You're feeling more calm now?"

"Much." Lottie quickly nodded. "Thank you for listening. I just had to tell you. I hope there's something you can do, Reverend."

Reverend Yates silently hoped so, too. When Lottie had taken her leave, he immediately went to work to find out if there was proof to substantiate her claims. There were precautions to be taken. Before he would risk going to the Remnant, he needed to be sure that Lottie was telling the truth.

☆☆☆☆☆☆☆

An urgent rapping on the cabin door woke Salina before dawn. It was soft at first but became more insistent, growing into a full-fledged pounding.

Taking her pistol from beneath her pillow, Salina slipped the pearl-handled weapon into the pocket of her robe. The wooden plank floor was cold against her bare feet, but she didn't bother to stop and put on her slippers. The banging grew louder and longer. Somebody obviously wanted her attention.

Duchess, anxiously growling, accompanied Salina to the door, which she opened a mere crack. "Reverend Yates?" She opened the door and let him inside. "It's okay, Duchess. Good girl. Go on, now."

"Morning, Miss Salina." Reverend Yates touched the brim of his hat and adjusted his spectacles. "I do apologize for calling at such an early hour, but I've come to collect you and Taylor Sue Carey—Taylor

Sue *Hastings*, rather. Tabitha is preparing a place for the two of you to hide. We have heard that Major John Barnes is in the area."

She covered her mouth to hide a sleepy yawn. "Jeremy hasn't been here in days..."

"It's not Jeremy he's after this time, Miss Salina. It's you." Reverend Yates patted her shoulder in a comforting gesture. "Major Barnes is going to submit your name as a suspect for questioning concerning the recent Rebel raid," he explained.

"But I haven't done anything!" Salina interrupted the Reverend. "I've behaved myself ever since I came back to Virginia. What Rebel raid are you talking about?"

"John Mosby's raid took place early yesterday," Reverend Yates clarified. "Mosby, with nearly thirty men, came into Fairfax Court House sometime around two in the morning. They came searching for a British officer serving with the Union army, a General Percy Wyndham. Wyndham has publicly labeled Mosby as nothing more than a common horse thief. In turn, Mosby replied that all of the horses he took had riders, and those riders were armed. At any rate, Wyndham was not in Fairfax when Mosby came for him. General Edwin Stoughton, however, was. He'd hosted another gala party at the house he uses as his headquarters. Stoughton was quite unaware of what was happening until Mosby went up to his chamber and captured him in his own bed. Quite a coup—a Yankee general. Mosby also got away with several other prisoners and more than fifty horses."

Salina was astounded. "Mosby captured all *that,* and the Yankees couldn't manage to get him?"

"Mosby surprised them on every side. He was there and gone again before those people knew what hit them." Reverend Yates nodded. "The Federal authorities suspect that someone living *locally* provided Mosby with intelligence."

Full comprehension settled on Salina. "Major Barnes will undoubtedly offer my name as a suspect. He's trying to have me arrested and thrown into jail again, isn't he?"

Reverend Yates sighed. "Something like that. How soon can you be ready to ride?"

Salina's eyes glittered with fury. "That sinister man is going to implicate me in order to strike against my family!"

"That's it in a nutshell," Reverend Yates agreed. "That's why time is a factor. I am of the opinion that John Barnes will make a strike at Taylor Sue, as well. Now that she has married Ethan, she will not be exempt from his twisted vendetta. Barnes is unstable, but especially so where your family is concerned. We must take greater care than ever before."

Disgust churned with apprehension in the pit of Salina's stomach. She clenched her teeth and refused the hot, angry tears. She was tired of running, yet once again she was left with no alternative. "I'll wake Taylor Sue," Salina said with a determinedly set jaw.

"No need. I'm awake. I can be ready in a few minutes." Taylor Sue, having overheard the majority of the conversation, yawned.

"Very well." Reverend Yates made a weak attempt to smile. "I'll wait for you outside."

Salina questioned the Reverend when he led them in the direction of Fairfax Court House. "Isn't it a little dangerous for us to go directly into Fairfax?"

"I'm taking you to Tabitha because we feel that Barnes won't think to search right under his nose, so to speak," Reverend Yates answered. "They will probably send a detail out to your cabin, to Little Ivy, and even Ivywood. Most likely they won't begin their search right in the thick of things. Besides moving you and Taylor Sue is just a precaution. Mosby and his band have been harassing the Union outposts for the past two months. This last raid has just particulary upset them. At the moment, the Yankees are in a dither trying to find a way to stop Mosby. I wish them all the best. I believe that Rebel partisan leader will lead them on a merry chase!"

Salina cast a backward glance at Shadowcreek, wondering if the Union detail would burn her home again. A hard lump formed in her throat that she could not swallow, and the thought of losing everything and having to start over again caused tears to well in her eyes. *Dear Lord,* she prayed silently, *it seems I am in trouble again. Only I haven't done anything this time. I pray that You will surround Shadowcreek with an invisible shield and block the Yankees from doing any more damage. I know that You are with me, and You watch Your children, who are the apple of Your eye. As always, I am in Your hand...*

☆☆☆☆☆☆☆

For three days, until the investigations into Mosby's raid ceased, Taylor Sue and Salina lived secreted away in the attic of Tabitha's boardinghouse. On the morning of March 13, Tabitha brought the girls the news that John Barnes had nothing left to hold over them. Miss Antonia Ford had been arrested and would be taken to the Old Capitol Prison in Washington.

Salina shuddered, as did Taylor Sue. They had been there, and knew firsthand what it was like to be locked up in the dark, dank cells. "How did they catch her?" Taylor Sue wondered aloud.

"The Federal Secret Service sent a female detective to Fairfax Court House to investigate." Tabitha explained. "The Northern woman posed as an ardent Confederate, and in convincing fashion spouted her Secessionist views. Supposedly traveling to Warrenton, the woman stopped in Fairfax and was given lodging at the home of the Fords. Antonia warmed up to the Yankee's lady detective and, believing her to be a staunch Southerner at heart, eagerly shared confidences with her.

"Antonia even went so far as to show the woman a commission of honorary aide-de-camp which had been bestowed on her by General Jeb Stuart. The commission was among the documents that were used against Antonia," Tabitha concluded.

Salina had her own letter of endorsement which General Stuart had written on her behalf. Could that document land her in the same predicament? She would be in as much trouble if the wrong people found her pardon and traveling papers signed by Lincoln. It was not a comfortable notion in either case. She made a mental note to guard her documents with utmost care.

Salina glanced out of the high attic window. She could see little, save for the shop across the street. But in front of the hitching rail, she spied Duncan Grant.

Duncan's in town, she mused. Well, that wasn't really so very surprising, considering all the action that had been going on in Fairfax the past few days. Lance Colby exited the shop and joined Duncan on the boardwalk.

Circling Colby's left ring finger was a telling gold band. Salina sighed over how closely Lottie had come to trapping Jeremy. Salina's heart thudded morosely at the very idea of Jeremy and Lottie together. *Thank God she was discovered, and Mary Edith was brave enough to stand up for what was right,* Salina thought pensively. She felt a pang of pity for Colby, who had done the honorable thing by marrying Lottie, honestly admitting his guilt to all charges. He willingly agreed to face the consequences of his actions. Salina believed what God's Word said about reaping what is sown: *The wages of sin are death,* Romans 6:23 declared, *but the gift of God is eternal life.* Unless forgiveness was sought and a truly repentant heart was offered before the Lord, punishment would be meted out.

Salina began to pray that Lottie would turn away from her willful wrongs and choose right instead. The Lord *could* heal a hard heart like

Lottie's. Salina prayed that He might reveal Himself to Lottie in a way that would make her stop hurting those around her.

From below and across the street, Duncan Grant must have sensed that he was being observed. His scrutinizing gray eyes roamed and uncannily settled upon the window of Tabitha's attic. Salina stepped away from the panes of glass, retreating into the shadows. She wondered how Duncan felt with the tables turned. He had watched and followed her on several occasions past. At present it was her turn to covertly study him. What was he *really* up to here in Fairfax?

☆☆☆☆☆☆☆

"Hello, Salina." Duncan's voice was so low it was hardly audible.

Pausing from the task of saddling Starfire, Salina looked up at her Yankee stepfather. "Duncan. How are you?"

"I am as well as can be expected. Thank you for asking." Duncan was inexplicably pleased to read in the emerald depths of her eyes an expression of implicit trust—an expression which reminded him of Garrett.

"How is Mamma? Have you seen her lately?" queried Salina.

"Annelise is doing well. So far it has been an easy pregnancy for her, and Jubilee fusses over her constantly. She is in good hands and under a watchful eye, to be sure," Duncan replied. With a sheepish grin he added, "I must say, it's still rather overwhelming to consider that I am to become a father this summer. I never would have believed it..." He smiled wistfully. "Annelise misses you more than ever."

Salina nodded, but she didn't regret coming back to Virginia. She had made her choice to be near Jeremy, and she would play it out resolutely. Salina withdrew a letter from the pocket of her coat and handed it to Duncan. "This is a letter for her with some photographs inside—if you wouldn't mind giving it to her the next time you see her."

"I'd be pleased to take it to her." Duncan nodded. "I'm certain it will cheer her considerably. I fear she still isn't happy living in Gettysburg, but hopefully one day that will change. For now, she relies on Jubilee a great deal."

Salina knew full well the depth of Jubilee's love and devotion to Mamma. Curiosity made her ask Duncan about another of Shadowcreek's former servants. "What ever became of Peter Tom?"

"I tried to get him to work for me," Duncan replied, "as a full-time agent, but he wouldn't have it. After you so successfully outmaneuvered him, he gave up the secret service. Peter Tom wanted to be a soldier. When he heard about a colored regiment being formed outside of Boston, he headed farther north and enlisted with the 54th Massachusetts. His last letter told of the drilling and training. He even has a blue uniform with shiny brass buttons bearing the letters 'U.S.' on them. Peter Tom is a very proud man. He will fight for the sake of freedom."

A knot twisted in the pit of Salina's stomach. She was not opposed to freedom for all men, but now there was the possibility that Peter Tom might one day end up fighting across a field from Jeremy or Ethan. "I'm sure Peter Tom will make a fine soldier," Salina murmured. She returned her attention to Starfire, but her next inquiry was directly to the point. "Why are you here, Duncan?"

"I came straight away when I heard a young woman was responsible for providing the Rebels information that led to the capture of General Stoughton," Duncan said plainly, adding ruefully, "President Lincoln was genuinely sorry when he heard of Mosby's raid. He said he could make new brigadier generals, but he couldn't make horses."

Salina turned to confront him. "You thought I had some part in it, didn't you?"

"I believed that you would honor your word to President Lincoln and that you would behave," Duncan replied. "It was only when I learned that Jeremy's uncle was in the vicinity that I came here. I couldn't just sit still as long as there was a chance he might succeed in implicating you."

"Well, as you have seen for yourself, I am still behaving." Salina met Duncan's gray eyes squarely.

"Yes, so you are. Reverend Yates was wise to move you from Shadowcreek," Duncan acknowledged.

"Why?" Salina interrupted, fearing the worst. "Have they burned the cabin too?"

"No, your little cabin is still safe." Duncan nodded. "I checked this afternoon, rest assured."

Salina sighed her relief.

"There's another reason I came looking for you. I've a favor to ask," Duncan murmured. "Salina, I need your help."

"My help?" Salina raised an eyebrow in question. "Rebels and Yankees working together?"

"Forget about Rebels and Yankees for a time, Salina," Duncan ordered softly. "This is a personal matter—which might well include you."

Salina crossed her arms determinedly over her chest.

"I want you to help me break the code in this book," Duncan continued. "I am unfamiliar with the cipher, but I was hoping you would help me with the translation."

She recognized the book Duncan held. It was the leather-bound one that Daddy had acquired last summer and asked her to hold for him. It had been taken from her room at Aunt Genevieve's house in San Francisco. "You're not afraid that if there's military information contained in the pages I might forward it to my people?" Salina couldn't help but taunt him just a little.

Duncan took her ribbing good-naturedly. "I think I know you better than that by now." His smile faded quickly. "Do you know what this book is, Salina?"

"It's the book Daddy smuggled inside of Celeste." Salina nodded with absolute certainty upon further examination. She thumbed through the pages. "Taylor Sue saw the Widow Hollis with a similar book, on Drake's stagecoach west. She said it had the same markings as this one does. Did the Widow own this?"

"No." Duncan shook his head. "If fact, she overlooked it altogether at your interrogation at Fortress Alcatraz. I came upon it by chance a few weeks ago when I was sorting through that crate again. I believe it belonged to Major Barnes. I'm thinking there's a connection there somewhere."

"There is. Jeremy told me that the Widow Hollis and Major Barnes are kin. He's her half-brother," Salina said evenly, watching for Duncan's reaction.

"That explains it, then." Duncan nodded. "Revenge is a very powerful motive. It's my opinion that the desire for vengeance against your family has begun to unhinge Major Barnes. He's a very dangerous man, and I want you to be extremely careful. Do you understand me?"

"Yes," Salina assured him. "I promise I'll be very careful."

"I don't particularly care for you living out there at Shadowcreek," Duncan remarked, unknowingly echoing Jeremy.

"Taylor Sue is with me. We have Duchess, and the Lord will watch over us," Salina said stubbornly.

"You could move back to Ivywood," Duncan suggested.

"Not while Lottie's still there." Salina put her foot down. "She hates me as much, if not more, than John Barnes does. I know what I'm up against. I don't want to leave my home just now."

Duncan realized that it was pointless to argue with Salina. She possessed a double dose of hard-headedness, from both her father and her mother. "I'll keep you in my thoughts and prayers," he resigned.

"I'll come back in a week to check on your progress with deciphering the book's code."

"You have no idea what this might be?" Salina inquired.

"No." Duncan shook his head. "That's why I've brought it to you. I'm hoping that you will be able to shed some light on *something*."

"I'm going to tell Jeremy about it," Salina stated, brooking no argument from Duncan.

"I expected that, and it's a chance I'm willing to take. *If* you can crack the code, Salina, and *if* there's some tiny little thing that will help keep all of you safe, then so be it." Duncan shrugged. "I know I'm asking a lot, but you're the only one I am able to turn to."

"As long as you know the conditions." Salina nodded. "I'll do what I can." She hugged Duncan. "Tell Mamma I love her."

Duncan held her for a moment, then he spontaneously kissed the top of her head. It was a gesture that seemed natural enough, but it surprised him nonetheless.

"Daddy used to do that to me all the time," Salina whispered.

"I meant no offense by it," Duncan quickly assured her.

"No, I know that," Salina said with a smile. "When the war is over, perhaps I'll call you Papa Duncan instead of Major Grant. If that would be all right with you."

"It will be all right." Duncan's heart brimmed with tenderness for Garrett's daughter.

"I'll see you in a week's time," Salina reiterated, slipping the leather-bound book into her pocket.

Duncan bowed at the waist. "Good-bye, Salina."

☆☆☆☆☆☆☆

Through the Remnant came the news of the fighting at Kellysville on March 17. The commander of Stuart's Horse Artillery had been mortally wounded in the skirmishing and later died at the home of Bessie Shackleford in Culpeper Court House. "The Gallant Pelham," as General Stuart often called him, was gone. His skill and presence would be sorely missed. General Stuart regarded the youthful artillery commander like a younger brother, and the pain of Pelham's passing rested hard with the daring cavalier. The cavalry put on their own show of mourning, and many whispered of the courageous cannonading Pelham had ordered during the Battle of Fredericksburg. Stonewall Jackson had wanted Pelham for his own artillery, but Stuart had refused to part with him.

Salina had heard Jeremy speak of John Pelham, the golden-haired "Boy Major" from Alabama, and she was sorry to learn of his death. *Lord Jesus, please keep Jeremy from harm. Let him live.* It was a common plea included daily in Salina's prayers.

Salina returned to the cabin after fetching two pails of water from the stream, near the footbridge. According to the routine the girls established, it was laundry day, and several of Jeremy's men left garments needing to be mended and cleaned.

The girls were vaguely aware of the frequent movements in and out of the tunnel-maze below the fireplace. Ever since Boone's discovery and Jeremy and Ethan's exploration, the tunnels had been put to regular use without full knowledge of the cabin's residents. It was only when Taylor Sue found the laundry or mending, or when Salina found meat, flour, coffee, and sugar from recent raids, that they were certain the horsemen had been nearby.

As she had each evening for the past six days, Salina labored diligently over the little leather-bound book Duncan had entrusted to her. She rubbed the back of her neck and pulled the kerosene lamp closer for more light.

"Still got you stumped?" Taylor Sue looked up from her work. She was knitting socks to send to Ethan, who had officially reported to Stonewall Jackson's corps.

"Maybe I'm trying too hard." Salina sighed. "I'm about ready to give up." She looked down dejectedly at the symbols, absently counting. *Twenty-six*—a number equal to the letters in the alphabet. *Alphabet...*

Randomly Salina assigned a letter to each symbol, manipulating them until the letters began to form words. Once she'd matched the symbols to the corresponding letters, it ceased to be difficult to form the translation. "Why didn't I see this *before*?" She laughed at herself.

"Maybe you were trying too hard." Taylor Sue shrugged. "But now that you know how to make sense of it, what does it say?"

"It seems to be a journal that Major Barnes kept during the early campaigns of the war," Salina replied. "He's listed Union victories in 1861, including Fairfax Court House and Cheat Mountain. He also talks about the victories at Fort Henry and Fort Donelson at the beginning of 1862. That's where their General U.S. Grant earned his nickname, 'Unconditional Surrender,'" she added.

Salina read further only to find a grisly account of the bloody Battle of Shiloh on April 6 and 7. Tucked between the ghastly, descriptive paragraphs was a rather peculiar passage:

> *My orders sent E.S. to the front at the head of the charge. He never had a chance. Got himself blown away in the first volley fired by them Rebs. He's dead 'n gone 'n he'll never find out thet he got himself a growed up son. J.'s secret'll go to the grave with her. She won't never let on thet her youngest boy weren't of C.'s seed. She mightn't care what folks'd say 'bout the whelp, but she cares mightily what folks'd say bout her. C. was a fool over her. J. preyed on his ignorance time 'n again. I swear I won't let J. or her Wrongful Act stain the proud name of Barnes she done covered herself with 'n passed on to her misbegotten brat. I shoulda kep her from mar-ryin' C. all them years ago. Besotted with her, thet he was—just like his likker 'n 'his cards. She was poison to him, the match doomed from the start, 'cept he wouldn't see it. At least I. made a good match with S. Til G.H. killed him outright. Things mighta been powerful difrent if H. hadn't killed B.J. in thet duel on account of A.S. Shoulda been the other way round. I swear I'll see G.H. an' his kin pay fer his deeds against us Barnes, one way or another...*

Salina shivered violently and slammed the book closed. John Barnes had deliberately ordered the death of a man with the initials E.S. *E.S...* Salina shrugged. She didn't know who that was. But knowing Jeremy's family history as well as her own, she could guess at the other names to replace the initials. She reread the paragraph inserting the names where they belonged. J. was Justine, Jeremy's mother. C. was Campbell, his father. I. was for Irene, and S. for Simon—the Hollises. G.H. could only stand for Garrett Hastings, B.J. for Beau Jefferson, and A.S. was none other than Mamma's maiden name, Annelise Spencer.

The dark inferences sunk into Salina's brain. If what was written was true, Campbell Barnes was *not* Jeremy's real father. E.S. was Jeremy's father, and John Barnes had *deliberately* had him killed because of it—even though the man apparently had no knowledge of ever having a son.

Salina set the leather-bound book aside. She didn't want to know anymore already about the twisted nature of John Barnes. He was bent on revenge and a strong sense of foreboding caused Salina to shudder involuntarily. It was only be a matter of time before he again would attempt to make good on his vindictive vow. She'd deciphered the code and had read her fill. If Duncan wanted the rest of the information contained in the pages, he was more than welcome to complete the transcription for himself.

☆☆☆☆☆☆☆

Duncan Grant sat in the rocker near the hearth, shaking his chestnut head. He was not surprised that Salina had successfully cracked the code. "I don't know why I didn't see it myself, but at least you did, Salina." He was working on plans to have Jeremy's uncle reassigned, away from Fairfax County and the Chantilly area. He'd spent the better part of the week pulling strings and calling in favors to people he knew in high places. He hoped and prayed that things would work out, but until they did, he could not share such information with Salina. He muttered, "John Barnes has killed before. I wouldn't put it past him to do it again." Duncan studied the journal again. "You see here, where the entries come to an end in the middle of April 1862?"

"Yes." Salina nodded. "Why do you suppose that is?"

"That's when your father snatched this from John Barnes's headquarters. I think Garrett knew even then that Barnes would try to use the war as a cover for his personal violence. Garrett smuggled the book south inside of Celeste. The untimely death of Simon Hollis in San Diego only added fuel to Barnes's already stoked fire of vendetta against your father, and the rest of the Hastings."

"You're thinking I should change my name again, aren't you?"

"Something like that," Duncan confirmed, uncomfortable with how easily she'd read his thoughts. "But we've argued about this before."

"I grew up here, Duncan," Salina reminded him. "Changing my name isn't going to have any effect. Too many people know who I am."

"Maybe it wouldn't matter here, but if you were to go somewhere else, you'd blend in easier," Duncan pressed the point, but stopped himself. "Never mind..."

"What else have you been up to this past week?" she inquired lightly, purposely changing the topic.

"Well, if you must know, I've been given a new assignment. It seems some of your Rebels have been quite successful in recent raids—namely Captain John Singleton Mosby, the one they call the Gray Ghost."

"I understand Captain Mosby is giving the Union scouts assigned to catch him a very rough time of it." Salina nodded. "I've even heard that the Federal authorities are afraid he'll ride right into Washington and capture government officials, or kidnap President Lincoln."

It was true. In fact, the planks on the bridge into Washington were taken up each night as a measure to guard against such an event. Duncan cleared his throat. "Leave it to you to be well informed. I suppose you know that the raids have gleaned powder, ammunition, arms, food, supply wagons, prisoners, and horses."

"Rumors do spread quickly," was all that Salina would say. She knew Mosby was successful because he had the assistance of the civilians all through an area coming to be known as "Mosby's Confederacy," in Loudon, Fauquier, and Fairfax counties.

"Well, I'm one of those scouts, Salina. For the time being, I'm one of those men who'll be hunting Mosby down," Duncan said with determination. "Where there's smoke, there's generally fire. And I have a hunch that where there's trouble, that's where Jeremy Barnes can be found."

"I haven't seen him lately," Salina evaded.

Duncan grinned. "I wouldn't expect you to answer any differently, and I won't press you for answers. I don't want to force you into lying. I'm indebted to you, though, for cracking the code. Hopefully, I'll be able to remedy the situation to the best of my ability. In the mean time..."

"I know," Salina put in, "watch my back."

"Precisely." Duncan saluted her.

Within three or four minutes Duncan was at the edge of the clearing, but he reined up when he came upon a horseless gray-clad soldier.

Jeremy Barnes glared at the Yankee Major. "What are you doing here?" he demanded coldly.

Duncan automatically touched the book in his pocket, reassuring himself that it was safely concealed.

Jeremy drew his revolver. He was at a definite disadvantage standing on the ground. "Put your hands where I can see them."

Obediently, Duncan raised both of his gloved hands. "I came here to warn Salina. Your uncle's presence has been threatening again, and I felt it my duty to let her know of the danger."

"Salina can take care of herself," Jeremy insisted. "You've done your good deed. Now go, before I change my mind about being hospitable."

"If something were to happen to you, Barnes, it might well destroy her." Duncan nodded toward the cabin. "Take care of yourself, if not for your own sake, then for hers," he said between clenched teeth. He rode on, quickly enveloped by the trees and the darkness.

Jeremy returned his gun to its holster. He looked toward the dark cabin, knowing that at least one candle burned behind the thick, light-blocking draperies. He did not go to the porch stairs but made a sweeping circle of the clearing and entered through the concealed tunnel.

Beneath the cabin, in the little alcove that served as both office and sleeping chamber, he stretched his long frame on the narrow cot and yawned. He'd lost track of the miles he'd walked from Kelly's Ford following the battle at Kellysville last week. During the fight, Comet had been shot out from under him. He was given the customary leave of sixty days to find a suitable horse, but he did not intend to be out of the action for that long. If Jeremy had returned to this area a day sooner, he could have gone on the raid Mosby ordered on a Federal camp in the woods near Chantilly a few short hours ago. Prisoners and horses had been taken. Jeremy was in need of a dependable, battle-tried steed, and a good one from a Union capture would certainly suffice. As it stood, he'd have to wait for word as to when Mosby planned another strike. Jeremy was reasonably sure he could talk Salina into letting him borrow Starfire for the job. He closed his eyes, sighing into the darkness.

The image of Salina's pretty face intruded his aimless contemplation. He silently thanked God that Duncan had not taken him prisoner, as he so easily could have done at the edge of the clearing. He thanked God, too, for Salina—for it was, without a doubt, because of her that Duncan had let him be.

Chapter Seventeen

*T*he secret door opened just a crack, letting a beam of light fall on the earthen floor below. Jeremy stirred, wakened by the growling of his stomach and the aromatic smell of coffee, bacon, and fried potatoes. Slowly he ascended the stairs to the cabin, and Salina greeted him with a sweet smile. "Hello there."

"How'd you know I was here?" he asked groggily, rubbing the sleep from his sapphire-colored eyes.

"I could feel it," she answered simply. "Sit down."

He did her bidding and ate heartily, recounting the battle at Kelly's Ford between bites—including how Comet had been shot out from under him. "So, here I am."

"Well, I suppose this is a blessing in disguise." Salina's eyes sparkled. She was sorry that Jeremy had lost Comet, yet she rejoiced at the gift of time they were miraculously granted. "If you'd like, I can fix a picnic lunch for us and we can go up to the ruins this afternoon, just the two of us. We'll figure out how to get you a new horse and send you back to General Stuart."

"I'd like that." Jeremy winked at her, restraining himself from rushing over to gather her into his arms to collect a good morning kiss. "I've got some business I must see to while I'm here, but I'll be back in a few hours," Jeremy assured her. It'd take him at least an hour to walk to Carillon.

"Take Mamma's horse," Salina suggested. "Daphne's not the fastest mare in these parts, but she'll get you where you're going quicker than on foot."

Jeremy didn't argue. They talked while he ate his breakfast, and then he kissed Salina's brow just before he descended into the tunnel again.

At Carillon's mill, Jeremy met up with Curlie and Bentley. He inspected the inventory sheets and examined the requests, prioritizing each one for delivery. They currently had more ordnance on hand than he was comfortable with having at their little armory. He wanted the inventory dispersed as quickly as possible. The risk of discovery was ever-present.

"Very good, sir." Bentley saluted. "And how are things over Shadowcreek way on this fine day?"

"Fine." Jeremy's lips twisted in a grin he couldn't contain. "Curlie?"

"Yes, sir?" Private Curlie Hawkins replied.

"Later on, when you're finished up here, go on back to Shadow-creek. Slip into the tunnels and go to the room under the cabin. In my saddlebags are some fairly recent newspapers from Washington and Richmond—also some maps and some orders contained in the pouch. You all can read the newspapers, and I want you to study the maps. If you'd be so kind as to make copies of the orders, I'll give them to Harrison and Kidd Carney when they arrive."

"Yes, sir." Curlie saluted.

"Boone's out on patrol with Cutter and Jake," Jeremy noted. "See if you can find out anything about where Pepper and Browne might be. I haven't heard from them in almost a week."

"I thought they were with you at Kellysville," Bentley said.

"That's what I'm afraid of," Jeremy admitted. "The last time I saw them, I'd just lost Comet near Kelly's Ford during the fight. I'm praying I haven't lost them as well."

"I suppose you've heard your uncle's been about these parts," Bentley gently but firmly reminded him. "Cutter saw him near Centreville two days ago."

"I know. He's hunting me down again," Jeremy said. It was common knowledge among his men that John Barnes was persistently in search of a way to kill him. "I'll be all right."

"Where you off to now, Lieutenant?" Curlie asked.

"I've an engagement for a picnic lunch." He chuckled and laughed harder when he saw Bentley roll his eyes. "I'll be back tonight, and we'll dispense with the bulk of this." Jeremy waved his hand in an arch which encompassed powder kegs and crates of repeating rifles.

"Beg your pardon, sir. But how is it you'll be joining us if you've not got a horse?" Bentley inquired.

"I'll have a horse. Don't worry," Jeremy said confidently. "Even if it is a temporary arrangement."

The afternoon sun was bright, the air pleasantly warm. Salina and Jeremy strolled up the slope hand in hand. They spread out a quilt in the overgrown yard of the former main house and had their picnic. Only the once-burnt trees and tall blackened chimneys bore mute witness to their laughter and conversation.

Salina unpacked a meat pie, bread rolls, sweet potato fritters, creamed peas, and peach cobbler. Jeremy ate until he couldn't take another bite, which meant there would be fewer leftovers to carry back to the cabin. He took a long drink of lemonade from a brown glass bottle and replaced the cork. "Sallie Rose, that was delicious." He rubbed his full stomach.

"Sallie Rose?" She smiled at the name. "Daddy used to call me Sally-girl."

"Ah, but you're a grown up now," Jeremy pointed out. He'd been watching her intently, as was his habit, during their shared meal. "Since Rose is your second name, it seems appropriate. My own Sallie Rose."

She smiled prettily and a pink flush crept across her cheekbones. Her pulse quickened when he looked at her like that, and she lowered her eyes self-consciously.

"I love you," he stated deliberately, entwining his fingers with hers. "You know I would do whatever I can to protect you."

"Such as altering my given name to a nickname that suits you?" she goaded, a defiant flash in her eyes.

"Clever little Salina." Jeremy's chuckles rumbled deep in his chest. He stretched his long legs out and propped himself up on his elbows. The green glint in her eyes was not lost on him. Her pride and her strength were only two of the reasons why he loved her. "And what if I were to change your name?"

Salina's temper flared instantaneously. "See here, Jeremy Barnes. I am proud to be Garrett Hastings's daughter! I've argued this with Duncan before. I'm not going to be a Grant..." She was on her knees, hastily clearing the leftovers, dumping the dishes unceremoniously into the wicker hamper.

Jeremy caught her wrist firmly. "Listen to me, Sallie Rose. I'm talking about changing your name to *mine*. Would that be so terrible? Could you be as proud to bear my name as you are to be a Hastings?"

Salina's eyes flew open wide, and she stared at him. Love twinkled merrily in his blue eyes. Her voice turned to a throaty whisper, "Are you asking me to marry you?"

"Yes, in a manner of speaking, I reckon I am." Jeremy rubbed his shadowed jaw and nodded once.

"You're asking me *now*?" Salina wanted to know.

"I want you to think on it for the time being, at least. I haven't officially asked Ethan for your hand yet, although he suspects that I will," Jeremy conceded. "He'll have my hide if I don't do this properly, you know. When I first came back from California last August, he assured me that I would have to deal with him should he find me guilty of trifling with your affections. I am a man of my word, and I will keep this respectable—especially in your brother's eyes!"

"Oh, Jeremy!" Salina harmlessly punched his shoulder. Then she laughed. It was a joyful sound.

"You'll consider it, then?" Jeremy fished for words of assurance.

"Yes, I'll consider it." She nodded, a bright smile illuminating her pretty face. She loved him, plain and simple.

Her sweet rippling giggle pleased him, and Jeremy tapped the end of her nose with his finger. She sat opposite of him, her skirts tucked under her crossed legs, and they talked of what their future might bring. After the war...after the war...*after this blasted war...*

Salina touched his cheek, gingerly caressing his beard with her fingertips, confiding, "I don't want to wait till the war's over to get married, Jeremy. We don't know when it will end. Ethan and Taylor Sue didn't wait until the fighting stopped. Who can say what might happen before then?"

Jeremy's fingers entangled themselves in her long, dark curls. "I'll talk to Ethan just as soon as I can," he promised a split second before he kissed her. "Rest assured," he murmured against her lips.

After the picnic basket was repacked, Jeremy lay with his head on Salina's lap as she read to him from Emily Brontë's *Wuthering Heights*. She absently stroked his sandy blond locks across his forehead. When she looked down, she found he was sleeping. It afforded her the opportunity to peruse his rugged features. Though Jeremy had light hair, his brows and whiskers were nearly black, a contrast which Salina regarded most arresting. In her eyes he was a handsome man—especially so when he flashed that disarming smile of his. If she didn't know the degree of boyish mischief that was hidden behind his closed eyelids, he might appear to be older than his twenty years.

She laid the book she was reading aside and contented herself with gently running her fingers through his hair, watching him sleep. In a way, it was amazing how full of joy her heart seemed to be in this moment.

"Sing for me, Sallie Rose." Jeremy's request startled her.

"You rascal. You're not asleep at all, are you?" she giggled softly.

An amused grin lifted the corners of his mouth, but his eyes remained closed. "Sing."

"What do you want to hear?" she asked.

Jeremy shrugged. "I doesn't matter. You choose."

Salina had learned a song from Tabitha, taken from a play called *The Virginia Cavalier*. It was a melancholy tune. She willed her voice to stay true and not tremble:

> *Bob Roebuck is my sweetheart's name,*
> *He's off to the wars and gone;*
> *He's fighting for his Nannie dear,*
> *His sword is buckled on;*
> *He's fighting for his own true love,*
> *His foes he does defy,*
> *He is the darling of my heart,*
> *My Southern Soldier Boy.*
>
> *Oh! if in battle he was slain,*
> *I am sure that I should die;*
> *But I am sure he'll come again*
> *And cheer my weeping eye;*
> *But should he fall in this our glorious cause,*
> *He still would be my joy,*
> *For many a sweetheart mourns the loss*
> *Of a Southern Soldier Boy.*
>
> *I hope for the best and so do all*
> *Whose hopes are in the field;*
> *I know that we shall win the day,*
> *For Southrons never yield.*

And when we think of those who are away,
We'll look above for joy,
And I'm mighty glad that my Bobby is
A Southern Soldier Boy.

Silence surrounded them. Duncan's words resounded in Jeremy's head: *It would destroy her if something happened to you...* He squeezed Salina's hand tightly and, hoping to convince himself as much as her, said aloud, "Nothing's going to happen to me—to us."

She looked away, picking at a blade of new grass. "Jeremy, you can't stay here. We both know it," she said firmly. "You've only got a limited time to get yourself a replacement horse." Her eyes, when she looked back at him, held a great degree of conviction. "I want you to take Starfire the next time John Mosby organizes a raid, so you can get a horse. He's been rather successful as of late, and I'm sure he'll be planning another strike very soon. I can find out when that will be and where they're meeting. I think it would be your best chance."

His blue eyes bore into her green ones. Here was evidence of his Salina—the *old* Salina—sharing confidences, volunteering pertinent information. Jeremy had to admit that they had worked well together when Salina had first been involved in her father's Secret Service activities. What was to prevent them from working together again?

"Can you read my thoughts so plainly to know that I've been considering doing just as you've said?" he asked. "Mosby's renown success comes from secrecy and surprise. If you know a way to find out about a raid, I'll go to wherever you say the rendezvous point will be."

"I don't know about reading your thoughts, but I know how you are." Salina nodded. "You're not content unless you're in the thick of it—just like Daddy was. You remind me of him in that way. Sometimes so much it scares me."

Jeremy had no words to allay her fears. He merely squeezed her hand in his, attempting to relay some sort of comfort to her.

Salina cupped her hand to his jaw and rubbed the coarse whiskers. "How soon before you to talk to my brother?" she inquired sweetly.

Jeremy threw his head back and laughed heartily. "I'll talk to Ethan. Don't you fret about it. But I've got to get a horse first. One thing at a time."

She giggled with him. She couldn't help but wish the afternoon would not come to its inevitable end.

☆☆☆☆☆☆☆

Following the fight at Miskel's farm, more than eighty Union soldiers had been wounded or captured. As a result, there were plenty of horses to choose from. Jeremy had no problem selecting a replacement for Comet.

Initially, when Jeremy rode to the meeting place at Rector's Cross Roads on Salina's horse, he hadn't known what to expect. Scores of other men had come as well. John Mosby, the Confederate partisan leader, was a small, wiry fellow, but undeniably the head of the operation. Mosby had examined each face amongst the group of "conglomerates." Discipline was demanded, and orders were expected to be obeyed without question.

Mosby had wanted to strike a Federal cavalry outpost at Dranesville, but due to recent raids, the Yankees had already abandoned this post and retreated closer to Washington. Nothing more could be done late on the night of March 31, so Mosby and his men bedded down at Miskel's farm. The Yankees learned Mosby was out and attempted to launch a surprise attack against the force of sixty-nine men under Mosby's command. At dawn on the first of April, one Rebel alerted all the rest that the Yankees were coming, and the sleepy raiders hurried to buckle on their weapons and to saddle their mounts.

One hundred and fifty blue-clad cavalrymen of the 1st Vermont outnumbered Mosby's Rebel raiders by more than two-to-one, and the situation did not look favorable. Mosby advanced on foot toward the gate to meet the oncoming Federal cavalry, pistol in hand, firing hotly. One of his followers leaped down from his horse and threw Mosby into the saddle in his place. From that point, the tide of the fight turned. The small force of Rebels charged headlong into a furious clash with the Vermonters.

In the fifteen-minute skirmish, which cost Mosby one dead and three wounded, more than eighty prisoners were taken as well as nearly a hundred fully-equipped horses. Two dozen Yankees lay dead or wounded along the roadside. When word of the clash arrived in Washington, the Union high command was utterly embarrassed by the rout.

The contraband horse Jeremy took a liking to was a big, mahogany-colored bay. The gelding had a black mane, tail, legs, and hooves, and had three distinct milky-white spots in a diagonal line across his rump on the left side. The horse seemed to have a good nature and was obviously a reliable, cavalry-trained mount. He possessed speed and endurance, and those were things Jeremy was certainly looking for.

When Mosby's force scattered, he rode away on the new gelding, leading Starfire along behind him.

Salina fed the newly-acquired horse a carrot and patted his neck when Jeremy brought him to the makeshift barn behind the cabin at Shadowcreek. "What will you name him?"

Jeremy shrugged. "I thought I'd let you choose a name for him."

Salina pondered the idea and then decided. "Those three spots in a row, they remind me of the stars which comprise the dagger sheath of the constellation of Orion."

"Hmmm." Jeremy nodded in agreement. He was familiar with the formation of stars and the tale of the mythological warrior. "Orion it is, then."

The mahogany bay nodded his head, seemingly a display of his consent. "Well." Salina laughed. "I guess that must mean he fancies his new name."

Jeremy eyed his new mount then checked the time on his pocket watch. "Now that I have a horse, I'll be leaving. I've been away as long as I dare from camp and General Stuart. I don't want him to think I've become one of Mosby's 'carpet knights' on a permanent basis."

Salina queried, "Carpet knights?"

"That's what some of the regular soldiers call the irregulars, especially since they have no camp, no headquarters. The irregulars hide with locals who are willing to take them into their homes to shelter them. Some prefer the great outdoors for their accommodations, but many hole up in safe houses," Jeremy explained.

"Like when you hole up here at Shadowcreek?" Salina prodded.

"Yes, I suppose you could say that," he admitted. He framed her pretty face in his hands and stared down into her eyes for a fair amount of time, not breathing a word. Bentley's words echoed in his mind: *You're just waiting for her to do something—either to slip up, or to prove her worth...* Salina'd done more than prove her worth. She believed in him, was willing to trust him. Each time he came here, it was harder and harder to leave her. He'd always considered himself so self-reliant. It took some getting used to, to admit that he needed her in his life. He felt an ache within his heart—the pain of separation mingled with the hope that they'd all live long enough to be together again. "Kiss me good-bye, Sallie Rose."

Salina readily obeyed without the slightest hint of argument.

☆☆☆☆☆☆☆

Barely three-quarters of an hour passed following Jeremy's departure when Salina spied horsemen at the edge of the clearing. Peeking through the heavy lace curtains with her field glasses, Salina saw that they wore blue uniforms, and she recognized Major John Barnes as their leader.

"I've got to get word to Jeremy," Salina told Taylor Sue. "He can't be that far off. I'm going after him."

"Salina, it's too dangerous for you to go," Taylor Sue protested.

"But it's more dangerous for Jeremy if I don't," Salina maintained.

"What if Major Barnes catches you?" Taylor Sue stepped in front of the door, blocking Salina's path. "What if..."

"He won't," Salina said confidently. "I've got to go!"

Taylor Sue lowered her eyes and nodded. She'd do the same for Ethan, if she had to.

Salina had seen Jeremy ride off in the direction of Carillon, and when she came upon Jeremy's new horse tethered outside the mill, she instantly knew he was inside. She entered the mill on tiptoe, so as not to disturb the muffled voices she heard. Salina found herself in the midst of a enormous cache of arms and ammunition. Her jaw slackened, and her mouth fell open in amazement.

The men's voices halted abruptly when they saw her there. Jeremy approached with brisk strides and a harsh scowl marring his brow. "Salina, what are you doing here?"

"I followed you...to warn you..." She looked up at him, apprehension visible in her green eyes. "Jeremy, this is *exactly* what you were doing in San Diego with Daddy, weren't you? Only this time you aren't buying and selling the goods, you're capturing them on raids and then making distributions."

"I'd have told you about it, eventually," Jeremy hedged. "I didn't want to see you tangled up in all that again..."

"I see," she replied with a sad nod, trying to quell the disquieting feeling that he might still hesitate trusting her. She took a deep breath and swallowed her disappointment. She thought they had come farther than that. "I rode out here because I had to tell you that your uncle is here. He's been at Shadowcreek. His men were all along the edge of the clearing. You and your men must leave this place before he finds you—and all of this!"

"You're not safe either, if he's as close as you say he is." Jeremy took her firmly by the elbow and led her back out to the horses. "I told you the other night I'd take you with me if I had to."

"No. Taylor Sue's by herself, and I won't leave her." Salina put her foot down. "We'll make it."

"But my uncle," Jeremy persisted.

"He's a horrid, horrid man, Jeremy." Salina shuddered. "We both know he'll kill you if given half a chance."

Jeremy muttered, "Tell me something I don't already know."

"I *can* tell you something that you don't know," Salina said ominously. "But you've got to listen to me. We haven't much time." Rapidly, Salina told him of the things she'd gleaned from the translation of John Barnes's journal.

"Don't you see, Jeremy?" Salina's eyes pleaded with him. "You're *not* his kin—and he knows it. That's why he's been so awful to you all these years. He resents you and your mother. And he probably held the details over your father's—over Campbell Barnes's—head before he died."

Jeremy felt as though he'd had the wind knocked out of him. "Campbell Barnes was *not* my father?"

Salina shook her dark head. "The journal entry did not specify a name, but the initials of the man are E.S. He was killed about a year ago, at the Battle of Shiloh in Tennessee. He was a Yankee officer, and Major Barnes deliberately assigned him to lead a charge he knew would cost E.S. his life."

Jeremy pulled away from Salina and brushed her hand off his arm. He tipped his head back, squeezed his eyes shut, letting all his breath out in a shaky gust. He'd known little but disdain and later cruelty from the people who constituted his "family." Campbell Barnes was a weak man, given to temper and habitual gambling. Often drunk, he took out his alcohol-induced rages on those around him. Campbell died when Jeremy was fifteen, and Justine had fled to England. She turned her son over to John Barnes, who was to serve as guardian until Jeremy came of age. After his mother's desertion, Jeremy found that the legacy from his father was immense gambling debts. There was no money to pay off the liabilities Campbell had incurred, so Jeremy was obliged to work them off, by any means available to him.

Jeremy had told only one person in advance of his plans to head west to California, and that person had been Salina. He knew she would keep his secret just as she had kept her mouth shut concerning his bruises caused by his uncle's repeated beatings. She'd cared for him back then as a true and compassionate friend. Thinking back, he couldn't remember a time when his own mother had shown even half the measure of concern for him as Salina had.

Jeremy had spent two years in California, working to raise enough money to pay off the insistent creditors. Eventually the debts were cleared. He'd stayed out west and managed to put away a tidy little sum for his future. He'd grown to rely on no one except himself and, every now and then, Drake. Jeremy's stomach churned with raw shame and deep-seated loathing. His mind was fixed on the suffering he'd endured at the hands of John Barnes—the vindictive man who was no blood relation to him whatsoever. A certain balm came from the new knowledge of who he *wasn't*, and that the lone bond Jeremy shared with the sinister man was their common surname.

At length Jeremy spoke with some difficulty, "I've been trying to convince you to consider taking my name—to be as proud of it as you are of your father's—only to learn it's not really my name at all."

"Of course it's your name. You know no other," Salina insisted. "I shall be proud to share it with you."

Jeremy rubbed his thumb across her cheek, smoothing away a tear she didn't know had fallen. "My own Sallie Rose..."

"Go," she entreated him. "Get away from this place quickly. I don't want him to kill you."

"I don't want to be killed either. I'm not in the mood to die today," Jeremy said gruffly. He pulled her to him, hugging her fiercely. "I appreciate your honesty and your courage in telling me of this, but it's bound to have ramifications."

"Of course it will. But we'll be strong for each other, and we'll get through it," she assured him. She would have held him in her arms a while longer, but she had to make do by whispering comfortingly, "I love you." There was nothing else she could do for him.

Jeremy nodded mutely, kissed her forehead, and swung himself into Orion's saddle. Resolutely he told her, "I'll see you when I've *properly* asked Ethan for his permission to make you my wife. Count on it." To one of his men standing nearby he commanded, "Boone! Follow Salina home. See she gets there safely. We'll wait for you near Frying Pan."

Boone Hunter replied by salute, then mounted and stuck his big feet into his stirrups. "Come on, Miss Salina. I'll see that you get back to Shadowcreek all safe and sound."

Salina left Starfire in the hidden corral and followed Boone through the tunnels until they arrived at the steps that led up to the fireplace entrance inside the cabin. "I'll make sure Taylor Sue is there alone," Boone told her, "and doesn't have any uninvited guests."

When Boone was convinced things were as they should be, he allowed Salina up the stairs. Before she could turn back to thank him, he was gone.

Taylor Sue hugged Salina tightly. "Praise You, Jesus!" she breathed a prayer of thanksgiving. "I had all sorts of imaginings that something terrible had happened to you—you've been gone for so long! Quick, gather some of your things, Salina. I've decided we're not staying here—not with Jeremy's uncle out there. We'll go to Little Ivy. There's security in numbers, even if we are only three women together. We'll take Duchess and the horses and whatever food we can carry. We'll pack a trunk between us."

Salina nodded, agreeing with her sister-in-law. "Perhaps it would be for the best. We'll leave after dusk and use darkness to our advantage. How long ago was Major Barnes here?"

Taylor Sue glanced at the clock. "Twenty minutes ago? Certainly not much more than that. I don't know what I'd have done if he'd come up to the cabin, Salina. I honestly don't."

"As soon as it's dark, we'll leave," Salina reaffirmed.

The only time Salina left the house that afternoon was to fetch a pail of water from the stream. They needed to wash the few dirty dishes and thoroughly douse the hearth. Salina left the door open, assuming Duchess would warn her if anything was amiss.

The dog barked noisily when a buggy approached. Salina was puzzled to see Mary Edith driving. "What on earth are you doing here?"

"I've been burned out," Mary Edith cried bitterly. "Those d-dirty Y-Yankees c-came, told me I had five minutes, and then they torched my little stone cottage. The outer structure is still standing, but everything else inside is lost..." Huge tears rolled down Mary Edith's flushed, smoke-stained face.

"Come inside and sit yourself down. Such strain probably isn't good for the babies..." Salina was rambling, and she knew it. The plans for going to Little Ivy evaporated. Salina held Mary Edith's hand, consoling her in gentle words, but inwardly her own anger raged. Her wild thoughts jumbled together in one eerie conclusion: What if the blue-bellies had mistakenly fired the *wrong* house?

Chapter Eighteen

$\mathcal{M}$ore raids by Mosby and his band of irregulars followed the incident at Miskel's farm. For two weeks following that April Fool's Day raid, Salina, Taylor Sue, and Mary Edith learned just how often the tunnels were being used by Jeremy's men for the purpose of hiding out from the Federal patrols. With increased frequency, the girls woke in the morning to find sacks of flour and sugar, hams and turkeys, sometimes vegetables, and once a keg of cider, neatly stacked on the hearth. The girls did not go hungry as the men kept them well supplied with food and staples. It became habit for the three young women to prepare large quantities of food at each meal, for they rarely ate by themselves. Jeremy's men came and went at will, and it gave the girls a certain comfort knowing they were in the area.

In addition to cooking for Jeremy's soldiers, the girls did sewing, mending and laundry for them. Mary Edith designed and stitched a miniature flag, the Confederate Stars and Bars, from scraps of cloth left over from mending. She presented it to Bentley, the honorary color-bearer, who tied it proudly to his horse's bridle, vowing not only to treasure it, but to never do anything that might bring dishonor to his country's flag.

Lulled into a dangerous sense of security with the men so regularly at hand, Salina was slow to notice that Duchess did not bark in the least when she opened the front door one morning. Shading her eyes from the sun, she looked for the big, lovable, hairy dog, but Duchess was nowhere in sight. "Probably off chasing a rabbit or something..." Picking up the pail from the corner of the porch, Salina skipped down the stairs and headed for the footbridge.

"Duchess?" Salina saw the dog, lying too still, near the edge of the stream. She screamed, horrified to discover that their loyal companion had been shot. Salina started to run back to the cabin, but she was encircled by half a dozen men, each holding a pistol or carbine trained at her heart.

"I'd be still, if I was you, Miss Salina," a harsh voice advised. Its owner spat out a stream of brown tobacco juice, the remaining drool disappearing into the scraggly graying beard. "Some of my boys got itchy trigger fingers."

Salina's heart was pounding so hard in her chest she was certain it was audible to the men surrounding her. "Major Barnes." She swallowed a large lump in her throat. "What a surprise to see you..."

"Oh, I hardly think so. But jist maybe it is a surprise after all. An' here you thought you was so safe tucked away in the woods, jist three pretty little ladies. We been watchin'. Bidin' our time. You forgot to be cautious this time, Miss Salina," he needlessly reminded her. "And this time, you're comin' with us."

Instantly a coarse gag and a thick blindfold were tied around Salina's head. Her hands were bound with tight coils of rope before she could offer even minimal resistance. She was roughly lifted up to a dirty, smelly man on horseback, whose arm about her shoulders was the only thing that kept her from falling off the rapidly moving beast. *Oh, God, help me!* She wanted to retch at the foul stench of body odor mingled with horse sweat and stale tobacco, but she thought better of it, fearing she might choke on the bandanna between her teeth.

Trepidation threatened to overwhelm her. Salina had the prickly feeling that she might not live through *this* and she groaned in earnest prayer. Her mind raced, conjuring up hundreds of horrific images. Major Barnes would probably kill her, but perhaps not too quickly. He would not want to eliminate her while there was a chance of using her as the bait to lure Jeremy into his clutches. *You, Lord, are my rock and my salvation. You are with me in times of trouble, You know what the future holds. Help me be brave and to draw on Your strength. Grant me peace if it is my time to meet You face to face, Jesus. Oh, Lord, I am terribly scared!*

Salina lost track of time and distance. At last she was handed down into the arms of a waiting rider. She was indelicately hauled into the main house of Carillon, where the blindfold was removed.

The interior of the once-beautiful home belonging to the Careys had been vandalized, and the sight brought a sad rush of tears to Salina's eyes.

"Take her upstairs. Tie her to one of the bedposts," Major Barnes ordered harshly. He took Salina's chin between his thumb and forefinger, jerking her head up to face him. "She's to be guarded constantly. Is that understood?"

"Aye, Major," came a reply in unison from the six men behind him.

A man called Farnham escorted Salina up the wide curving staircase, careful to avoid steps which were broken. Salina thought he seemed to be the least hardened of the bunch, and although he was loathe to show it, Salina sensed he didn't quite cotton to what was going on.

"Please, may I have some water?" she requested hoarsely when he removed the gag from her mouth.

"I reckon." Farnham nodded brusquely, rechecking the knots he'd used to anchor her securely to one of the posts of the bed in Jennilee's room. He left Salina under the watch of a second soldier, but he was back in a few minutes with a tin mug filled to the brim with well water. Farnham held the mug to her lips, and she swallowed greedily until she had drained the contents. She wiped her mouth on the torn shoulder of her dress and expressed her thanks.

Farnham merely grunted.

"Why am I being held captive? What does the Major hope to gain by holding me here?" Salina dared ask in a small voice.

Farnham hesitated, debating whether or not it was prudent to answer. He decided there was no harm in allowing her to know. "He's using you to trap a certain Rebel scout—one of Stuart's own," Farnham replied gruffly, but then stopped abruptly. "I don't have to tell you anything, little lady. You just hush up. Don't try anything stupid, and you might live through this—maybe."

Salina shook her head slowly. "I don't think so. I think Major Barnes will kill me anyway, perhaps along with that scout he's trying to catch." She was shocked at how calm she sounded. "Hasn't the Major told you who I am?"

"It doesn't make a bit of difference who you are, just so long as this scout shows up," Farnham shot back.

"Have you ever heard of a Rebel captain named Garrett Hastings?" Salina queried.

Guilt flashed in Farnham's eyes, and he stepped closer to the bed. "How would you know about *that* incident?" he strained through clenched teeth.

Salina raised an eyebrow. "Which incident?"

Before he could stop himself, Farnham answered, "I was only following my orders. I didn't want to kill him, but I was told to shoot if he made any attempt to escape. Hastings knew that," Farnham declared. "He knew I had no choice but to shoot him down."

Salina blinked as her breath caught in her throat. "*You* killed him." Her heart slammed against her ribs. "You shot Garrett Hastings as he tried to escape."

"I had to," Farnham reluctantly admitted. He snapped his head up and demanded sharply, "How do you know about that? What has this got to do with you?"

Salina was stunned by Farnham's confession, and she felt as if she were being suffocated. "Captain Garrett Hastings was my daddy."

Farnham wriggled uncomfortably, his ice-cold eyes narrowed in careful scrutiny. "Who's the scout that Major Barnes is after?"

"Jeremy Barnes, his nephew," Salina replied uneasily. "The Major didn't tell you that either?"

"He tells us what he deems is necessary for us to know. We follow orders without question," Farnham responded in monotone. He did know about Barnes's nephew, but he wouldn't disclose the fact to Salina. "You've done enough talking for one day," he decided, replacing the bandanna gag.

Farnham angrily marched to the door, but he stole a backward glance at the young lady who was their captive. He didn't like this, not one bit. But he had no say in the matter. He couldn't help but think of his own daughter back home. His Elinor was about the same age as this young lady, and he tried not to think of what he'd do if anyone ever laid a hand on her. Major Barnes had gone too far this time, Farnham resolved. An unexpected and unwelcome feeling of compunction pierced him. He had tried desperately to shake the vivid memory, but Hastings's death had plagued him unmercifully for the last seven months. Belatedly, Farnham arrived at the sickening conclusion that it was probably *because* he'd killed Hastings that Major Barnes had recruited him to assist in the abduction of the Rebel's daughter. No, he didn't like it one bit.

☆☆☆☆☆☆☆

The door swung open with an abrupt crash, startling Salina into sudden awareness. Major John Barnes, drunk and reeking of whiskey, approached the corner bedpost where Salina was securely tied.

The Major insolently took one of Salina's disheveled curls, twisting it around his bony finger. "Such a purty little thing," he fumed thickly. "*His* darlin' daughter... an' *hers*."

Salina turned away from him in an effort to prevent having to breathe his nauseous exhalations. He stank of alcohol and was sorely in need of a bath. The huge wad of tobacco that made the side of his cheek protrude was positively repulsive and caused his ugly features to appear more distorted than ever.

"Such a *fine* young lady." Major Barnes yanked on her hair. "Your high an' mighty family has always thought itself far above us. In fact, I'm surprised the *honorable* Master Garrett would allow his sweet little girl to associate with the likes of my nephew."

"That's easily explained. Jeremy is *not* your nephew," Salina whispered, taking no thought of what his reaction might be to such a statement.

"Who told you that?" Major Barnes demanded fiercely. "Justine?"

"No." Salina shook her dark head. "I learned it from the same source where you recorded having a hand in orders that ensured that Jeremy's father was killed at Shiloh."

The major's hand clamped tightly on her arm. "Surely Jeremy didn't tell you this. He don't even know it himself," John Barnes ground out between his tobacco-stained teeth.

"He does now," Salina replied evenly. "It's no secret that you've hated him for years and have attempted to beat the life from him on more than one occasion. He knows you're after him, and now he knows the reason why. And I also know why you are so obsessed with attacking my family. Even if you do succeed in getting all of us, we Hastings will still plague you..."

Major Barnes' eyes narrowed dangerously. "Your family's been trouble ever since they come here from Alexandria some fifty years ago. It started back when yer granddaddy bought up the Shadowcreek land—land which belonged to my pa an' should rightfully be mine. The acreage was put up as collateral when we didn't have enough to make the mortgage payments. Yer granddaddy, Henry Hastings, he were a good friend of the circuit judge who'd come to Fairfax Court House on Court Day. I ain't never been able to prove it, but I swear there was finaglin' goin' on. Henry Hastings wanted that property in the worst way 'cause he knew its value. An' when my pa couldn't pay up what he owed, Hastings was quick to step in an' offer ta buy him out—at a portion of what the land was worth! So that's what he did. He bought out my pa, an' he built up Shadowcreek an' harvested the farmlands. Then, Henry's firstborn, Garrett, he fell in love with Miss Annelise Spencer even though she was promised to Beau Jefferson. My sister loved Jefferson, but she didn't have the dowry Annelise would bring him. There was that fuss over honor, an' a duel, an' Garrett killed Jefferson on Annelise's account..."

Salina listened intently, being ever so quiet so she wouldn't interrupt his telling of the familiar story from his view. He seemed to have forgotten she was there.

John Barnes went on in his slurred, slow speech. "If it weren't bad enough Garrett shot Jefferson, then he was responsible for takin' the life of the man Irene eventually married. Both the men my sister has loved have their deaths to your daddy's credit..." Major Barnes took a long draw from the whiskey bottle. "The way I see it, all the hurt an' misfortune my family suffered is by the hands of Hastings. It's high time they pay up for inflictin' us Barnes..."

"By striking back at us, you're trying to avenge wrongs that are beyond your control—or mine, for that matter," Salina said simply. "What purpose will eliminating us serve? If you manage to kill us all, what then?"

"What then?" Major Barnes looked at her with a glassy-eyed stare. "Why then, you'll all be wiped out, and I'll not have ta be bothered with any of ya ever again! You gotta pay fer what ya've done. We Barnes lost land, loves, an' dignity, an' ya *will* pay. I can tell you this one thing—we ain't goin' to take it no more. No, Miss Salina, not no more!"

"You won't get away taking the law into your own hands," she whispered ominously. "Too many people know what you've done."

The Major's reply was a backhanded fist to her jawline, and her head smacked the bedpost. "You guard that tongue, Missy. No man likes a babblin' woman."

Salina's face smarted where he'd hit her, and she was sure there was a growing lump on the back of her head. She refused to cry. Wisely she kept quiet, even as he glared at her.

"Justine's boy loves ya, thet I know." Major Barnes shook a finger at Salina. "Thet's his misfortune. I'll make him suffer an' wish he was never born. His ma was a bright woman, but not enough so. She carried on behind Campbell's back, knowin' he couldn't produce his own offspring, an' when she turned up in the family way...well, she had the audacity to pawn it off on my brother, an' he weren't man enough to call her bluff. Justine enchanted Campbell an' nearly had him convinced that maybe that boy of hers *was* his after all—until I made him see otherwise. That boy is no more related to me than Robert E. Lee is! No sir! Jeremy's no more than the misbegotten result of an adulterous tryst between Justine Barnes and..."

"And who?" Salina dared ask. "What's the man's name?"

"No." Major Barnes shook his head. "I don't see no cause fer ya ta know the man's name. All ya need ta remember is thet I took care of him, an' rest assured, I'll see thet his boy is taken care of, in like manner. Jeremy's gotta pay, jist as his father had ta."

"You hold that the sins of the father are visited on the son?" Salina quipped.

"His father is dead, killed at Shiloh. When I kill Jeremy, then there will be no more disgrace brought to the name of Barnes..."

You are the disgrace, you evil man! Salina wanted to scream it at the top of her lungs. But she knew such an action would more than likely earn her another bruising blow, and so she said nothing.

Major Barnes continued to mumble, something about those who have and those who have not, about the rich and the poor, and about those in power and those who had none. "Us Barnes have got pride!" the drunken major exclaimed. "Honor an' duty—Jeremy'll see it as his duty ta come after ya, Missy." The Major stroked her cheek where a red welt showed along her jaw. "An' then he'll pay fer his pa's sins with his own life."

Goose flesh crept along Salina's arms and a chill crept round her heart. "But it's already been four days. What if Jeremy doesn't come after me?" she inquired.

"He'll come," Major Barnes vowed, malice burning in his bloodshot eyes. "He'll be here, 'cause this is where ya are. Ya wait an' see. He'll come jist in time to watch ya die, Missy. An' then he'll get what he's got a-comin'!" The Major left in a fury, slamming the door on the way out just as loudly as he had on the way in.

☆☆☆☆☆☆☆

"He ain't coming." Farnham pounded his fist against the table. "It's been nearly a week, and there's no sign of him. *If* he got the note, and *if* he cares at all for the girl, he should've been here by now!"

"Shut up!" Major Barnes leveled a menacing glare at Farnham. Then he glared at each of the others.

Farnham had voiced what the other men had already begun to think. Jeremy Barnes was probably too far south to receive the message that Salina was their hostage. Each day the bickering increased among John Barnes's men, and they now questioned the practicality of the endeavor.

Salina could hear the argument raging downstairs. The man posted as her guard heard the loud exchange of voices as well. "What will you all do since Jeremy's not coming after me?" she asked between spoonfuls of the broth he fed her.

"None of your business," he retorted. "The Major will have a plan, never fear."

Salina swallowed the lukewarm broth and noticed that there were fewer pieces of chicken floating in it. Their food supply must be dwindling. Major Barnes hadn't expected Jeremy to take so long. She desperately wished that he would come to rescue her, yet at the same time Salina prayed fervently that Jeremy wouldn't come after her. It would spell certain disaster for both of them.

Following the meager lunch, Salina rested her forehead against the bedpost and hummed to herself. Hymns ran through her mind—*All Hail the Power of Jesus Name; O, The Deep, Deep Love of Jesus; Rock of Ages, Cleft for Me.* The church music mingled with military tunes, waltzes, and other songs of the homefront.

She wondered idly if Taylor Sue and Mary Edith were still safe at the cabin. And she wondered if Tabitha or Reverend Yates knew what had become of her. Ethan, thankfully, was too far away. When this was all over, he would undoubtedly become Major Barnes's next target.

As the men following Major Barnes fought amongst themselves, Salina could hear the dissension among them. They wanted to abandon the kidnapping, but Major Barnes wouldn't hear of it. He felt he was so close to his success that he could taste it.

From eavesdropping, Salina also learned that the armies were moving toward another clash. Earlier that day she'd heard them speak of "Fighting Joe" Hooker, who was the new commander of the Army of the Potomac—Burnside had been relieved in the wake of the Union debacle at Fredericksburg. Hooker was still somewhere along the Rappahannock River, heading toward the Wilderness area, near a place called Chancellorsville, where he bragged that he would bag the Army of Northern Virginia.

☆☆☆☆☆☆☆

Jeremy struggled to keep Orion under control. The skittish horse outwardly displayed the agitation of his rider and continued to shift impatiently. Holding the reins tightly, Jeremy felt his insides twisting into a hard, uneasy knot. He refused to meet Bentley's questioning glance. Bentley wisely held his tongue. He could plainly discern his lieutenant's anguish. Salina Hastings was a captive in that house on account of Jeremy's uncle, and it was tearing Jeremy apart.

Reverend Yates moved his steed beside Jeremy's. The Reverend had led them here, having discovered only yesterday where Salina was being held. He brought along a haversack Tabitha had the foresight to pack with food, a spare canteen, a small flask of whiskey, an extra shirt, and a few miscellaneous items donated from her carefully-hoarded medical supplies. The Reverend waited, with the other seven horsemen, to see what Lieutenant Barnes would have them do. "Don't throw caution to the wind, Jeremy," the minister advised. "You can't just go storming in there and get her. Your uncle must have been planning this for some time—certain you'd come after her. We both know why he's taken such pains to draw you here, and he's used Salina as the device which would ensure your arrival. We can't give him the satisfaction of an emotional, ill-planned counteraction. Think what to do carefully—that way we'll lessen the chance that he'll kill you."

"He'll have to catch me first," Jeremy said with deadly calm. "If he's harmed her in any way, Reverend, he's going to regret it. I promise you that!" He was not angry anymore. Jeremy had spent most of his anger on the ride from Culpeper. Yet the burning intensity in his sapphire eyes bespoke his restrained rage. Cool sureness and unfailing calculation were necessary at this point.

Jeremy was unsure why his *uncle* settled on Carillon as the place to hold Salina. It was the closest estate, but perhaps Major Barnes had gained the knowledge of the arms and ammunition stored at the mill. Jeremy couldn't afford to take any unnecessary chances. He commanded his men to keep watch of the house, determine a routine, and as soon as they could ascertain a weak link, they'd exploit it and free Salina. Duty beset him, and right then and there Jeremy vowed to torch the arms depot himself if it was the only means to prevent the Yankees from reacquiring the stolen weaponry.

Bentley leaned over in his saddle and asked, "How do ya reckon we're gonna get her outta there, Lieutenant?"

Reverend Yates said confidently, "The Lord will provide a means."

Jeremy wanted to believe that, and he tried to with all his heart, but it didn't stop him from formulating plans of his own and asking God to bless the attempt.

Incredibly, in the very next moment, Jeremy saw the front door open. Salina was roughly led, under guard, out of the main house to the privy in back.

Quick orders had Bentley and the Reverend following Jeremy while Boone, Harrison, Curlie, Jake, Kidd Carney, and Cutter fanned out and surrounded the house, staying hidden in the cover of the trees.

Reverend Yates put a hand on Jeremy's arm. It seemed the young lieutenant was going to charge. "Look!" The Reverend pointed toward the outhouse.

Jeremy witnessed a second miracle. With his own eyes, he watched the man who was Salina's guard take out his knife and slit the ropes that bound her wrists. "Run!" The Yankee urged her to do his bidding. "Run as fast and as far away from here as you possibly can!"

Salina glanced up at Farnham in utter disbelief. "You know what you're doing? You'll very likely forfeit your life for this."

Farnham nodded. "Consider it a belated attempt in asking for forgiveness. One day, you might be able to remember me with kindness. Major Barnes has gone too far this time."

"He'll kill you," Salina stated plainly. "If not today, then another time. He'll hunt you down in revenge."

"Better me than you." Farnham shrugged. "I deserve it for some of the things I've done in his service."

"What of your daughter?" Salina asked, recalling that only yesterday he'd mentioned he had family somewhere in southern Pennsylvania.

"She'll be better off without me," Farnham declared. "I was reading the Testament you gave me, and perhaps there's still a chance for this hardened heart." He handed her a small, bound package. "If you ever have a chance, I want you to take this to my Elinor. It's the little Bible, a faded *carte de visite*, and a letter that hopefully will explain. She and her grandparents live near Fairfield. Promise me?"

Salina nodded vigorously, tucking the small parcel into the pocket of her dress.

"Now, get on with you. The Major will come looking for us in a minute. Go!" Farnham urged, shoving her away from him. "And take this with you!" He returned her confiscated pearl-handled pistol.

Salina shook off the ropes and started running just as fast as she could. Major Barnes and the others in his command spilled from the doorway swearing, yelling, and shooting.

As the first shots rang out, Salina dropped to the ground, looking back over her shoulder. She saw Farnham fall, the fatal bullets killing him instantly. Attempting to rise, she stumbled on the hem of her skirt and landed hard, face down in the dirt. When she gained her footing, she ran—but Major Barnes was not far behind. She had no time to load or aim her gun.

Simultaneously, the Union men and the Confederates opened fire on one another, and soon a full-fledged skirmish erupted. Bullets flew fast and furious, whistling through the night air.

Salina was terrified, her heart thudding wildly. She heard a horse and rider plunge into the woods after her, and she was afraid that one of the Major's men was closing in on her. She tried to run faster, stuffing the gun in her pocket, using both hands to gather her skirt to her knees, and she pushed on.

Jeremy rode close, reached out, and snatched her up. "I've got you now!" He swung Salina up onto Orion's back, landing her behind him. "Hang on!" he ordered needlessly.

Salina's arms encircled his middle and squeezed tightly. She rested her cheek against his back, and the tears of thankfulness flooded unchecked down her cheeks. *Thou, O Lord, art a shield about me...* She hung onto Jeremy desperately, bullets whizzing all around them amongst the shouting and fighting. While only a handful of men were engaged, the ferocity rivaled that of a clash between much larger forces.

Jeremy maneuvered Orion through a sparsely wooded grove. John Barnes pursued them relentlessly in his alarming obsession. Jeremy kept his head low and urged Orion onward.

Salina felt a bullet slice though the fabric of her sleeve then heard it slam into the sapling on the right of her as they passed by. "Where are we going?" she screamed.

"Back to the mill," Jeremy yelled over his shoulder.

"But he'll get us!"

"And the ammunition." Jeremy hoped she would understand that it was his duty, his responsibility, to see that the supply depot did not fall into his uncle's hands.

Boone, Curlie, and Kidd Carney had circled back to the mill and were already dumping powder stores, emptying the kegs around the outside of the structure.

"Get back! Get back!" Kidd Carney put a torch to the black powder, and a trail of sputtering sparks flared into a fire that raced furiously into the mill. Kidd Carney sprinted with all his might to put distance between himself and the impending destruction.

Jeremy rode frantically past the gate. He pulled Salina down from Orion's back, practically slamming her to the ground, shielding her with his own body. In a split second, a deafening, heart-stopping B-O-O-M! thundered all around them, and the entire mill exploded in a gigantic, glowing eruption of orange flame and black smoke. Salina felt the ground tremble with reverberation, and Jeremy held on to her tightly. She hid her face beneath Jeremy's shoulder as the charred debris showered upon them.

Still the carbines and pistols exchanged fire, amid the cloud of falling ash and burnt fragments raining down.

"Come on." Jeremy yanked Salina up by one arm and was dashing after Orion. He pulled her up behind him again, and his fingers came in contact with a warm wetness. The substance was sticky and, though it was dark, Jeremy instinctively knew what he felt was blood.

He hadn't been shot—he'd been injured before and knew the sensation. Had Orion taken a stray bullet? He didn't have time to worry about that just now. He pressed on through brush and brambles, ducking low-hanging branches, and warning Salina to lean close.

"He's still coming, Jeremy! Major Barnes is still after us!" Salina shrieked.

"I know!" he tossed back angrily. "I'm going as fast as I can!"

Orion reared as a bullet grazed his withers, and he nearly dislodged Jeremy and Salina from his back altogether. Jeremy managed to steady the injured horse, wheeling him around to one side. He listened for the slightest sound. He saw a flash of fire out the corner of his eye, then he aimed, firing his revolver. The shot seemingly went astray. Jeremy anxiously spurred Orion forward to get away.

Major John Barnes spurred his horse unmercifully, holding the reins in his crooked, stained teeth. He held a pistol in one hand and used the other hand in an attempt to stop the heavy flow of blood oozing from the bullet-hole in his opposite arm. He emitted a low, guttural groaning, and he hurled obscenities at his prey. He came close enough to Salina to reach the length of her fluttering skirt with his bloody, outstretched hand.

Salina screamed horrendously, kicking furiously, while the Yankee major pulled at her from behind.

Jeremy drove Orion relentlessly, creating a mere yard or two of separation between the churning hooves of the two horses. When he had a clear shot, he turned and fired again into the darkness.

John Barnes was unseated, falling hard to the ground. His horse veered away from Orion's pounding pace. Jeremy did not slow or even look back. He only wanted to get Salina out of harm's way.

Jeremy temporarily lost his sense of direction, and his chest was still heaving when they happened upon a deserted barn. The cloud cover was thick, the moon all but invisible. He lifted Salina from Orion's back.

"Oh, Salina," he whispered her name hoarsely, tucking her dark head just beneath his chin. His hands rubbed her shoulders, but he stopped abruptly when she winced at his touch. He set her away from him and attempted to examine the sticky wetness that covered the palm and fingers of his left hand. He took her into the barn and lit a lantern. It was blood, no mistake about it—*her* blood.

Salina was in a mild state of shock, and she suddenly felt the cold-warmth of the blood oozing through the right sleeve of her blouse.

"You've been hit." Jeremy turned her around so the lantern light would shine on the wound.

"Shot? Are you sure it's not just a cut?" she asked in a small voice. "We rode though some thick brambles, and some of those trees had some low branches..."

"No," he said with certainty. "This was a bullet you took—and it was one that had been meant for me." His blue eyes flashed with renewed anger. Every day and every night he took the risk of being shot at by the enemy. But this time Salina was involved, and that rankled him to no end. She had taken a bullet that had been directed at him. "Seems like you've saved my life, Salina."

The wound was in a place that was difficult for Salina to see without a looking glass. "I don't feel much pain, though it does burn some. Certainly it can't be very deep..."

"It isn't. It's not much more than a graze, but there's quite a bit of blood," Jeremy confirmed. He retrieved Tabitha's haversack, impatiently searching for the small medical kit. "I should be able to fix it up with just a few stitches at the most. Can you manage to get that blouse off?"

Salina swallowed with difficulty. With shaky fingers she undid the button at her throat first. Pulling the left sleeve off easily, she had to peel the blood-drenched right sleeve away from the open wound on her shoulder. She could see now where the blood had soaked through to her corset cover, but she would not take that off in front of Jeremy. The very thought of it sent a rush of color to her cheeks.

Jeremy's fingers were almost as gentle as Ethan's when it came time for the stitching. She tried desperately not to flinch each time she felt the needle slide through her torn flesh, and Jeremy clenched his teeth so tightly that the muscles along his jaw twitched. He knew he was hurting her, and he was helpless to ease her pain—until he remembered the flask of whiskey.

"Here." He removed the cork stopper. "Take a sip of this—a sip, mind you. I'll not have you getting drunk."

Salina hated the smell of whiskey, but she doubly hated the burning taste of it. She felt the hot, fiery trail that it made down the back of her throat all the way to the pit of her empty stomach. She coughed and sputtered. "People drink that for enjoyment? That's positively nasty!"

"Nasty or no, it is all I've got to help alleviate some of the pain." Jeremy completed his task. "If you could see this, you'd compliment me on my fine handiwork—nice, small, even stitches. I don't reckon your brother the doctor could have done any better, or your sister-in-law the seamstress, if I do say so myself."

"Quite proud of your stitchery, are you?" Salina answered. "Well, I'll have to take your word for it because I can't see what it is that you've done, but I do thank you for it."

Jeremy nodded and packed away the needle and thread into the medical kit. "Stay here. I'll go to the pond and see if I can't get some of the blood out of that sleeve."

Salina swayed on her feet. "Maybe you could stitch up that hole as well..." She put a shaky hand to her forehead. "I think I'll lie down right over there and wait for you..."

Jeremy caught her in his arms just as her knees buckled. He laid her down in a relatively clean pile of straw, and then he covered her with the quilt from his pack. "I'll be right back," he told her. "You rest."

"No, please." She was crying now. "Don't leave me. I...Please don't leave me in here alone."

Jeremy nodded, settling himself down at her side, taking her hand in his own. He pressed it to his lips and gave her a reassuring smile. "You're safe, Sallie Rose."

"I think I'm bleeding again," she sniffed.

Jeremy helped her sit up. She was bleeding. Once more he delved into the haversack, withdrawing additional rolled bandages and a length of clean muslin. He bound her shoulder securely "All right?" he asked.

"Thank you," Salina murmured, her eyes fixed intently on his.

Jeremy sighed unevenly. He didn't move away.

"Would you..." She swallowed, tearing her eyes from his handsome face.

"What, Sallie? What do you want me to do?" he asked anxiously, trying to help as best he could.

"Could you just...hold me?" She sighed raggedly, fresh tears welling in her emerald eyes. "Please?"

Jeremy obliged, gingerly taking her into his strong arms, mindful of her wound. She leaned against him, weary and drained from their harrowing escape. Gently he touched her bruised face, allowing his fingers to trail through her unkempt curls. "You're a sight, Sallie Rose," he mused softly.

Salina felt warm, loved, protected in the circle of his embrace. "I'm s-so v-very g-glad you f-found me." The tears escaped her watery eyes, making salty streams down her flushed cheeks. "I p-prayed you wouldn't c-come b-because I knew the risk you'd be t-taking, but I really thought he m-might m-make good his awful th-threats..."

"I've killed him," Jeremy said with cold certainty. "He can't hurt us anymore, Sallie."

"He was crazy with b-bitterness and h-hatred for us." She shuddered. "He was g-going to w-wait until you arrived b-before he k-killed me. I wondered if I was ever g-going to s-see you alive again..."

"Hush now." Jeremy wiped her tears away. "Don't think on it anymore. Just thank the good Lord that we live to tell the tale." Yet behind his brave words, his heart wrenched at the very thought of how close he'd come to losing her. If the worst had happened, if John Barnes had killed her, Jeremy would have snapped. "I love you so much," he whispered, his lips tarrying near her brow, alongside the bridge of her nose.

She burrowed her head against his shoulder, heart racing, head befuddled. Words, inadequate to describe the things she was feeling, thinking, failed her. She didn't know what to say, except, "Thank you for what you've done." Her tears moistened the front of his shirt.

He, too, seemed unable to express himself with mere phrases. There was so much he wanted to tell her, yet he didn't know how. He continued to hold her, protected and close, even as exhaustion and weariness overtook them both.

☆☆☆☆☆☆☆

Jeremy woke with a start. Salina was nestled in his arms, and he was loathe to disturb her, but they had to move. They couldn't remain here. He had to find his men and get Salina back to where she could get decent treatment for her injury. Instinctively, he caressed her cheek, then traced her lips before he stole a kiss.

Salina's long-lashed eyes fluttered open. She'd been dreaming of kissing him. In fact, she'd been dreaming lots of things, and she flushed scarlet as she met his inquisitive blue eyes, fearful he might see her innermost thoughts reflected in her own.

Jeremy saw the high color stain her cheeks. His mind, as well, had traveled where it ought not. He possessed a vivid imagination and a healthy desire. Both were brought sharply under control. Wisely, he created space between them, and he cleared his throat. "Reckon I should see about washing out that blouse of yours right about now."

She made no move to stop him from leaving this time. Alone, she flung her arm over her eyes. She was flustered by the forbidden path her mind traveled. She scolded herself and reined her thoughts into a more acceptable line of thinking. Slowly she got up, aching everywhere, and tried to restore some semblance of order to her appearance. She found a chambray shirt in Tabitha's haversack and draped it over her shoulders. It was of little use to try to comb through her tangled hair with her fingers.

When Jeremy reentered the barn, he felt much calmer, more assured. How often Bentley taunted him for allowing her to tie him up in knots. "I did what I could, but the bloodstain might be set in. Maybe you should just go on and wear that shirt. I can rig a sling from the rest of this muslin for you."

Salina nodded, silently following his soft commands. She pretended that she was merely one of his men, obeying orders, but she found she was not immune to the allure of his nearness. She chided herself: What would the others say, once they were all together again, about Jeremy and Salina being out alone all night together? She could guess the answer. Ethan, she assumed, would be furious. And it might take much to assure her brother that nothing had happened between them.

Chapter Nineteen

I could have you punished for taking absence without leave—severely." General Stuart delivered a stern rebuke to his truant lieutenant scout. "I ought to have you arrested for such behavior."

"With all due respect, General, I only did what I believed to be the right thing," Jeremy replied, rightly penitent. "If I had not acted when or as I did, the cache of weapons and supplies at Carillon's Mill would have fallen to the Yankees for sure. It was only a matter of time. I felt it my duty to prevent that from happening. And as I and my men were the only ones who were aware of the location of the depot, it rested with us to see the matter through."

"You went on your own, with no orders and no permission," General Stuart unnecessarily reminded him. "However, I need you too badly to punish you. It would be a bigger crime to deprive the cavalry of your services at this point. See that it doesn't happen again."

"Yes, sir." Jeremy nodded.

General Stuart continued, "While you were off doing what you perceived as your duty, General Stoneman has gone out and is headed toward Richmond. It is our obligation to see what he's up to. Take a handful of your men and scout the Federal cavalry position. If you are in need of maps, then get them. I want a full report by morning. Don't disappoint me again, Barnes. I trust you, and I trust that while there might have been more to the escapade than the depot at Carillon, I choose to rely on your good judgment as to what is recorded in your report of the action. Do I make myself clear, Lieutenant?"

"Perfectly, General, sir." Jeremy saluted. "I'll include the necessary details in my report and leave you to determine whether or not my absence was worth the risk."

"I will at that," General Stuart assured him. "You're dismissed, Barnes. Take your men, and God go with you."

"Thank you, sir." Jeremy nodded. "My men and I will depart within the half hour."

"Carry on, Lieutenant." General Stuart nodded brusquely.

Jeremy detailed Bentley, Boone, and Cutter to accompany him on the reconnaissance mission, informing them of their impending departure. In the meantime, he went to the hospital tent to see Kidd Carney. He had been sent to the doctor to be treated for burns he sustained in the explosion at Carillon's mill.

"Where have you been?" Ethan demanded. "Have you the slightest notion of the stir you've caused by disappearing for the better part of a week?"

"I've been reprimanded by the General already. I don't need it from you, too," Jeremy said tightly.

Ethan stepped in front of Jeremy, blocking the way to the cot where Kidd Carney lay sleeping. "What's happened this time?"

Jeremy recounted the majority of the details of the last few days. "According to Salina, the whole tangled mess stems back to the land and the loves lost. John Barnes's bitter, vindictive ways have corrupted his mind, the hatred eating away at his reasoning..."

"You've killed him," Ethan stated the natural conclusion.

Jeremy shrugged his broad shoulders. "I reckon I did. I shot at him. I know he fell, because he didn't come after us any more."

"But you're not quite certain?"

"I'm fairly sure I got him. I'm a good shot, and even though we were moving fast...Look, if I didn't kill him, it would be nothing short of a miracle," Jeremy said tersely.

Ethan's mouth twisted into a wry smile. "We've both witnessed miracles before, though, haven't we?"

"If John Barnes isn't dead, then he's certain to be out of commission for quite some time," Jeremy said confidently. "No, I think I killed him." He swallowed bitterly. This was war, and he'd killed before in the line of duty—but the guilt assailed him. He could derive no pleasure or reassurance in killing the man he'd been raised to believe was his uncle.

"Did your men go back?" Ethan questioned.

"Yes." Jeremy nodded.

"And how many bodies were accounted for?" Ethan pressed.

"All but his." Jeremy had to acknowledge the fact that had been torturing him. "I have no proof, but I can't say for sure that he didn't hole up somewhere. Even if he found a place to slither off and hide, I don't think his chances are very good for survival, if you know what I mean."

Ethan finally let it go. He studied his friend. Jeremy was a crack shot with his nine-round LeMat revolver. He knew Jeremy would not brag about killing his uncle. But there was something else—something *different* in Jeremy's demeanor. "What is it that you're not telling me?" Ethan prodded. "You and Salina aren't at odds again, are you?"

"No, we're not at odds again, but there's something you should know. And I'd rather you hear it from me than anywhere else: Salina was shot during our escape. I took her to a deserted barn, stitched and dressed her wound, and slept for a couple of hours holding her in my arms. We didn't get back to Shadowcreek until dawn the following morning."

Ethan's eyes flashed dangerously. "Are you telling me something happened between you and my little sister? Because if you are, I'll..."

"No, Hastings. I'm trying to tell you, up front, that nothing happened between us." Jeremy swallowed. "I love your sister very much, but I know what is right and what isn't. I promised her I would talk to you..."

"About?" Ethan raised an eyebrow in question.

"I intend to make her my wife. I want to ask you for her hand," Jeremy stated firmly.

"Well, it certainly has taken you long enough, Barnes." Ethan finally allowed his grin to show. "Consider it given."

"You mean it?" Jeremy asked, relieved that Ethan offered no opposition.

"Of course," Ethan assured him. "Tell me you're not so blind that you can't see you're the only one she's loved since she was twelve years old. And I suspect that you're the only one she'll ever love.

Makes sense to see the two of you married—soon, I trust. My sister's a good girl...young woman, rather. She'll make a fine wife."

"Better than I deserve," Jeremy admitted.

"I'll agree. In the meantime, I want your word that you'll refrain from any improper activities, hmmm?" Ethan's statement was hardly more than a thinly concealed threat. "No more stealing away to deserted places and staying out all night until after you're wed to each other, hear?"

"I'll wait." Jeremy nodded his sandy-blond head, smiling wistfully. "She's worth it. She's a regular trooper, your sweet little sister, but she was quite shaken by the ordeal, just as I was. It's unnerving to know that someone wants you dead in a very desperate way." He took his plumed hat off and ran his fingers through his hair. "I honestly thought a part of me had died when I got word that John Barnes had kidnapped her. It's the sort of adventure I hope never to repeat."

"Stuart was heartily displeased when he discovered you were gone," Ethan reiterated.

"Yes, I know. He's already told me so himself. In fact, I'm supposed to be leaving again—on his orders this time. We've got to locate Stoneman and his blue cavalry, determine their intentions. Then I've got reports to write upon our return."

"Tell me quick, then, what happened to the depot?" Ethan wanted to know.

"We blew it up. There was no justification in letting all that go back to the Union. You know as well as I do that the Yankees would have used it all against us anyhow. We destroyed it. More accurately, Kidd Carney did. He saw the sense in it and was the one to carry out the action that I gave the orders for. How's he doing?"

"The burns are minor," Ethan assured Jeremy. "Carney will ride another day. He just needs time to heal. What about the girls? They're at Shadowcreek now?"

Jeremy nodded affirmatively. "Salina and I made a discovery when we returned to the cabin. Charlie Graham has taken up residence at Shadowcreek. He's pitched his tent right out front."

"What do you make of that?" Ethan rubbed his chin.

"Well, Salina told me about the train ride she'd accompanied him on, and how she had saucily invited him to stop by for tea whenever he felt he was ready to be sociable again. Charlie meant to take Salina up on her challenge, but when he arrived on horseback, it was only to learn that Salina had been kidnapped and Mary Edith and Taylor Sue were there alone. He's adamant about staying on to serve as the girls' protector. He says he might be missing a leg, but that has no bearing on his ability to shoot straight."

"Really now? Well, knowing that does make me feel somewhat better." Ethan sighed. "Besides, it will do Charlie good to feel useful again. I thought he might do himself some unspeakable harm when he was in the hospital in Richmond. He was rather upset with me for saving his life. Perhaps Charlie feels he's fulfilling what he considers a debt."

"Maybe," Jeremy agreed. "But at least he's there, and they have someone nearby in case of trouble. Charlie's already preparing for the spring planting and helping keep the place up. We really don't have anything else to worry about, I don't think..."

Ethan nodded. "We'll continue to keep the girls in our prayers. I know they keep us in theirs."

"Yes, they do—constantly. Thank God for that." Jeremy grinned, replacing his hat and pulling on his gloves.

"So, you're off again." Ethan clapped Jeremy's shoulder. "When do you suppose you'll find time to get around to making my sister your wife?"

Jeremy shrugged. "At this point, I don't rightly know. Look how long it took you and Taylor Sue to finally get your vows said and done."

"I had hoped you two wouldn't have to wait that long." Ethan was characteristically optimistic.

"It's not by choice that we're waiting," Jeremy admitted. "But sometimes certain situations are beyond our poor, feeble attempt at controlling them."

"Yes, I think having the two of you married might be the best thing." Ethan winked. "Godspeed, my friend."

"Take care, Captain." Jeremy saluted briskly.

☆☆☆☆☆☆☆

Instead of writing the first of his two reports upon returning from his scouting assignment, Jeremy penned the lines that had invaded his thoughts. Bentley wasn't the only one who could wax poetic on occasion. Jeremy was sure his own verse could improve with adequate practice. He reread the lines he'd written:

The Horse Soldier's Bride

> *Stars which glitter in deep, inky skies*
> *Cannot truly compare with the sparkle in her eyes;*

Her curls are as dark as the raven's glossy wing,
Raising her soft, sweet voice she oft will sing.

Longing to hear the joyous lilt of her laughter,
Yearning for war to be over, then in the days after
We'll share many long hours, perhaps days on end,
Yet for now by post and letter all my love I must send.

She alone is the cause that quickens this heart,
Of my thoughts she occupies more than a small part,
Her endearing smile and winning ways earned my pride,
If she will but say Yes,
I would make her this Horse Soldier's Bride.

He smiled to himself, pleased. These were the kinds of words Salina deserved to hear from him.

Jeremy sighed. It was almost disconcerting, how she affected both his mind and his heart. John Barnes had known what kind of hold Salina Hastings had over Jeremy—even before Jeremy fully realized it for himself. He was already willing to lay down his life for his country, and he would lay it down for her as well. He loved her so much that there was almost a physical ache within him. Love, strangely enough, was the culprit, guilty of bestowing both joy and anguish. For twenty years, he'd lived just fine without the emotions and the feelings. But Salina's love made Jeremy see what he'd been missing.

While the rest of his men gathered around the fire and fixed their breakfast of bacon and biscuits, Jeremy hurriedly put the finishing touches on his reports. He dipped the quill into the inkstand and signed his name and rank to the bottom of the page. He sincerely hoped Stuart would think that the scouting assignment had been worth it, that the information he brought back from reconnaissance would be of use. Otherwise, he had little doubt his commander would let him know differently.

As Jeremy turned in his reports to the adjutant, he received new orders in exchange. Union General Hooker was crossing the Rapidan River, and Jeremy was assigned to investigate the Federals' movements and position. It promised to be a very busy next few days. He studied the map of the route he was to follow, and all thoughts of making another run to Shadowcreek were quickly abandoned. Being unable to personally make a run up Chantilly way, Jeremy arranged to have his poem delivered by one of his men instead.

☆☆☆☆☆☆☆

Salina's nimble fingers plaited her curls into a thick braid. The cracked looking glass threw back a distorted reflection, but it was the only mirror in the rustic cabin. She took a closer look at the purplish-yellow bruise along her jawline and bramble scratches across her cheek. The moist tobacco poultices Taylor Sue insisted she apply had helped to heal her wounds over the past few days. Discontented, Salina sighed while she bound the end of the braid with a fraying satin bow. "Dear Lord," she whispered earnestly, "give me the strength to make it through this day..."

"Salina! Breakfast is ready!" Mary Edith called up into the loft. "Hurry, silly, or we'll be late for Sunday church service."

Salina's stomach churned rebelliously at the idea of eating. She wasn't hungry. She'd been too upset to eat, and it showed. During her week-long captivity, John Barnes hadn't provided much food to speak of, and now she simply didn't care whether she ate or not. If Jeremy were here, he'd declare she was his little scarecrow—as he had when she'd first come back to Virginia. And if Jeremy were here now, well...she wanted to be with him, to find out if he'd gotten Ethan's blessing. Salty tears stung her emerald eyes. The reflection in the mirror wavered out of focus. She thought about him constantly and replayed the scene of their parting in her head at least a hundred times a day. She touched her mouth, where Jeremy's lips had kissed her farewell. She'd worried about him before, but now her fears seemed more out of control than ever. Mentally she scolded herself for such foolishness. He'd be fine. They'd both be fine...

"Are you up here?" Taylor Sue poked her russet head above the loft's floor boards. "Salina?"

"Yes." Salina quickly dabbed a bit of rose water on her neck and wrists. "I'm coming."

Taylor Sue ascended the ladder rungs and joined Salina in the low-ceilinged loft. "Have you been crying again? Oh, Salina, what is it? Won't you tell me?" Taylor Sue squeezed her shoulder with tender concern. "You've been so withdrawn since your return. It's not like you at all."

Salina groped for words, trying impossibly to say what was on her heart. "I fear for Jeremy. What if Major Barnes really *didn't* die that night? Sometimes I can't help thinking Jeremy might be killed before we can have our wedding, before...Oh, Taylor Sue. You're married now. It's not wrong for you and Ethan to be together," Salina whispered hesitantly, "to want and desire and love each other."

"Did something...happen...between you and Jeremy?" Taylor Sue dared ask.

"No!" Salina quickly shook her head, the end of her braid swinging to and fro against her shoulders. "It could have. I mean...I think we both were *thinking* of what could have happened between us, but it didn't." Her eyes fell to the floorboards, and her cheeks flushed hot crimson.

"So that's it." Taylor Sue nodded in immediate understanding. "It's not always easy to control our thoughts, or sometimes our actions, but you both know there's been no wrong committed. Salina, it's obvious that Jeremy Barnes is a normal, hot-blooded young man, and you're a healthy young lady. Those things are natural between a man and a woman—within the context of marriage, as the Bible says."

"I know." Salina nodded slowly, then confided, "But I feel so impatient. When will he talk to Ethan? When will he be back? When can we marry? When can be alone?"

Taylor Sue confessed, "I know precisely what you're going through. Ethan and I were highly sensitive to the attraction we felt for each other before we said our vows. I know what you're feeling—the longing and the loneliness."

"You don't think I'm wicked?" Salina asked.

Taylor Sue shook her head but cautioned, "I think you're honest, Salina. It might be wise, however, for you to keep from putting yourself in situations where temptation might get the better of you. In the first book of Corinthians, the apostle Paul wrote: 'There hath no temptation taken you but such as is common to man: but God is faithful, who will not suffer you to be tempted above what ye are able; but will with the temptation also make a way to escape, that ye may be able to bear it.' We're only human, each one of us. We make our choices, and if they aren't the right ones, there are consequences that follow. Forgiveness of sins is ours through Jesus' blood, but that's not to say there's no price for wrongdoing."

"Such as the consequences Lottie finds herself in," Salina murmured.

"She is a willful soul," Taylor Sue agreed. "And yes, I'd say she's paying the consequences for her wanton actions. But let's don't spoil the morning by talking of Lottie. She's almost enough to take the sunshine out of a perfectly glorious day!"

Salina nearly giggled.

"Oh! Do I detect a hint of a smile?" Taylor Sue jabbed sarcastically. "It's been days since you've worn one at all, Salina. I was beginning to wonder if you'd forgotten how."

"I've been miserable since that night in the barn," Salina admitted "I keep thinking about it—about him and us. I guess I'm just being hard on myself, as usual."

Taylor Sue hugged her friend. "I still see that strength in you, you know. It's there. It's what gets you through the difficult times. From what you told me of the way Farnham released you, the skirmishing, the chase through the woods, the explosion, being shot—I'd have been a wreck if it were me in your place. How I prayed and prayed, and Mary Edith with me, the whole time you were gone, that God would not let you die at the hand of Major Barnes. I praise Him for honoring our prayers and delivering you from that horrid man."

Salina squeezed Taylor Sue's hand. "Thank you," she whispered softly. "I certainly needed the encouragement."

"Any time." Taylor Sue hugged her. A twinkle lit her eyes.

"What are you thinking?" Salina asked.

"Something mean. I shouldn't say anything," Taylor Sue hedged.

"What?" Salina pressed.

"I was just thinking that if your Aunt Genevieve ever found out you'd spent the night in an abandoned barn without a proper chaperone, you'd get another good scolding for sure!" Taylor Sue said irreverently.

Salina laughed out right. "I'm sure I would have!"

Mary Edith's voice came from below. "If the two of you don't come down here anytime soon, there won't be time to eat breakfast before we have to leave for church!"

☆☆☆☆☆☆☆

After going to church and listening to Reverend Yates's sermon, the girls found a visitor awaiting them at Shadowcreek later that same afternoon.

"Aunt Ruby!" Salina exclaimed. "What are you doing here? Come in, won't you?" Salina opened the door of the cabin and invited Daddy's sister-in-law inside. She made the introductions. "You know Taylor Sue, and my cousin Mary Edith, and this is Charlie Graham, one of our neighbors."

"Pleased to meet you, ma'am." Charlie nodded. "If you all will excuse me, I think I'll go out on the porch and smoke my pipe for a while. Let you ladies talk freely without a man underfoot."

Ruby Tanner smiled at Charlie. "How very thoughtful, Mr. Graham."

Salina noted that the smile did not reach Ruby's eyes, and she wondered at the reason behind this unexpected visit. She was sensitive to the despondency her aunt was trying bravely to hide. Earlier this morning, Taylor Sue had supplied encouragement when Salina needed it. It seemed to be Salina's turn to pass along some uplifting words.

Ruby nursed a speckled blue enamel mug filled to the brim with steaming hot tea as she told of the events that had transpired in Alexandria. "They finally made the connection," Ruby explained softly. "Those Yankee officials might not have realized that your Daddy occasionally posed as the reporter *Gary Hayes*, but they put the pieces together and pinned down Will as the true author of the controversial editorials. I warned him constantly, but he kept telling me it was for the sake of duty. Will was arrested, imprisoned for over a month. While he was there, he caught pneumonia. Last week he mercifully died, God rest his soul."

"Why didn't we hear any of this through the Remnant?" asked Salina. "If we'd have known, we'd have tried to help you somehow."

"Child," Ruby said fondly, "there's little *you* could have done. Almost immediately after Will's arrest, they came and took the printing press, destroyed whatever else they had no use for, and issued an order that I was to be taken behind enemy lines—our lines. It's for the best, Salina. When God closes a door, He opens another one somewhere else. I'm in a position where I must rely on Him to show me the direction of that other door. In the meantime, I'd written to your mamma. She says there's plenty of room for me there, but I can't go North. Will would never have wanted me to do that. I'm refugeeing to Culpeper Court House instead."

"Culpeper," Salina repeated then realization dawned. "Of course—to Aunt Tessa's house."

"If I'm not imposing, I was wondering if I might stay with you, just for a while. I don't know how well the trains are running, but I'll get to Culpeper by foot if I have to," Ruby determined.

"You're more than welcome to stay, Ruby," Taylor Sue assured her. "It's the least we can do to reciprocate your hospitality toward us when Salina and I were in Alexandria."

"Invitation accepted." Ruby smiled genuinely this time.

The afternoon hours passed rapidly, filled with talking, mingled with both tears and laughter. Taylor Sue showed Ruby the photograph of her and Ethan, taken the night of their wedding. "He's a captain, now," Taylor Sue said proudly, gingerly fingering the *carte de visite* print.

"And a handsome one at that." Ruby nodded. "Captain Hastings..." Her voice trailed into silence. She cleared her throat. "How like Garrett he has indeed grown to be. Have you heard from Ethan recently?"

"No," Taylor Sue replied. "Although Reverend Yates told us this morning after church that the army is moving out from Fredericksburg. Only a small force is left on Marye's Heights under Jubal Early's command. Ethan will be with the Second Corps. He's attached to Stonewall Jackson's medical staff."

"I, too, had heard the armies were moving—both of them. That Yankee Joe Hooker has been quoted as saying that he has the finest army on the planet! Wait until he gets into a tangle with our General Lee," Ruby said confidently. "Now that they're out from winter quarters, the armies will launch into their spring campaigns—and more blood will be shed."

Salina shivered at the ominous, prophetic words, but her mind lingered on Culpeper Court House. Stuart's cavalry was reported to be in that area from time to time. Jeremy would be where Stuart was. She sighed softly. The mere thought of a journey of any distance tuckered her out before she even took the first step. Yet if traveling would afford her the opportunity to see Jeremy, she reckoned any amount of exhaustion would be well worth the effort.

Taylor Sue would object loudly over such an idea, Salina knew. She could imagine the protestations and insistence that she was not strong enough to undertake such a journey on the heels of her kidnapping and subsequent release. Tomorrow, Salina determined, she would rest as much as possible, and she would force herself to eat.

☆☆☆☆☆☆☆

Rest, however, was not to be had during the next day. At least an hour before sunup, Salina was awakened to the sound of the secret door opening at the base of the hearth and the shuffling sounds of feet. "Jeremy?" she called into the stillness.

"No, miss," a husky voice replied. "It's me, Pepper. And I've got Browne with me."

Salina scrambled out of bed and quickly pushed her arms through the sleeves of her wrapper, knotting the sash around her slim waist. In an instant she found her slippers and was descending the ladder from the loft. "Jeremy's been so worried about the two of you! Where have you been?"

Pepper Markham answered in a scratchy voice, "We were captured at Kelly's Ford, but we escaped. Browne took a hit in his thigh, and his fever's been pretty hot. I'm no doctor, and I don't know what to do about him. He keeps bleeding. He's not doing very well. Can you help him?"

"Bring him up, quickly!" Salina instructed. By now Taylor Sue and Ruby were awake, and Mary Edith was rubbing the sleep from her eyes.

The girls did what they knew how to do for Browne, stitching his wound and bathing him with cold cloths. Taylor Sue dispensed what little laudanum she had, and at last Browne slept, albeit fitfully. Pepper seemed somewhat relieved, and he collapsed from sheer exhaustion. Charlie took him to his tent and let him sleep there, out of the way and undisturbed.

Ruby and Taylor Sue busied themselves with preparations for food for their increased numbers. Barely a quarter of an hour passed before Mary Edith waddled into the kitchen with her hands splayed across her extended belly. "I think it's time," she whispered hoarsely, her cornflower blue eyes wide in anxiety. "I've been having pains, on and off, for the last day and a half, but they've gone as quickly as they would come. This is different. I can feel it."

"If there's a doctor to be had in these parts," Ruby aided Mary Edith into the wide-seated rocking chair, "now would be a good time to ride after him—for Browne's sake and for Mary Edith's. I've had four of my own children. Birthing is no easy accomplishment."

"I'll go find Doc Phillips," Charlie volunteered, ably crutching his way across the floor.

"Go, Charlie." Taylor Sue nodded, whispering, "And hurry. I fear twins might make this more difficult for her."

Dr. Phillips examined Mary Edith when he arrived. "Water's not broke yet, but soon. If that happens before supper, I'd reckon you'll be delivered before daybreak. You'll move fast—and you're early."

"About three weeks," Mary Edith confirmed, alarm glowing in her eyes. "Will they be all right?"

"Time will tell. I've got a few other house calls to tend to, but I'll stop by on my way back to Centreville." Dr. Phillips told Charlie where he was headed, just in case he needed to be found.

Ruby sat with Browne Williams. She watched Salina tend to her cousin, making an effort to comfort the travailing girl. Taylor Sue was gathering things she thought might be needed for the birthing, including clean sheets, twine, a pair of scissors, and the small nightshirts sewn by Mary Edith's loving hand. "I'll go fetch some water," Taylor Sue said, taking the pail with her.

"Taylor Sue has quite a skill with nursing," Ruby observed aloud. "In truth, you both possess a very tender, gentle touch with your patients."

"We've had our share of practice, that's for sure. They say Ethan's a good doctor, so maybe we've managed to pick up a thing or two from him." Salina shrugged and set her sewing kit down on the edge of the hearth. There were several items that required mending.

"What's this?" Ruby picked up a garment from the pile of clothes next to the sewing box.

"That's a blouse I must repair, if I can," Salina answered.

Ruby held up the once-white garment. The shoulder seam on one side boasted a jagged tear, the other had a hole in it, the fabric blood-stained. "This blouse is telling me a story that you have failed to."

Salina nodded, averting her eyes.

"I've been out of touch with the Remnant. What would they know about this?" Ruby persisted.

Salina resigned herself to the retelling of her ordeal at the hands of Major John Barnes, and she shuddered yet again at the memories.

"Salina, I had no idea..." Ruby hugged her gently. "Is what we're all fighting for truly worth it?"

"I don't know sometimes," Salina admitted. "But this is a personal fight. This is about my family. Jeremy shot at John Barnes in self-defense. We think Major Barnes is dead, and I would be lying to you if I said that I was sorry about that. If he's dead, he can't hurt us anymore."

Ruby touched Salina's cheek. "No wonder you look so forlorn, so pitifully thin and pale. I think you could use a change of pace, a change of scenery. Come with me to Culpeper," she suddenly suggested. "Perhaps some time away from this place and these memories might be good for you."

"But what about Taylor Sue and Mary Edith—and the babies that are coming?"

"They'll manage. Charlie's here, and now Pepper and Browne," Ruby pointed out.

Salina shook her dark head. "Pepper will leave as soon as he's able. I don't think Browne will be with us in the morning."

"Please, think on what I've said," Ruby encouraged. "Besides, when's the last time you saw Tessa and all her brood?"

"Christmas before the war," Salina remembered. "It has been a long time." *Culpeper is not so far as Richmond,* she thought. *Why shouldn't I go?*

Pepper came in after his lengthy nap, looking much better for it, and sat near Browne. Browne's eyes opened briefly, and he whispered hoarsely, "I have fought the good fight."

Taking his friend's hand in his own, Pepper squeezed reassuringly. He could feel the hotness of the skin and sensed Browne wasn't going to get any better.

"Give the ladies my compliments," Browne continued. "I know that they tried...Tell Lieutenant Barnes...that we did all we could...he must keep fighting," Browne's words were faint. "Give him...my regards..." When Browne closed his eyes this time, he opened them no more.

Tears streamed down Salina's and Taylor Sue's cheeks as Pepper agonizingly pulled the sheet over Browne's head. Ruby came out from behind the partition of quilts, where Mary Edith lay writhing in a bed of pain. "Birth and death—they are inevitable," Ruby remarked sagely. "One life in exchange for another—two in this case." She put a hand on Salina's shoulder. "Pepper, Charlie, and I will see to Browne's burial. In the meantime, Mary Edith calls for you."

Salina slipped past the quilted divider. "I'm here, Mary Edith," she said gently. *Please God, help her through this difficult time. Browne is dead, and I don't think I could bear losing another friend today...*

Mary Edith squeezed Salina's fingers in so tight a clasp that the circulation was cut off. Salina extracted her fingers from Mary Edith's hand and gingerly stroked her cousin's perspiring forehead with a damp cloth. "I want to help you, if I can, Mary Edith. Is there something you want me to do?"

"Mama," Mary Edith breathed. "Will you...get her...for me? Ride to...Ivywood...tell her...I need her here..."

"Of course, I'll ride to Ivywood," Salina promised, knowing that she risked facing Lottie, yet glad of the excuse to get away from the cabin even for a short time. "I'm sure Dr. Phillips will be back soon. You hang on, Mary Edith. Everything's going to be just fine."

Chapter Twenty

*T*aking the cold cloth from her eyes, Lottie squinted into the dim room. Stripes of bright sunlight pierced through the lowered window shades. *Where was Maraiah? Why didn't she answer the bell?* Lottie felt downright awful. Downstairs the doorbell sounded, and a scuffle of activity greeted a caller. It was a struggle, but Lottie roused herself up from the bed and went into the hall. Peering over the railing, down into the entryway below, Lottie saw Salina Hastings being led into the house by Maraiah.

"Miss Salina." Maraiah swung the door open. "Wontchya cum on in?"

"For only a minute, Maraiah. Where's Aunt Priscilla? I've come to fetch her. Mary Edith's time has come. She's having her babies, and she wants Aunt Priscilla to come be with her."

"Ya stay put right here, Miss, an ah'll gatha Miz 'Scilla fer ya. Massah Caleb, he be in da study wid sum o' dem blockadin' gemptamums. He callin' em bizniss 'quaint'nsez. Ah call'em pirates," Maraiah said conspiratorially. "All but one, dat is. Ya wait here, Miss Salina. Ah'll git Miz 'Scilla," the slave called over her shoulder as she scurried toward the kitchen.

Salina studied Ivywood's stately hall. Mary Edith and Randle Baxter had been married on these very steps, and she had been a bridesmaid, proud to stand up with her cousin on that special day. Salina could almost hear echoing strains of the *Palmyra Schottische* and the other noises of the ballroom that night. Belatedly, Salina's glance ascended the banister, locking with Lottie's pained expression. "Hello, Lottie," Salina managed calmly.

"Salina." Lottie's acknowledgment was in the form of a near-imperceptible nod. "Is she in great pain, my sister?"

"She's not having an easy time of it," Salina responded. "Every few minutes, the pains come hard. It's been this way since..."

"Since before dawn," Lottie interjected. She closed her eyes and rubbed the small of her back. Mama had always said that the twins could feel each other's joys and sorrows. Lottie had been feeling a severe measure of pain since long before sunup. At least she knew the reason why. "No sign of the babies yet?"

"No." Salina shook her dark head. "Hopefully soon, though. She calls for your mother, and for Randle." Salina's inquisitive eyes settled on her cousin's perspiring face. "Lottie, are you well? You look a little peaked."

If Lottie hadn't felt so poorly, she might have unleashed a sharp rejoinder, telling Salina that *she* looked like a battered, half-starved little waif. Instead she merely said, "I've been awake most of the night."

"Oh." Salina didn't know what else to say. Civil conversation was a rare occurrence where Lottie was concerned. She didn't want to do anything to spoil it.

"I'll send mama over," Lottie said. "I'm sure she can help Mary Edith if anyone can."

"Thank you, Lottie. I know Mary Edith will take some comfort with her there." Salina nodded.

"If that's all you've come for, then I suggest you go now," Lottie said coolly. "You know your way out."

Salina felt as though she'd been dismissed. "I do hope you feel better soon, Lottie."

Her cousin made no reply. She simply tossed her blond curls and turned her back on Salina. Lottie leaned against the door as a fresh rush of pain hit her. "Oh, God, please let Mary Edith be through with the birthing soon. I can't take much more of this," she petitioned. A certain horrific realization came to mind: If these sympathy pains were this strong, how much more so would real labor be? She shuddered. There were months and months before Lottie's baby was due, but she fiercely dreaded the inevitable.

Ringing the bell again, she berated Maraiah under her breath. When at last the housekeeper arrived, Lottie was snappish and rude. "Where have you been! I've been calling and calling."

"I been servin' the blockade runna gemptamums, Miss Lottie," Maraiah answered, eyes downcast. "Dey's three of 'em here, two down in da study."

"Blockade runner gentlemen? Who are they, Maraiah?" Lottie insisted.

"One of 'em's Capt'n Randle—he be home from da sea. Ah done sent 'im on over ta Shadowcreek wid Miz 'Scilla. Da Good Lawd musta knowed dat Miss Mary Edith'd be needin' her man. He sent Capt'n's blockade runna home jist in time."

"Fancy that," Lottie grumbled.

"Now Missy, ya look like ya'd be havin' need of ya own man. Should ah send ta Washington fer him?" inquired Maraiah. She rinsed the washcloth out in the basin and handed it back to Lottie.

Lottie paused, but then she nodded, agreeing with Maraiah. Maybe she would feel better if Lance was here with her. He professed to care for her, and this would be a test of his devotion. Maraiah scurried off to do Lottie's bidding, and Lottie replaced the cold cloth. At least with Lance by her side, she was assured of at least *one* person's undivided attention...

☆☆☆☆☆☆☆

Nothing had changed. The Army of the Potomac was in much the same position as it had been just a few hours ago, when Jeremy had made his first reconnaissance in the company of General Stuart and other members of his staff. The Union right was "in the air," meaning it was virtually unprotected. It did not rest on any natural barrier, such as a body of water or the slope of a hill. It was just *there*—and seemingly not on its guard. There was a good chance, if strategic action were taken at once, the Union right could be flanked.

The catch was that the Army of Northern Virginia was not close enough to attempt such a strike at the moment. But *something* had to be done. With the armies in the proximity that they were, the inevitable clash was coming. Earlier in the day Stonewall Jackson's corps had already clashed with General George Meade's forces near Zoan

Church. Tomorrow, the fighting would be renewed in all its infernal fury.

It was not good ground to fight on—this wilderness surrounding a mansion known as Chancellorsville. It was a dense, heavy forest combined with thick, thorny underbrush which provided limited visibility. It was not flat land. Marshy streams crossed through it, and miles of tangled vines wove their way amidst the darkened timber, over hills, down ravines. Few roads cut through the vast, cluttered acreage, sprinkled with even fewer clearings. Chancellorsville was the home of a Southern woman, Mrs. Sanford Chancellor, who lived there with her six daughters. The house, situated where the Plank Road intersected the Orange Turnpike, was now headquarters for the Yankee General Joseph Hooker.

Jeremy reined Orion, tethering the horse to a nearby tree, and dismounted. Quietly he approached the circle of wavering light thrown out by one particular campfire.

Near that fire, Generals Robert E. Lee and Stonewall Jackson were seated on upended cracker boxes. General Jeb Stuart, one knee to the ground, leaned over a parchment map sketched by Jackson's topographical engineer, Jed Hotchkiss. Stuart watched intently as Jackson outlined a vague woodcutter's road with the point of a long stick.

Jeremy knew the road. He'd been on part of it not more than an hour ago. He could not clearly hear the words the generals shared as they were obviously deciding on their next course of action, but he recognized the burning intensity in each of the commanders' eyes. Battle plans were certainly in the making. Jeremy managed to read a phrase from Jackson's lips, "My whole corps." Jeremy guessed that General Lee must have inquired as to which troops Jackson intended to use in the proposed flanking maneuver, and Jackson had committed his 30,000 men to the task.

Shivering slightly, as though someone had walked over his grave, Jeremy stepped hesitantly closer to the warmth of the fire. If Jackson's corps went ahead with the march, General Lee would be left with only two divisions, roughly 13,000 men, under Anderson and McLaws. The Confederates, as usual, had far fewer troops than did the Federals, who outnumbered them more than two to one. This mathematical equation did not distress Jeremy in the least. He, along with the better part of the Army of Northern Virginia, had come to share Lee's belief that this army was invincible. It was merely a matter of time before the plans for attack would be put into effect. Jeremy felt strongly that they would be triumphant when the battle was spent.

General Stuart caught Jeremy's eye. "Any change?" the cavalry commander inquired.

"No, sir. Those people are right where we left them," Jeremy reported.

"Very good," General Stuart replied. "Tomorrow, the Eleventh Corps of the Union Army will be in for a rude awakening."

"Surprise will be a key factor," General Lee reiterated.

"Yes, sir," General Stuart nodded. "You've done well, Barnes. I'll send for you again later, if need be."

"Thank you, sir. My compliments, General Lee, General Jackson." Jeremy swallowed self-consciously, bidding the generals goodnight.

General Lee nodded in slight acknowledgment, but Stonewall Jackson's brilliant blue eyes remained focused on the parchment map. An unintelligible reply was uttered, his attention otherwise confined to the business at hand. Jeremy walked away, headed in the direction of his own tent.

"Halt!" a thin voice called from the darkness. "Stop where you are and identify yourself!"

"Lieutenant Jeremy Barnes, 1st Virginia Cavalry," Jeremy answered the invisible picket on duty.

"Beg yer pardon, Lieutenant," the young private said sheepishly. "We're all on our guard, sir."

"Yes, Private, we are." Jeremy knew they were all a little jumpy, nervous tension was at a peak. "At ease, Private. With your permission, I'll be moving along to my quarters."

"Yes, sir." The private saluted. "Of course, sir."

"Carry on." Jeremy returned the salute, too tired to grin. He found Curlie and Boone sacked out near the dying campfire. Bentley, on the other hand, was wide awake and whittling under the stars.

"Evening, Lieutenant," Bentley acknowledged. "What word?"

"None yet. I'm sure we'll have our orders come morning." Jeremy yawned. "Harrison back yet?"

"Got back just a few minutes before you did," Bentley replied. "Those Yankees are making a foray down toward Richmond. Stoneman's cavalry has been dispatched to harass our communication lines and the capital itself. Jubal Early's still up on Marye's Heights up above Fredericksburg."

"So much for the good news." Jeremy shrugged, casting aside the memories he carried of that frozen night back in December, when showers of light illuminated the sky as the eerie moans of dying soldiers punctuated the frigid air. "G'night Bentley."

"G'night, Lieutenant." Bentley continued to apply the sharp edge of his pocketknife to the hunk of wood he held firmly in his opposite hand. With a cocky grin he added, "Sweet dreams."

Jeremy was too weary to respond to Bentley's teasing, and when morning broke, he would never admit to his riding companion that his dreams of Salina had been very sweet indeed.

☆☆☆☆☆☆☆

May the second was a long, grueling day. Jeremy licked his dry lips, then wished he hadn't. A thin layer of dust clung to him, his hat, his uniform, his skin. He had no call to complain. If it hadn't rained recently, the dirt roads they traveled would have been much worse than they were. Thousands of men, trekking barefooted over dry narrow pathways, would have created sizable clouds of dust, and thus given away their position. *Surprise will be a key factor...*

Jeremy and the rest of his men rode along. Stuart's orders were to screen the infantry march. If the Yankees had sent out scouts, how long could they truly keep their movements hidden? It was only a matter of time before Hooker would discover what Stonewall was up to, which was probably the reason the wily Southern General had twice led his troops in southward counter marches and then back on course—feigning retreat, hoping Hooker would bite at the ploy.

The gray columns marched at a rate of two miles an hour, with ten minutes of rest. Jeremy was once again thankful that he was a horse soldier in the cavalry and not in the ranks of the infantry. As they passed the Catharine Furnace, an ironworks that supplied materials for the Confederacy, Jeremy prayed silently. In a few hours, the fighting would commence, and while the cavalry might not play an active role, he would be called upon to carry dispatches between the commanders. He had studied the roads and lanes on the map in Stuart's possession. He knew what would be required of him.

A while later, merely a few yards from where he had reined Orion to a pause, Jeremy saw Stonewall Jackson ride alongside the marching men. Had this been any other occasion, the men would have erupted in boisterous enthusiasm and acclaim, but Jackson held his finger to his lips, calling for quiet. Through the brush, they could hear the enemy plainly. They were not far from their quarry.

Surprise was not fully achieved by the Rebel troops. Hooker's scouts had managed to discover the Confederate movements, but time and speed were still on the Rebels' side. The Federal commanders seemed to disregard the warning signs. It was later told how small game raced through the Yankee camp, and the blue-bellies cheered heartily, laughing at the spectacle. Those scurrying animals were followed by a flood of gray- and butternut-clad soldiers wailing the Rebel yell. The Yankees were properly stunned—not to mention routed.

Ethan knew that darkness was falling. The orderlies were bringing lanterns that did little to stave off the growing dimness. In a little while, he would be unable to work here, and he would fall back from this dressing station to a field hospital somewhere behind the lines. There were so many men yet to tend to. He'd been up to his elbows in blood for hours and would be for hours yet to come.

This is what I'm here for, he reminded himself. This was what he'd studied for, joined the army for. He wanted to be involved in the conflict, to serve. This was the best way he knew how. *Father God, help me help these men!*

"Next!" Ethan yelled out to an orderly, the kerosene lantern throwing eerie shadows across his operating table. He took the time to clean his instruments carefully, and then he washed the blood from his hands. He knew that cleanliness increased his patients' chances for survival.

Ethan worked on a steady steam of men, one closely followed by another, and another, and another. "Next!" he cried out, wiping his forearm against his brow, leaving a bloody streak behind.

"That was the last one, Captain," the orderly at last replied to Ethan's repeated command, some hours later. "All the others have been loaded into ambulance wagons and will be taken to the field hospital. You're to join Dr. Shields as soon as you're able to do so."

"Tell Dr. Shields I'll be there shortly." Ethan nodded. "I'll finish up here and ride over."

"Very good, sir." The orderly saluted and departed.

"You do like living dangerously, don't you, Captain?" Jeremy Barnes entered the makeshift shelter. Many times he'd envisioned Ethan—blood-stained apron, wielding the silvered tools of his practice—somewhere safely conducting surgeries at a field hospital. To find him here, less than a hundred yards from the front line, well, that was another matter. It was too jarring a reminder that they were only human, and in constant peril for their lives. Jeremy shrugged the niggling fears aside. There was work to be done.

Ethan glanced over his broad shoulder. "Lieutenant Barnes. What a time for a social call," he remarked dryly.

"This is not a social call, I can assure you. It's official business." Jeremy clicked the heels of his boots and snapped a smart salute. "What are you doing here?"

"I volunteer for dressing station duty. I get the men directly from the battle. I do what I can for them immediately then send them on behind the lines. Hopefully my ministrations will have laid the groundwork for their recovery."

"So many of them die anyway, some even before they reach the hospitals," Jeremy noted grimly.

"I know. That's why I'm here. To help them. Yet for each one who dies of battle wounds, two others die of disease. At times this line of work is very discouraging..." Ethan sighed, weary and tired. "What're *you* doing here? Why aren't you on a reconnaissance mission monitoring the Federal troops?"

"I've done my reconnaissance," Jeremy replied tightly. "It wasn't until I returned to camp that I learned the news. That's why I'm here. I'm to accompany you to the field hospital to pick up what supplies are available and then take you on to the Wilderness Tavern."

Ethan began to pack his instruments. "Wilderness Tavern? What news? I'd heard we were gloriously victorious today. Hooker abandoned the offensive and has taken up defensive positions. All we have to do is press him, and he'll go running right back to Washington."

"Yes, we were successful today, but there's tomorrow to contend with. We're in a bad way. A.P. Hill is injured, Ethan, and Stonewall's been shot," Jeremy told him.

"What?" Ethan's eyes blazed with disbelief. "General Jackson is down?"

"Come on. I'll tell you how it happened along the way. They've taken General Jackson to the Wilderness Tavern. As soon as he's able, he's to be taken farther behind the lines. General Lee doesn't want to risk his capture by the Union. It sounds like you might be one of the doctors ordered to accompany the ambulance."

Ethan hurried his packing. "Tell me what happened."

"I can only tell you what I know," Jeremy said, and he began his tale.

Stonewall Jackson had wanted to press the Yankees, but his troops were too worn out to be effective. A.P. Hill's reserves were ordered to come forward to complete the attack and crush the Federals. In the meantime, Jackson and a handful of staff members went out between the lines to scout the positions. Jackson's aide cautioned the General about the danger, but Stonewall insisted that the danger had already passed. When he had seen what he went to see, Jackson wheeled and returned to his own lines. It was Lane's Georgians who were on the picket line, and they opened fire into the returning Confederates. Two of Jackson's staff were killed instantly. Another yelled repeatedly, "Cease firing! You're firing into your own men!"

The Georgians, thinking it to be a Union prank, swept the wooded area with heavier fire. Jackson, hit once in the right hand and twice in the left arm, was carried on his frightened horse through the thick tangle to trees until he was miraculously able to gain control of his mount.

A stretcher was procured after the firing finally halted. Jackson was at length taken on a hazardous journey to the Wilderness Tavern.

"General Lee's understandably grieved over the situation." Jeremy shook his sandy-blond head. "A corps commander has to be found. A.P. Hill would have been the next in succession..."

"But he's wounded, too," Ethan interrupted. "General Rodes is next after Hill, I think, but he has never led a division in battle before, let alone an entire corps."

Picking their way through the forest, Ethan and Jeremy passed pickets from both sides and finally came upon the clearing. They entered the Tavern just as one of Jackson's aide's was asking for some advice on behalf of General Stuart. Jeb Stuart held the confidence of Jackson's men, and he had been placed in temporary command of Jackson's corps for the fight that was sure to ensue in a matter of hours.

The room was silent, all anxiously waiting for Jackson to reply. For a moment, his eyes burned brightly with the heat of battle, but then he looked puzzled, and he sighed wearily. "I don't know. I cannot tell. Say to General Stuart that he must do as he thinks best."

The aide, Sandy Pendleton, prepared to return to Stuart. Jeremy bade Ethan farewell, glanced at Stonewall Jackson one last time, and then rode off with Pendleton. This situation was certainly an unexpected blow. General Stuart had a challenge ahead of him—he, a cavalry commander, was to lead infantry and artillery. Jeremy knew Stuart, though, and he knew full well that the General never did anything in half measures. He would lead the men in a fierce fight, if nothing else.

Chapter Twenty-One

*T*abitha Wheeler was the first visitor to pay a call on Mary Edith and Randle's new little daughters. She brought with her two lovely crocheted blankets and took great joy in wrapping each of the babies up in one. She sat in the rocking chair by the fireplace with a sleeping girl in each arm. They were darling girls, identical replicas of Mary Edith, but they had Randle's slate-colored eyes right from the start. Both were healthy, as was their mama, though she was quite weak. Randle ministered to his wife with great tenderness, and he was clearly proud of being a new papa.

Salina sat down on the hearth near Tabitha, busying herself with a fresh batch of mending to be done.

Tabitha smiled fondly. "We were so very worried, Salina. The Remnant put out word to Jeremy as soon as we learned of your capture. Now with that Yankee uncle of his dead, you should get on tolerably well, I reckon. Word has it that Lieutenant Barnes has asked your brother for your fair hand in matrimony. Is this true?"

Salina gasped, wide-eyed. "How did you know that?"

"Ah, so it is true." Tabitha smiled her toothless smile and shook her finger at Salina. "Good news travels quickly."

"Ethan may have given his blessing, but Jeremy has yet to ask me officially. He keeps telling me he wants to do this properly," Salina clarified, restlessness evident in her tone.

Tabitha patted her hand. "Patience is a virtue, dear one. Time has a way of passing. I'm certain the two of you will get your chance to be wed all right and nicelike. With the war on, you'll have to find a way to make an opportunity, as Ethan and Taylor Sue have done," Tabitha suggested. "What with the smashing victory at Chancellorsville, things are looking very good for the Confederacy. The spirit of the troops and of the folks on the homefront has never been better. It will be a spring of celebration for the South!"

"God willing." Salina nodded. "We're praying that Stonewall Jackson will recover swiftly. There's been nothing new since he was moved to Guinea Station?"

Tabitha's tone returned to a realistic level and she replied, "They say that pneumonia has set in. But perhaps he'll recover from that. You did."

"But I wasn't shot at the same time," Salina said. "Oh, he can't die, Tabitha. We need him too badly."

Tabitha shrugged, silently committing the matter to Providence.

Charlie Graham poked his head into the cabin. "There's someone here to see you, Salina, but I suggest you see him out here."

Salina set her mending aside and went out onto the porch. Lance Colby stood there, hat in his hands.

"I came to pay my respects to you, now that you're back safely, and to the new parents." Colby made an honest attempt to be cordial. "Lottie's feeling much better than when you were last at Ivywood, almost back to her old self. She wanted to know if they'd named the twins yet."

"No, not yet." Salina shook her head. "They're still trying to decide." She glanced back to the cabin door, which was open just a crack.

"If I didn't know any better, Salina, I'd almost think that you didn't want to be seen with me," Colby quipped, amusement easily read in his pale blue eyes.

"While we might be related distantly by marriage, you still wear a blue uniform. Some of my family, friends, and neighbors don't quite appreciate that," Salina pointed out.

Colby laughed outright, not offended by her accurate remarks. "Yes, I'm well aware of that." He looked over his shoulder to where Charlie sat on a stump, deliberately whittling away at a chunk of wood with a very large knife. "I'll be leaving soon." Colby knew better than to wear out his welcome. "I only came to Ivywood because Lottie needed me. When I return to Washington, I've decided to take her with me. I think she might enjoy the parties and festivities there when we Yankees aren't too busy being horrendously defeated by Lee and his Army of Northern Virginia."

"Dinners, parties, dances, theater. If you furnish Lottie with an allowance and give her the name of a good dressmaker, she'll be quite content," Salina predicted. She tipped her head to one side, contemplating the man before her. "Do you care for Lottie? I mean, you were honorable enough to marry her, just shy of being prodded into it at the muzzle end of Uncle Caleb's shotgun..."

"Since our wedding, even while I've been in Washington these past few weeks, I found I actually started to miss her," Colby confessed. "I suppose I *do* care for her. You might not see it, but underneath her meanness is a charming young lady. I think she just goes about things the wrong way more often than not. She craves attention, which in her eyes always seems to rest with you. She's spent most of her life being jealous of you, Salina. Perhaps there's something I can do to remedy that. *I* can give her the attention she seeks. If Lottie's happy, then she'll have no cause to lash out at others." Colby shrugged sheepishly. "I know, I must be out of my mind to put up with her. You know that I've a weakness for Southern ladies. Now that I've got one of my own, I don't intend to let this one get away. And while she'll never admit it, I believe Lottie needs me. I took my vows seriously the day we wed, albeit hastily, and I mean to honor them."

Salina nodded. "I wish you well. You certainly have your work cut out for you." Then she requested, "If you see Duncan or my mamma, please give them my best."

"I will." Colby nodded. "Farewell, then." He pressed her fingers briefly to his lips, and he rode away.

Salina found Randle in the shadow of the porch roof, watching intently. "Are you spying on me?"

"Just making sure he minds his manners, that's all," Randle said gruffly. "I can't deny he's my brother-in-law, but that doesn't mean I have to like him."

"He's a Yankee," Salina stated with a shrug, perceiving the reason for Randle's defensiveness. "But I guess he's not such a bad sort after all."

Randle chuckled. "No, I suppose he's not. I just haven't been able to give him a legitimate chance. I can't get past the blue of his uniform, though I'm sure the gray of mine sets his teeth on edge in much the same fashion. For now, we'll just have to keep our silent truce and let each other be."

Salina understood and shared his dilemma. Wistfully she added, "Someday we'll all be able to be friends again, perhaps."

"Perhaps." Randle shrugged noncommittally.

After supper, Boone Hunter arrived. His visit was just as brief as Colby's had been. He stopped only long enough to collect the mending Salina had completed, eat a plateful of stew, and have Pepper get ready to ride. Under the cover of darkness, Boone visited Browne's grave, paying respects. Just before the two men departed, Boone handed Salina a thin envelope. "Regards from the Lieutenant."

Salina smiled, recognizing the slanted handwriting which comprised her name. "Where is he?"

"Near Chancellorsville. It was a hard-won fight. The rumors say Stonewall Jackson may be on the mend. It still remains to be seen, however. And then there's U.S. Grant, out there in Mississippi. He's besieging Vicksburg. Something will have to be done about that."

"We can't afford to lose control of the Mississippi at this stage in time, that's for sure," Randle commented, hands balled tightly into fists. "Godspeed, Boone. You, too, Pepper."

Each of the riders saluted. "Take care of those precious little girls." Boone nodded. He tipped his hat. "Miss Salina."

Salina retreated to the loft to read her letter from Jeremy. It was filled with details of the battle at Chancellorsville, but at the bottom was another poem he'd written for her. As she read the touching lines, her eyes grew misty, and she whispered to herself, "I will say *Yes*, and I'll be my Horse Soldier's bride." She giggled softly. She didn't know when she would see him again, but she prayed it would be soon.

The next morning, Salina was awakened by the cry of one of the babies. No one had had much sleep since the twins arrived eight days ago.

Salina descended the ladder from the loft and found that the other occupants of the cabin were already in a flutter of activity—Ruby at the stove, Taylor Sue with one baby in her arms, Mary Edith with the other. "I want to hold one of them," Salina declared.

Taylor Sue relinquished the twin she was holding into Salina's arms. "You went to bed early last night, before I could share the letter from my mama with you. It's on the table if you'd care to read it."

"Things are well in Richmond?" Salina asked, plopping down in the rocking chair Taylor Sue had vacated.

"Well enough, I guess. But read," Taylor Sue instructed. "Keep rocking, and you'll have Annie Laurie asleep in no time."

"Annie Laurie?" Salina tickled the chin of the little girl nestled in the curve of her arm. She cooed, "Mama and Papa finally got around to giving you girls names? Well, little Miss Annie Laurie—that's no surprise since Papa Randle sings that song much of the time.

Maxwelton braes are bonnie, and early fa's the dew,
And it's there that Annie Laurie gave me her promise true;
Gave me her promise true, which ne'er forget shall be
And for bonnie Annie Laurie, I'd lay me doun and dee!"

Mary Edith laughed. "That is *precisely* where she got her name. And this little girl is Bonnie Lee. We've named partly for after a song as well, *The Bonnie Blue Flag*, but also in honor of General Lee's recent victory over the Yankees. Why, Salina, you do make a picture with that little one."

Salina's eyes grew round, and she shook her head. "Not yet I don't! Taylor Sue is a much more likely candidate for motherhood than I. Besides, she's got a husband already."

"But you will have a husband, Salina—providing Jeremy Barnes is ever in one place long enough to ask you, and then make good his word." Taylor Sue laughed.

Salina smiled secretively, recalling the lines of Jeremy's poem. She fell silent as she read Mrs. Carey's month-old letter. It was filled with news from the Confederate capital—of the shortages, the throngs of refugees, of an act of violence brought on by an oppressed, unruly crowd...

I'm not sure that you would have heard of this inci-
dent called the Bread Riots, as great pains were taken to
keep the news from being published by the press. Presi-
dent Davis doesn't want the North to know just how bad
off we stand, and so has dictated that this must not be
read by those who would use it as war propaganda to
their advantage. Last Thursday morning, April 2, a mob
comprised of over 400 women marched on Capitol
Square and then on down 9th Street. Along the way, they
picked up a fair number of vagrants, and their numbers
swelled to 500 or so. The initial purpose might have been

*just, but the looting and breaking into shops and stores
along the way was merely an act of taking the law into
their own hands. They went to bakeries and other stores,
smashing windows and taking whatever they desired.
They say hunger and starvation drove them to this, but
that doesn't justify their acts. The city militia was called
out, and President Davis threw what money he had in his
own pockets to the angry crowd. He addressed the mob,
begging them not to blame the government for such conditions, but to blame the Yankees who had inflicted this
plight onto the Confederacy. Tensions rose, and the mob
was ordered to disperse. A warning was issued, then
force would be used to dissolve the crisis. It was only
when the command of "Load!" was sounded and the militia prepared their arms that the mob finally disbanded...*

Mrs. Carey closed the letter by writing:

*Please do write and let me know how you girls are
faring. I don't suppose you've given any thought as to
when you might return for a visit. Before you should
come, I beg advance notice, as there might be things you
would be able to bring with you that are impossible to obtain here in Richmond. Of course, you shouldn't attempt
to come, if it isn't safe to do so.*

Give our best—mine, papa's, and Jennilee's—to
Ethan, and greet Salina fondly for us. Do write soon, as I
miss you.

> *Affectionately,*
> *Your loving mamma*

"I thank my God upon every remembrance of you"
Philippians 4:3

"Perhaps one day we will go back to Richmond and visit," Taylor
Sue murmured when she saw Salina look up from the pages. "Obviously, Mama would want that time to be sooner rather than later."

Salina nodded sympathetically, knowing what is was like to be
separated from loved ones by far distances. She wondered if she'd ever
visit Mamma in Gettysburg. She did have her traveling papers from
President Lincoln, and she knew Duncan would provide her with safe
conduct if she ever changed her mind about going North.

☆☆☆☆☆☆☆

The pendulum clock on the fireplace mantle ticked loudly enough to be heard over the murmur of voices drifting from the next room. Mrs. Anna Jackson read psalms from her Bible, her tone barely concealing the rattled, labored breathing of her wounded husband, General Thomas Jonathan "Stonewall" Jackson.

A sense of depression, perhaps even of foreboding, hovered in the corners of the small clapboard building which served as an office for the Chandler plantation until Jackson was brought here almost a week ago. Death was in the air.

Ethan, seated near the brick hearth in the room opposite the one where General Jackson laid, couldn't help but smile down at the happy little blue-eyed baby he held. Even as he bounced the General's daughter gently on one of his knees, Ethan keenly felt a degree of sadness on her behalf. She would grow up without fully realizing how much her father loved her. One day little Julia Jackson would be told of the celebrated campaign Stonewall led in the Shenandoah Valley, of the fierceness of some of the other battles he'd survived: both battles at Manassas, Cedar Mountain, Chantilly, South Mountain, Antietam, Fredericksburg. Then they would tell her of the brilliant flank march he led around the right of the Union Army at Chancellorsville, and how he was felled by his own men. Someone would tell her of the Mighty Stonewall, including his peculiar eccentricities, his deep faith, and his military fame, North and South. The little five-month-old girl would never know her heroic father beyond the retold stories. It was whispered that Stonewall Jackson would not live beyond this day.

"I admire your daddy, Miss Julia, very much. During the time I've served in his corps, I've learned there's no one else quite like him," Ethan whispered to the tiny little girl. He sighed, remembering a phrase contained in General Lee's dispatch to Jackson: *"You have lost your left arm, but I have lost my right..."*

Robert E. Lee had written those words to Jackson before the pneumonia had set in, and the ailment was now robbing the legendary Stonewall of life. The amputation of his left arm had been a successful operation, as had been the removal of a bullet from his right hand. The scratches on his face, acquired while crashing through thick brambles, were healing. But the new wounds inflicted by Dr. McGuire in the distasteful practice of cupping and bleeding had been administered in an effort to make him well again.

A few hours ago, Dr. McGuire informed Mrs. Jackson that her husband would die today. When she relayed the message to the General, he seemed to be rather at peace. He was not afraid to die—and if he were to have any say in the matter, he preferred to die on a Sunday anyway.

It was a Sunday, the tenth day of May. Ethan had been at the plantation office near Guinea Station since Stonewall Jackson was brought here on the night of May 4 from Wilderness Tavern. For a few days, the staff doctors were convinced the General might recover, but then he grew steadily worse. At times he rambled on about the war, and his mind wandered. Other instances found him very focused, but that was before the illness overtook him and the fever usurped his reason.

Ethan glanced at his own watch, which indicated ten minutes past the hour of three. Little Julia's fingers immediately curled around the shiny gold fob, her bright smile appearing. She looked up at Ethan with those vivid blue eyes—those which were inherited from her father—and he hugged her gently.

The General was speaking, and Ethan strained to hear the words, but he could not. Ethan settled the baby into the crook of his arm and quietly walked to the doorway, standing inconspicuously amid the others present, watching and waiting. Ethan looked into the General's daughter's eyes again, and her fingers curled tightly around his little finger with a firm grip. He heard the faint words fall from Jackson's lips, "Let us cross over the river, and rest in the shade of the trees..." A dreadful and calm stillness followed.

Ethan's eyes flew to the face of Stonewall Jackson. He suffered no more. The South, Ethan was sure, would suffer instead as a result of his passing. *There is no one else like this man,* he thought and didn't realize he was shedding tears until one dripped onto Julia's cheek. Swiftly, Ethan used his thumb to wipe his tear from the baby's rosy face, then dabbed at his own cheeks. When he stole a glance at the others, he took heart. They were all weeping, and with good cause. The sounds of soft sobbing were accompanied by the ceaseless ticking of the clock on the mantle. At 3:15 in the afternoon, Jackson was recorded as dead. Ethan prayed fervently that Stonewall's fighting spirit would live on.

In the hours following Stonewall Jackson's death, arrangements were made, travel plans verified, new orders issued. Ethan stood outside on the porch of the whitewashed office and absently stared out across the nearby tracks of the Richmond, Fredericksburg, & Potomac Railroad. Mrs. Jackson would go south with little Julia and have her husband buried at Lexington, even though his amputated left arm would remain where it had been interred a week ago at a neighboring plantation. A dull ache spread through Ethan, penetrating the numbness of disbelief. He shook his dark head mutely. God alone knew how very much the Confederates would miss Stonewall. General Lee had no one else like him, and he would prove impossible to replace.

☆☆☆☆☆☆☆

Major General Jeb Stuart was in his tent, unusually sullen. Deep in thought, he stroked his cinnamon-colored beard and reread the sobering lines delivered from General Lee: *"I regret to inform you that the great and good Jackson is no more. He died yesterday, at 3:15 p.m., of pneumonia, calm, serene, and happy. May his spirit pervade our whole army; our country will then be secure."* Included in the letter were instructions: The cavalry was to rendezvous at Culpeper Court House. The Rebels were on the move with the taste of victory still sweet in their mouths. A fight had been won around Salem church, but the Confederate soldiers had yet to partake in a major engagement without Jackson commanding his corps. When that time came, and Stuart sensed it was to be soon, then the true depth of the absence of Jackson's leadership would be measured.

"You wanted to see me, sir?" Lieutenant Jeremy Barnes poked his blond head through the tent flap.

"Take three of your men, deliver this to General Lee's headquarters, and then you're to depart at once," Stuart ordered briskly.

"Where are we going, General?" Jeremy raised a dark eyebrow in question.

"On a ride along the Rapidan River," General Stuart replied. He smoothed a map across the camp table and positioned the lantern. "Here." He pointed to the map, tapping his finger on a particular area. "This is where I want you to go—find out whatever you possibly can. Do not engage the enemy if it is avoidable. This is reconnaissance only, not a skirmish line. Report back to me immediately of your findings."

"Yes, sir." Jeremy saluted. His General was up to something, Jeremy could see it burning and glittering in the commander's eyes.

"When you get back," Stuart continued, "I'll have another assignment for you. You've ridden with Major Mosby before, yes?"

Jeremy nodded. "Yes, sir, I have. Quite an experience," he added with a wry grin.

"I've decided to provide Mosby with the howitzer he's requested. I've ordered him to harass the railroad. He says he would have increased success if he was in possession of a gun with more firepower than a handful of carbines can provide. I suggest you go along with the gun when it's delivered. It might provide another experience for you. That will be all, Barnes," Jeb Stuart dismissed the young horse soldier. "Have a care. You and your men be on your guard," he admonished.

Once Jeremy exited the tent, Stuart rested his head against one hand, pinching the bridge of his nose between his thumb and first finger, closed his eyes and sighed. Essentially, Jackson had gone in the midst of a fight. He himself wished to go the same way—in the heat of battle, gloriously leading a charge against the enemy. He wanted to win this fight for Virginia's sake, for pride's sake, and for the sake of honor and duty. He had already made it quite clear that he would rather die fighting than lose the war and suffer defeat at the hands of the Yankees. The South was at stake, and he was bound to do all he could to aid her cause.

General Stuart looked again at the map. Lieutenant Barnes was among a handful of scouts he'd sent out in hopes of discovering Yankee troop positions. In the next few days they should learn something decisive. He took out a bottle of ink, a quill, and a few sheets of paper. He wrote, *My Dearest One...* Visions of home and his wife combined with remembrances of his children momentarily superseded the activity in the cavalry headquarters surrounding him.

Chapter Twenty-Two

Closing the cabin door, Salina dropped her basket on the settee near the window. She pulled off the leather work gloves she'd worn while working in the garden with Charlie, leaving them next to the basket. She loosed the strings of her bonnet, and it, too, landed discarded on the bench seat. Salina's purposeful steps stopped abruptly at the bottom of the ladder. "What are you doing up there, Taylor Sue?"

"Packing," came the simple reply.

"Packing? Where are you going? To Richmond? Are you going to see Ethan?" Salina hurriedly ascended the ladder rungs to the loft.

"I'm not going anywhere." Taylor Sue shook her russet head. "You are."

"Me? What on earth are you talking about?" Salina's hands curled into fists which rested on her slim hips. "That's your dress, not mine."

"I know. I'm letting you borrow it, just in case." Taylor Sue's golden-brown eyes danced with mischief.

"What's going on?" Salina demanded. "Just in case what? I don't understand what you mean."

"We've been talking it over—Mary Edith, Randle, Ruby, and I—and we think it's best if you go to Culpeper with Ruby for a while. She's going first thing tomorrow morning, and you're going to go with her." Taylor Sue made it sound as though the decision was not Salina's.

"Oh, really?" Sarcasm edged Salina's words. "And *when* exactly were you planning to let me in on it?"

"Simmer down, Salina. Don't get your back up." Taylor Sue grinned. She pulled another dress from her own trunk, refolded it, and packed it in Salina's satchel. "This one is such a lovely shade of sky blue, and the bold green plaid brings out the emerald color of your eyes. This will be very pretty on you."

"*That* is your wedding dress," Salina objected. "Besides, I can't wear bright colors. I'm still in mourning over Daddy. You know that."

"He's been dead for over six months, Salina. I don't think your daddy would mind. I'd wager that Captain Hastings would want you to enjoy whatever pleasures might happen along your way. Goodness knows they're few and far between these days. Don't let them pass you by, Salina, or you might live to regret it," Taylor Sue said meaningfully.

Salina studied her sister-in-law's face carefully. "There's something you're not telling me. Out with it, Taylor Sue."

"Yes, I *do* know something. What about stockings?" she again changed the subject.

"I've two pair in the bottom drawer of the dresser," Salina grumbled impatiently, "Taylor Sue!"

Another grin lifted the corners of Taylor Sue's mouth. She finally shared what she had gleaned from Reverend Yates, who had briefly visited the cabin while Salina and Charlie were tending the gardens on the far side of the creek. According to the Remnant, Stuart's cavalry headquarters had moved from Orange Court House to the vicinity of Culpeper Court House. Rumors had the armies were moving north again.

"General Stuart will be screening any infantry movements, at least Reverend Yates seems to think so. Wouldn't you think so, too?" Taylor Sue's question was a leading one.

"North?" This was indeed news to Salina. She contemplated aloud, "Another attempt at an invasion into Maryland—or maybe even Pennsylvania?"

"It's possible," Taylor Sue confirmed. "Forage is scarce, and the men and horses need food to survive. Reverend Yates said General Lee was in Richmond on May 15 to meet with President Davis. The Yankees have laid siege to Vicksburg on the Mississippi. The South can't afford to lose such a stronghold to the Union under General U.S. Grant."

" '*Unconditional Surrender,*' himself, eh?" Salina raised an eyebrow in question. "So General Lee proposes an invasion in hopes of drawing Yankee troops away from Vicksburg," she pondered the situation. "At this rate, the future of the Confederacy might be settled before the summer's over—providing whatever General Lee's got planned succeeds. Maybe the North would sue for peace if we bring the battle to them. There was talk of that last year before Antietam, remember? Another triumphant victory like Chancellorsville would certainly put those Yankees in their place."

Taylor Sue shrugged her shoulders. "Could be. As I mentioned, Reverend Yates has confirmed accounts that the cavalry has moved to Culpeper Court House, or thereabouts. It's good ground there, he says. The horses and men will be able to feed themselves and perhaps get some much needed rest to recuperate from Chancellorsville. Reverend Yates also explained that since Stonewall Jackson's death, General Lee has reorganized his army. Instead of two corps like before, now there are three. One is led by General James Longstreet, another by General A.P. Hill, and the last by General Richard Ewell. Ewell's troops are in the Shenandoah Valley, near Winchester, even now."

"But the cavalry is at Culpeper," Salina whispered, a bright intensity sparking in her eyes.

"I'm about finished with your packing." Taylor Sue's lips twisted into an amused smile. "Randle will drive you and Ruby over to the depot in the buggy. The train leaves Fairfax Station in the morning."

"But what of you? Randle's leave expires soon, and he'll have to go back to sea. That would leave you and Mary Edith, the twins, and Charlie here alone," Salina pointed out.

"Charlie knows how to handle a gun, Salina. He's been teaching Mary Edith and me how to use a revolver," Taylor Sue disclosed. "We'll be fine."

"Taylor Sue, what if Jeremy's uncle," Salina corrected herself, "what if John Barnes isn't really dead? And what if he were to come after *you* now that you're a Hastings?"

"We'll be on our guard, Salina. Don't fret. Besides, from the way you described it, I hardly think it's likely the man survived. Jeremy is prone to hit what he's aiming at—you know as well as I do he's an excellent marksman."

Salina bit her lip, thinking. They would be all right. She believed it. Charlie had long since paid the debt he felt he owed to Ethan for saving his life, but as long as he chose to stay in the clearing near the cabin, they would certainly benefit by his company. And with the cavalry near Culpeper Court House, being at Aunt Tessa's would certainly position Salina in the area to run into Jeremy. "All right. I'll go with Ruby."

Taylor Sue's grinned impishly. "Do give the good Lieutenant my best when you see him."

☆☆☆☆☆☆☆

With the local telegraph wires cut and a selected section of rail loosened, forty-some-odd Rebels under the command of Major John Singleton Mosby lay anxiously in wait to strike the next train bound this way on the Orange & Alexandria Railroad. Jeremy Barnes, Boone Hunter, Weston Bentley, and Curlie Hawkins were among the men hiding in a stretch of pines roughly a hundred yards from the tracks. Tense and perspiring, trigger fingers itching, the men watched anxiously for the anticipated train to make its appearance. A short time ago, they'd been awakened by the blast of enemy bugles calling reveille. It had not taken long to get into position amid the thick pines. In the distance, a screeching whistle sounded, and above the trees an inky cloud of smoke oozed from a smokestack, dimming the bright sunny morning. Jeremy checked his watch. The hour of nine a.m. had passed. The rails began to hum, the earth vibrated—the chugging train was coming at last.

The little twelve-pound mountain howitzer cannon stood primed, loaded, and aimed. Mosby was prepared to wreak havoc on the approaching Federal supply train, just as Jeb Stuart instructed.

The advent of destruction opened with the derailment of the southbound locomotive. The artillery crew shot a shell from the fire-belching cannon directly into the boiler of the steam engine, abruptly halting its forward motion. The attached cars collided in a tumultuous, metal-grinding crash. In wild, hair-raising fury, Mosby's men descended on the wrecked train like a swarm of angry hornets. Amid the ensuing confusion, the unsuspecting passengers, predominantly Union soldiers, spilled from the derailed cars, running for the cover of trees on the opposite side of the tracks. The bark and crackle of carbine and pistol fire rent the tranquillity of the bright May morning.

The Rebel raiders gleefully ransacked the train cars, seizing bags of mail, oranges, lemons, candies, shoe leather, and barrels packed with fresh shad. It was a prosperous menu of spoils, and the Rebels threw any and all salvageable items from the train, yelling and cheering, but wasting no time as they quickly torched the wreckage. Time was a key factor. It would be only a short while until the enemy camps detected the smoke and fire of destruction and no doubt would descend upon the raiders with all the alacrity they could muster.

The uniformed prisoners were rounded up, but there were a handful of civilians mixed in. Mosby's men herded them all together and moved them away from the present danger.

"Major Mosby, sir." One of the raiders approached the partisan leader. "There's a couple of ladies among the prisoners, sir, and one of them has papers I think you ought to see."

The short, wiry, gray-clad major found the two women in question standing huddled together but apart from the others. His hard glance swept over the two in swift appraisal. They appeared to be uninjured but unmistakably shaken. The younger of them produced a letter of endorsement signed by the Army of Northern Virginia's Chief Cavalry Commander.

"You're acquainted with General Stuart." Mosby made it a statement, folding the letter, returning it to Salina's hand.

"Yes, I am." She quickly nodded. She watched the partisan leader scan the area with his stern eyes, looking for any sign of enemy patrols or approaching Union cavalry. She explained, "My aunt and I were on our way to Culpeper Court House, with hopes of having a chance to visit the General at his headquarters there."

Mosby barked out a rapid command to a nearby ranger, "Get them horses, and get them gone!" He turned back to Salina and brusquely ordered, "Go, then. Get from here as quickly as you can. You'll find General Stuart's encampment at Afton. My apologies for the inconvenience, ladies, but this is war."

"Thank you for your trouble, Major," Ruby hastened to acknowledge her gratefulness.

"Yes, thank you." Salina grasped Major Mosby's implication that traveling on a Yankee-infested train was not without personal risk.

"Convey my compliments to General Stuart." Mosby touched the brim of his plumed hat.

"I shall do so with pleasure and gratitude, Major Mosby." Salina and Ruby lost no time in securing their satchels and mounting the horses generously provided by Mosby. They rode from the crash site just as fast as the steeds would carry them, the deafening sounds of firing and fighting resounding in their wake.

Curlie Hawkins rubbed his eyes with his sleeve. The combination of smoke and sweat must be playing tricks with his vision. For the moment he chose to keep to himself that he thought he'd seen Salina Hastings on horseback galloping away from the wrecked and burning train. It was impossible—wasn't it?

Warning shouts and yells of caution drove the unlikely ideas from Curlie's head. The Yankees were charging, and it was every man for himself. The Rebels had a prearranged meeting place where they would gather later on, but presently they lit out in every direction. The raiders dispersed quickly to escape both the onslaught of Federal-aimed bullets and the risk of capture.

☆☆☆☆☆☆☆

A few days following their arrival at Aunt Tessa's house, Salina and Ruby read an account in a Richmond newspaper that cited Mosby's latest raid.

> *The fight took place at Catlett's station and Bristoe on Friday last, in which Maj. Mosby's force and a large body of Yankees were engaged. We learn that Mosby attacked the passenger train coming from Alexandria, containing a large number of soldiers and civilians. With a light mountain piece he put a ball through the boiler of the locomotive, which disabled the train. He then captured between two and three hundred prisoners, and burnt the train. While removing his prisoners and stores, a heavy force of Yankees, supposed to be a brigade, attacked Mosby, who charged upon the Yankees twice, but finding his enemy too much for his small force, he was compelled to fall back. While doing so, his men scattered to save themselves from being overwhelmed by the Yankees, and his prisoners succeeded in making their escape.*

Delia and Clarice Carpenter, Aunt Tessa's two daughters nearest Salina's age, marveled in awe over the venturesome episode. They pleaded with Salina to retell her account of such a hair-raising experience.

"You must rest, both of you," Aunt Tessa had firmly maintained when Salina and Ruby first arrived, completely disheveled, only slightly injured, and certainly out of breath. Daddy's sister solicitously tended to their purplish bruises and to the cut Ruby sustained in the train crash.

That first day in Culpeper Court House, Salina slept the sun around and felt exceedingly better for it. Now, lingering over the remains of breakfast, she reread the newspaper article and shook her head in mute amazement. *Dear Lord, I must thank You for seeing me through another time of difficulty. How often You intervene on my behalf, and You have once more set Your angels between me and grave danger. I am reaffirmed in my belief that You still have my life in Your hand, and I am convinced that You will guide me, dependent wholly on Your strength and not my own weakness. Thank You, Father, for Your everlasting love, and certainly for Your continued protection! In Jesus' precious name ...*

☆☆☆☆☆☆☆

Uncle Saul, the Carpenters' butler, answered a brisk knocking upon the front door. Boone Hunter was ushered into the entryway, and Salina hugged him in warm greeting. "Boone!"

"Miss Salina." Boone smiled sheepishly, ducking his head in acknowledgment.

"How did you know we were here?" Salina asked.

"Well, we didn't believe him at first, but Curlie *insisted* that he'd seen you after we attacked the train from Alexandria. Lieutenant Barnes was in a state. He must have searched those woods a hundred times looking for any evidence of you. Incidentally, we found Mrs. Tanner's trunk, and I've got it outside."

"It wasn't burned?" Ruby was incredulous.

"No, ma'am. It survived the fire." Boone grinned. "I'll bring it in for you."

Ruby was pleased beyond words to have her trunk recovered. She stood on tiptoe and kissed Boone's cheek out of gratitude, causing the young rider to blush profusely. He shrugged shyly and studied the scuffed toes of his long boots.

"Stay to dinner, then, won't you?" Salina suggested. "It's the least we can do in return for your delivering the trunk."

Boone reluctantly declined. "Actually, I haven't time to stay, but I thank you just the same. I've been detailed to deliver an invitation to you, Miss Salina, and to this household, from General Stuart. All you ladies are invited to a ball tonight at Town Hall, and tomorrow there's to be a Grand Review of Cavalry on the plain near Auburn. Do you know of it?"

"Yes!" Delia clapped, excited over the prospect of a social event.

"General Stuart's inviting us?" Clarice asked.

"Yes, miss." Boone could barely meet her eye. "All the women-folk in these parts and beyond—for nearly a hundred miles—have been invited. General Stuart's even issued invitations to the dignitaries and high command, including General Lee himself."

Ruby and Tessa smiled, and Clarice and Delia giggled in delight.

Salina's smile appeared more slowly. She recalled the insistence of Taylor Sue, now she was thankful that she had borrowed a festive dress. "Boone?"

"Yes, miss?"

"Lieutenant Barnes—he'll be at the ball tonight, won't he?" Salina wanted to know.

Boone assured her, nodding. "Of course he will, along with Bentley, Jake, Curlie, Cutter, Pepper, Harrison, Kidd Carney, and myself. All the boys are back together now, save for Browne."

Salina nodded sadly. "Is there no one to take Browne's place?"

Boone snapped his fingers. "I nearly forgot. We have acquired a new rider. Carter Jameson is his name, but we all call him C.J. for short. You'll meet him this evening as well," Boone told Salina. "I'll be pleased to go back and tell Lieutenant Barnes you'll be there tonight. Shall I relay any other message, miss?"

"Oh, yes." Salina returned Boone's smile. "Do tell him that I am *most* anxious to see him this evening. And, please, indicate to him I'll have an answer. He'll know what I mean."

Boone grinned lopsidedly, touching the brim of his gray slouch hat in salute. "I reckon he will, miss."

☆☆☆☆☆☆☆

Lieutenant Jeremy Barnes lifted a cup of cool, tangy cider to his lips. His sapphire eyes darted anxiously about the room, skimming over the myriad of guests who had accepted General Stuart's invitation and flocked to his ball. Judging by the number of hoop skirts swishing on the dance floor, Jeremy reckoned every female in Culpeper County must be present. The ladies, beautifully coifed and elegantly dressed, were held in the arms of smartly uniformed officers and select staff members—each of whom displayed their best military spit and polish.

It was no secret that General Stuart greatly enjoyed a good party. Tonight would prove no exception.

Culpeper Court House's Town Hall was filled to capacity. A near-palpable, romantic ambiance settled over the dazzling spectacle, due in part to the shimmering light exuded by the tallow candles illuminating the hall. Melodies from Sweeney's banjo, accompanied by the rest of the musicians, occupied the entire room and surrounded the dancers already swirling on the floor.

Jeremy felt Salina enter the hall before he actually found her with his eyes. In his opinion, she was the prettiest belle of the ball, his own Sallie Rose.

Bentley spied Salina Hastings at the same instant Jeremy had. More sharply than he intended, Bentley nudged Jeremy's elbow. He failed to notice that the cider in Jeremy's cup sloshed over the brim. "There she is, Lieutenant!" Bentley turned to encounter Jeremy's icy glare, then observed the spilled golden liquid as it was absorbing into the front of his lieutenant's relatively new gray wool jacket.

"Bentley," Jeremy muttered under his breath, quite obviously annoyed.

"Beg your pardon, sir." Bentley pulled his handkerchief from his back pocket and hurriedly attempted to mop up the spilled cider.

Jeremy snatched the bandanna from Bentley's hand and finished wiping up himself. "I've got eyes, Bentley. I knew she was here."

Bentley grinned, glancing over his shoulder at his lieutenant's lady. "Aye, she's here all right. And you're wound up tighter than the springs in that watch she gave you. Relax. She's probably as nervous about this little reunion as you are."

"I'm not nervous," Jeremy declared, but he knew it wasn't true. His pulse raced; his mouth went dry. He was overjoyed to see her and had so much he wanted to say to her, but his mind stubbornly refused to form a coherent thought. Chances were that his voice might fail him if he tried to speak so much as her name.

He shoved the mostly empty cup into Bentley's hand. Shouldering his way through the throng of guests, he paused every few feet, saying, "Beg your pardon...May I pass, please...Excuse me...Pardon me...excuse me..." The last ten yards were the easiest because those who saw the look of steely determination in his eyes instantly parted to make way.

At last Jeremy stood before Salina. Instead of words he offered his arm. Accordingly she slipped her arm though his—without greeting, without hesitation, but with love shining in her eyes. As they danced, they stared into each other's faces. Neither saw anyone or anything else.

Her smiles warmed him. They laughed together softly, a shade conspiratorially. Simultaneously, they both attempted to initiate conversation.

"I understand you've read my poem," he began.

"I have an answer to your poem," she said in the same breath.

Her laughter bubbled between them, then Jeremy quoted, " '*If she will but say, Yes; I would make her this Horse Soldier's Bride.*'"

"Yes," she whispered in his ear, so he alone would hear her. "Yes," she repeated, dissolving into mirthful giggles.

Throwing convention and caution to the wind, he kissed her right there in the middle of the dance floor and grinned quite broadly afterwards.

"Jeremy!" Salina offered mock protest. "People will say it's improper!"

"Tonight I don't care what people say." Jeremy chuckled, his eyes glinting with challenge, as though daring anyone to make even the slightest comment. "I'll gladly explain to them that you've said yes!"

Salina flushed a pretty shade of pink, and she fitted her small hand into his larger one. "Come, I want you to see my family. I know my aunts and my cousins want a chance to visit with you."

Jeremy had become acquainted with most of Salina's family through various holiday gatherings over the years, and he greeted them in a manner befitting an old friend. When the polite chatter ceased, he excused himself, claiming Salina for several sets of dancing. But he never finished an entire set as her partner. His men repeatedly and purposely cut in on them.

Weston Bentley was the ring leader of the mischief, of that Salina was sure, but she didn't mind. It was worth seeing the impatience flare across Jeremy's features, and she had to laugh. She danced not only with Bentley, but with Boone, Jake, Cutter, Curlie, Kidd Carney, Harrison, Pepper, and the new man, the one called C.J.

"I've heard you're from Texas," Salina said conversationally.

"Yup." The freckle-faced red-head nodded. "San Antone. Ever hear of the Alamo?"

"Yes," Salina replied. "My daddy used to tell the story of the place—of the Mexican dictator, Santa Anna, and of those who gave their lives for Texan independence: Crockett, Bowie, Travis. '*Cross this line,*'" she quoted. "Those who willingly answered Travis's challenge were massacred for the sake of freedom."

"I'm impressed, miss. You know a bit of our glorious history, to say the least. At any rate, the Alamo's right close to where I hail from. I came east on the recommendation of a friend of mine—a mutual friend you might say." C.J. winked.

"Mutual friend? Who might that be?" Salina couldn't imagine who she might know in common with the Texan.

"Drake would be mighty crushed if he ever learned you'd forgotten him so quick like," C.J. drawled. "I'm trying to convince him to give up that stage route and come on and join us. Drake always did love a good fight."

"Drake." Salina smiled as she said the name. "I have *not* forgotten him. So if you tell him so, you'll be lying. I can't forget him. He's been too good to me and my sister-in-law. We owe Drake a great debt for aiding us on a journey we took last fall to San Francisco."

"Yes, he did mention that you were one who enjoyed adventure. Intrepid, I believe, was one of the terms he used to describe you. Beautiful was another." C.J. continued before Salina could protest his offhanded compliment. "Needless to say, Drake was a bit put out when he got back from his run only to find that the Yankees had sailed you away." C.J. nodded. "And I suppose I needn't tell you that Drake's a feisty soul. I honestly believe he intended to rescue you all singlehandedly."

"I held that very same notion." Salina's cheeks flushed. "In truth, I didn't realize how much I'd missed him until just now."

C.J. grinned. "No disrespect, Miss Salina, but having met you, I can understand how it is that you made such an impression on Drake—and Lieutenant Barnes."

Jeremy appeared on cue, and Salina didn't doubt that he'd overheard C.J. mention his name. He reclaimed Salina for the last of the quadrille, and C.J. was wise enough to refrain from hooting loudly over Jeremy's displayed possessiveness. At the end of the set, Jeremy led Salina outside, retaining a firm grasp on her elbow.

Spanning her waist with his hands, Jeremy lifted Salina onto one of the many conveyances that was parked in the street. Her feet dangled over the end of the wagon bed, her hoops settled to one side, Jeremy stood near her on the other side. He held one of her gloved hands, cupping her cheek with his other hand. "I love you, Sallie Rose."

"I know," she answered pertly.

"I want you to be my wife," he stated, blue eyes penetrating the very depths of her soul.

"I know that, too," Salina replied saucily.

His arms circled round her, hugging her close.

"Ouch." Salina sucked in a pained breath. "Not so tight, Jeremy. I think I bruised a rib or two in that train wreck last week."

"You should never have been on that train in the first place," Jeremy scolded. "I told Curlie he was crazy, that you'd never pull a stunt like that..." His tone softened. "I stand corrected, for here you are. I should have known better. You're not hurt anywhere else, are you?"

"No." Salina shook her dark head. "Some scratches and bruises, nothing more. Aunt Ruby and I were fortunate—blessed."

"Indeed," Jeremy wholeheartedly agreed. "My own Sallie Rose. What am I going to do with you?"

"Unless I miss my guess, your recent poem intimated that you plan to wed me," she replied, her green eyes sparkling.

"I do." Jeremy hugged her more gently this time.

Salina rested her cheek on the top of his sandy head, glorying in their quiet time together. "You smell of apples," she remarked, threading her fingers amid his tawny locks.

"Compliments of Bentley and his misplaced elbow." Jeremy rolled his eyes. "I ended up wearing almost the entire contents of my cup, thanks to him."

Salina giggled, imagining Bentley's momentary lack of grace. "Can you recite my poem? I want to hear you say the lines."

Jeremy repeated each stanza from memory.

Intently, Salina listened to each word, each tone and inflection of his deep, clear voice. "Yes," she answered affirmatively once again. She had no doubts. She knew he had obtained her brother's blessing. "I do love you, Jeremy Barnes."

"I know." He cleared his throat, then said, "We've been through quite a bit—some good, some not so good. I'm afraid I can't promise that the future will be any less difficult for us."

"Perhaps not. We're each too stubborn for our own good, but we know better now than to let small misunderstandings grow into huge barriers between us. I'll not keep anything from you again," Salina vowed. "Of course, time and distance will keep us apart until this fight for independence is done. We'll just have to do the best we can with what we're given. Take happiness wherever we can find it."

"You're not afraid to take my name, even if it isn't really mine?" Jeremy asked, chagrined at sounding so unsure of himself when he customarily displayed a much higher level of confidence.

"I'll take your name regardless. If you don't like the one you have, then change it to one of you'd rather call your own," Salina suggested. "Whatever it is, I shall bear it proudly."

"As proudly as you do Hastings?" he challenged openly. He needed to be sure, no reservations.

Salina nodded. "Maybe prouder. I had no choice in the matter of being born a Hastings, but I consider it an honor that you would choose me to share your name."

Jeremy smiled lopsidedly. "You trust me?"

"With my life," she said, sensing his inherent need for reassurance. "And I know you trust me, too. You don't have to say it with words." She put her hands on either side of his bearded jaw, looking deep into his eyes and whispered with sincere conviction, "Jeremy, I'm not like your mother. She might not have wanted you or loved you, but I do—on both accounts. You may never know who your real father was, but that doesn't matter to me. I love you for who you are, for yourself, for what you mean to me. I've probably loved you since I was twelve years old."

Her admission made Jeremy chuckle lightly. "So your brother tells me."

"Oh, he does, does he?" Salina cocked her head to one side, her fists resting on her hips. "And what else does Ethan have to say?"

"He says we should be married—the sooner the better." Jeremy nodded, containing his grin. "I've not been able to figure out just when yet, or where, but I'll have a better idea tomorrow after the cavalry review. In the meantime, I have something for you." Jeremy fished in the pocket of his patched gray trousers until he retrieved a small, leather drawstring pouch. "I must be losing my sanity to have nearly forgotten about this."

"About what?" Salina queried anxiously. "What's in there?"

From the pouch Jeremy withdrew a shiny gold ring set with a deep red garnet, his birthstone, flanked by two smaller, winking diamonds. "I bought it at a store down in Richmond because I'd wanted to give it to you, to declare my intentions. But the timing wasn't right, and I was foolishly believing Lottie's lies. We've changed, grown up, you and I both, and the timing is right for us now." He slipped the ring on her left hand. "Perfect," he said, pleased.

Salina bit her lip, blithely studying the beautiful ring, the tangible testimony of their betrothal. "Taylor Sue told me recently that I'd get my husband in time, providing you were ever in one place long enough to make good your word. I reckon she was right." Salina bestowed a tender kiss on Jeremy's smiling lips. "All you have to do now is determine when and where."

"Trust me." Jeremy's mischievous wink accompanied a disarming grin. "I'll see to it."